Gasolina

CREATED BY SEAN MACKIEWICZ & NIKO WALTER

SEAN MACKIEWICZ
CREATOR, WRITER

NIKO WALTER
CREATOR, ARTIST

MAT LOPES
COLORIST

RUS WOOTON
LETTERER

ARIELLE BASICH
EDITOR

ANDRES JUAREZ
LOGO & PRODUCTION DESIGN

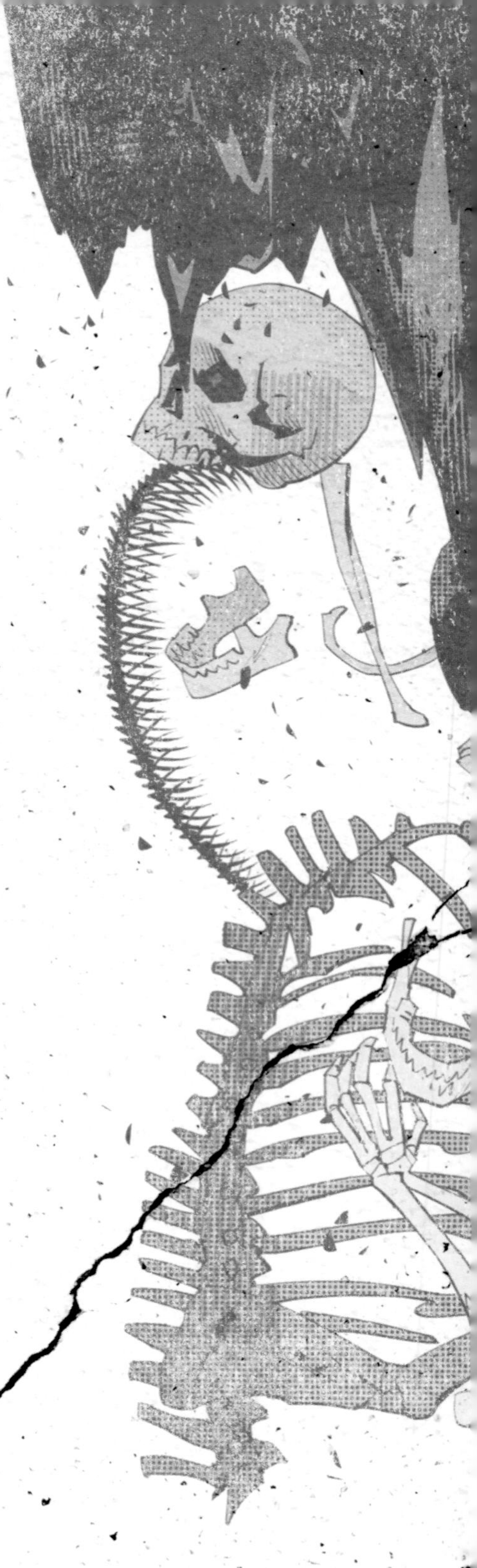

FOR SKYBOUND ENTERTAINMENT

Robert Kirkman *Chairman*
David Alpert *CEO*
Sean Mackiewicz *SVP, Editor-in-Chief*
Shawn Kirkham *SVP, Business Development*
Brian Huntington *VP, Online Content*
Shauna Wynne *Publicity Director*
Andres Juarez *Art Director*
Jon Moisan *Editor*
Arielle Basich *Associate Editor*
Kate Caudill *Assistant Editor*
Carina Taylor *Production Artist*
Paul Shin *Business Development Manager*
Johnny O'Dell *Social Media Manager*
Dan Petersen *Sr. Director of Operations & Events*

Foreign Rights Inquiries: ag@sequentialrights.com
Other Licensing Inquiries: contact@skybound.com

WWW.SKYBOUND.COM

IMAGE COMICS, INC.
Robert Kirkman *Chief Operating Officer*
Erik Larsen *Chief Financial Officer*
Todd McFarlane *President*
Marc Silvestri *Chief Executive Officer*
Jim Valentino *Vice-President*

Eric Stephenson *Publisher / Chief Creative Officer*
Jeff Boison *Director of Publishing Planning & Book Trade Sales*
Chris Ross *Director of Digital Sales*
Jeff Stang *Director of Specialty Sales*
Kat Salazar *Director of PR & Marketing*
Drew Gill *Art Director*
Heather Doornink *Production Director*
Nicole Lapalme *Controller*

WWW.IMAGECOMICS.COM

GASOLINA VOLUME 3. FIRST PRINTING. July 2019. Published by Image Comics, Inc. Office of publication: 2701 NW Vaughn St., Ste. 780, Portland, OR 97210. Copyright © 2019 Skybound, LLC. Originally published in single magazine form as GASOLINA #13-18. GASOLINA™ (including all prominent characters featured herein), its logo and all character likenesses are trademarks of Skybound, LLC, unless otherwise noted. Image Comics® and its logos are registered trademarks and copyrights of Image Comics, Inc. All rights reserved. No part of this publication may be reproduced or transmitted in any form or by any means (except for short excerpts for review purposes) without the express written permission of Image Comics, Inc. All names, characters, events and locales in this publication are entirely fictional. Any resemblance to actual persons (living or dead), events or places, without satiric intent, is coincidental. Printed in the U.S.A. For information regarding the CPSIA on this printed material call: 203-595-3636. ISBN: 978-1-5343-1231-9

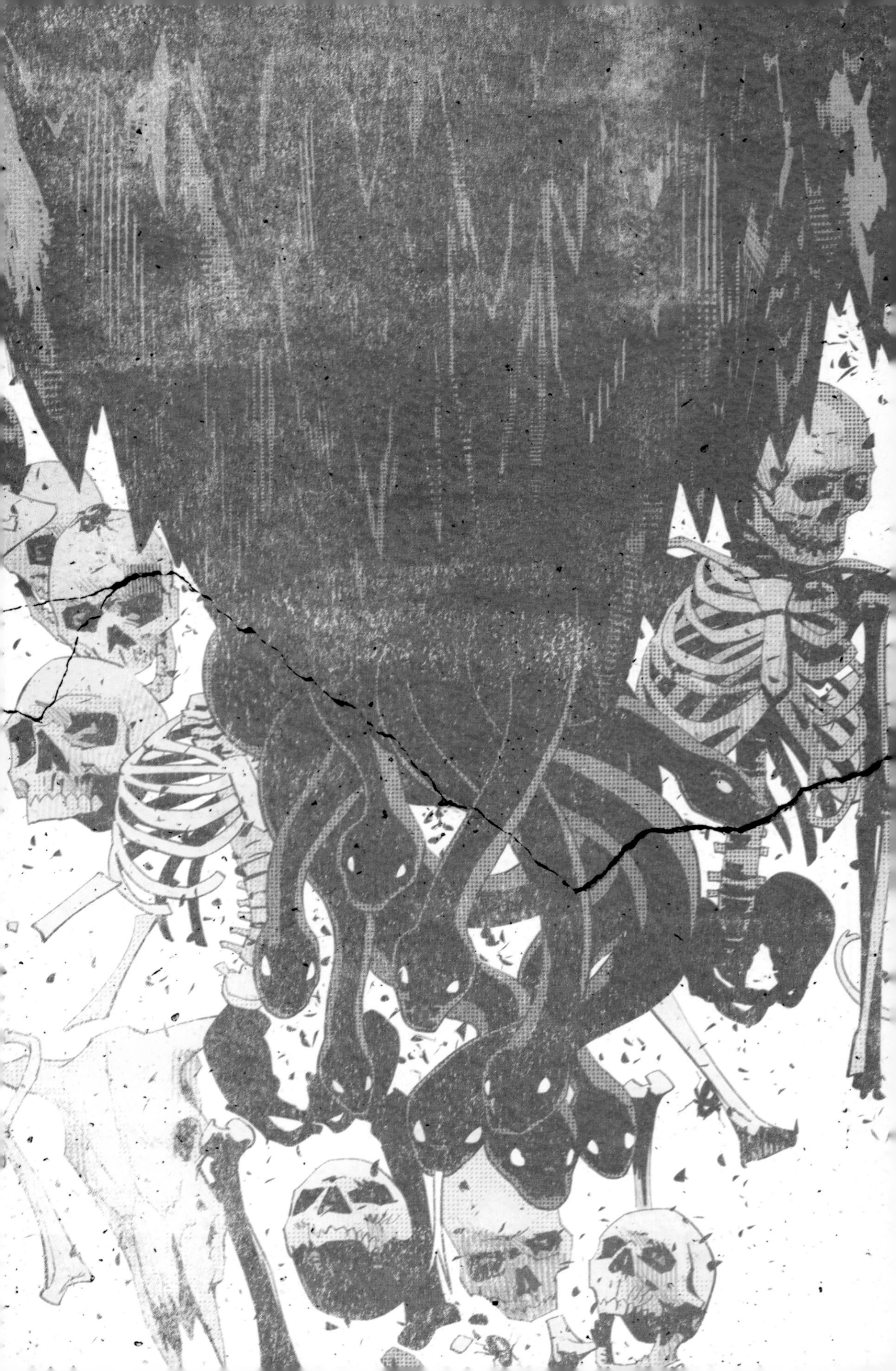

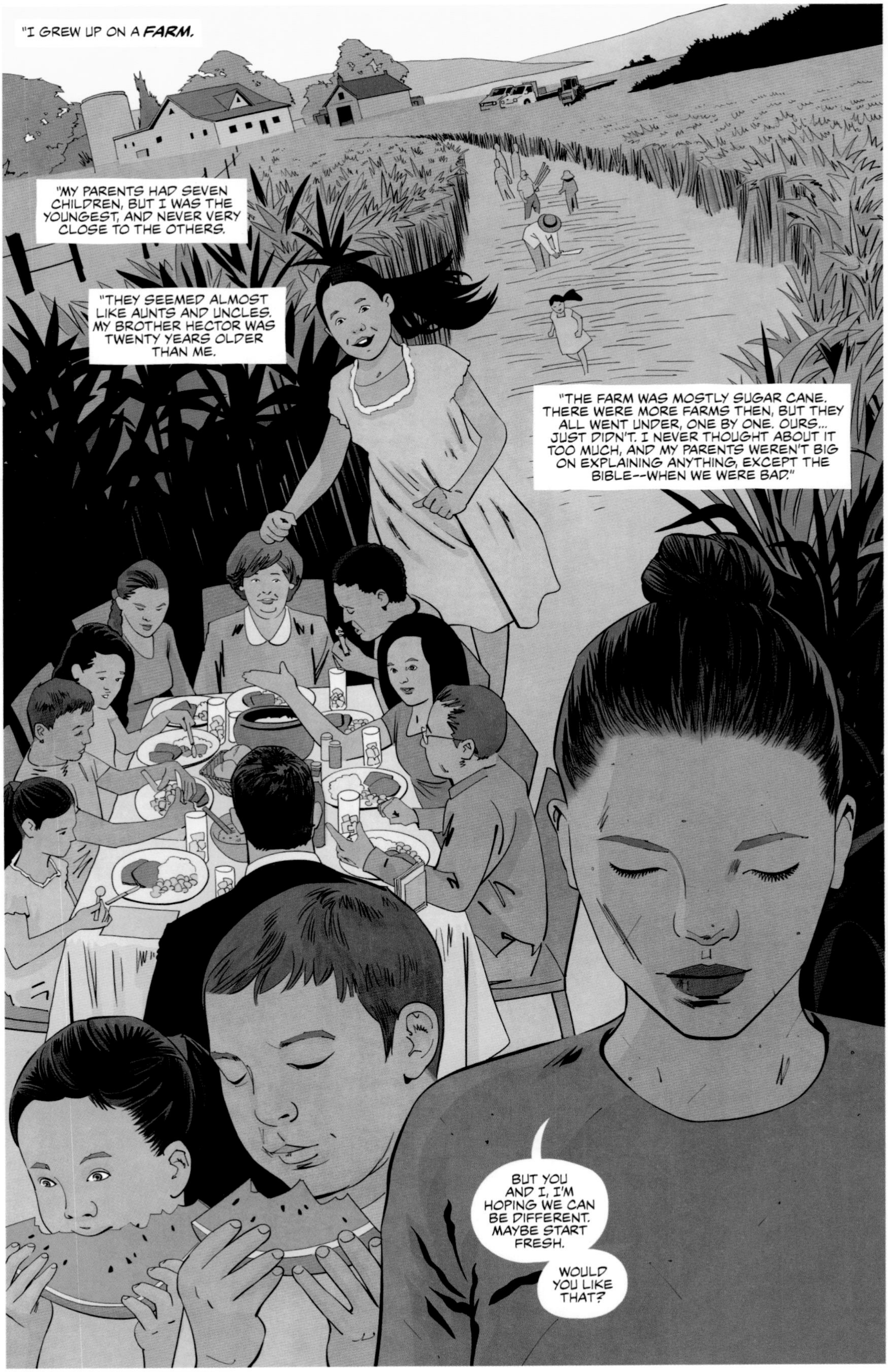
"I GREW UP ON A *FARM.*
"MY PARENTS HAD SEVEN CHILDREN, BUT I WAS THE YOUNGEST, AND NEVER VERY CLOSE TO THE OTHERS.
"THEY SEEMED ALMOST LIKE AUNTS AND UNCLES. MY BROTHER HECTOR WAS TWENTY YEARS OLDER THAN ME.
"THE FARM WAS MOSTLY SUGAR CANE. THERE WERE MORE FARMS THEN, BUT THEY ALL WENT UNDER, ONE BY ONE. OURS... JUST DIDN'T. I NEVER THOUGHT ABOUT IT TOO MUCH, AND MY PARENTS WEREN'T BIG ON EXPLAINING ANYTHING, EXCEPT THE BIBLE--WHEN WE WERE BAD."
BUT YOU AND I, I'M HOPING WE CAN BE DIFFERENT. MAYBE START FRESH.
WOULD YOU LIKE THAT?

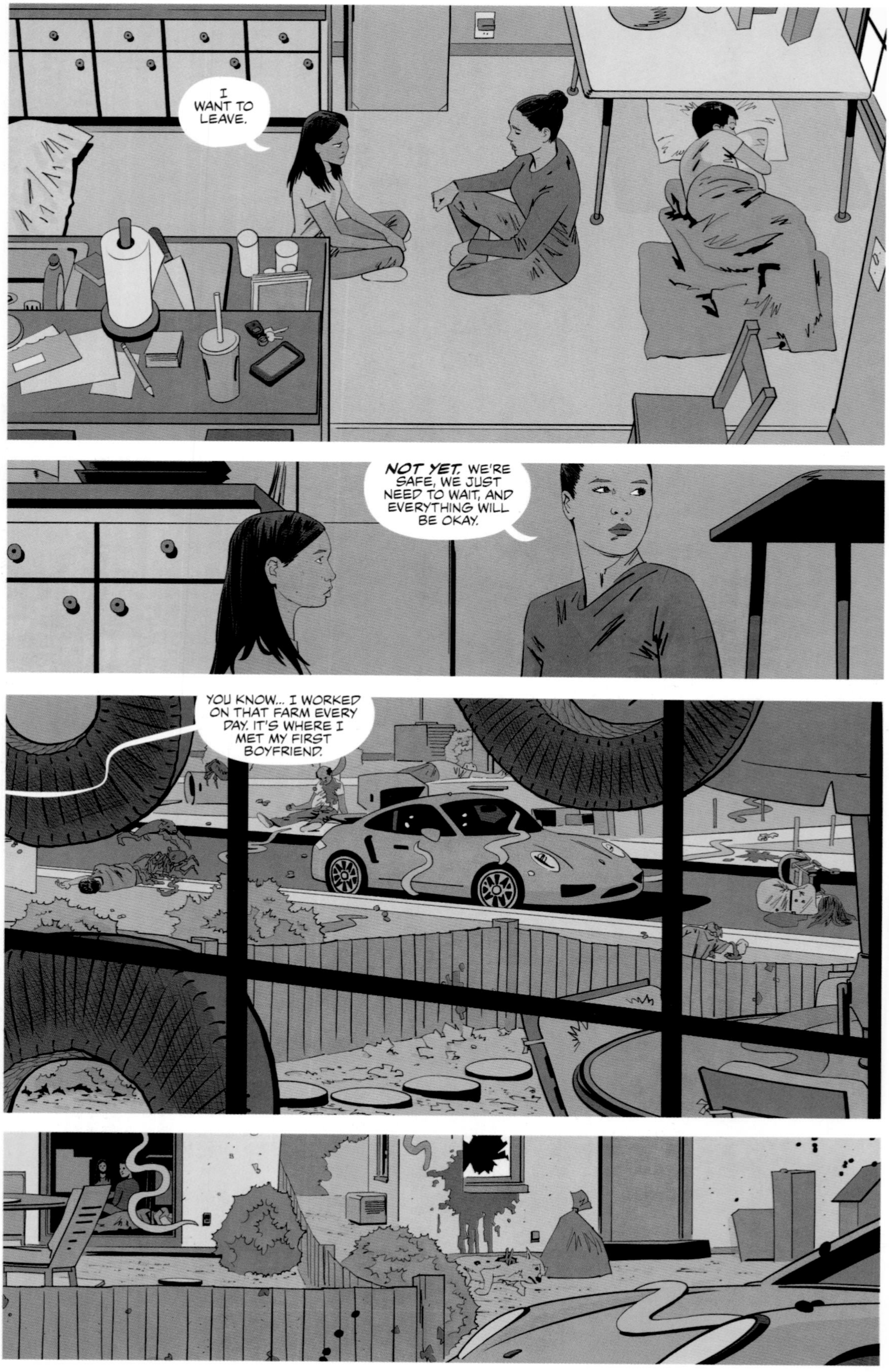
I WANT TO LEAVE.
NOT YET. WE'RE SAFE, WE JUST NEED TO WAIT, AND EVERYTHING WILL BE OKAY.
YOU KNOW... I WORKED ON THAT FARM EVERY DAY. IT'S WHERE I MET MY FIRST BOYFRIEND.

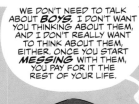

WE DON'T NEED TO TALK ABOUT **BOYS.** I DON'T WANT YOU THINKING ABOUT THEM, AND I DON'T REALLY WANT TO THINK ABOUT THEM, EITHER. ONCE YOU START **MESSING** WITH THEM, YOU PAY FOR IT THE REST OF YOUR LIFE.

I'VE... LOST PEOPLE BEFORE, TOO. I KNOW HOW THIS FEELS.

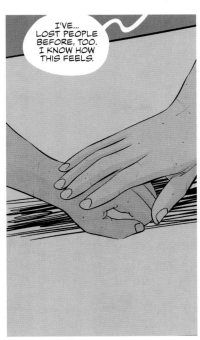

I HAD A LIFE ON THE FARM, AND THEN I **RAN AWAY** FROM IT.

I WAS IMPULSIVE. I THOUGHT I KNEW BETTER. AND THEN, I JUST HAD TO GIVE IT ALL UP... MY MOTHER, MY FATHER... **YOU AND YOUR BROTHER.** I COULDN'T HANDLE ANY OF IT.

WHY?

EVERYONE GOES CRAZY SOMETIMES.

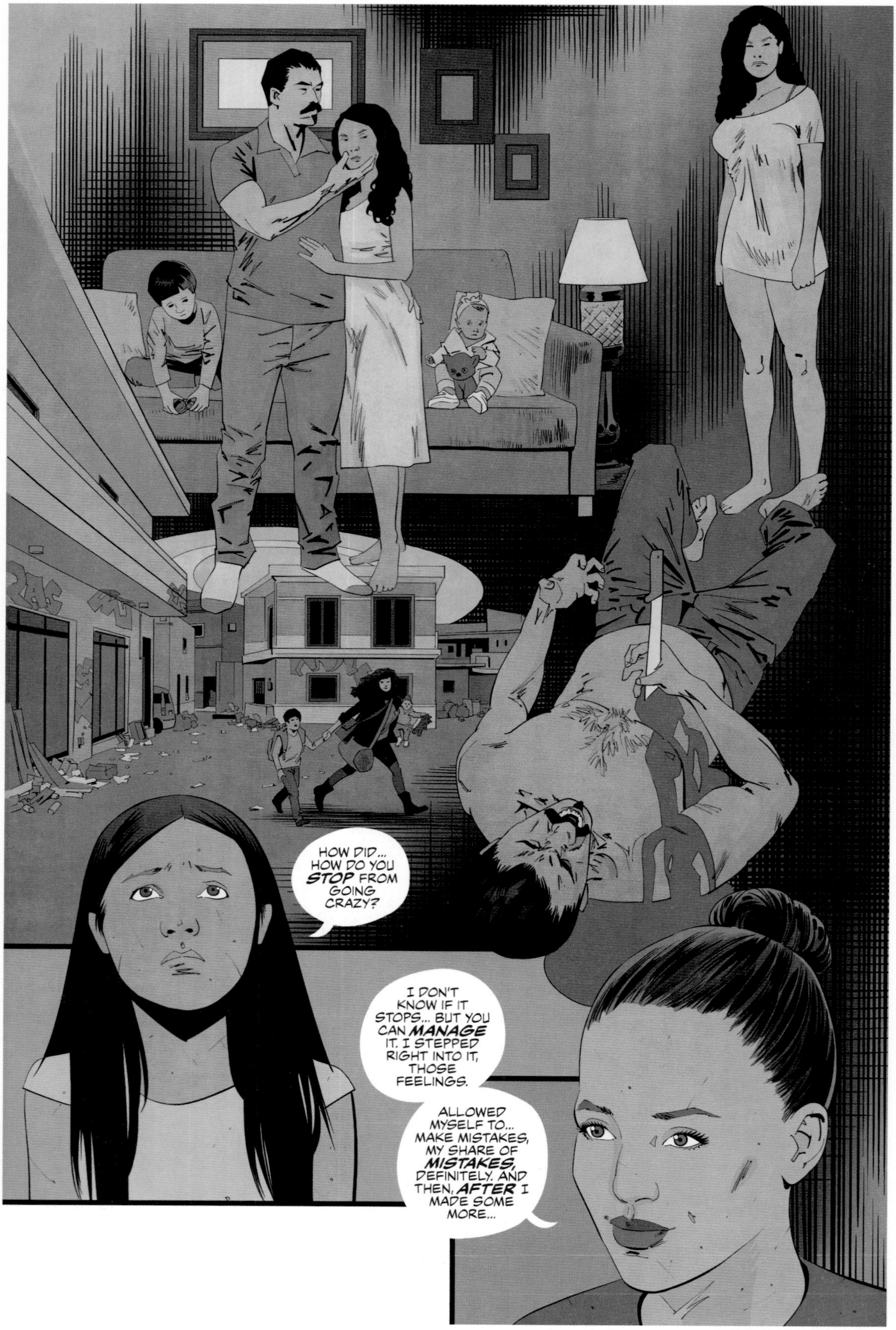
HOW DID... HOW DO YOU STOP FROM GOING CRAZY?
I DON'T KNOW IF IT STOPS... BUT YOU CAN MANAGE IT. I STEPPED RIGHT INTO IT, THOSE FEELINGS.
ALLOWED MYSELF TO... MAKE MISTAKES, MY SHARE OF MISTAKES, DEFINITELY. AND THEN, AFTER I MADE SOME MORE...

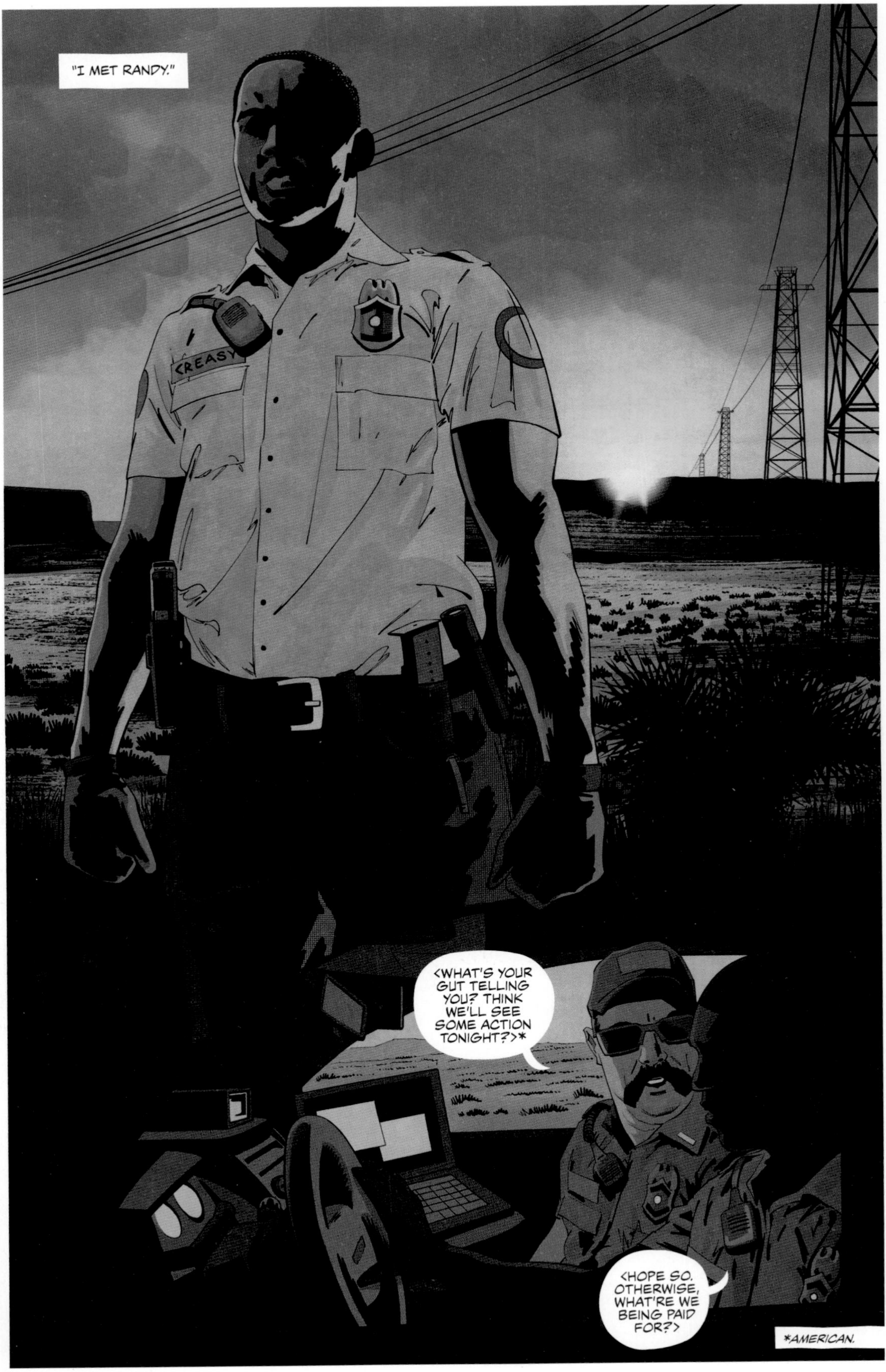
"I MET RANDY."
<WHAT'S YOUR GUT TELLING YOU? THINK WE'LL SEE SOME ACTION TONIGHT?>*
<HOPE SO. OTHERWISE, WHAT'RE WE BEING PAID FOR?>
*AMERICAN.

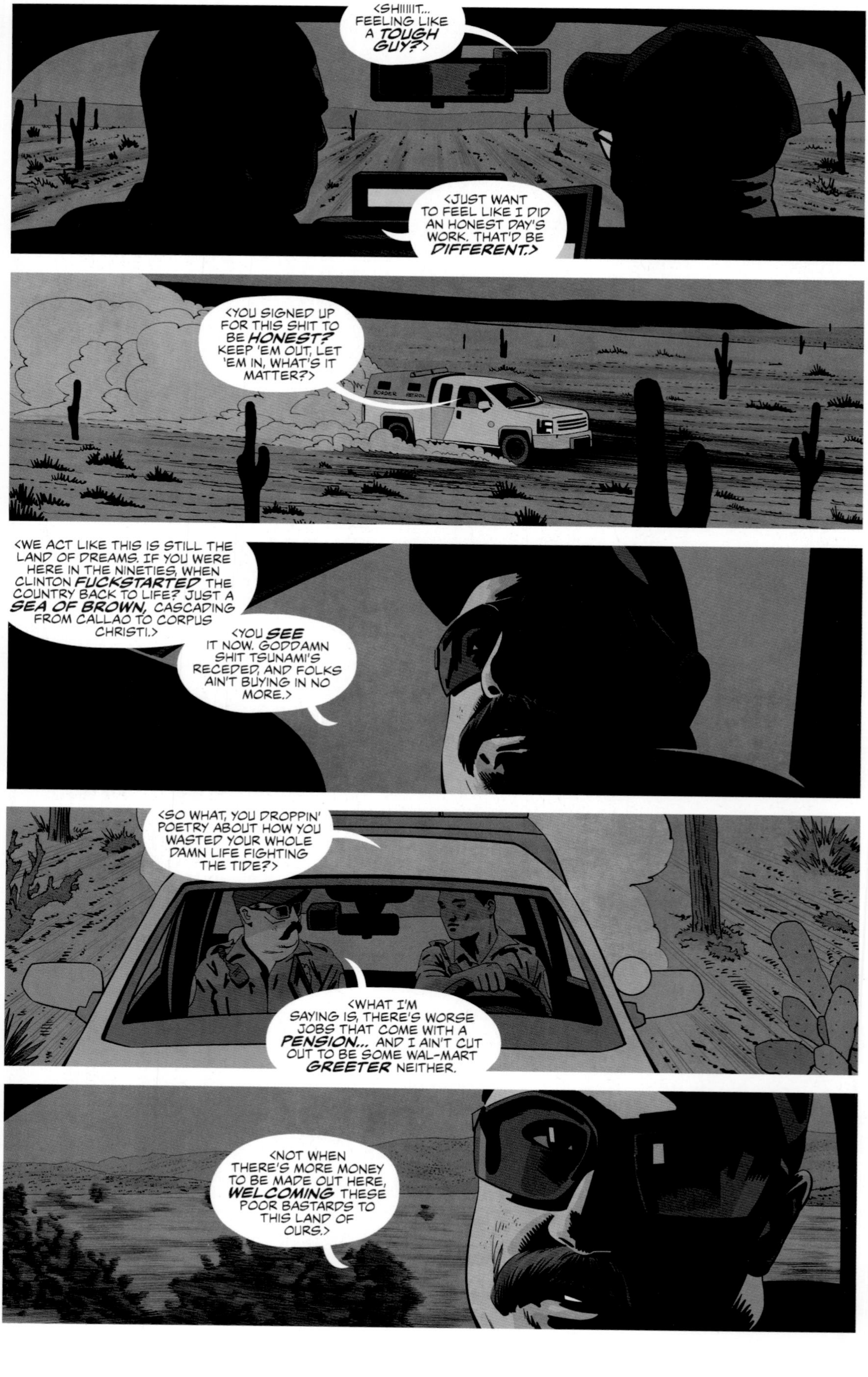
<SHIIIIIT... FEELING LIKE A TOUGH GUY?>
<JUST WANT TO FEEL LIKE I DID AN HONEST DAY'S WORK. THAT'D BE DIFFERENT.>
<YOU SIGNED UP FOR THIS SHIT TO BE HONEST? KEEP 'EM OUT, LET 'EM IN, WHAT'S IT MATTER?>
BORDER PATROL
<WE ACT LIKE THIS IS STILL THE LAND OF DREAMS. IF YOU WERE HERE IN THE NINETIES, WHEN CLINTON FUCKSTARTED THE COUNTRY BACK TO LIFE? JUST A SEA OF BROWN, CASCADING FROM CALLAO TO CORPUS CHRISTI.>
<YOU SEE IT NOW. GODDAMN SHIT TSUNAMI'S RECEDED, AND FOLKS AIN'T BUYING IN NO MORE.>
<SO WHAT, YOU DROPPIN' POETRY ABOUT HOW YOU WASTED YOUR WHOLE DAMN LIFE FIGHTING THE TIDE?>
<WHAT I'M SAYING IS, THERE'S WORSE JOBS THAT COME WITH A PENSION... AND I AIN'T CUT OUT TO BE SOME WAL-MART GREETER NEITHER.
<NOT WHEN THERE'S MORE MONEY TO BE MADE OUT HERE, WELCOMING THESE POOR BASTARDS TO THIS LAND OF OURS.>

"I'D MOVED UP TO TAMAULIPAS BY THEN. I TRIED LIVING IN *A LOT* OF PLACES--RIO BRAVO, REYNOSA.

"I HAD SOME COUSINS THERE. I LIVED WITH THEM FOR AS LONG AS IT'D LAST, THEN I'D MOVE ON.

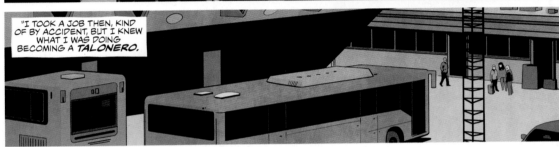

"I TOOK A JOB THEN, KIND OF BY ACCIDENT, BUT I KNEW WHAT I WAS DOING BECOMING A *TALONERO.*

"A FRIEND OF MY COUSIN TOOK PEOPLE TO *EL NORTE.* IT'S A LONG JOURNEY, ALL KINDS OF DANGEROUS... SO YOU NEEDED A *MAN* LIKE HIM, WHO WAS GOOD AT WHAT HE DID. HE WORKED MAINLY OFF REFERRALS.

"IF YOU CROSSED SUCCESSFULLY, YOU WOULD TELL YOUR FAMILY MEMBERS WHO TO *TRUST* SO THEY COULD COME JOIN YOU. HE CROSSED THREE, SOMETIMES FOUR, TIMES A WEEK.

"I WOULD TRAVEL THE NORTHERN TOWNS, TALK TO PEOPLE IN THE BUS STATIONS, PLACES LIKE THAT, SEE WHO NEEDED HELP CROSSING. THE ONES THAT CAME UP FROM VERACRUZ WERE EASIER TO PULL.

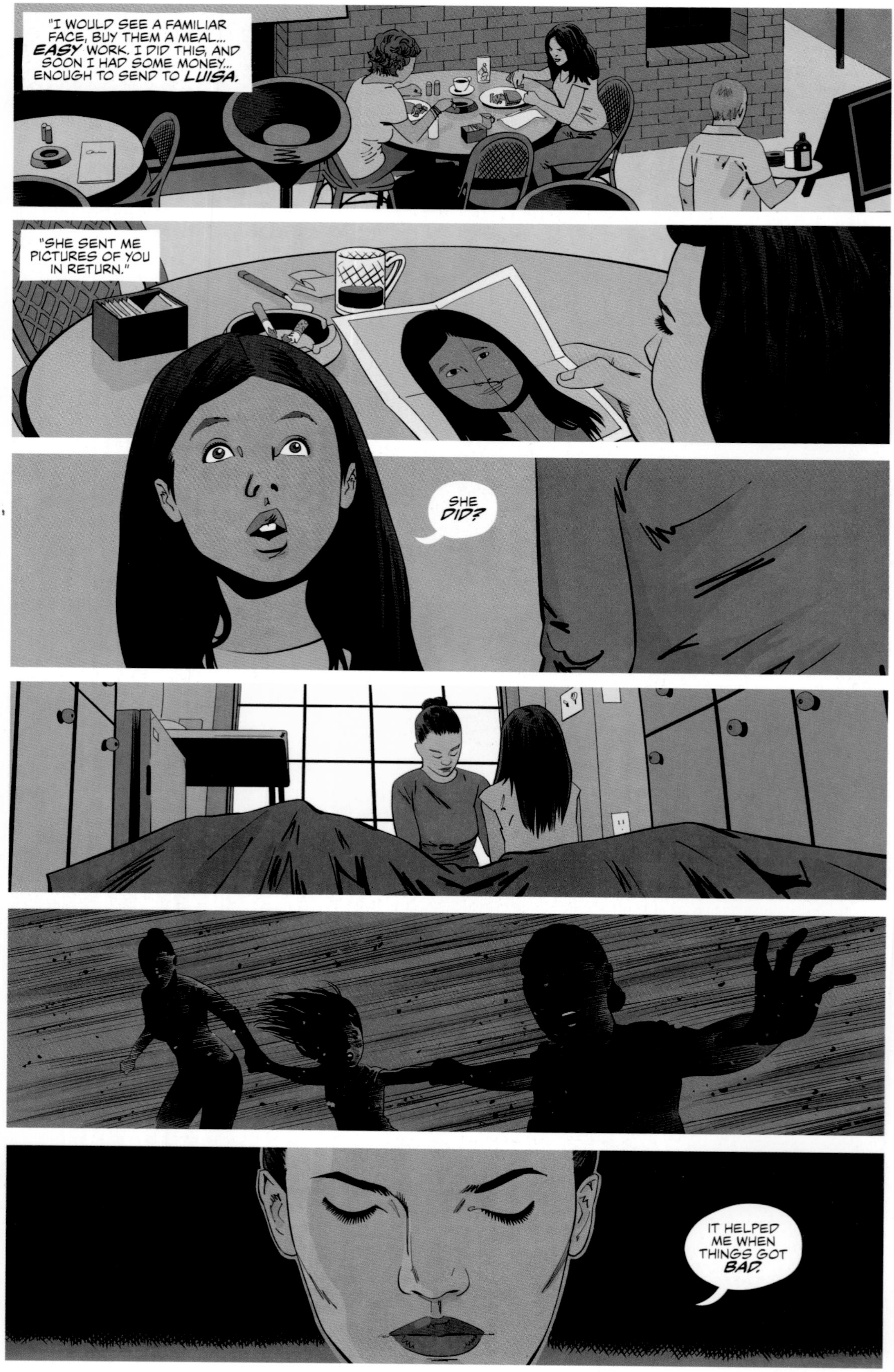
"I WOULD SEE A FAMILIAR FACE, BUY THEM A MEAL... EASY WORK. I DID THIS, AND SOON I HAD SOME MONEY... ENOUGH TO SEND TO LUISA.
"SHE SENT ME PICTURES OF YOU IN RETURN."
SHE DID?
IT HELPED ME WHEN THINGS GOT BAD.

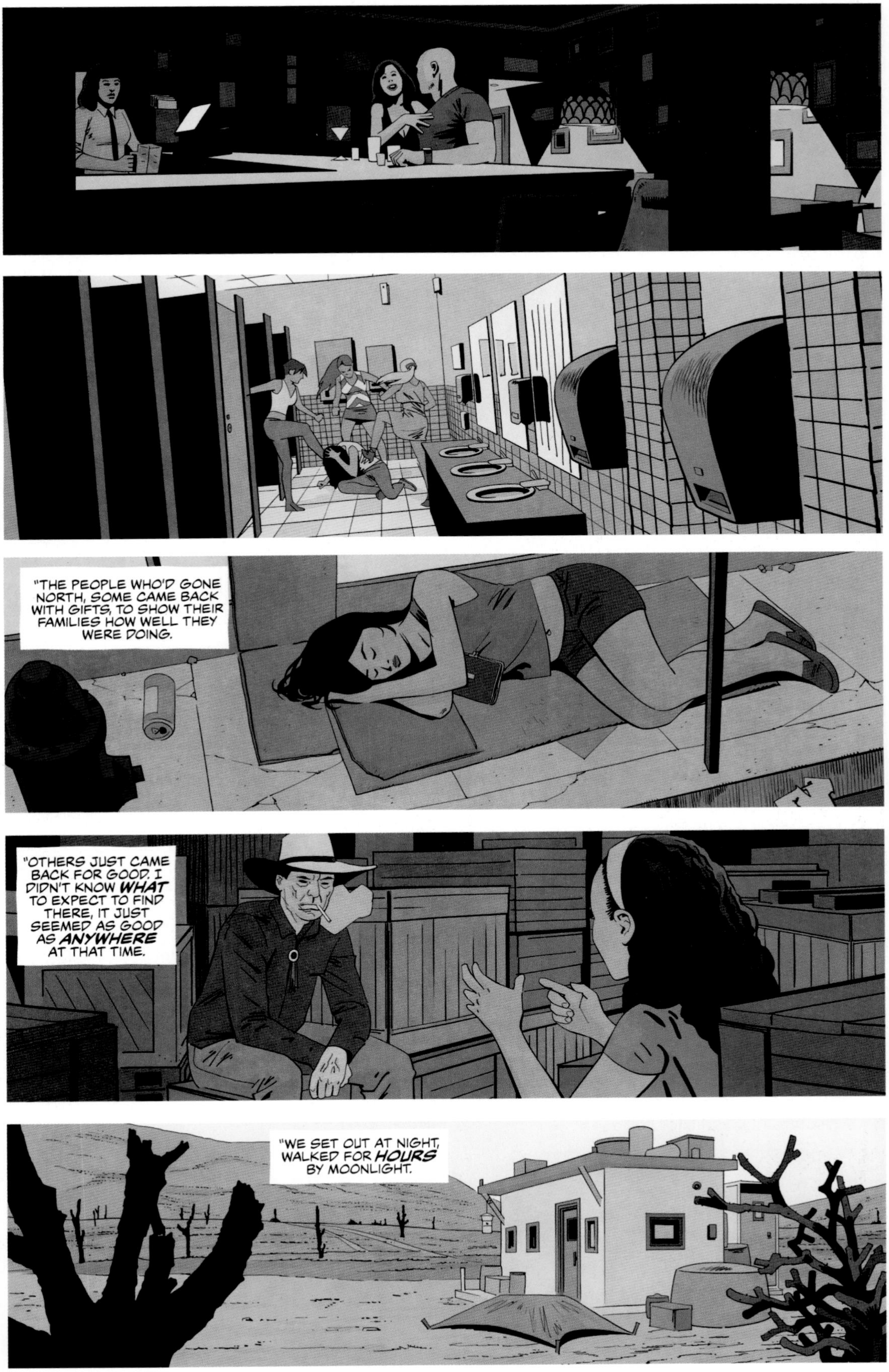
"THE PEOPLE WHO'D GONE NORTH, SOME CAME BACK WITH GIFTS, TO SHOW THEIR FAMILIES HOW WELL THEY WERE DOING.
"OTHERS JUST CAME BACK FOR GOOD. I DIDN'T KNOW WHAT TO EXPECT TO FIND THERE, IT JUST SEEMED AS GOOD AS ANYWHERE AT THAT TIME.
"WE SET OUT AT NIGHT, WALKED FOR HOURS BY MOONLIGHT.

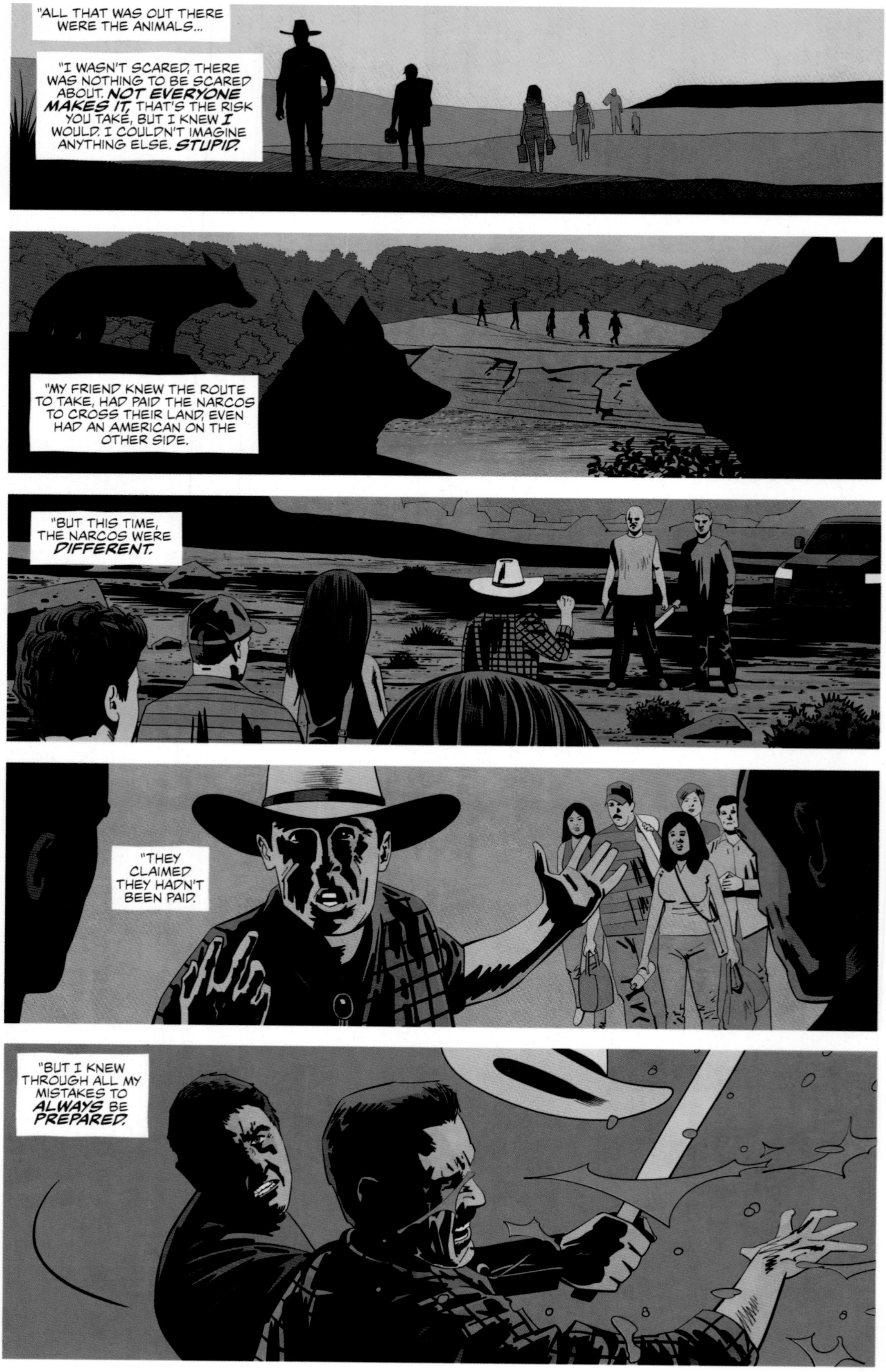
"ALL THAT WAS OUT THERE WERE THE ANIMALS...
"I WASN'T SCARED, THERE WAS NOTHING TO BE SCARED ABOUT. NOT EVERYONE MAKES IT, THAT'S THE RISK YOU TAKE, BUT I KNEW I WOULD. I COULDN'T IMAGINE ANYTHING ELSE. STUPID.
"MY FRIEND KNEW THE ROUTE TO TAKE, HAD PAID THE NARCOS TO CROSS THEIR LAND, EVEN HAD AN AMERICAN ON THE OTHER SIDE.
"BUT THIS TIME, THE NARCOS WERE DIFFERENT.
"THEY CLAIMED THEY HADN'T BEEN PAID.
"BUT I KNEW THROUGH ALL MY MISTAKES TO ALWAYS BE PREPARED.

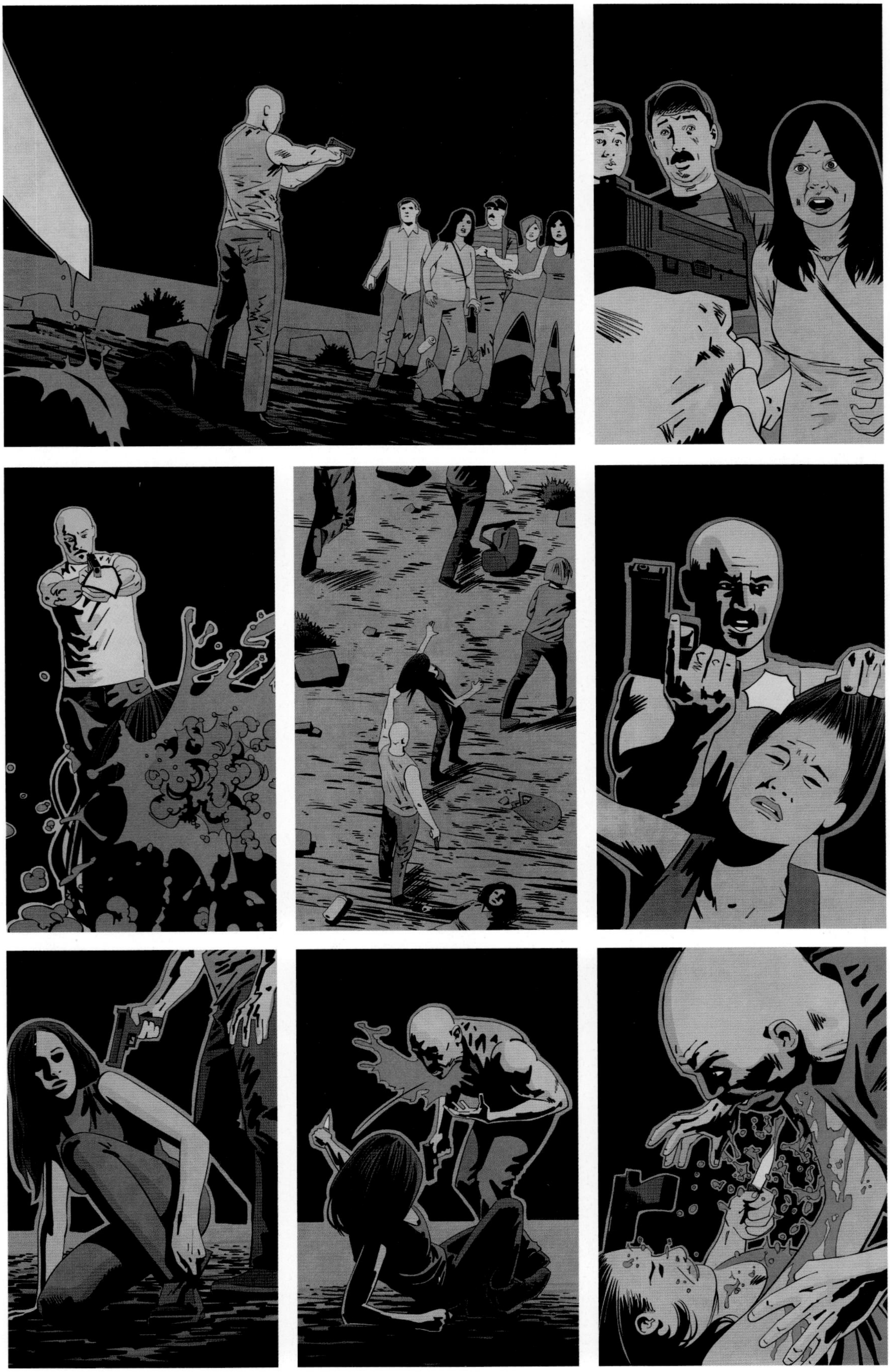

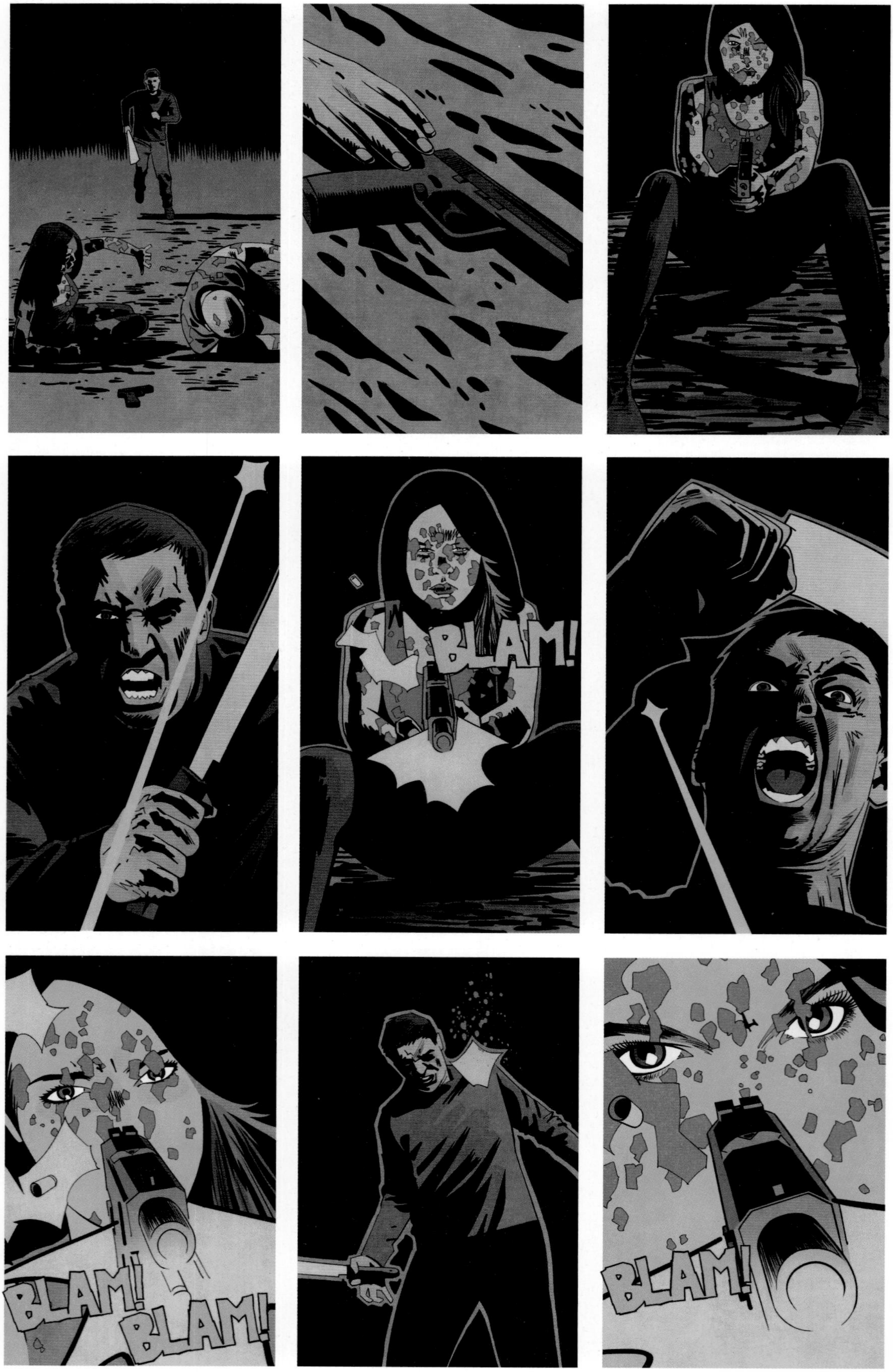
BLAM!
BLAM!
BLAM!
BLAM!

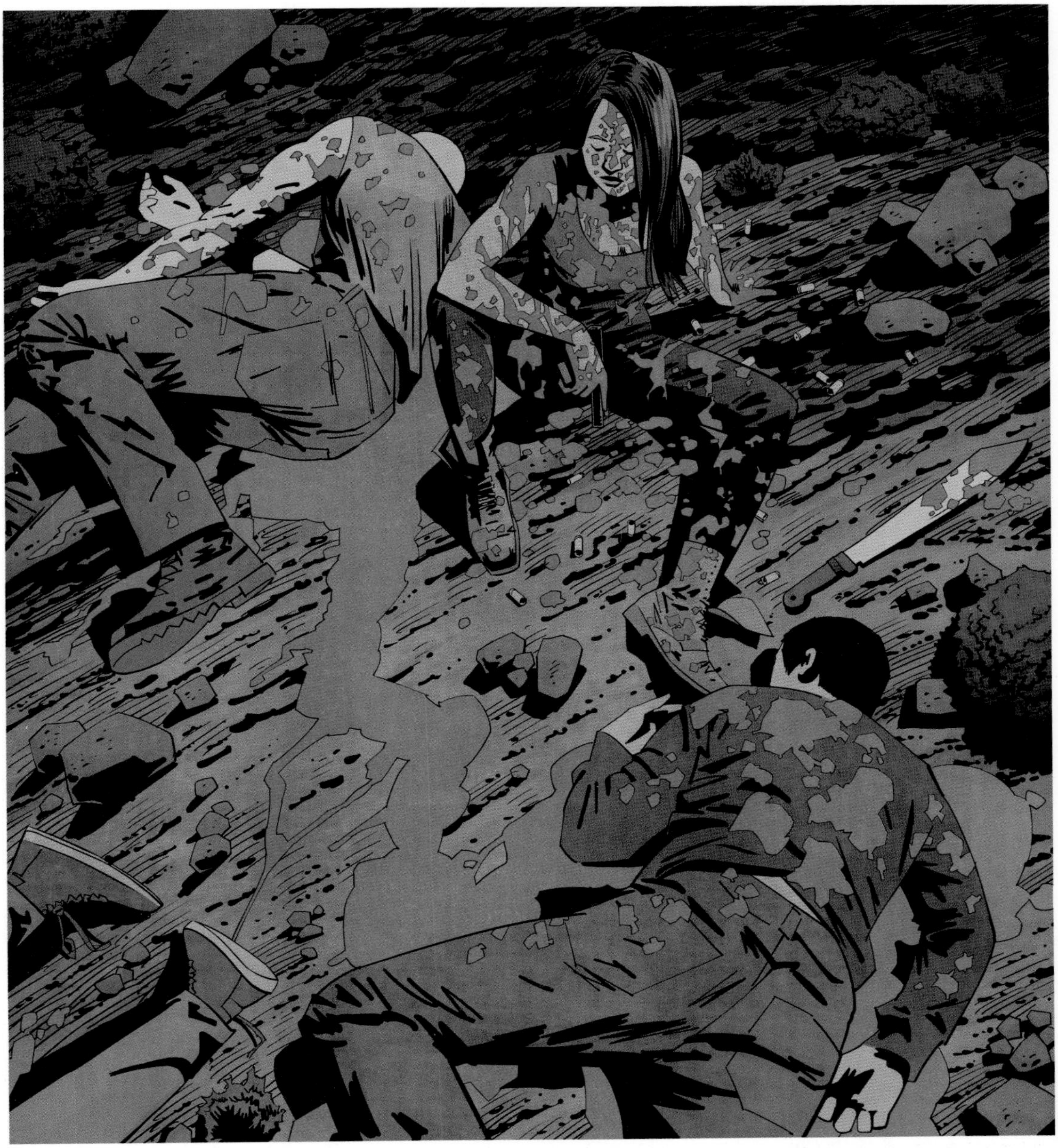

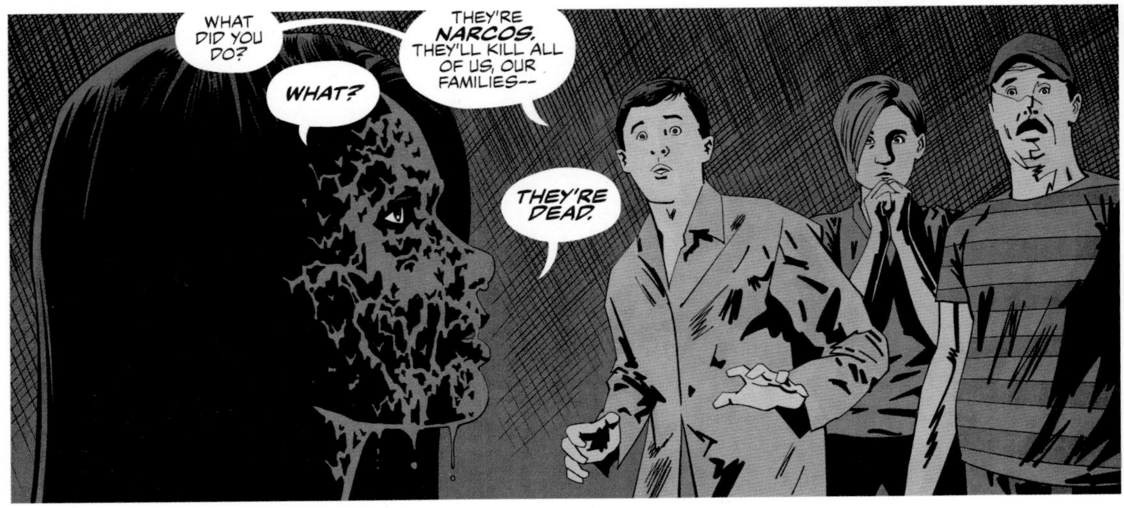
WHAT DID YOU DO?
WHAT?
THEY'RE NARCOS. THEY'LL KILL ALL OF US, OUR FAMILIES--
THEY'RE DEAD.

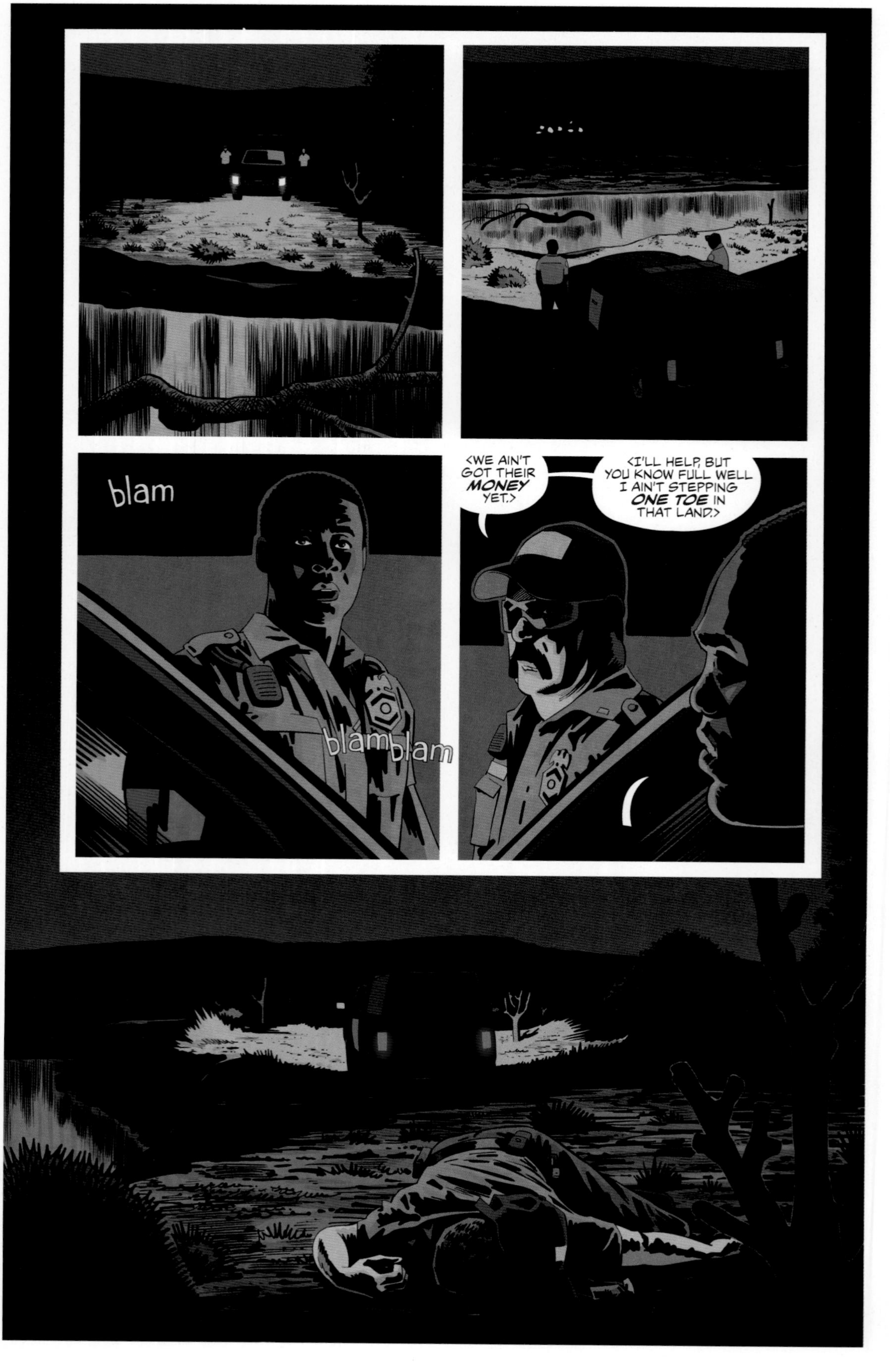

blam
blamblam
<WE AIN'T GOT THEIR MONEY YET.>
<I'LL HELP, BUT YOU KNOW FULL WELL I AIN'T STEPPING ONE TOE IN THAT LAND.>

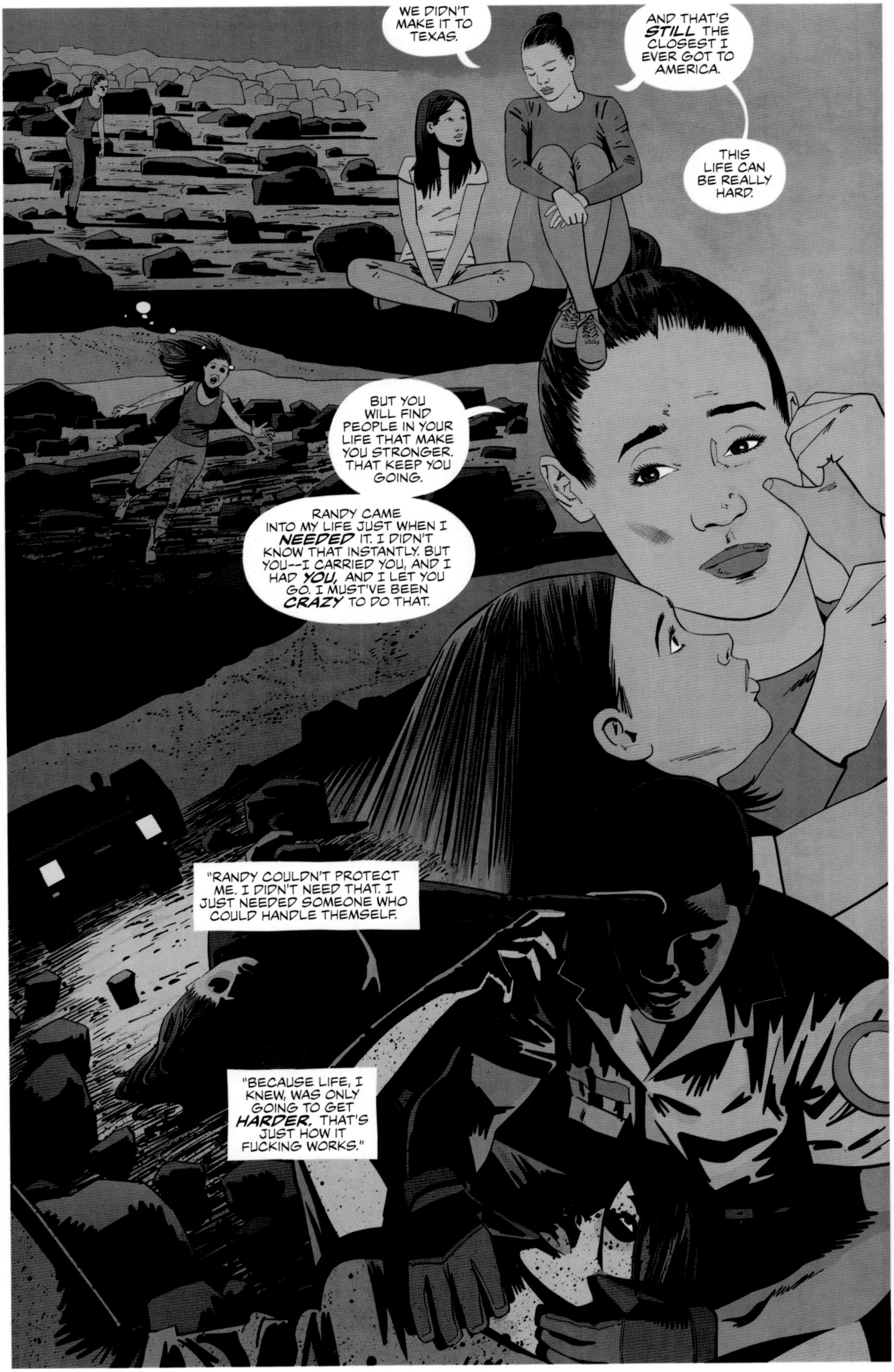
WE DIDN'T MAKE IT TO TEXAS.
AND THAT'S STILL THE CLOSEST I EVER GOT TO AMERICA.
THIS LIFE CAN BE REALLY HARD.
BUT YOU WILL FIND PEOPLE IN YOUR LIFE THAT MAKE YOU STRONGER. THAT KEEP YOU GOING.
RANDY CAME INTO MY LIFE JUST WHEN I NEEDED IT. I DIDN'T KNOW THAT INSTANTLY. BUT YOU--I CARRIED YOU, AND I HAD YOU, AND I LET YOU GO. I MUST'VE BEEN CRAZY TO DO THAT.
"RANDY COULDN'T PROTECT ME. I DIDN'T NEED THAT. I JUST NEEDED SOMEONE WHO COULD HANDLE THEMSELF.
"BECAUSE LIFE, I KNEW, WAS ONLY GOING TO GET HARDER. THAT'S JUST HOW IT FUCKING WORKS."

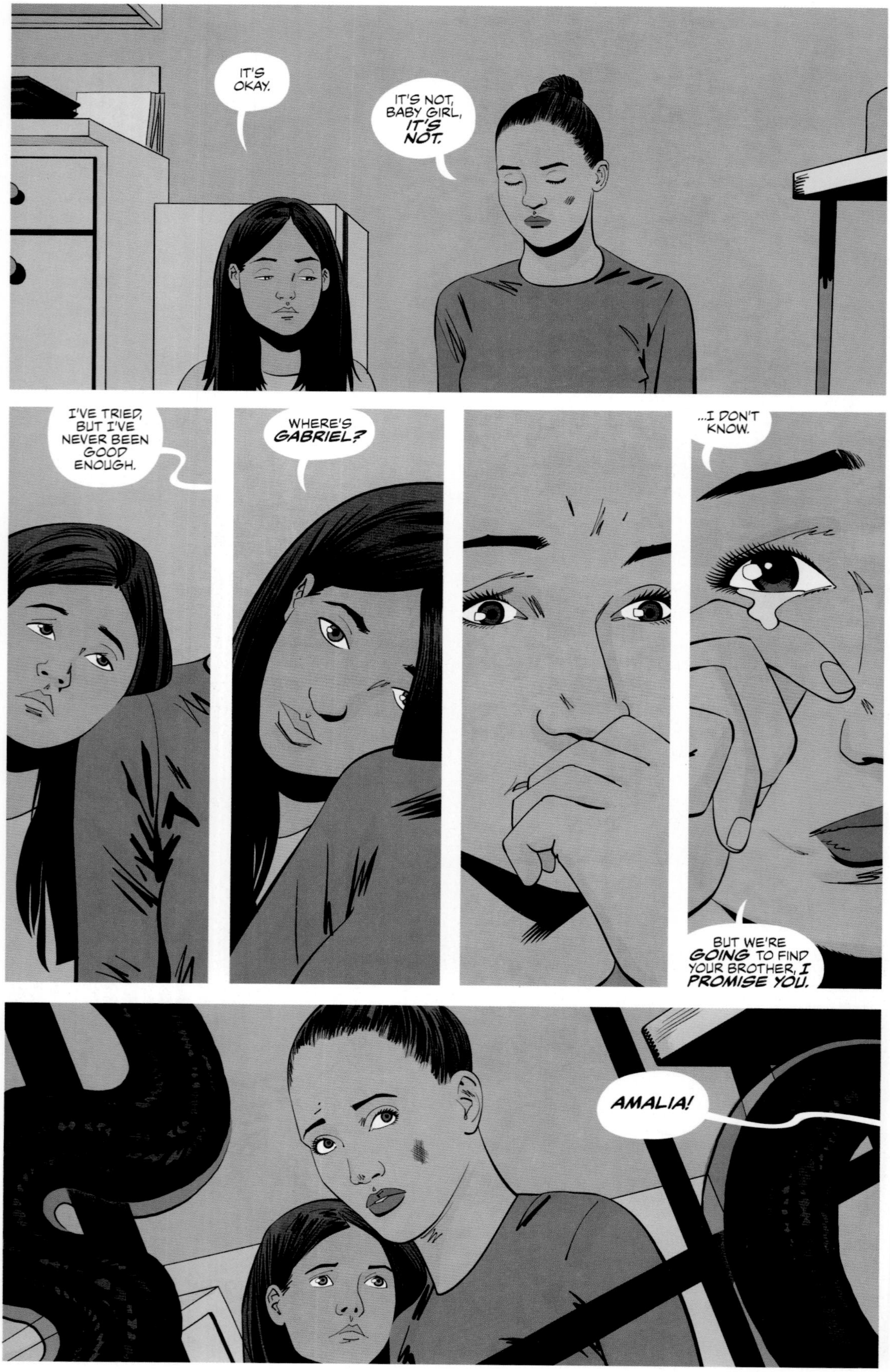
IT'S OKAY.
IT'S NOT, BABY GIRL, IT'S NOT.
I'VE TRIED, BUT I'VE NEVER BEEN GOOD ENOUGH.
WHERE'S GABRIEL?
...I DON'T KNOW.
BUT WE'RE GOING TO FIND YOUR BROTHER, I PROMISE YOU.
AMALIA!

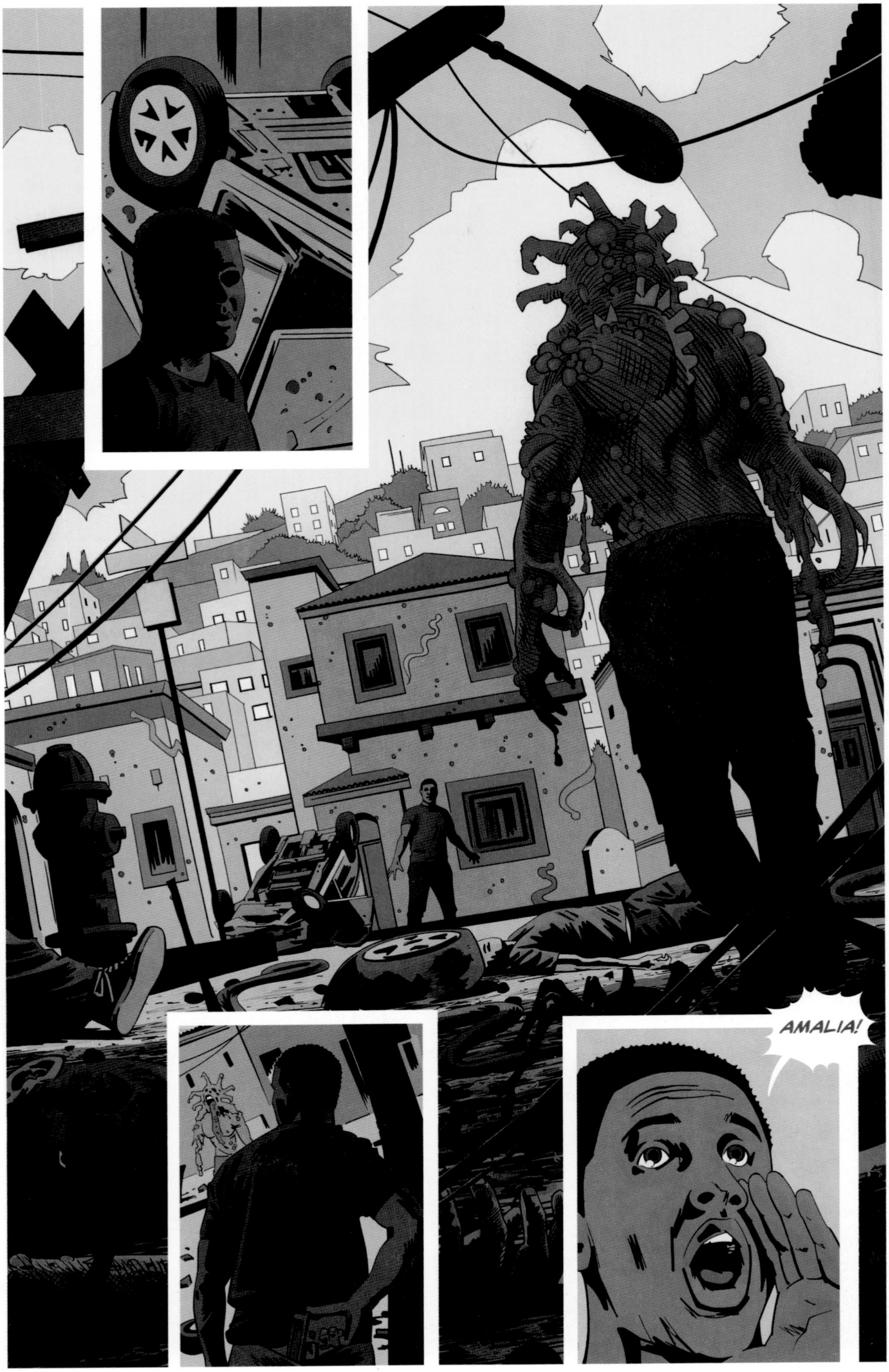
AMALIA!

FSISSS
CLAP CLAP
RANDY'S BACK. **COME ON.** HE NEEDS US.

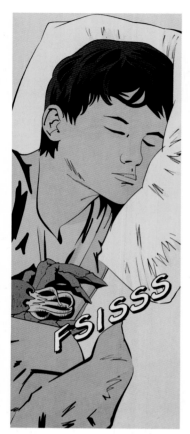

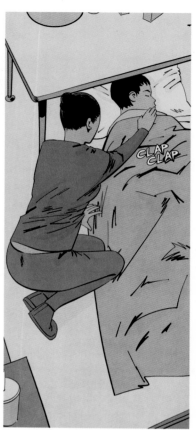

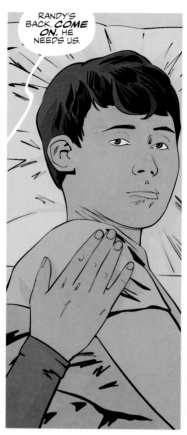

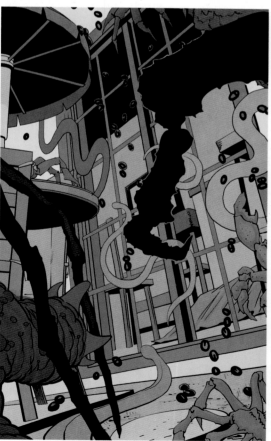

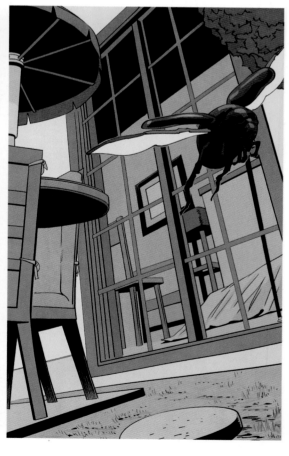

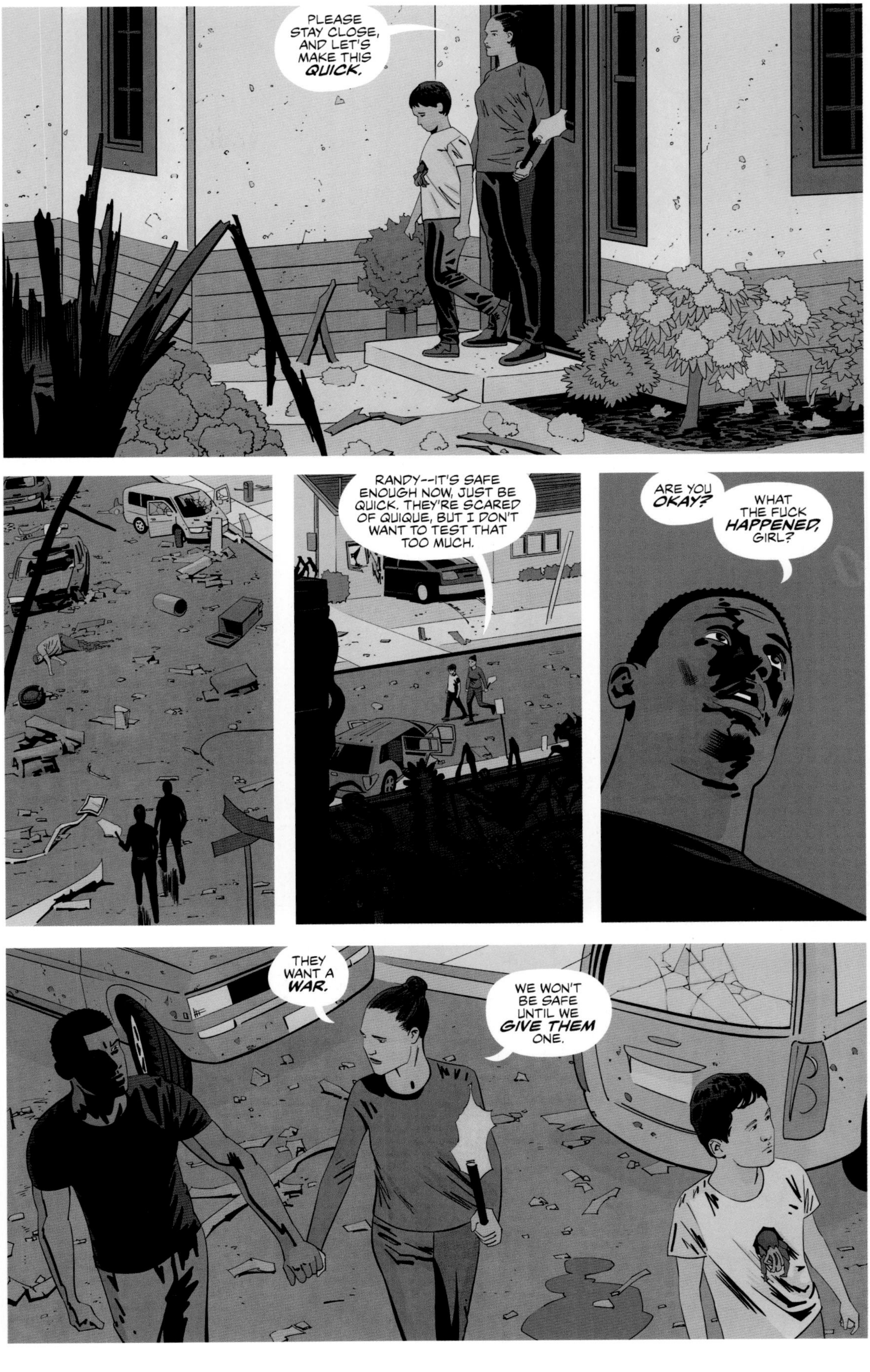
PLEASE STAY CLOSE, AND LET'S MAKE THIS QUICK.
RANDY--IT'S SAFE ENOUGH NOW, JUST BE QUICK. THEY'RE SCARED OF QUIQUE, BUT I DON'T WANT TO TEST THAT TOO MUCH.
ARE YOU OKAY?
WHAT THE FUCK HAPPENED, GIRL?
THEY WANT A WAR.
WE WON'T BE SAFE UNTIL WE GIVE THEM ONE.

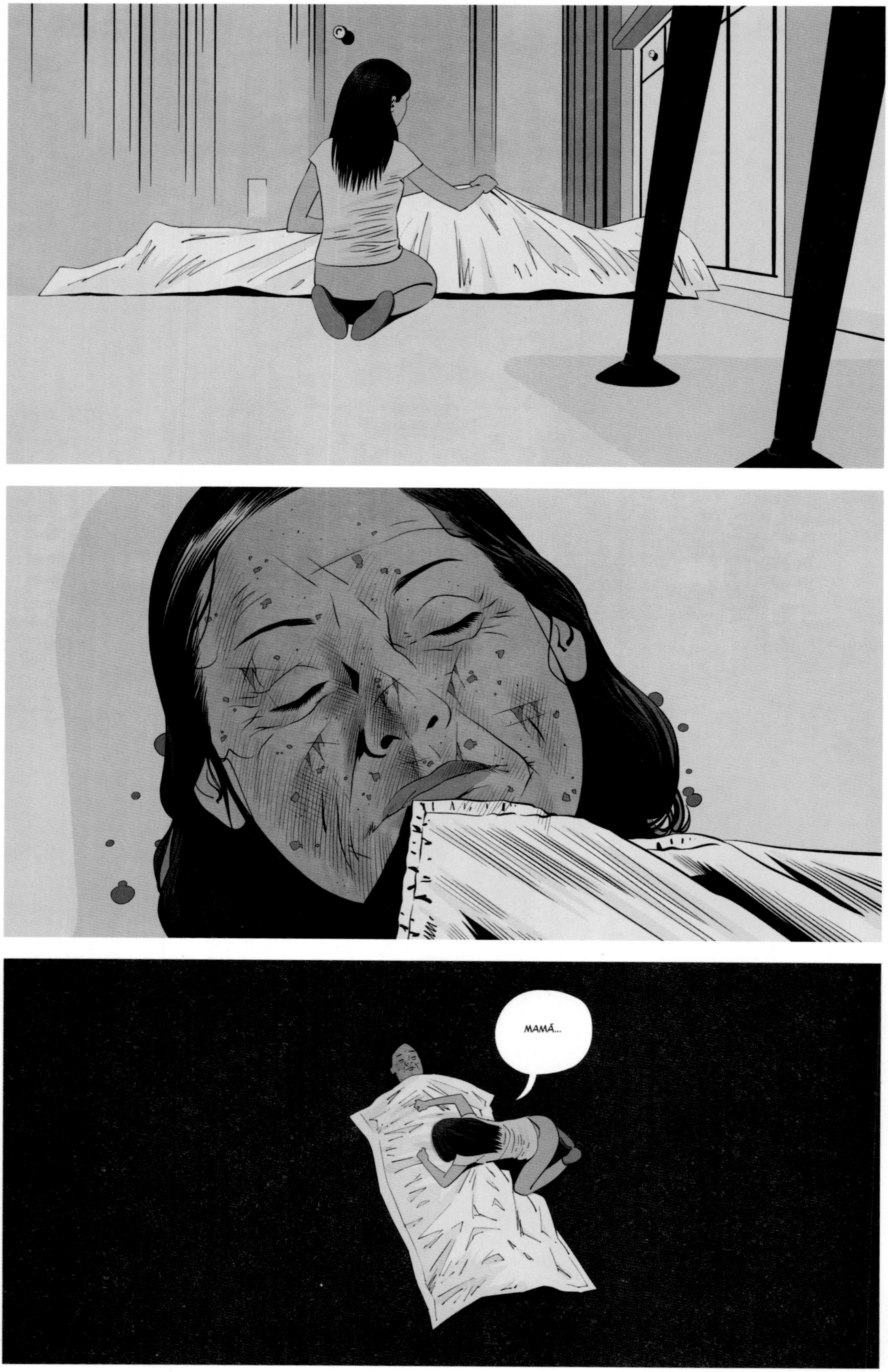
MAMÃ...

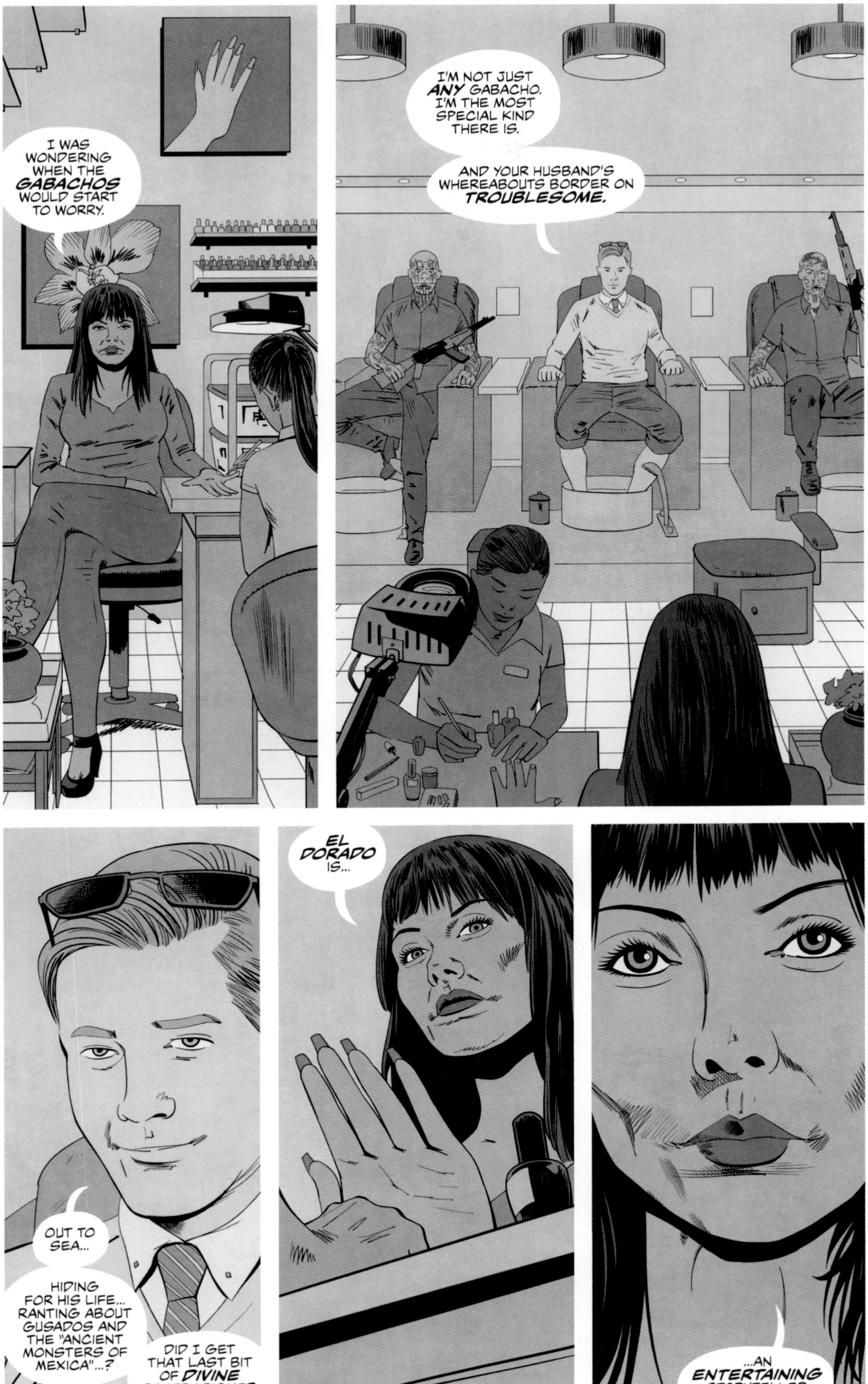
I WAS WONDERING WHEN THE GABACHOS WOULD START TO WORRY.
I'M NOT JUST ANY GABACHO. I'M THE MOST SPECIAL KIND THERE IS.
AND YOUR HUSBAND'S WHEREABOUTS BORDER ON TROUBLESOME.
OUT TO SEA...
HIDING FOR HIS LIFE... RANTING ABOUT GUSADOS AND THE "ANCIENT MONSTERS OF MEXICA"...?
DID I GET THAT LAST BIT OF DIVINE POETRY RIGHT?
EL DORADO IS...
...AN ENTERTAINING STORYTELLER.

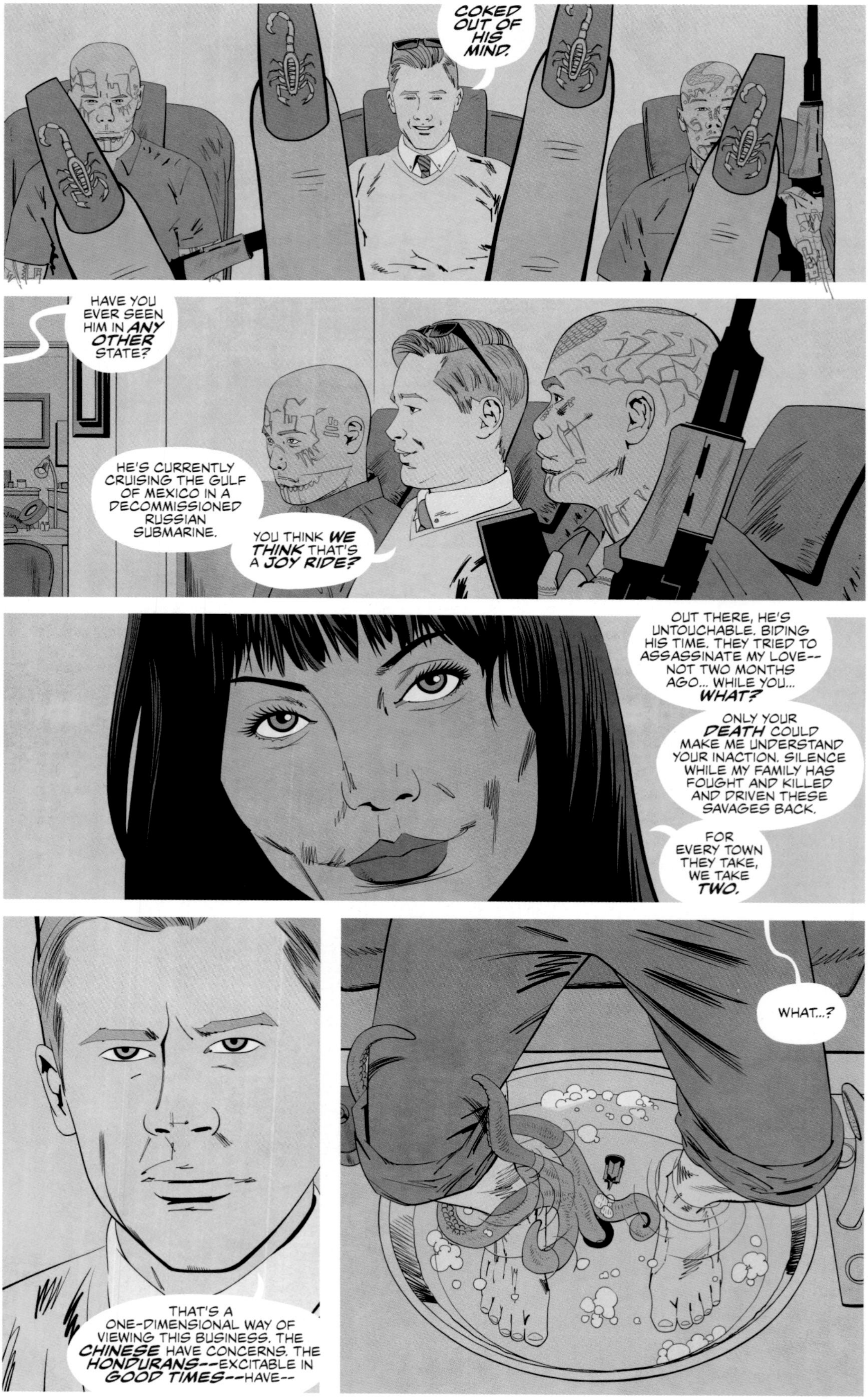
COKED OUT OF HIS MIND.
HAVE YOU EVER SEEN HIM IN ANY OTHER STATE?
HE'S CURRENTLY CRUISING THE GULF OF MEXICO IN A DECOMMISSIONED RUSSIAN SUBMARINE.
YOU THINK WE THINK THAT'S A JOY RIDE?
OUT THERE, HE'S UNTOUCHABLE. BIDING HIS TIME. THEY TRIED TO ASSASSINATE MY LOVE-- NOT TWO MONTHS AGO... WHILE YOU... WHAT?
ONLY YOUR DEATH COULD MAKE ME UNDERSTAND YOUR INACTION. SILENCE WHILE MY FAMILY HAS FOUGHT AND KILLED AND DRIVEN THESE SAVAGES BACK.
FOR EVERY TOWN THEY TAKE, WE TAKE TWO.
THAT'S A ONE-DIMENSIONAL WAY OF VIEWING THIS BUSINESS. THE CHINESE HAVE CONCERNS. THE HONDURANS--EXCITABLE IN GOOD TIMES--HAVE--
WHAT...?

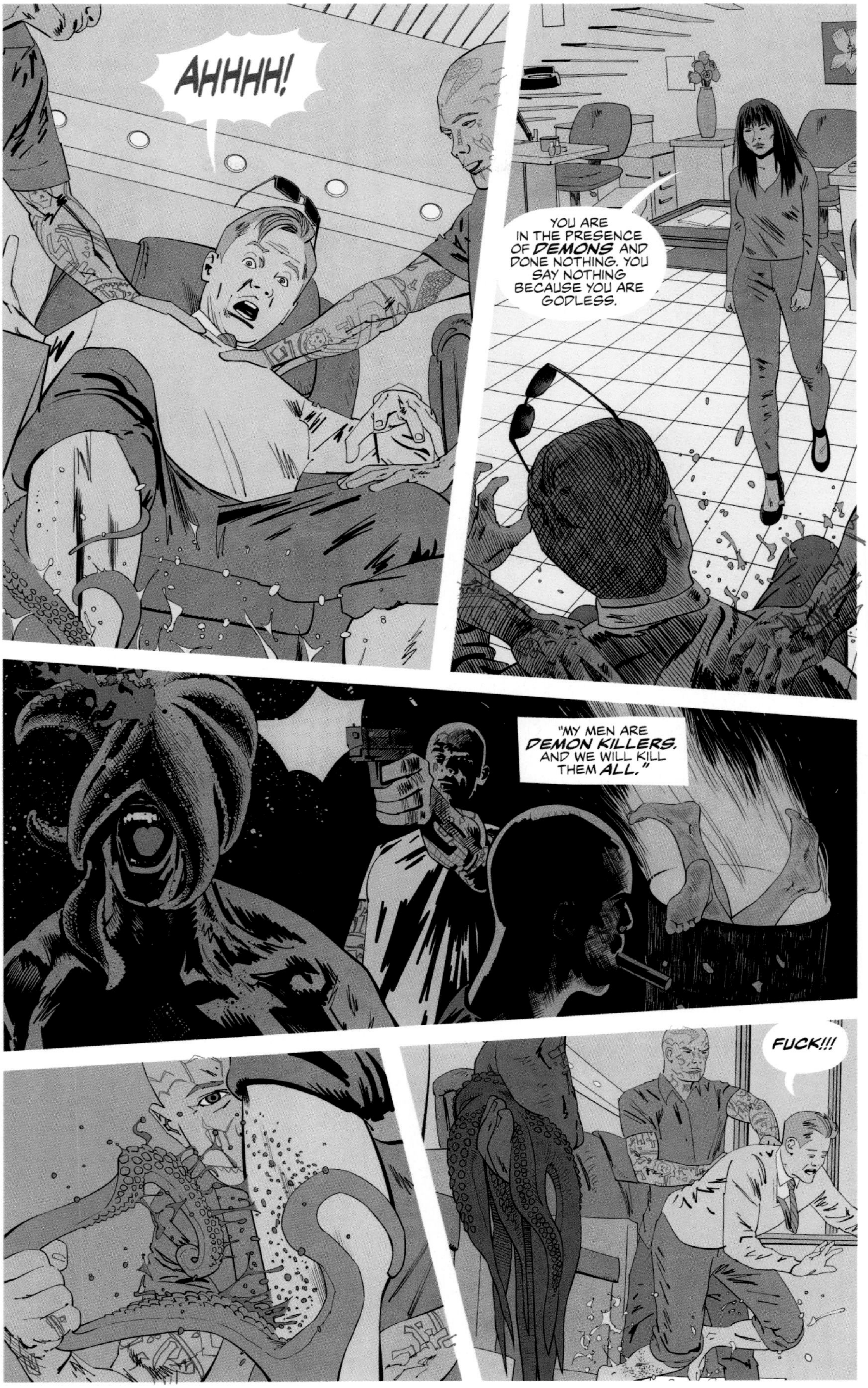
AHHHH!
YOU ARE IN THE PRESENCE OF DEMONS AND DONE NOTHING. YOU SAY NOTHING BECAUSE YOU ARE GODLESS.
"MY MEN ARE DEMON KILLERS. AND WE WILL KILL THEM ALL."
FUCK!!!

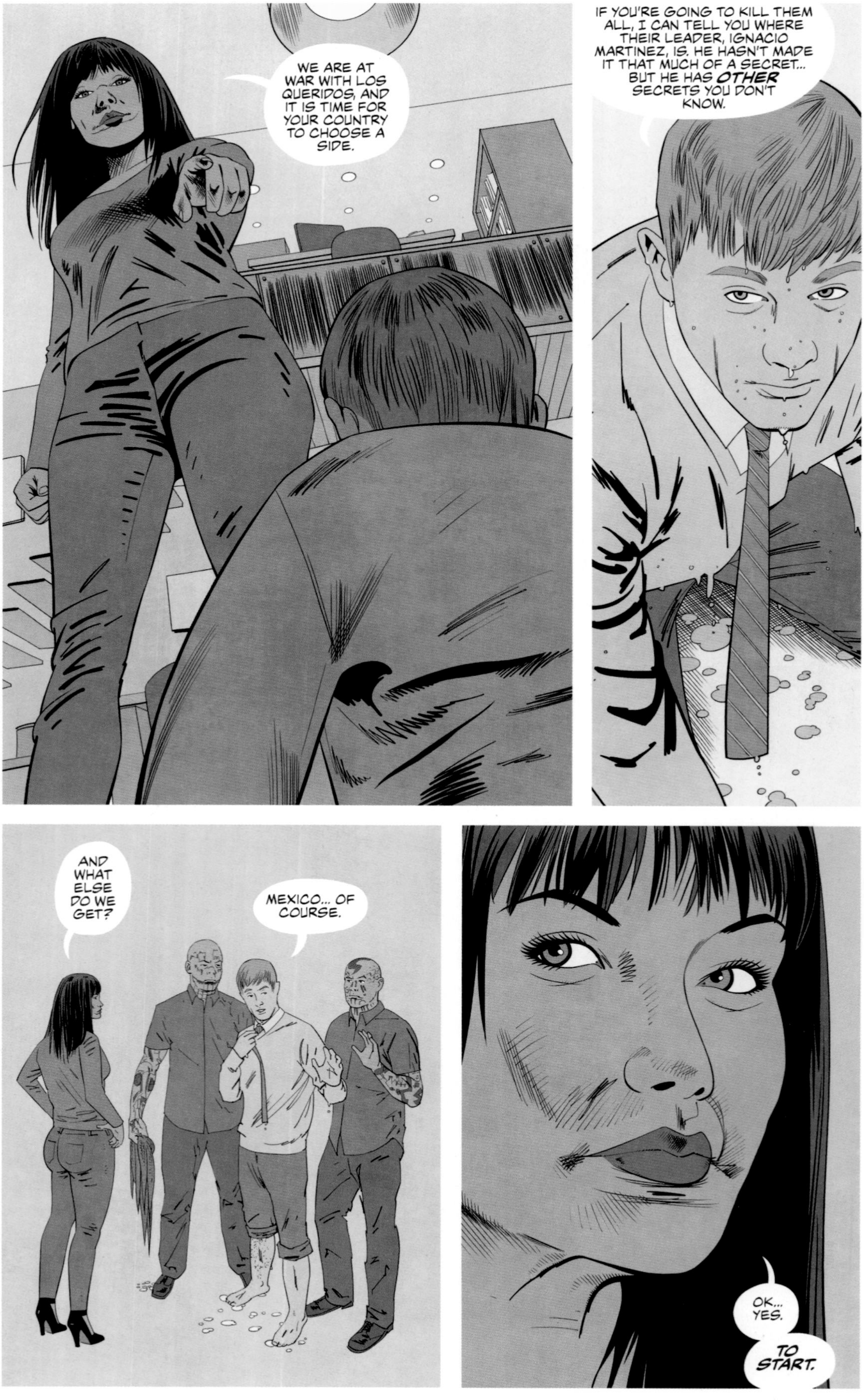
WE ARE AT WAR WITH LOS QUERIDOS, AND IT IS TIME FOR YOUR COUNTRY TO CHOOSE A SIDE.
IF YOU'RE GOING TO KILL THEM ALL, I CAN TELL YOU WHERE THEIR LEADER, IGNACIO MARTINEZ, IS. HE HASN'T MADE IT THAT MUCH OF A SECRET... BUT HE HAS *OTHER* SECRETS YOU DON'T KNOW.
AND WHAT ELSE DO WE GET?
MEXICO... OF COURSE.
OK... YES.
TO START.

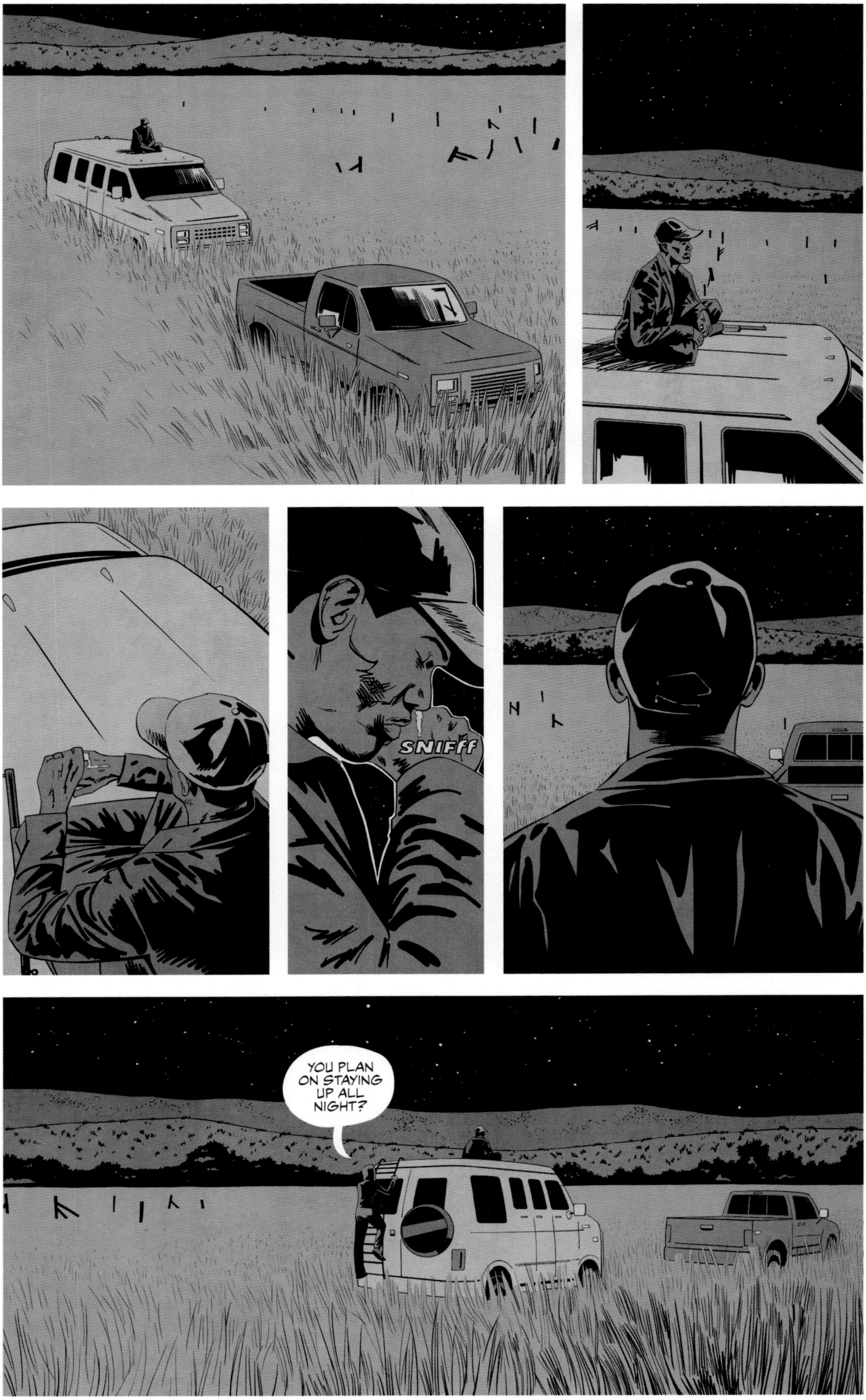
SNIFFf
YOU PLAN ON STAYING UP ALL NIGHT?

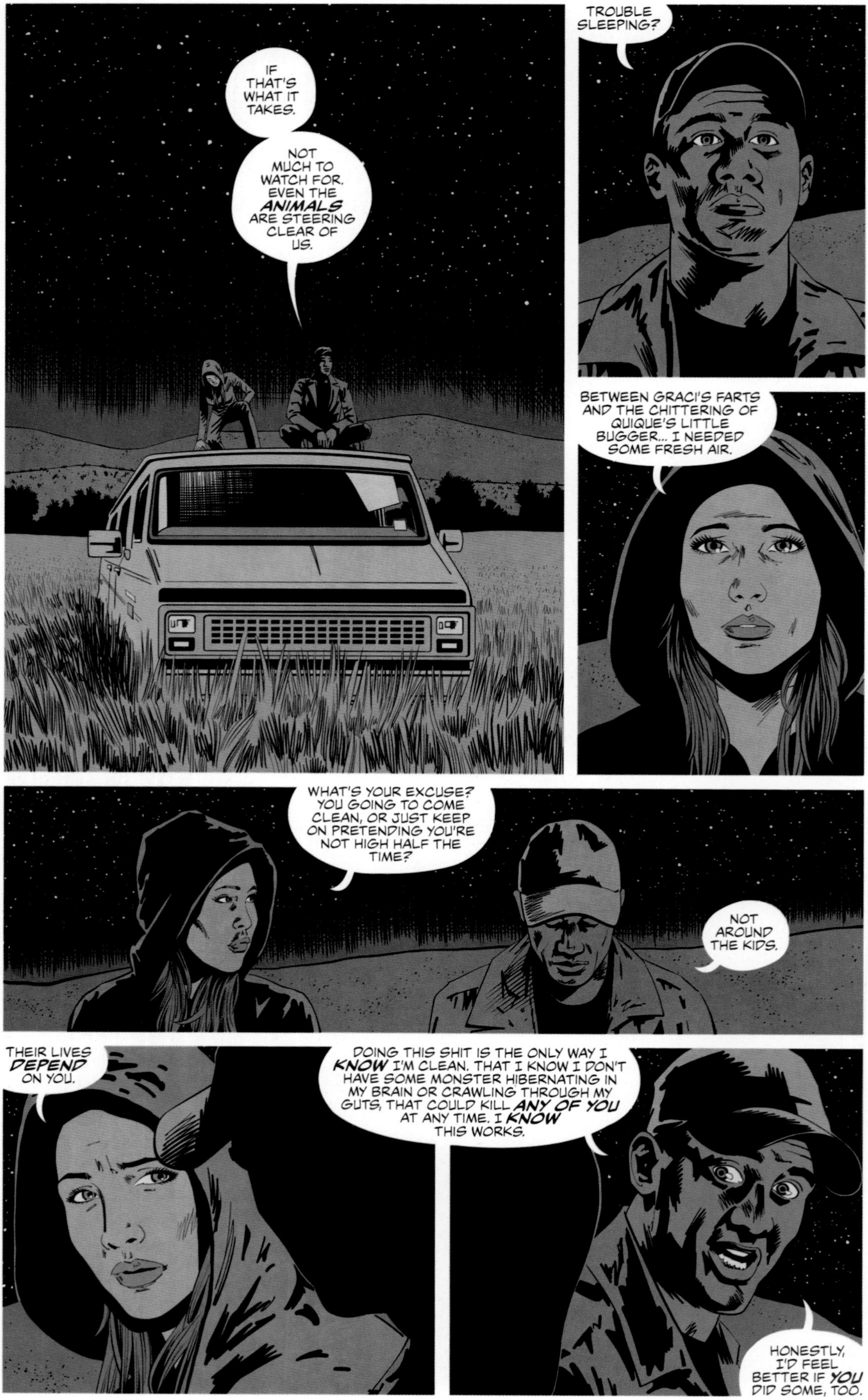
IF THAT'S WHAT IT TAKES.
NOT MUCH TO WATCH FOR. EVEN THE ANIMALS ARE STEERING CLEAR OF US.
TROUBLE SLEEPING?
BETWEEN GRACI'S FARTS AND THE CHITTERING OF QUIQUE'S LITTLE BUGGER... I NEEDED SOME FRESH AIR.
WHAT'S YOUR EXCUSE? YOU GOING TO COME CLEAN, OR JUST KEEP ON PRETENDING YOU'RE NOT HIGH HALF THE TIME?
NOT AROUND THE KIDS.
THEIR LIVES DEPEND ON YOU.
DOING THIS SHIT IS THE ONLY WAY I KNOW I'M CLEAN. THAT I KNOW I DON'T HAVE SOME MONSTER HIBERNATING IN MY BRAIN OR CRAWLING THROUGH MY GUTS, THAT COULD KILL ANY OF YOU AT ANY TIME. I KNOW THIS WORKS.
HONESTLY, I'D FEEL BETTER IF YOU DID SOME, TOO.

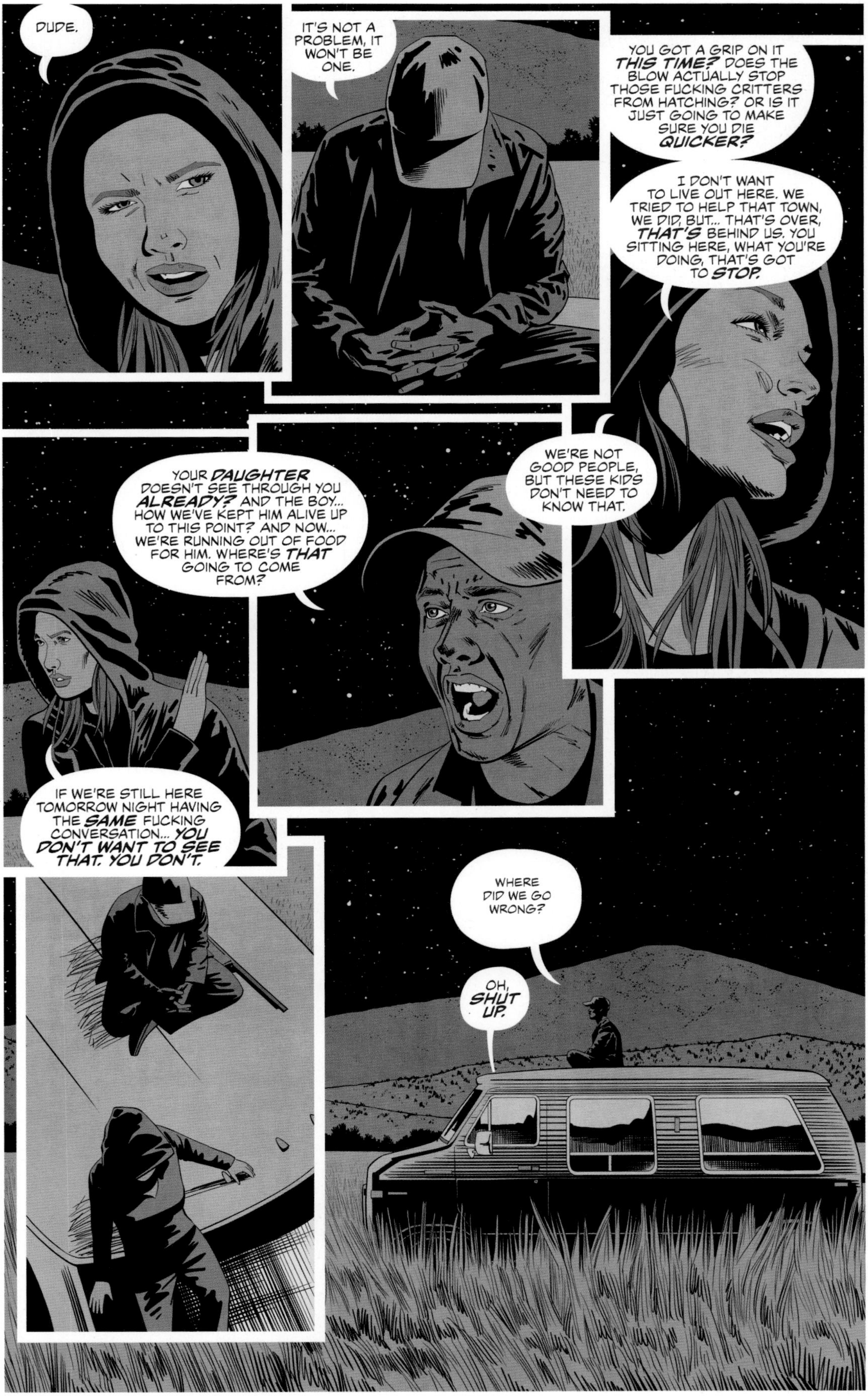
DUDE.
IT'S NOT A PROBLEM, IT WON'T BE ONE.
YOU GOT A GRIP ON IT THIS TIME? DOES THE BLOW ACTUALLY STOP THOSE FUCKING CRITTERS FROM HATCHING? OR IS IT JUST GOING TO MAKE SURE YOU DIE QUICKER?
I DON'T WANT TO LIVE OUT HERE. WE TRIED TO HELP THAT TOWN, WE DID, BUT... THAT'S OVER, THAT'S BEHIND US. YOU SITTING HERE, WHAT YOU'RE DOING, THAT'S GOT TO STOP.
WE'RE NOT GOOD PEOPLE, BUT THESE KIDS DON'T NEED TO KNOW THAT.
YOUR DAUGHTER DOESN'T SEE THROUGH YOU ALREADY? AND THE BOY... HOW WE'VE KEPT HIM ALIVE UP TO THIS POINT? AND NOW... WE'RE RUNNING OUT OF FOOD FOR HIM. WHERE'S THAT GOING TO COME FROM?
IF WE'RE STILL HERE TOMORROW NIGHT HAVING THE SAME FUCKING CONVERSATION... YOU DON'T WANT TO SEE THAT. YOU DON'T.
WHERE DID WE GO WRONG?
OH, SHUT UP.

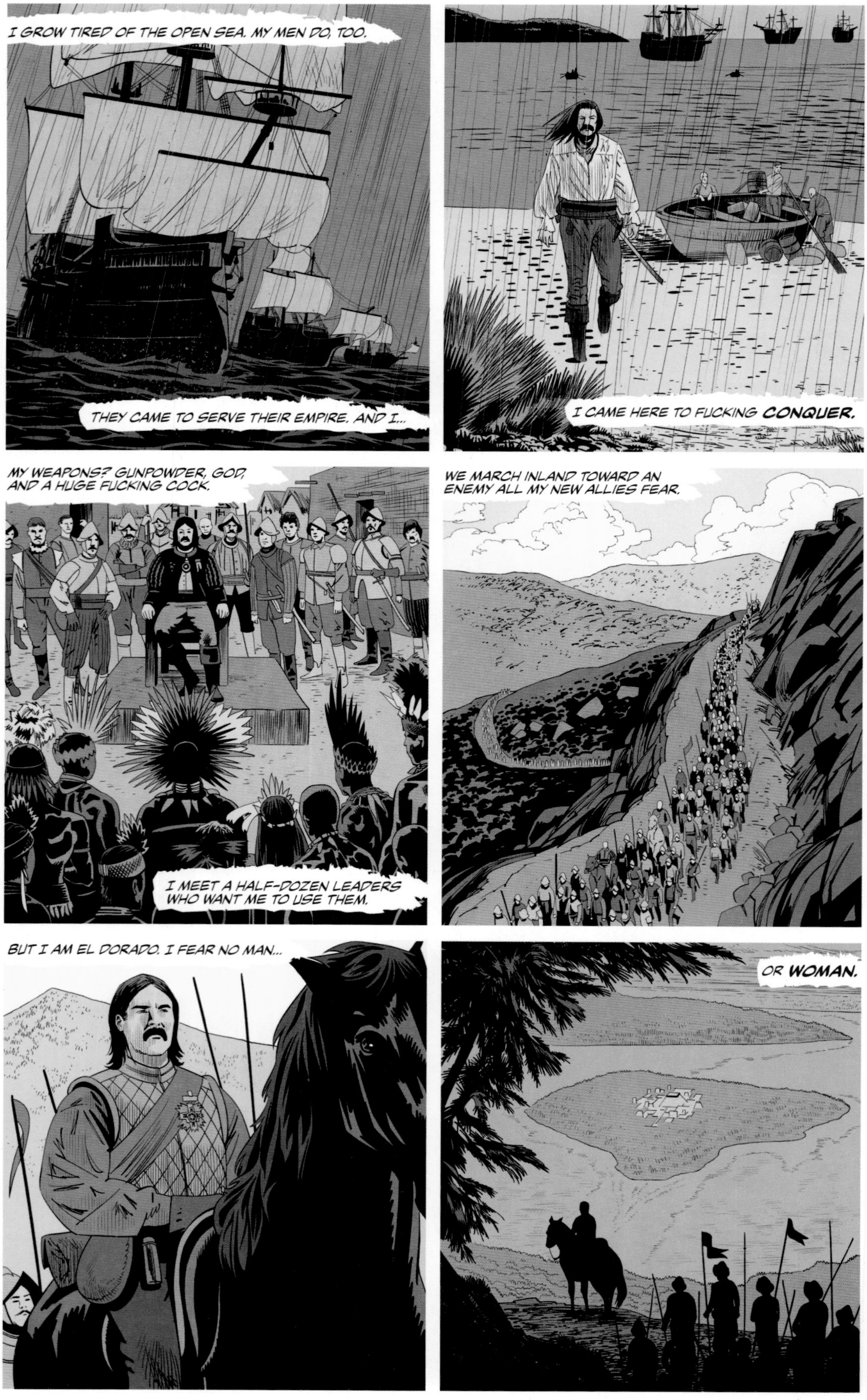
I GROW TIRED OF THE OPEN SEA. MY MEN DO, TOO.
THEY CAME TO SERVE THEIR EMPIRE. AND I...
I CAME HERE TO FUCKING **CONQUER.**
MY WEAPONS? GUNPOWDER, GOD, AND A HUGE FUCKING COCK.
I MEET A HALF-DOZEN LEADERS WHO WANT ME TO USE THEM.
WE MARCH INLAND TOWARD AN ENEMY ALL MY NEW ALLIES FEAR.
BUT I AM EL DORADO. I FEAR NO MAN...
OR **WOMAN.**

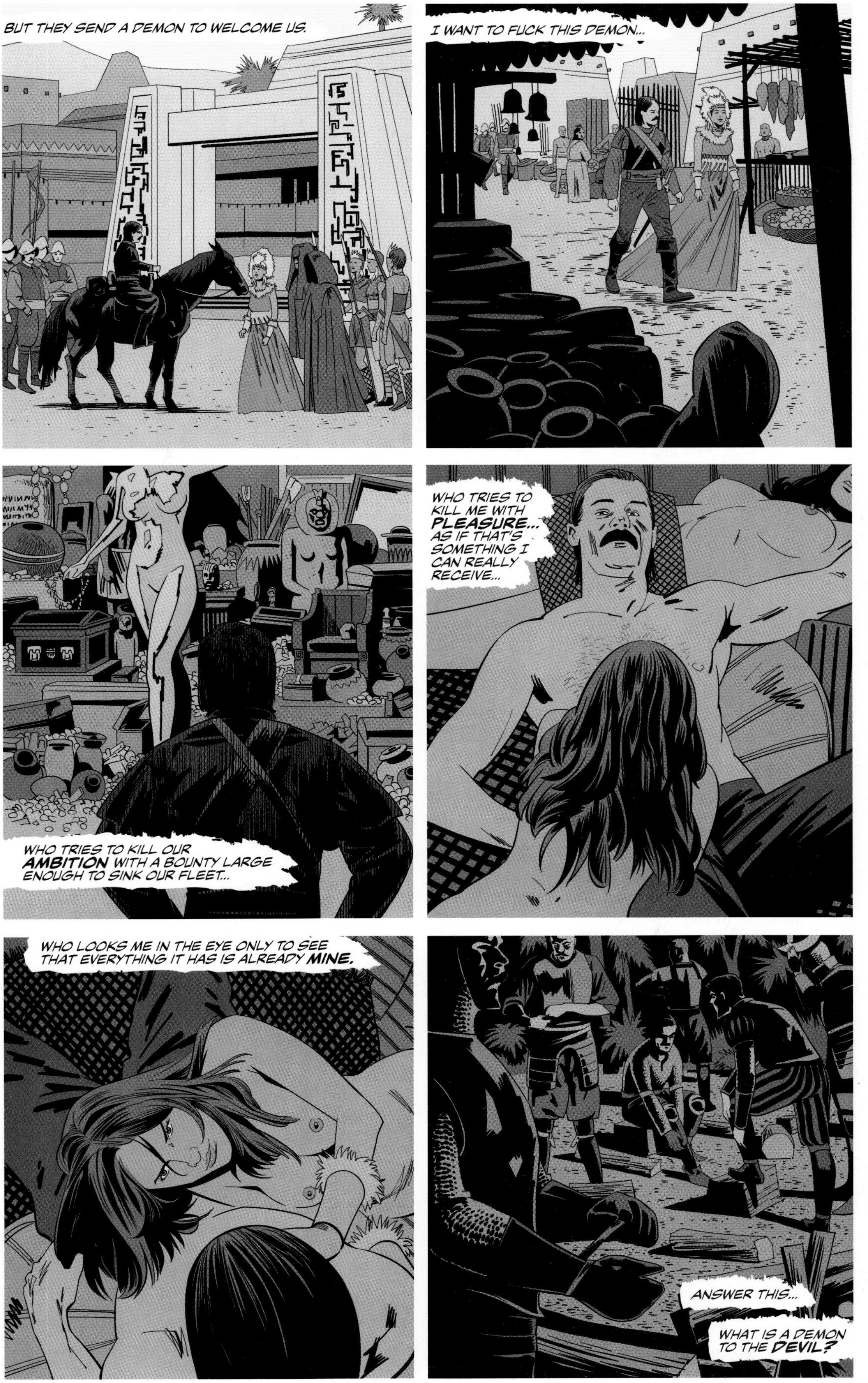
BUT THEY SEND A DEMON TO WELCOME US.
I WANT TO FUCK THIS DEMON...
WHO TRIES TO KILL OUR AMBITION WITH A BOUNTY LARGE ENOUGH TO SINK OUR FLEET...
WHO TRIES TO KILL ME WITH PLEASURE... AS IF THAT'S SOMETHING I CAN REALLY RECEIVE...
WHO LOOKS ME IN THE EYE ONLY TO SEE THAT EVERYTHING IT HAS IS ALREADY MINE.
ANSWER THIS...
WHAT IS A DEMON TO THE DEVIL?

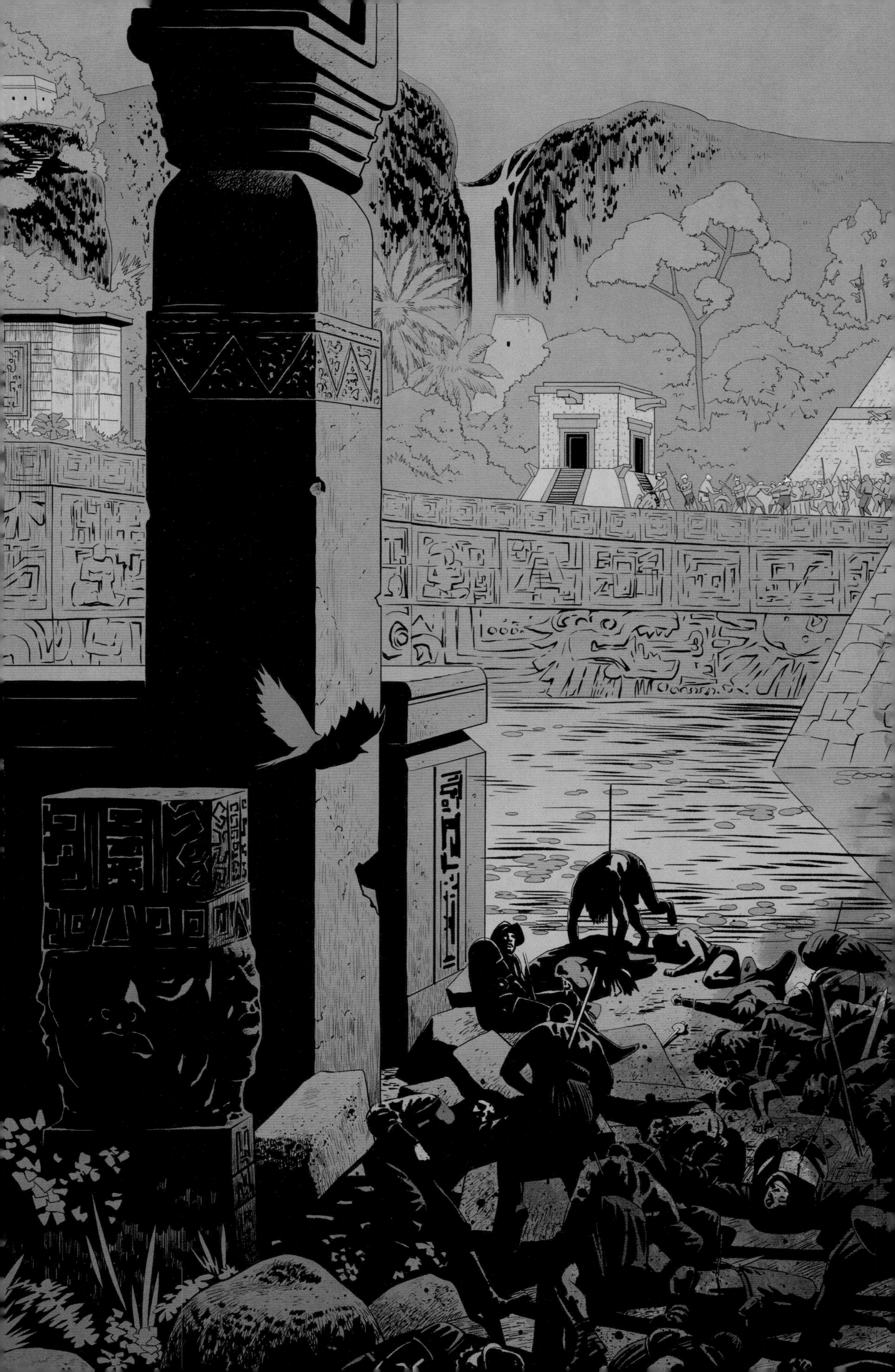

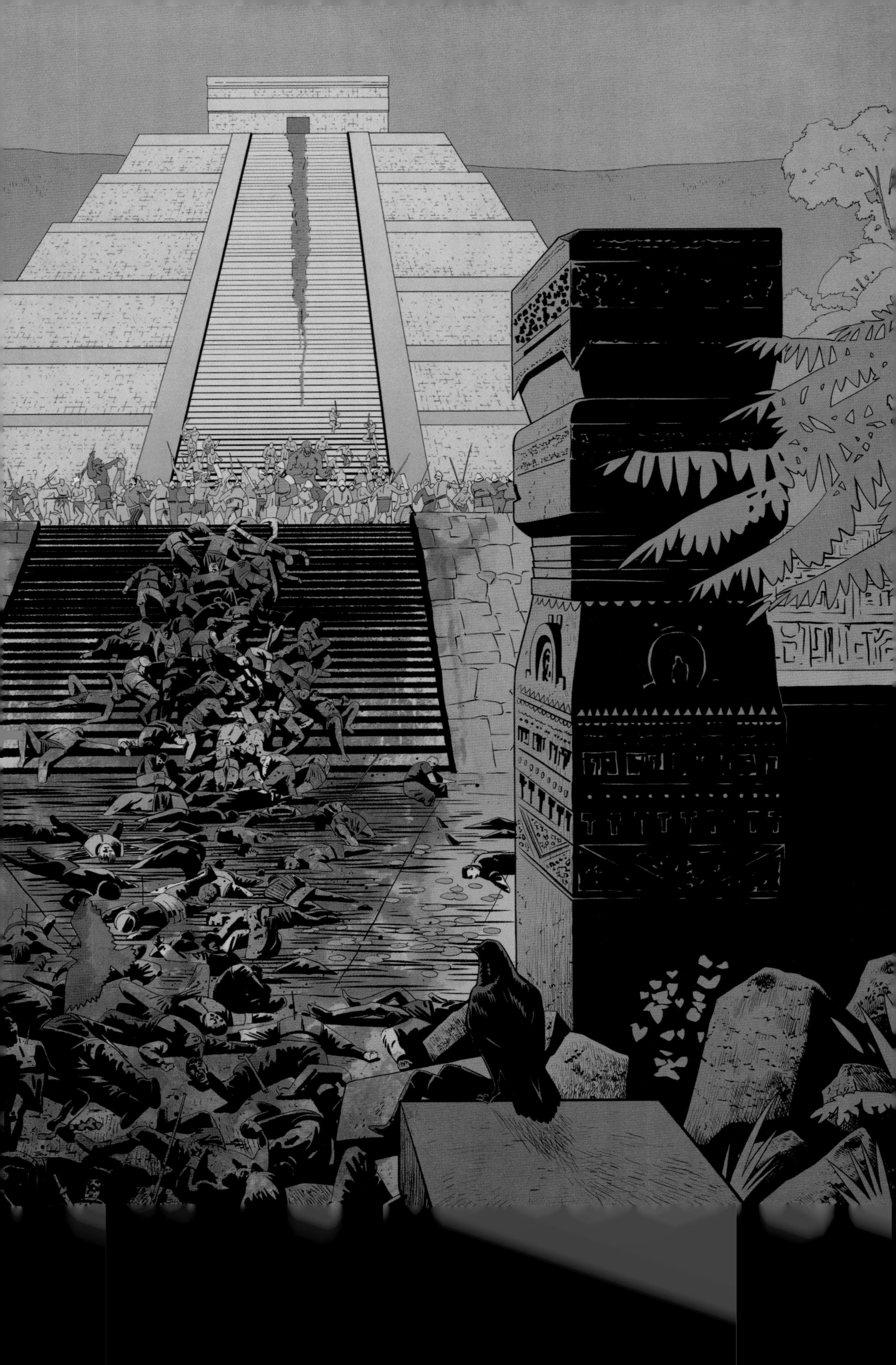

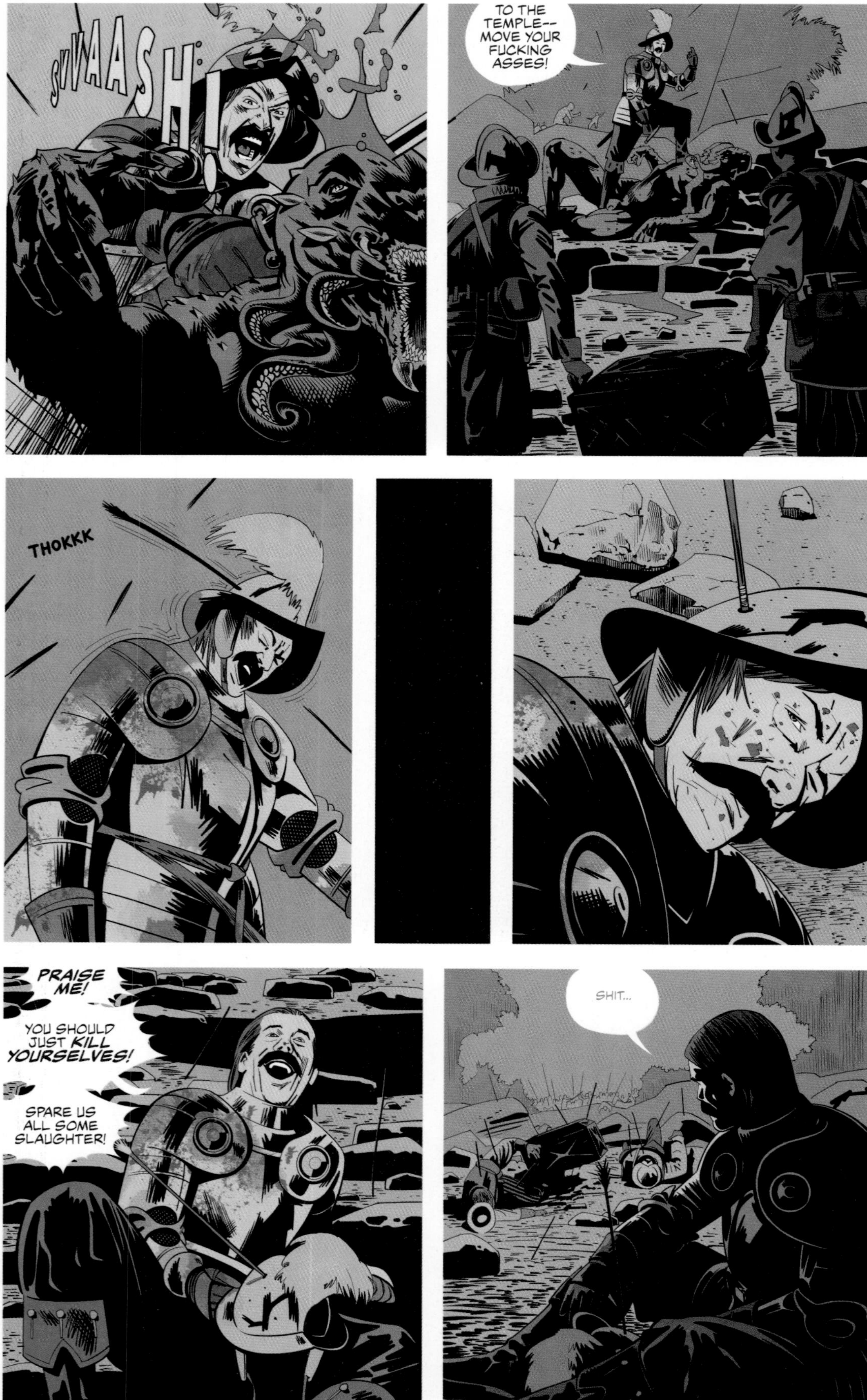

SWAASH!
TO THE TEMPLE-- MOVE YOUR FUCKING ASSES!
THOKKK
PRAISE ME!
YOU SHOULD JUST KILL YOURSELVES!
SPARE US ALL SOME SLAUGHTER!
SHIT...

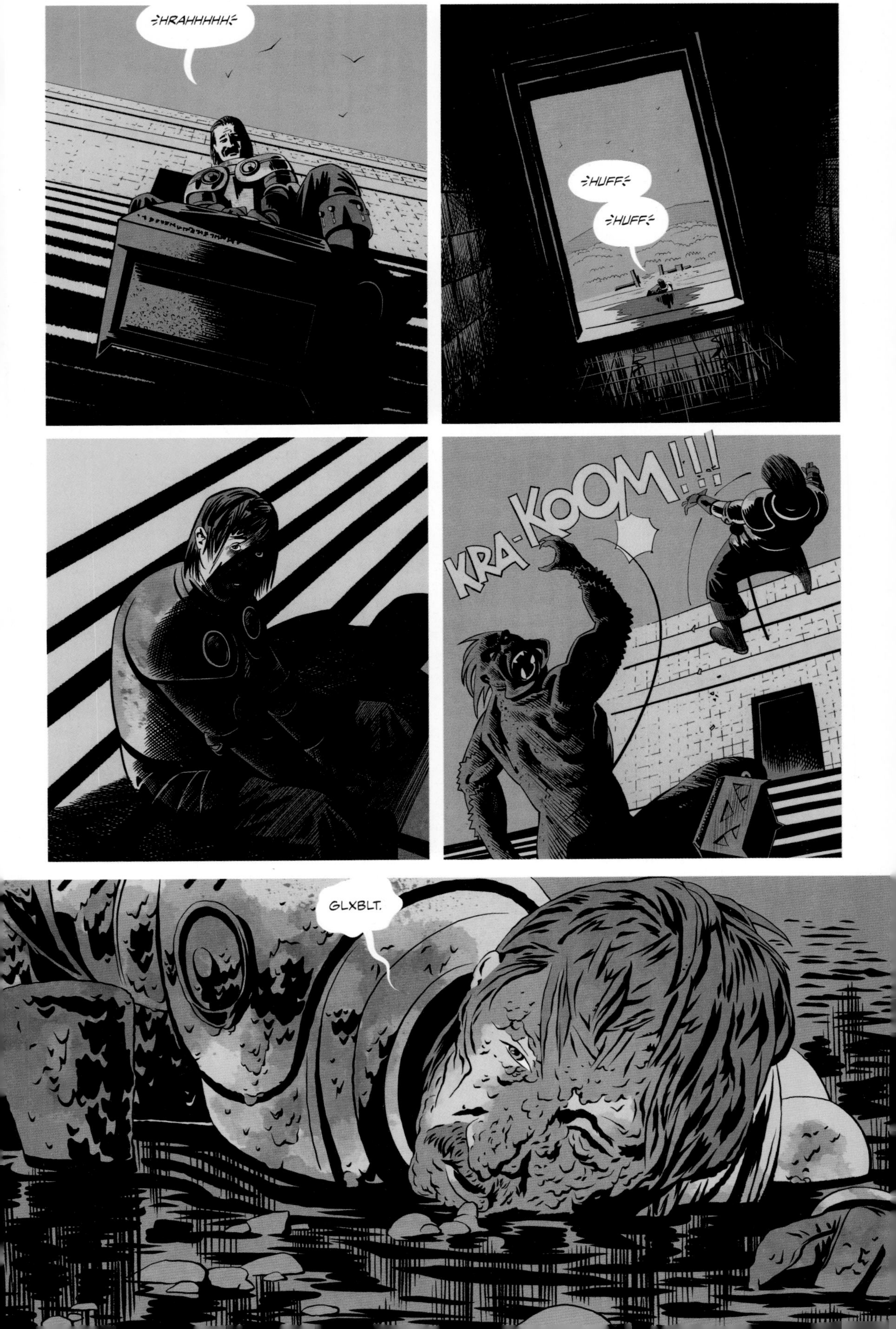
HRAHHHHH
HUFF
HUFF
KRA-KOOM!!!
GLXBLT.

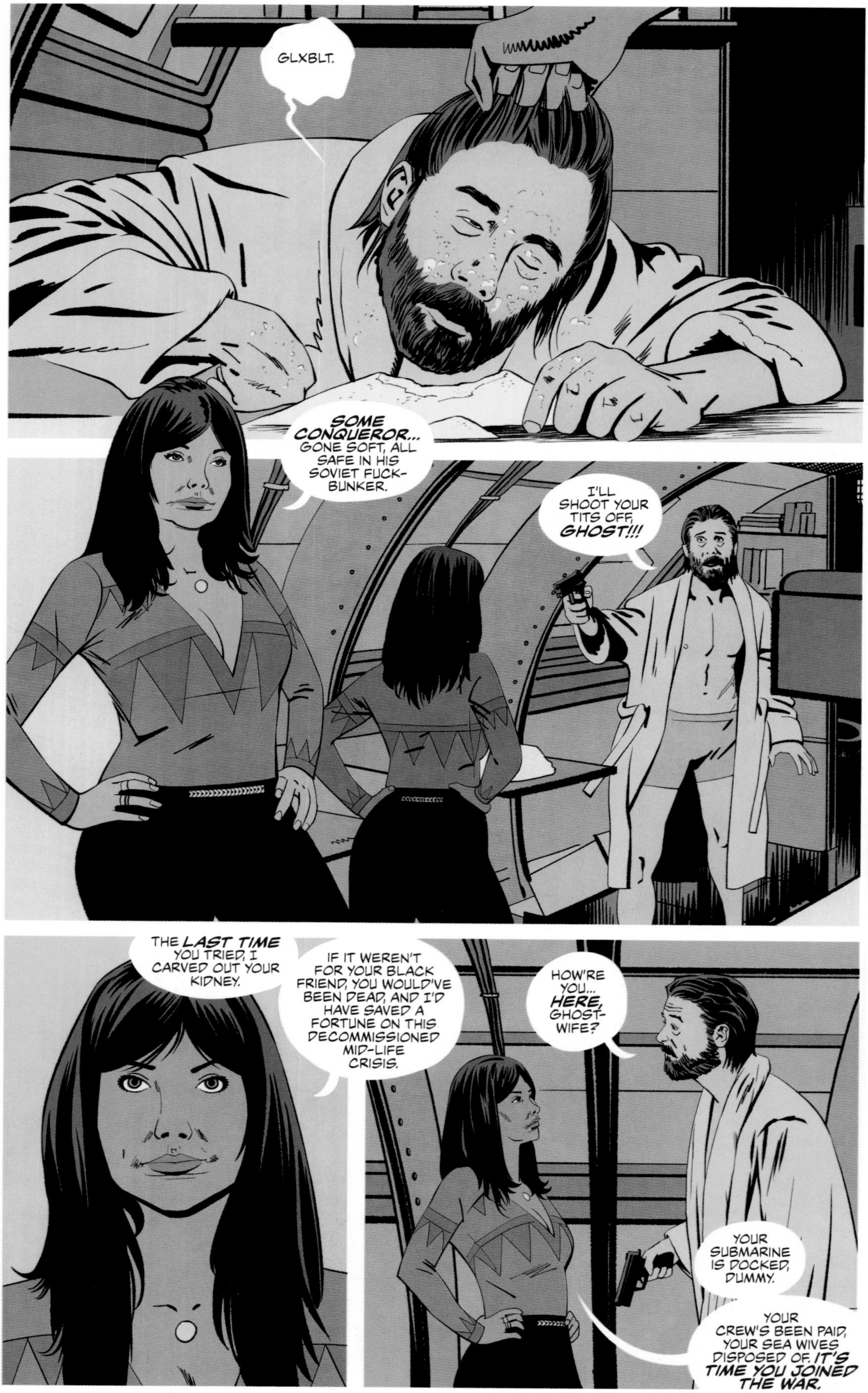
GLXBLT.
SOME CONQUEROR... GONE SOFT, ALL SAFE IN HIS SOVIET FUCK-BUNKER.
I'LL SHOOT YOUR TITS OFF, GHOST!!!
THE LAST TIME YOU TRIED, I CARVED OUT YOUR KIDNEY.
IF IT WEREN'T FOR YOUR BLACK FRIEND, YOU WOULD'VE BEEN DEAD, AND I'D HAVE SAVED A FORTUNE ON THIS DECOMMISSIONED MID-LIFE CRISIS.
HOW'RE YOU... HERE, GHOST-WIFE?
YOUR SUBMARINE IS DOCKED, DUMMY.
YOUR CREW'S BEEN PAID, YOUR SEA WIVES DISPOSED OF. IT'S TIME YOU JOINED THE WAR.

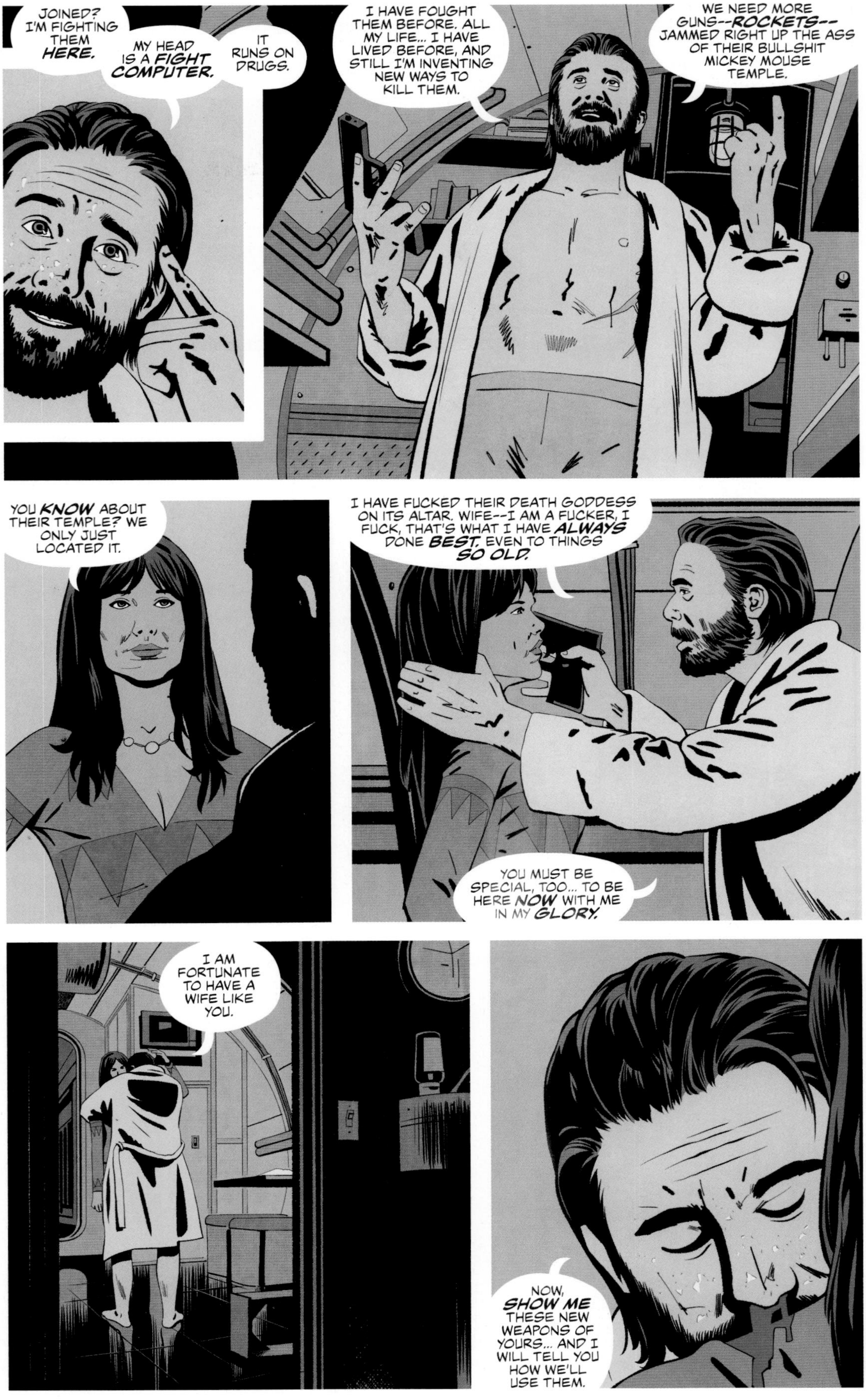

JOINED? I'M FIGHTING THEM HERE.
MY HEAD IS A FIGHT COMPUTER.
IT RUNS ON DRUGS.
I HAVE FOUGHT THEM BEFORE. ALL MY LIFE... I HAVE LIVED BEFORE, AND STILL I'M INVENTING NEW WAYS TO KILL THEM.
WE NEED MORE GUNS--ROCKETS--JAMMED RIGHT UP THE ASS OF THEIR BULLSHIT MICKEY MOUSE TEMPLE.
YOU KNOW ABOUT THEIR TEMPLE? WE ONLY JUST LOCATED IT.
I HAVE FUCKED THEIR DEATH GODDESS ON ITS ALTAR. WIFE--I AM A FUCKER, I FUCK, THAT'S WHAT I HAVE ALWAYS DONE BEST. EVEN TO THINGS SO OLD.
YOU MUST BE SPECIAL, TOO... TO BE HERE NOW WITH ME IN MY GLORY.
I AM FORTUNATE TO HAVE A WIFE LIKE YOU.
NOW, SHOW ME THESE NEW WEAPONS OF YOURS... AND I WILL TELL YOU HOW WE'LL USE THEM.

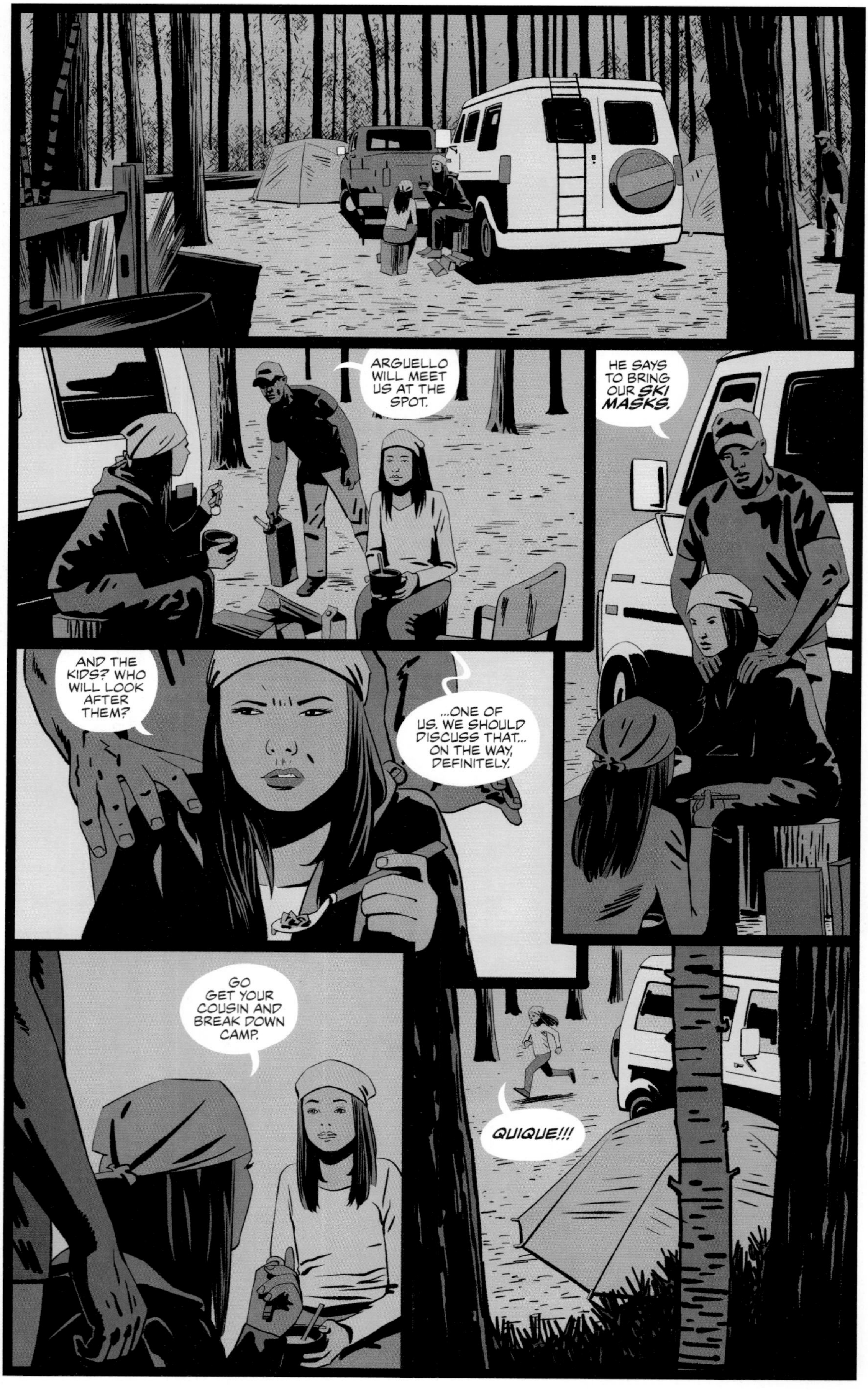

ARGUELLO WILL MEET US AT THE SPOT.
HE SAYS TO BRING OUR SKI MASKS.
AND THE KIDS? WHO WILL LOOK AFTER THEM?
...ONE OF US. WE SHOULD DISCUSS THAT... ON THE WAY, DEFINITELY.
GO GET YOUR COUSIN AND BREAK DOWN CAMP.
QUIQUE!!!

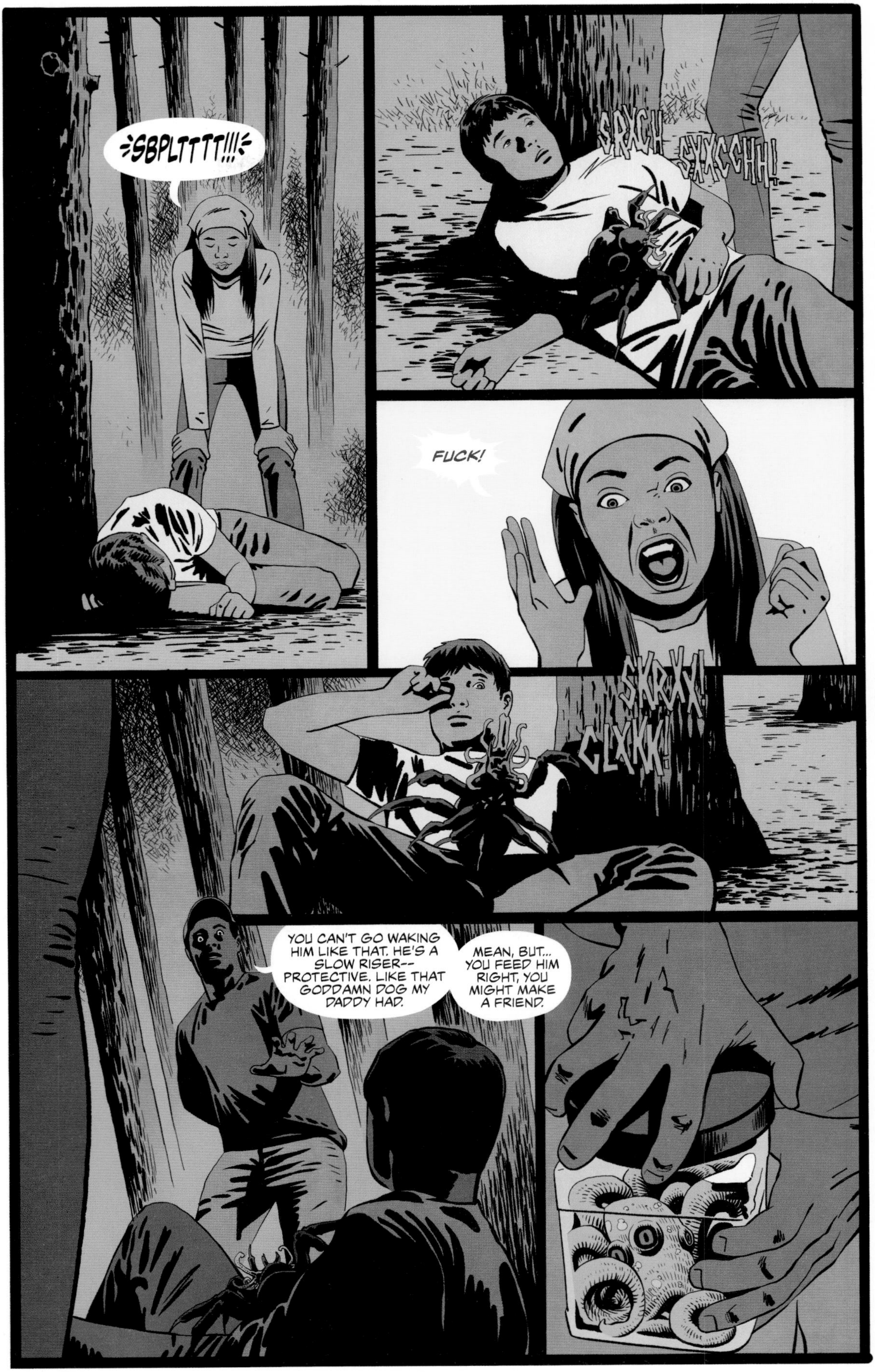
SBPLTTTT!!!
SRXCH
SXXCCHH!
FUCK!
SKRXX!
CLXKK!
YOU CAN'T GO WAKING HIM LIKE THAT. HE'S A SLOW RISER-- PROTECTIVE. LIKE THAT GODDAMN DOG MY DADDY HAD.
MEAN, BUT... YOU FEED HIM RIGHT, YOU MIGHT MAKE A FRIEND.

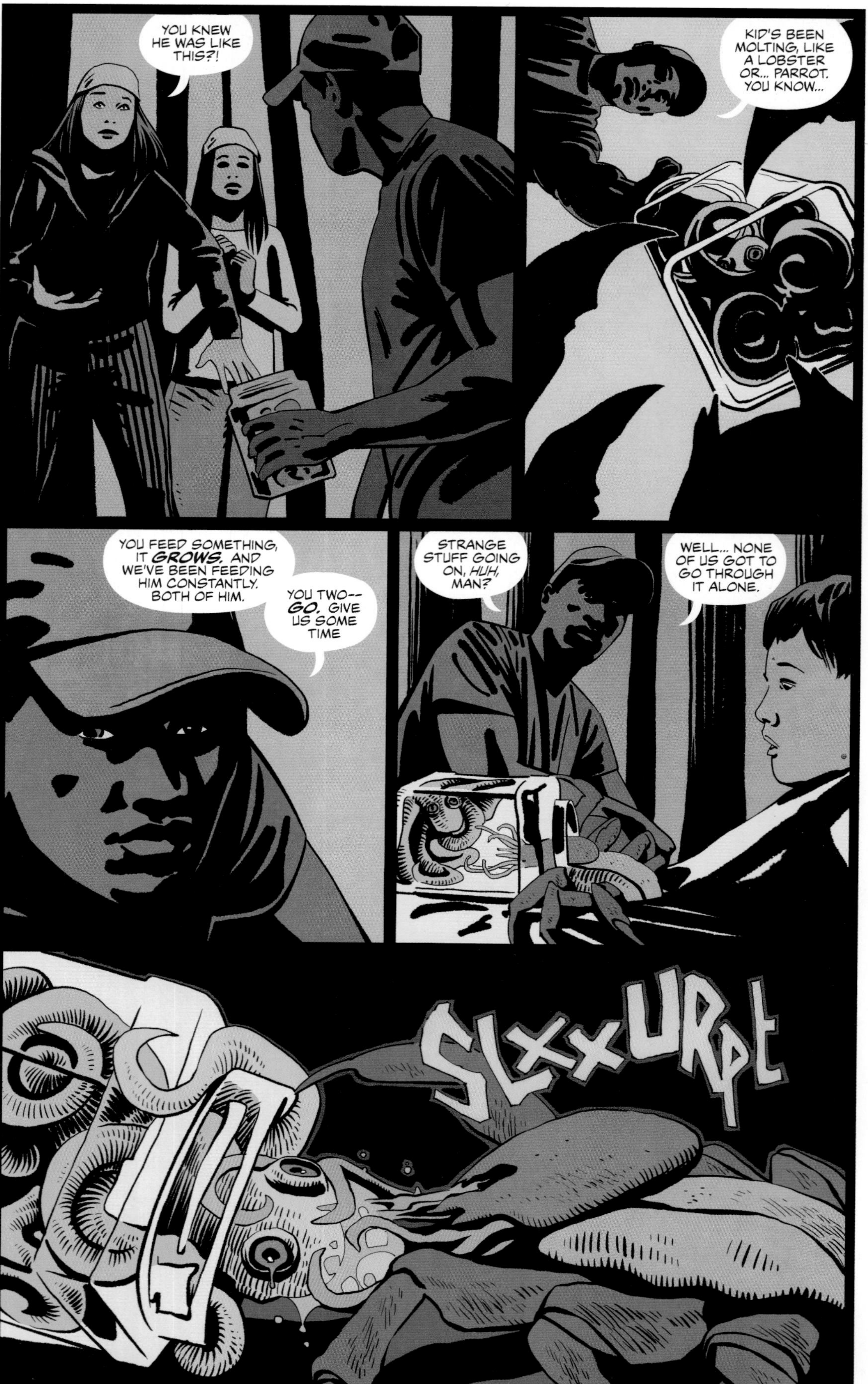
YOU KNEW HE WAS LIKE THIS?!
KID'S BEEN MOLTING, LIKE A LOBSTER OR... PARROT. YOU KNOW...
YOU FEED SOMETHING, IT GROWS. AND WE'VE BEEN FEEDING HIM CONSTANTLY. BOTH OF HIM.
YOU TWO-- GO. GIVE US SOME TIME
STRANGE STUFF GOING ON, HUH, MAN?
WELL... NONE OF US GOT TO GO THROUGH IT ALONE.
SLXXURPT

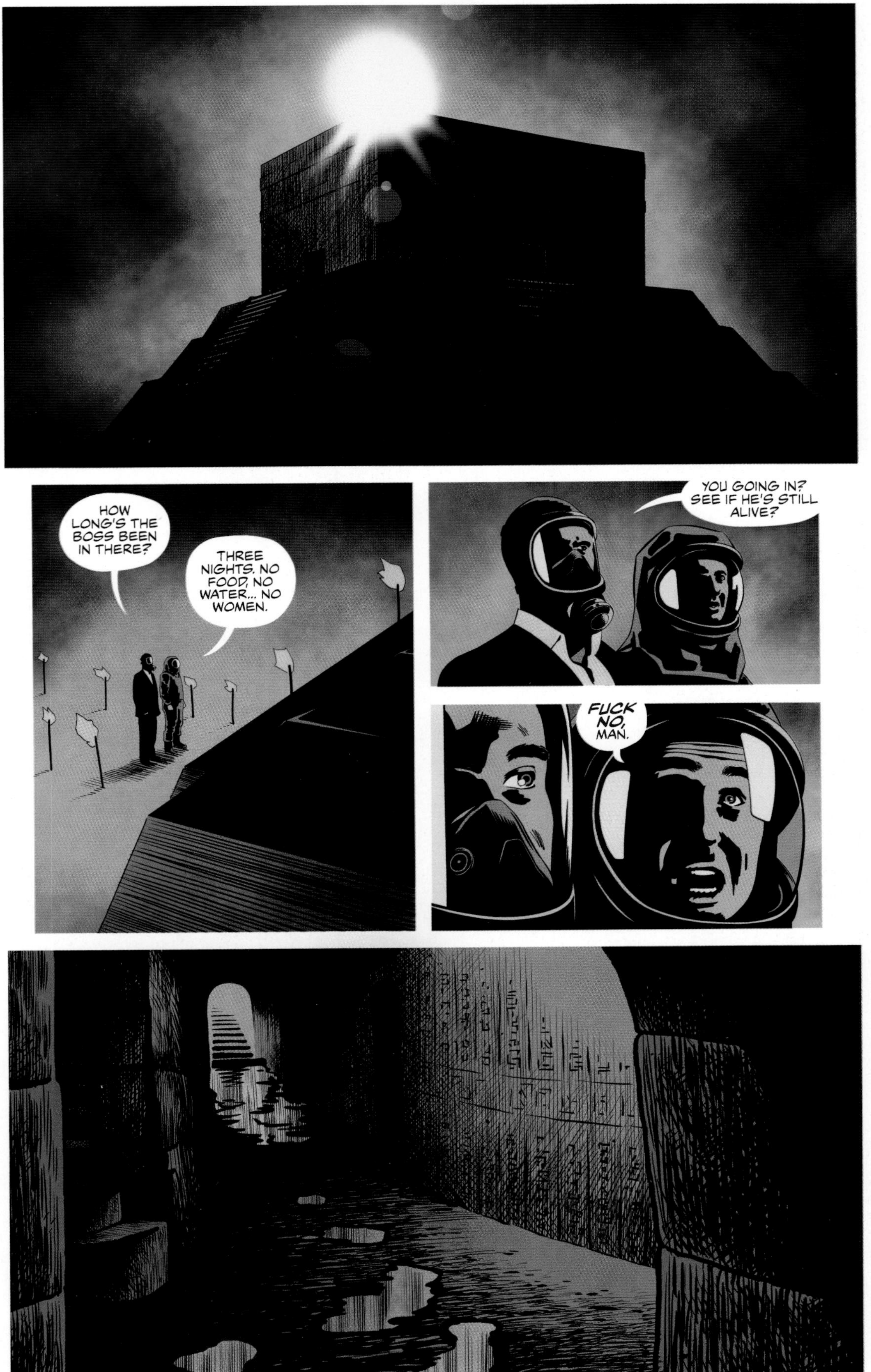
HOW LONG'S THE BOSS BEEN IN THERE?
THREE NIGHTS. NO FOOD, NO WATER... NO WOMEN.
YOU GOING IN? SEE IF HE'S STILL ALIVE?
FUCK NO, MAN.

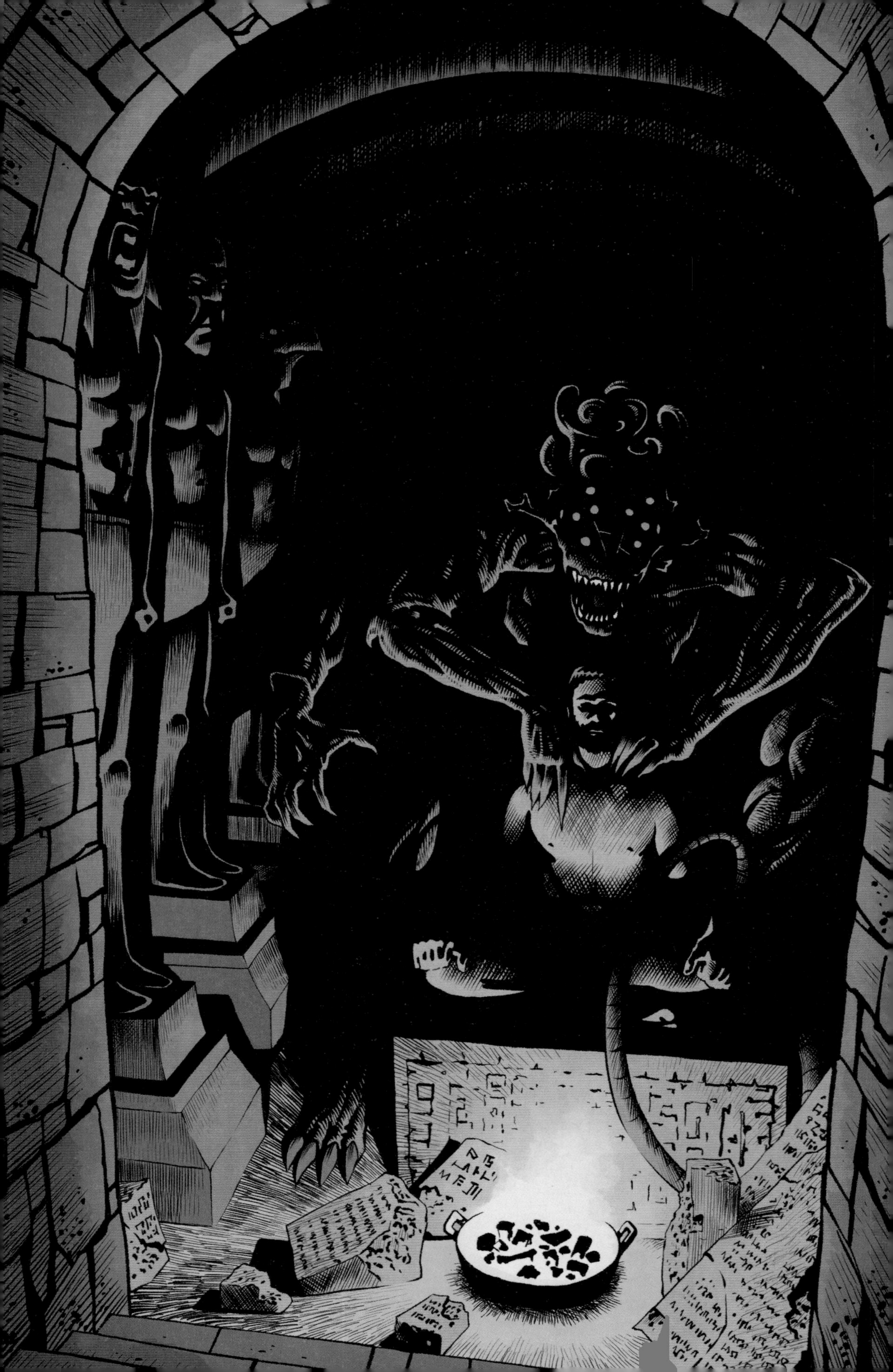

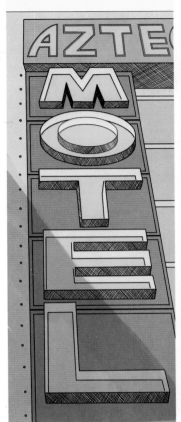

ONCE UPON A TIME IN NOGALES...

TIME FOR YOU TO GO HOME.

<WHAT?>*

*AMERICAN!

STUPID FUCKING GABACHO.

<ENGLISH--YEAH, I SPEAK IT. I'VE BEEN TO CALIFORNIA-- LOS ANGELES... THE VALLEY.>

<EVERYWHERE THERE'S CUSTOMERS. THEY ALWAYS TOLD US WHERE TO GO NEXT-- WHO NEEDED THE *GOOD SHIT.* GOT AS FAR AS OHIO. OHIO *FUCKS WITH THE GOOD SHIT.* YOU FROM THERE?>

<...TEXAS.>

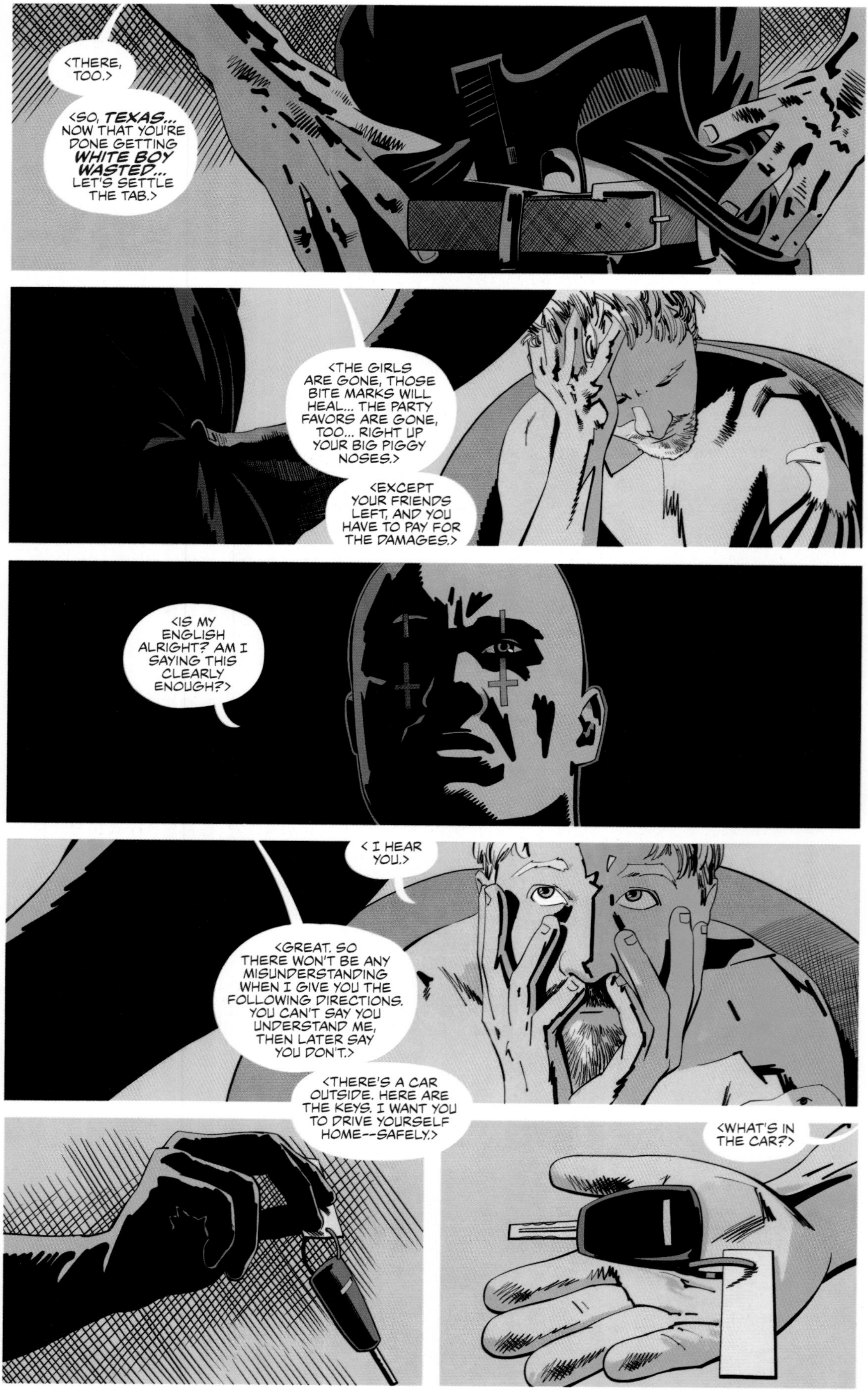
<THERE, TOO.>
<SO, ***TEXAS...*** NOW THAT YOU'RE DONE GETTING ***WHITE BOY WASTED...*** LET'S SETTLE THE TAB.>
<THE GIRLS ARE GONE, THOSE BITE MARKS WILL HEAL... THE PARTY FAVORS ARE GONE, TOO... RIGHT UP YOUR BIG PIGGY NOSES.>
<EXCEPT YOUR FRIENDS LEFT, AND YOU HAVE TO PAY FOR THE DAMAGES.>
<IS MY ENGLISH ALRIGHT? AM I SAYING THIS CLEARLY ENOUGH?>
< I HEAR YOU.>
<GREAT. SO THERE WON'T BE ANY MISUNDERSTANDING WHEN I GIVE YOU THE FOLLOWING DIRECTIONS. YOU CAN'T SAY YOU UNDERSTAND ME, THEN LATER SAY YOU DON'T.>
<THERE'S A CAR OUTSIDE. HERE ARE THE KEYS. I WANT YOU TO DRIVE YOURSELF HOME--SAFELY.>
<WHAT'S IN THE CAR?>

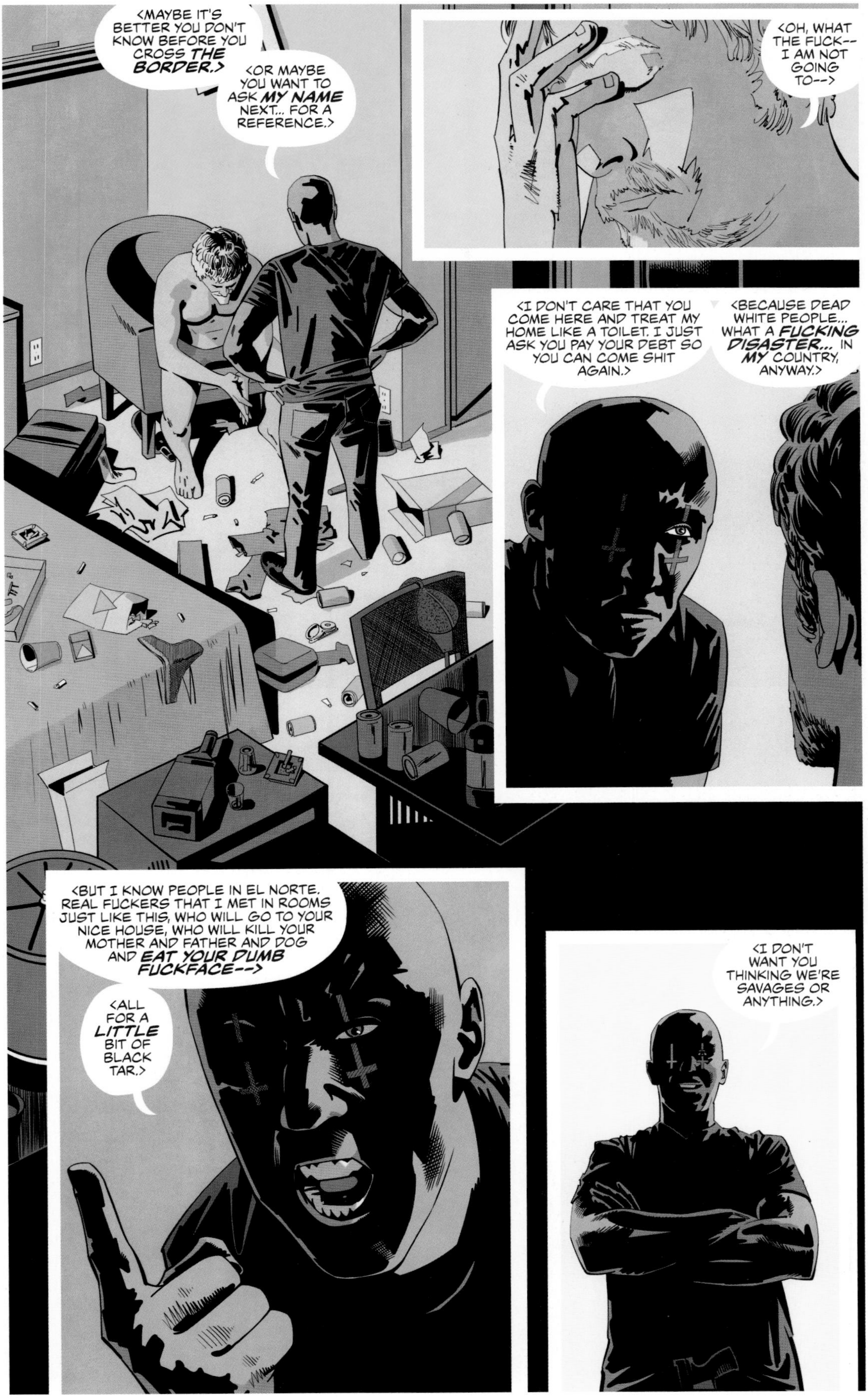
<MAYBE IT'S BETTER YOU DON'T KNOW BEFORE YOU CROSS THE BORDER.>
<OR MAYBE YOU WANT TO ASK MY NAME NEXT... FOR A REFERENCE.>
<OH, WHAT THE FUCK-- I AM NOT GOING TO-->
<I DON'T CARE THAT YOU COME HERE AND TREAT MY HOME LIKE A TOILET. I JUST ASK YOU PAY YOUR DEBT SO YOU CAN COME SHIT AGAIN.>
<BECAUSE DEAD WHITE PEOPLE... WHAT A FUCKING DISASTER... IN MY COUNTRY, ANYWAY.>
<BUT I KNOW PEOPLE IN EL NORTE, REAL FUCKERS THAT I MET IN ROOMS JUST LIKE THIS, WHO WILL GO TO YOUR NICE HOUSE, WHO WILL KILL YOUR MOTHER AND FATHER AND DOG AND EAT YOUR DUMB FUCKFACE-->
<ALL FOR A LITTLE BIT OF BLACK TAR.>
<I DON'T WANT YOU THINKING WE'RE SAVAGES OR ANYTHING.>

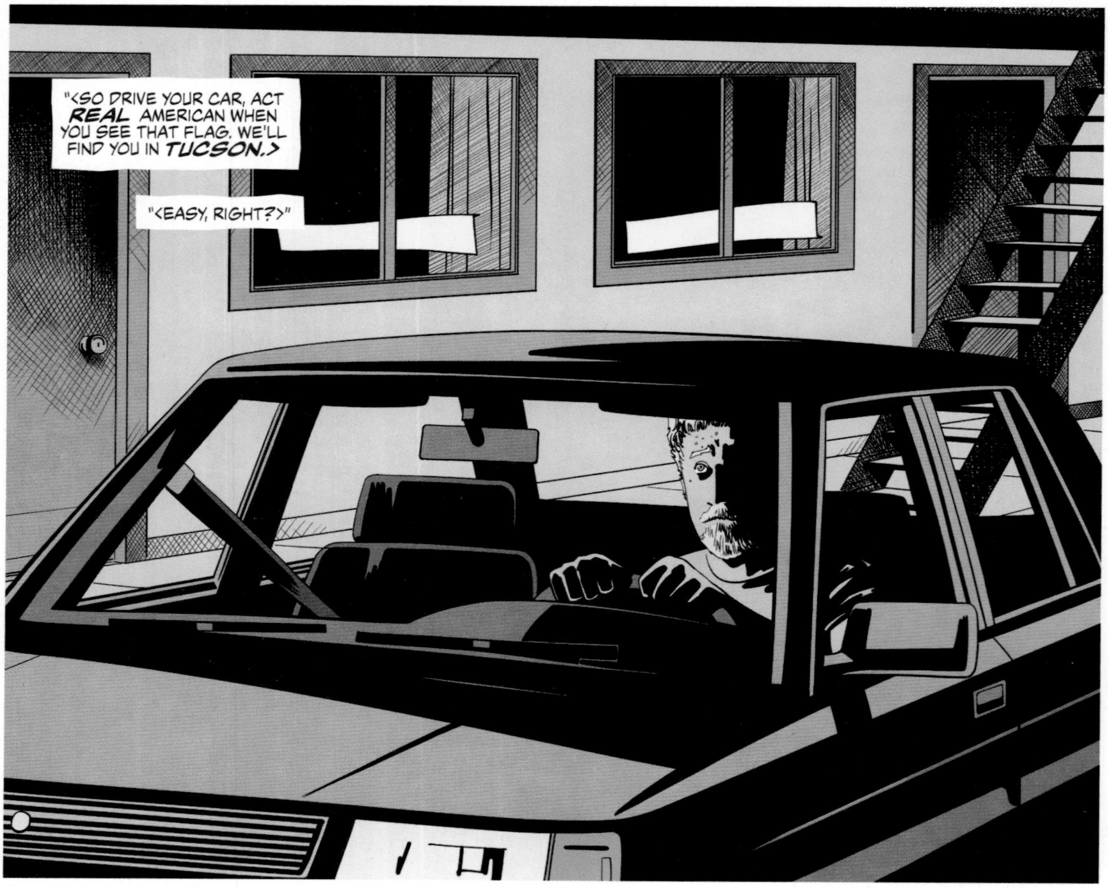
"<SO DRIVE YOUR CAR, ACT **REAL** AMERICAN WHEN YOU SEE THAT FLAG. WE'LL FIND YOU IN **TUCSON.**>
"<EASY, RIGHT?>"

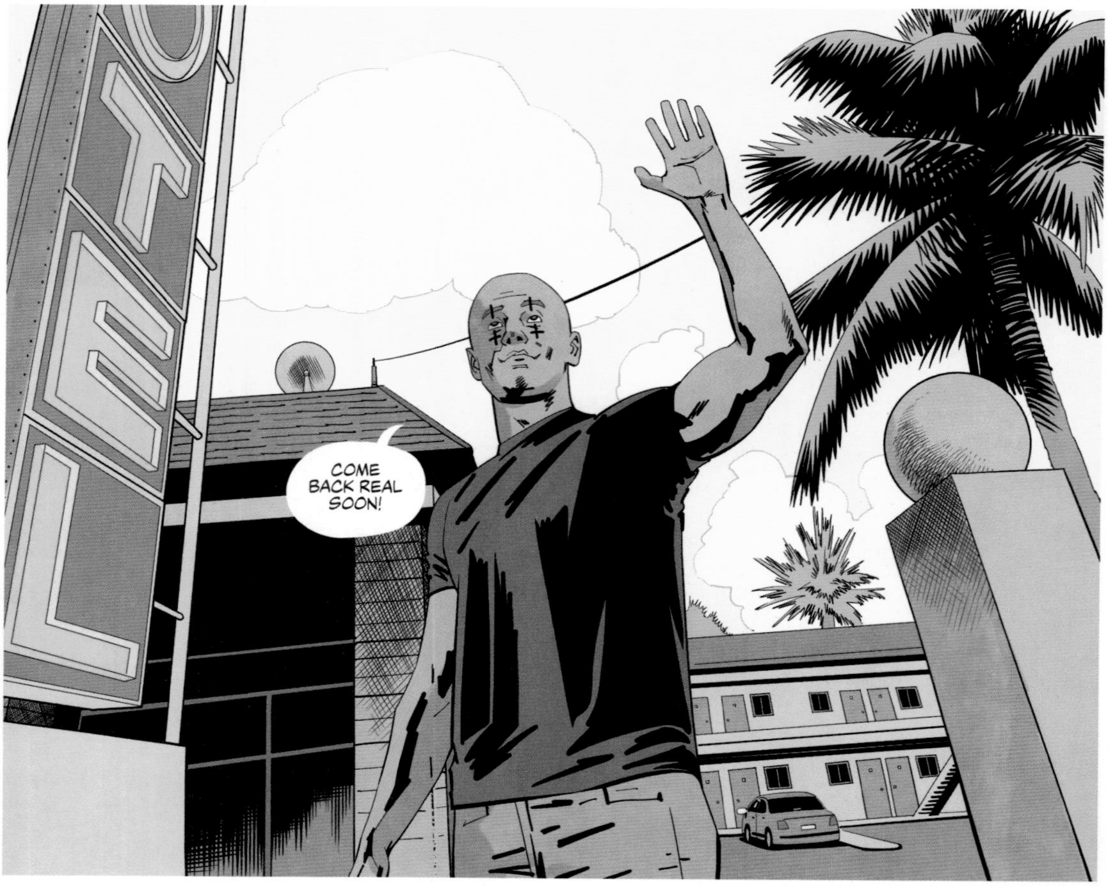
COME BACK REAL SOON!

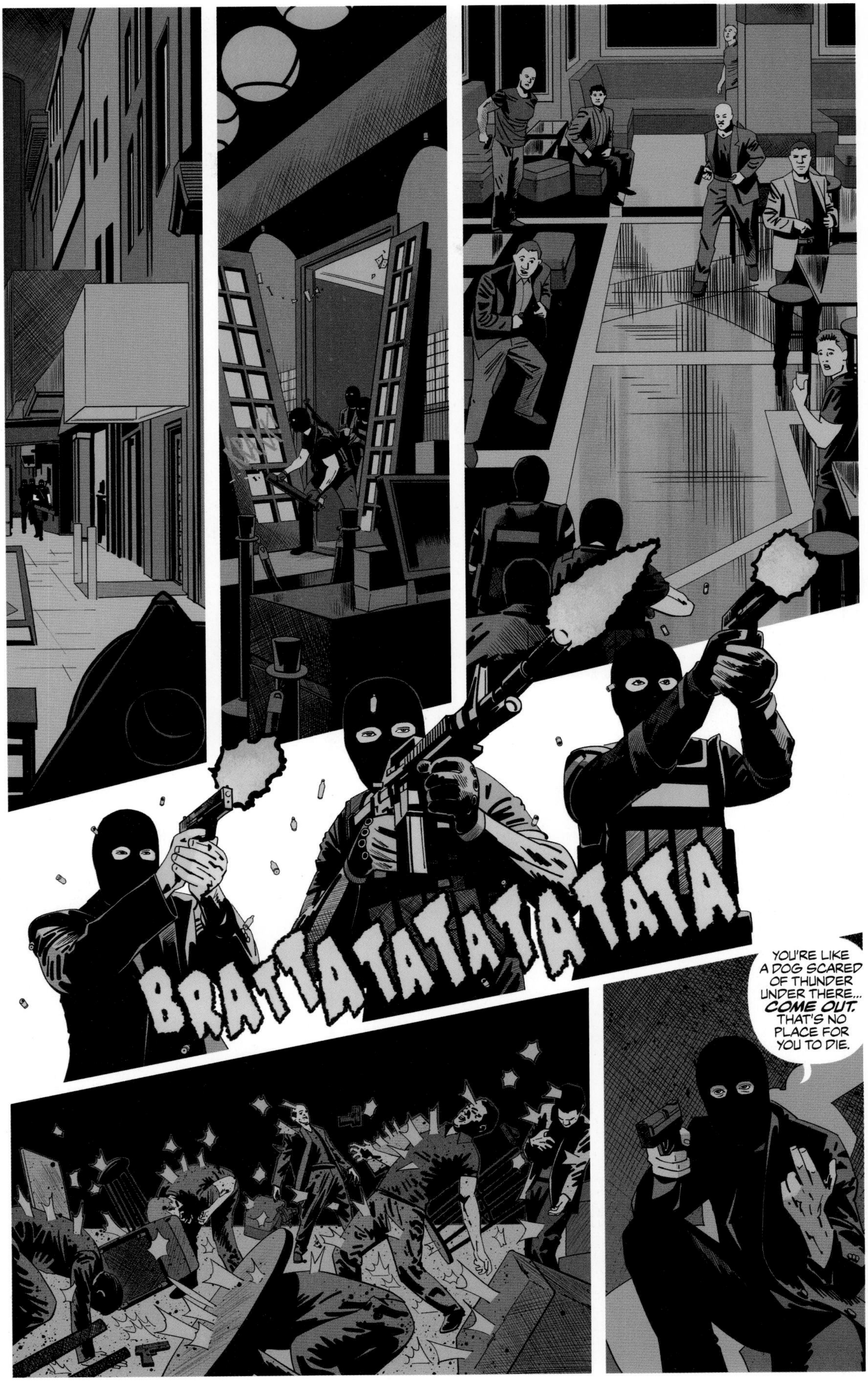
BRATTATATATATATA
YOU'RE LIKE A DOG SCARED OF THUNDER UNDER THERE... ***COME OUT.*** THAT'S NO PLACE FOR YOU TO DIE.

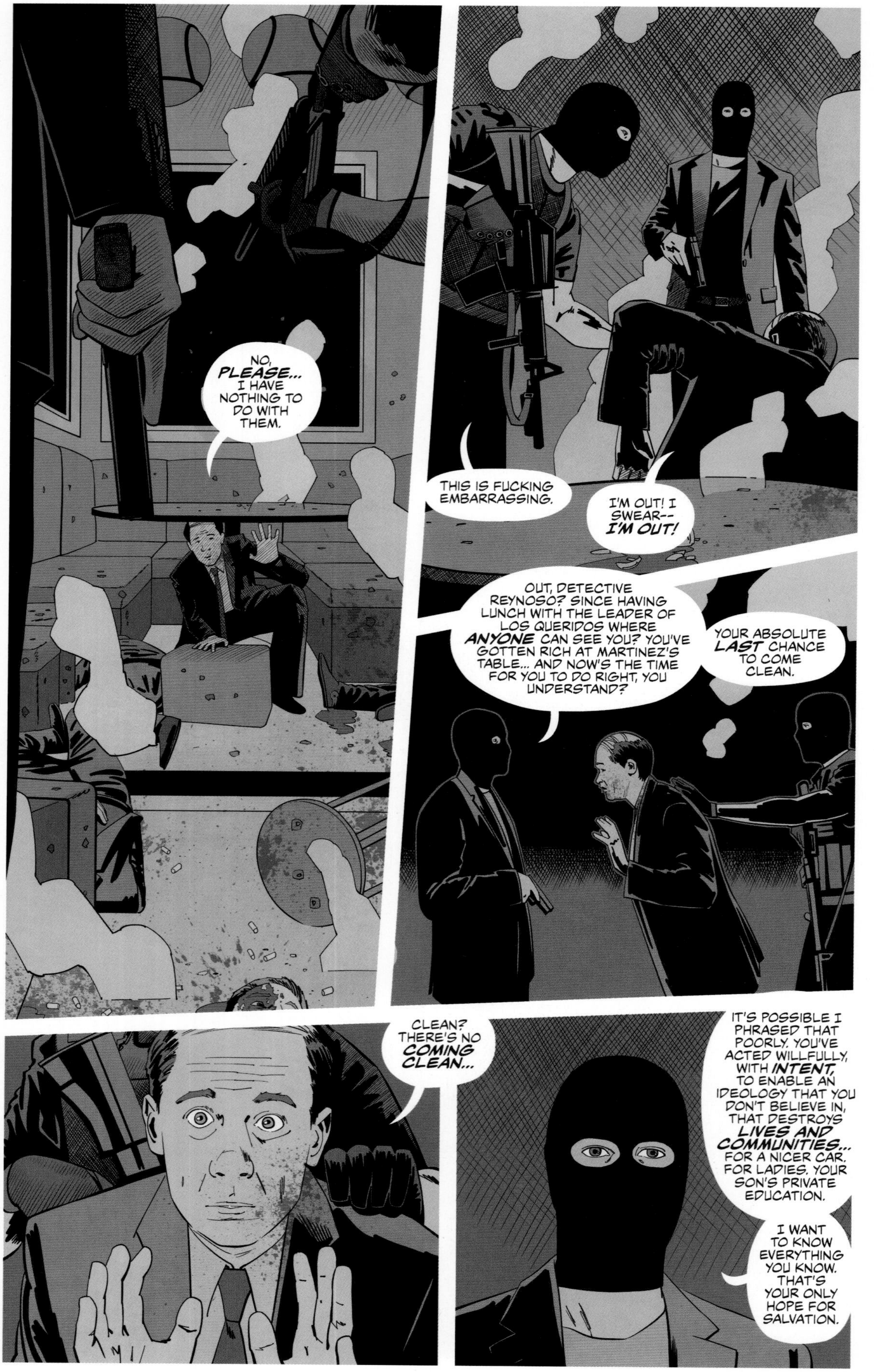
NO, PLEASE... I HAVE NOTHING TO DO WITH THEM.
THIS IS FUCKING EMBARRASSING.
I'M OUT! I SWEAR-- I'M OUT!
OUT, DETECTIVE REYNOSO? SINCE HAVING LUNCH WITH THE LEADER OF LOS QUERIDOS WHERE ANYONE CAN SEE YOU? YOU'VE GOTTEN RICH AT MARTINEZ'S TABLE... AND NOW'S THE TIME FOR YOU TO DO RIGHT, YOU UNDERSTAND?
YOUR ABSOLUTE LAST CHANCE TO COME CLEAN.
CLEAN? THERE'S NO COMING CLEAN...
IT'S POSSIBLE I PHRASED THAT POORLY. YOU'VE ACTED WILLFULLY, WITH INTENT, TO ENABLE AN IDEOLOGY THAT YOU DON'T BELIEVE IN, THAT DESTROYS LIVES AND COMMUNITIES... FOR A NICER CAR. FOR LADIES. YOUR SON'S PRIVATE EDUCATION.
I WANT TO KNOW EVERYTHING YOU KNOW. THAT'S YOUR ONLY HOPE FOR SALVATION.

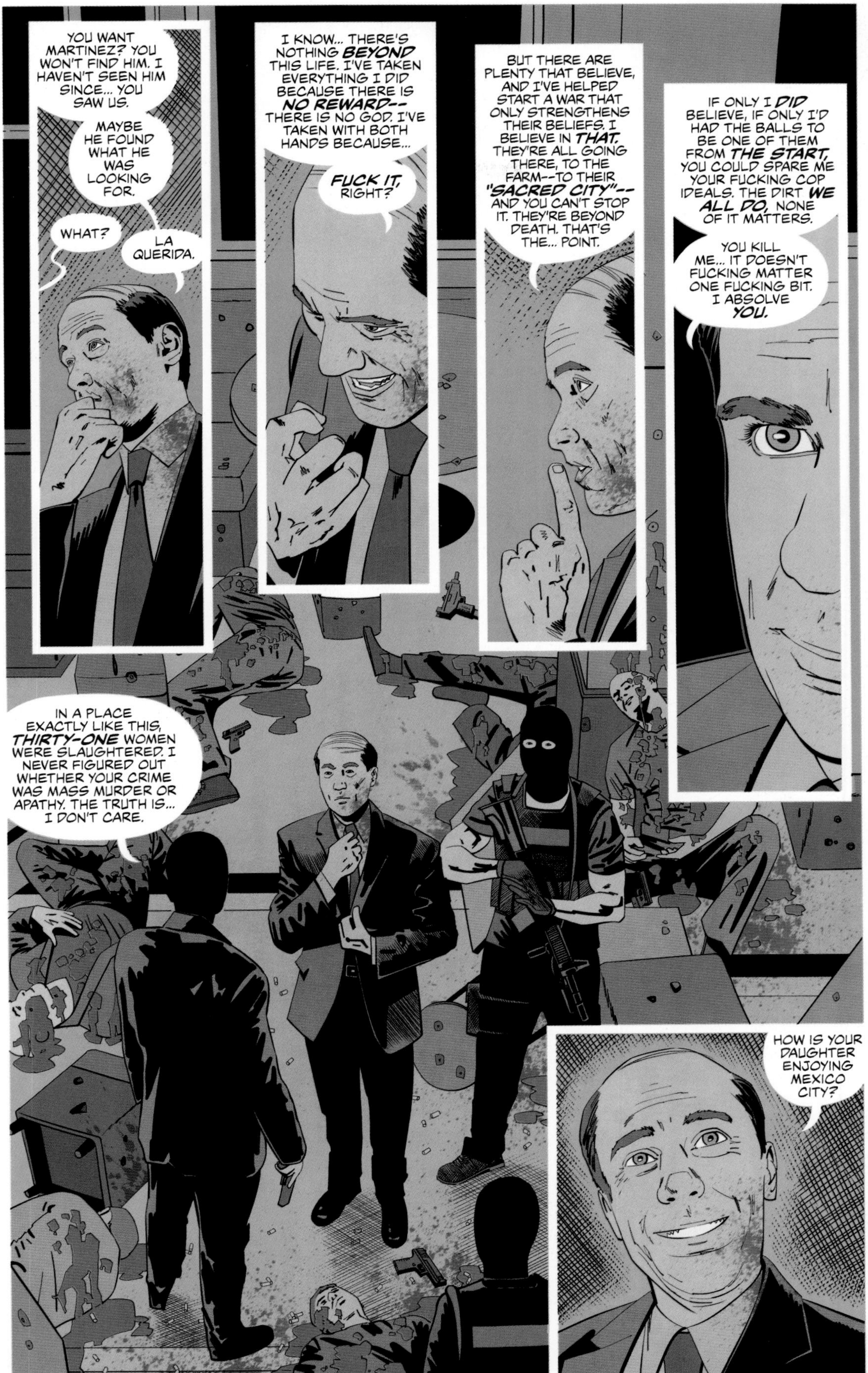
YOU WANT MARTINEZ? YOU WON'T FIND HIM. I HAVEN'T SEEN HIM SINCE... YOU SAW US.
MAYBE HE FOUND WHAT HE WAS LOOKING FOR.
WHAT?
LA QUERIDA.
I KNOW... THERE'S NOTHING BEYOND THIS LIFE. I'VE TAKEN EVERYTHING I DID BECAUSE THERE IS NO REWARD-- THERE IS NO GOD. I'VE TAKEN WITH BOTH HANDS BECAUSE...
FUCK IT, RIGHT?
BUT THERE ARE PLENTY THAT BELIEVE, AND I'VE HELPED START A WAR THAT ONLY STRENGTHENS THEIR BELIEFS. I BELIEVE IN THAT. THEY'RE ALL GOING THERE, TO THE FARM--TO THEIR "SACRED CITY"-- AND YOU CAN'T STOP IT. THEY'RE BEYOND DEATH. THAT'S THE... POINT.
IF ONLY I DID BELIEVE, IF ONLY I'D HAD THE BALLS TO BE ONE OF THEM FROM THE START, YOU COULD SPARE ME YOUR FUCKING COP IDEALS. THE DIRT WE ALL DO, NONE OF IT MATTERS.
YOU KILL ME... IT DOESN'T FUCKING MATTER ONE FUCKING BIT. I ABSOLVE YOU.
IN A PLACE EXACTLY LIKE THIS, THIRTY-ONE WOMEN WERE SLAUGHTERED. I NEVER FIGURED OUT WHETHER YOUR CRIME WAS MASS MURDER OR APATHY. THE TRUTH IS... I DON'T CARE.
HOW IS YOUR DAUGHTER ENJOYING MEXICO CITY?

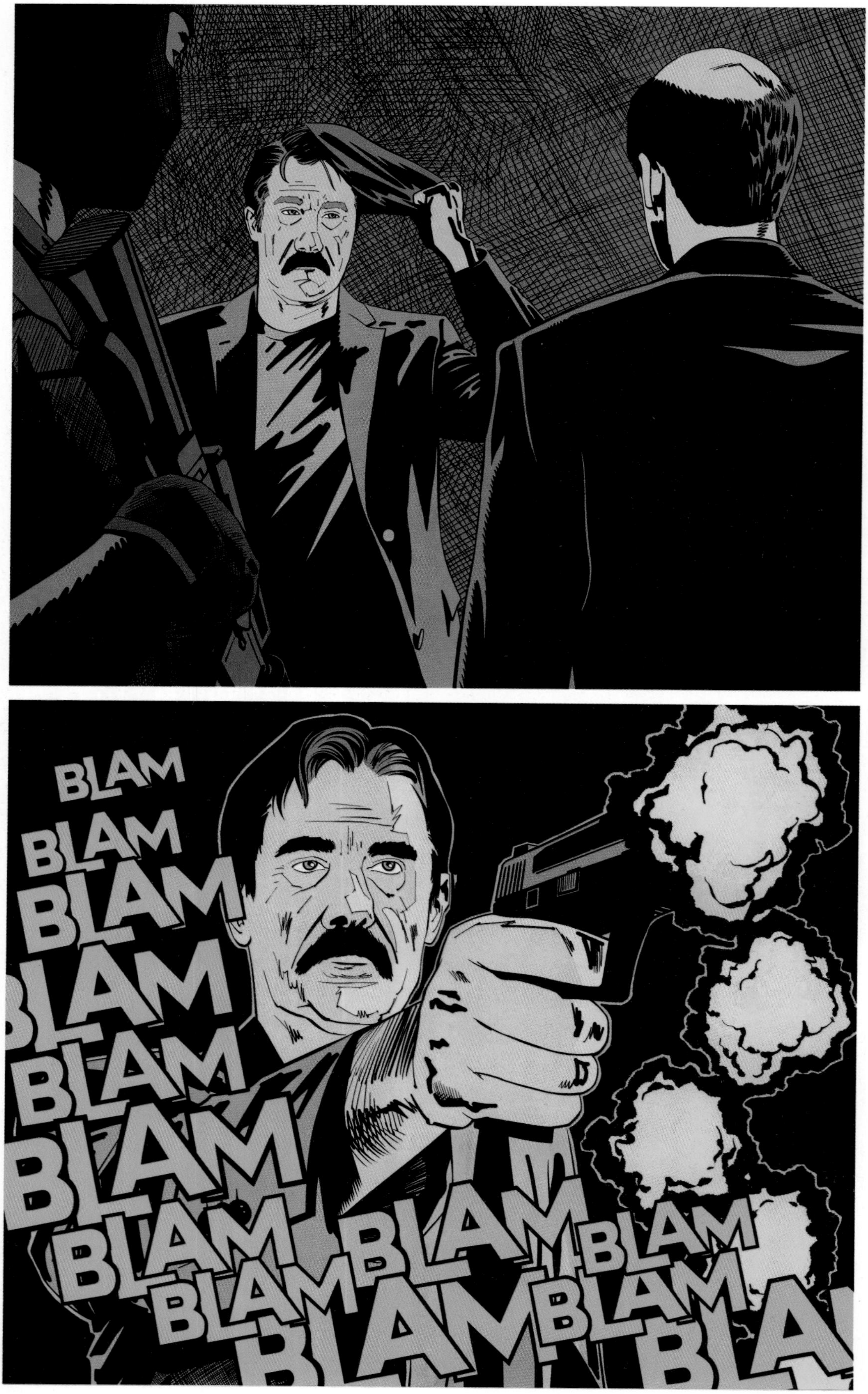
BLAM
BLAM
BLAM
BLAM
BLAM
BLAM
BLAM
BLAM BLAM BLAM
BLAM BLAM BLAM

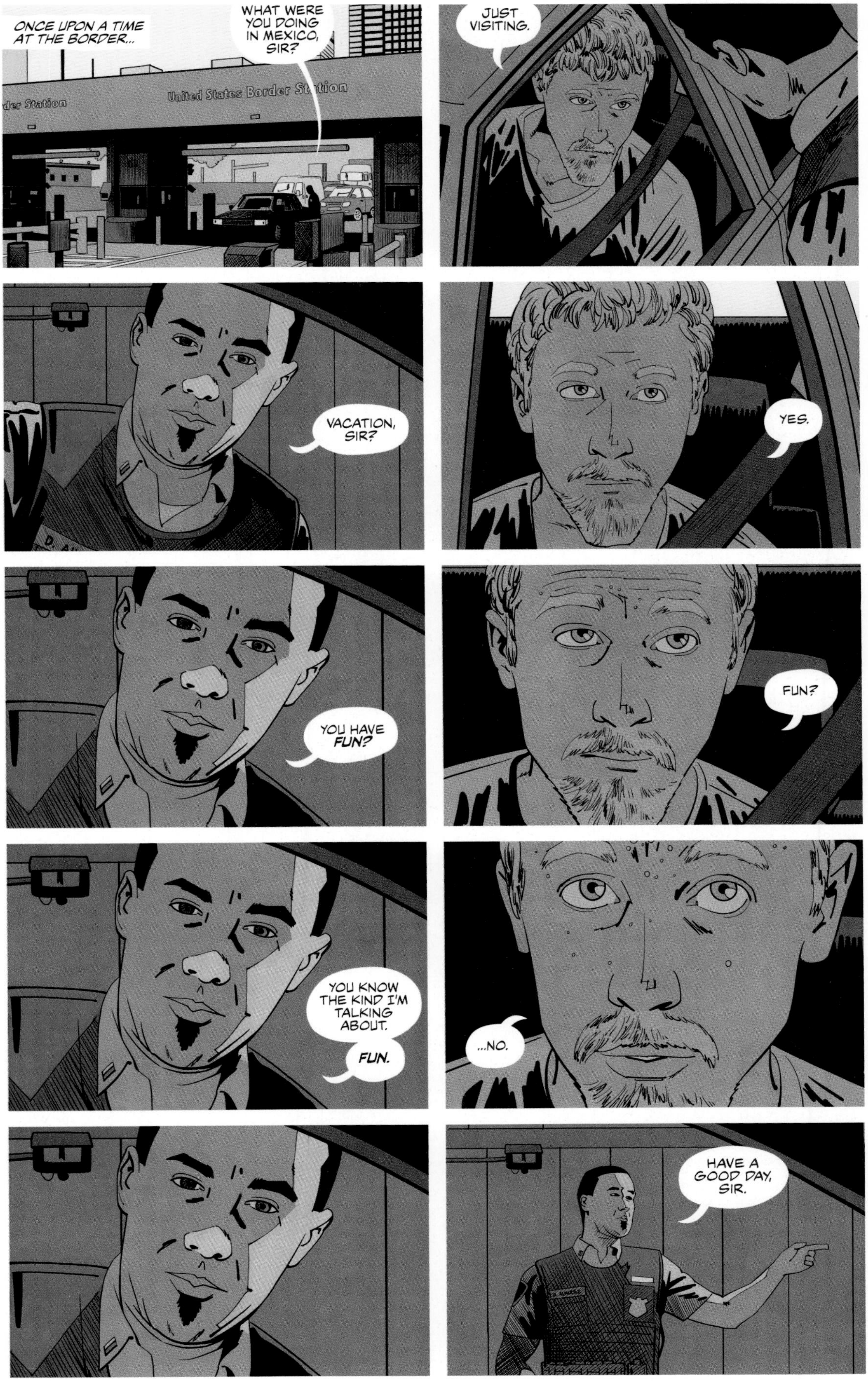
ONCE UPON A TIME AT THE BORDER...
WHAT WERE YOU DOING IN MEXICO, SIR?
United States Border Station
JUST VISITING.
VACATION, SIR?
YES.
YOU HAVE *FUN?*
FUN?
YOU KNOW THE KIND I'M TALKING ABOUT.
FUN.
...NO.
HAVE A GOOD DAY, SIR.

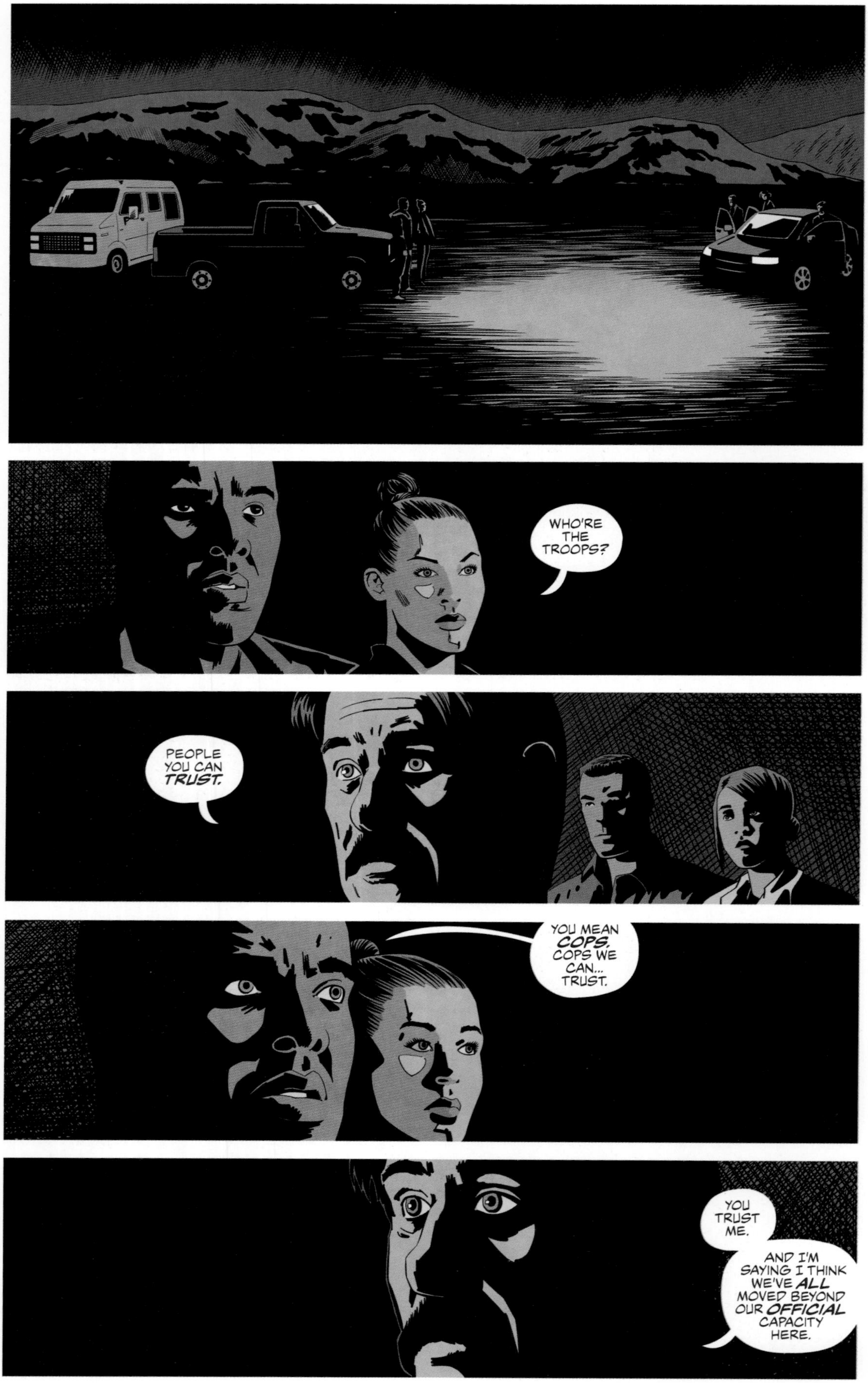
WHO'RE THE TROOPS?
PEOPLE YOU CAN TRUST.
YOU MEAN COPS. COPS WE CAN... TRUST.
YOU TRUST ME.
AND I'M SAYING I THINK WE'VE ALL MOVED BEYOND OUR OFFICIAL CAPACITY HERE.

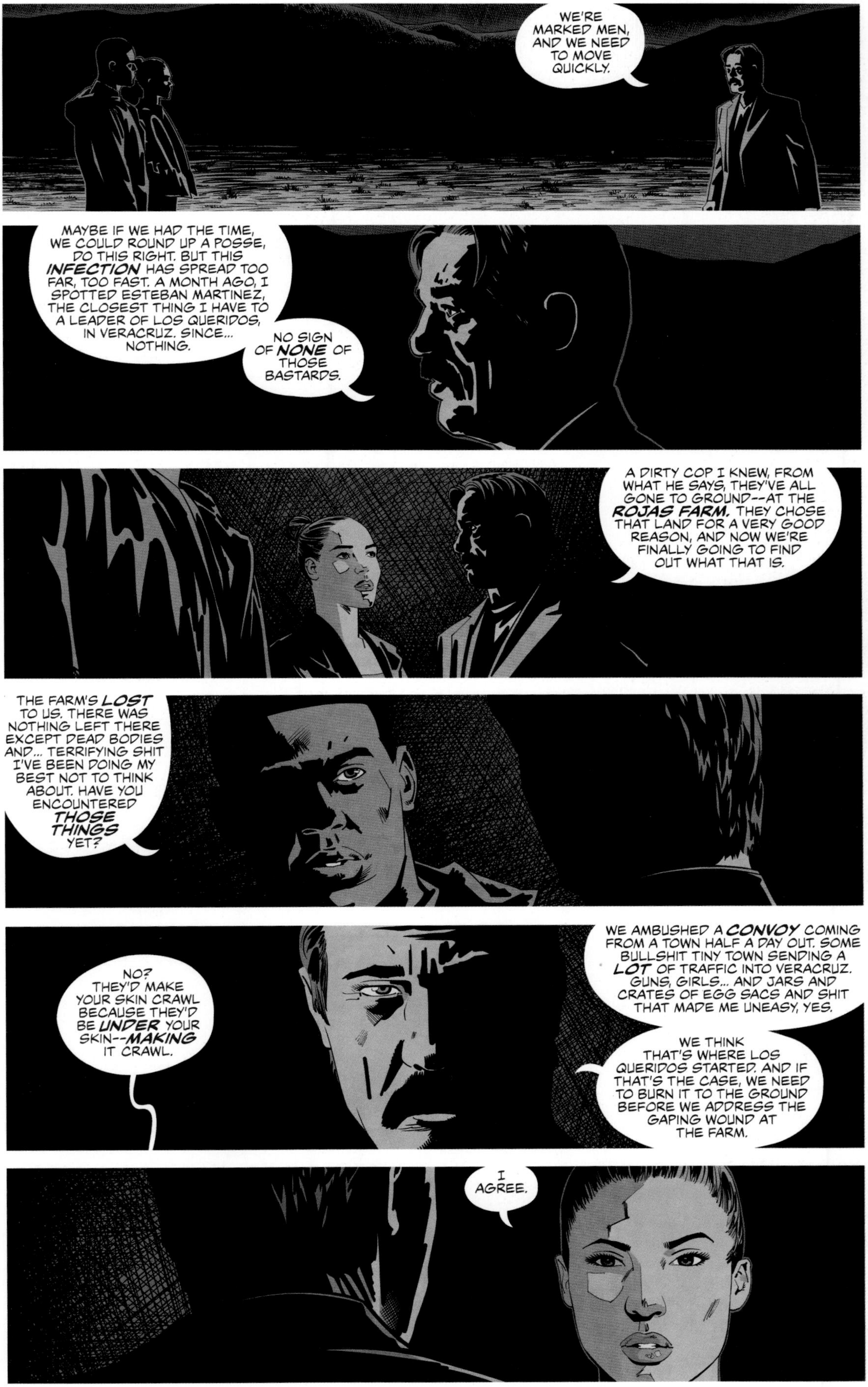
WE'RE MARKED MEN, AND WE NEED TO MOVE QUICKLY.
MAYBE IF WE HAD THE TIME, WE COULD ROUND UP A POSSE, DO THIS RIGHT. BUT THIS INFECTION HAS SPREAD TOO FAR, TOO FAST. A MONTH AGO, I SPOTTED ESTEBAN MARTINEZ, THE CLOSEST THING I HAVE TO A LEADER OF LOS QUERIDOS, IN VERACRUZ. SINCE... NOTHING.
NO SIGN OF NONE OF THOSE BASTARDS.
A DIRTY COP I KNEW, FROM WHAT HE SAYS, THEY'VE ALL GONE TO GROUND--AT THE ROJAS FARM. THEY CHOSE THAT LAND FOR A VERY GOOD REASON, AND NOW WE'RE FINALLY GOING TO FIND OUT WHAT THAT IS.
THE FARM'S LOST TO US. THERE WAS NOTHING LEFT THERE EXCEPT DEAD BODIES AND... TERRIFYING SHIT I'VE BEEN DOING MY BEST NOT TO THINK ABOUT. HAVE YOU ENCOUNTERED THOSE THINGS YET?
NO? THEY'D MAKE YOUR SKIN CRAWL BECAUSE THEY'D BE UNDER YOUR SKIN--MAKING IT CRAWL.
WE AMBUSHED A CONVOY COMING FROM A TOWN HALF A DAY OUT. SOME BULLSHIT TINY TOWN SENDING A LOT OF TRAFFIC INTO VERACRUZ. GUNS, GIRLS... AND JARS AND CRATES OF EGG SACS AND SHIT THAT MADE ME UNEASY, YES.
WE THINK THAT'S WHERE LOS QUERIDOS STARTED. AND IF THAT'S THE CASE, WE NEED TO BURN IT TO THE GROUND BEFORE WE ADDRESS THE GAPING WOUND AT THE FARM.
I AGREE.

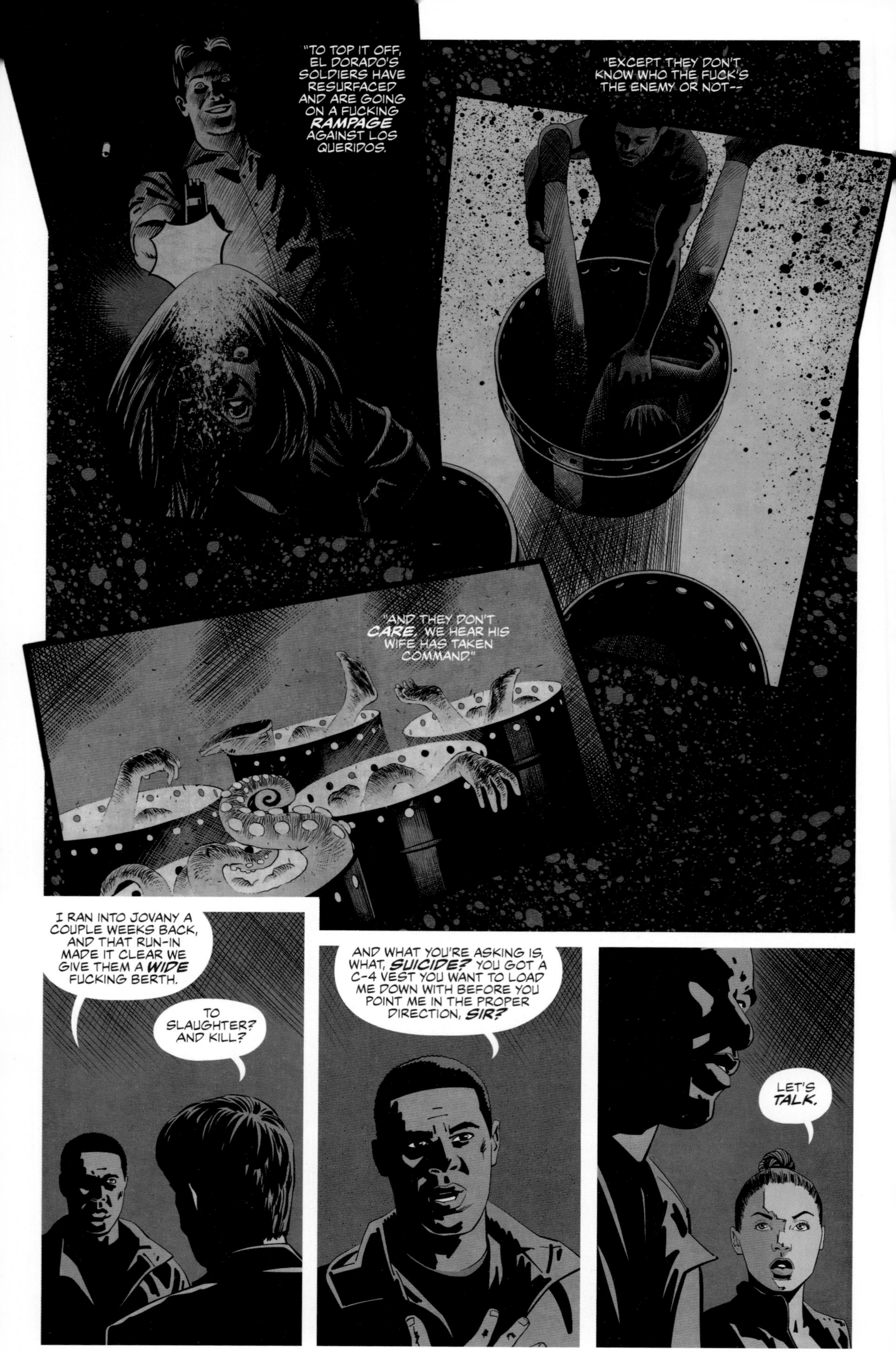
"TO TOP IT OFF, EL DORADO'S SOLDIERS HAVE RESURFACED AND ARE GOING ON A FUCKING RAMPAGE AGAINST LOS QUERIDOS.
"EXCEPT THEY DON'T KNOW WHO THE FUCK'S THE ENEMY OR NOT--
"AND THEY DON'T CARE. WE HEAR HIS WIFE HAS TAKEN COMMAND."
I RAN INTO JOVANY A COUPLE WEEKS BACK, AND THAT RUN-IN MADE IT CLEAR WE GIVE THEM A WIDE FUCKING BERTH.
TO SLAUGHTER? AND KILL?
AND WHAT YOU'RE ASKING IS, WHAT, SUICIDE? YOU GOT A C-4 VEST YOU WANT TO LOAD ME DOWN WITH BEFORE YOU POINT ME IN THE PROPER DIRECTION, SIR?
LET'S TALK.

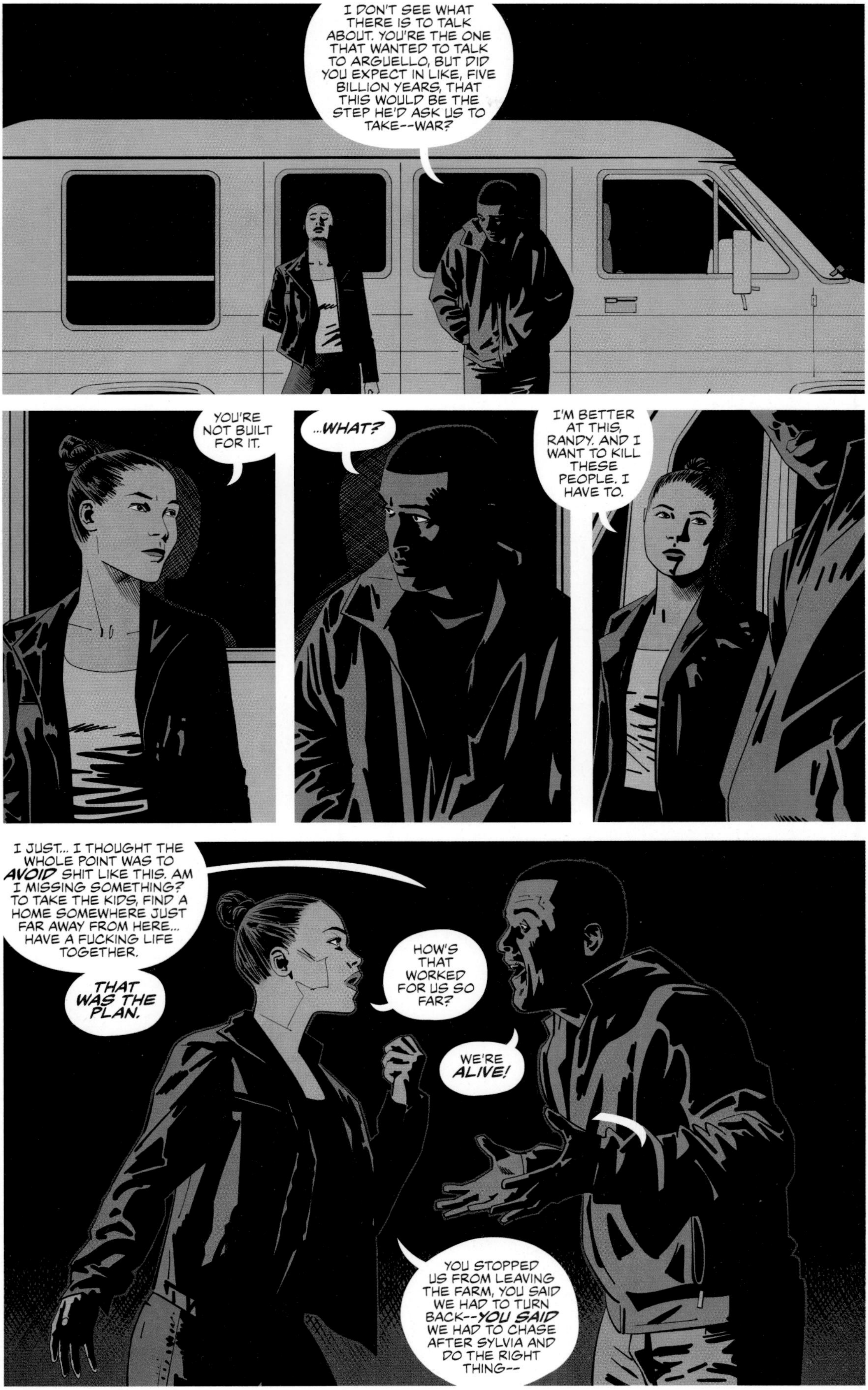
I DON'T SEE WHAT THERE IS TO TALK ABOUT. YOU'RE THE ONE THAT WANTED TO TALK TO ARGUELLO, BUT DID YOU EXPECT IN LIKE, FIVE BILLION YEARS, THAT THIS WOULD BE THE STEP HE'D ASK US TO TAKE--WAR?
YOU'RE NOT BUILT FOR IT.
...WHAT?
I'M BETTER AT THIS, RANDY. AND I WANT TO KILL THESE PEOPLE. I HAVE TO.
I JUST... I THOUGHT THE WHOLE POINT WAS TO AVOID SHIT LIKE THIS. AM I MISSING SOMETHING? TO TAKE THE KIDS, FIND A HOME SOMEWHERE JUST FAR AWAY FROM HERE... HAVE A FUCKING LIFE TOGETHER.
THAT WAS THE PLAN.
HOW'S THAT WORKED FOR US SO FAR?
WE'RE ALIVE!
YOU STOPPED US FROM LEAVING THE FARM, YOU SAID WE HAD TO TURN BACK--YOU SAID WE HAD TO CHASE AFTER SYLVIA AND DO THE RIGHT THING--

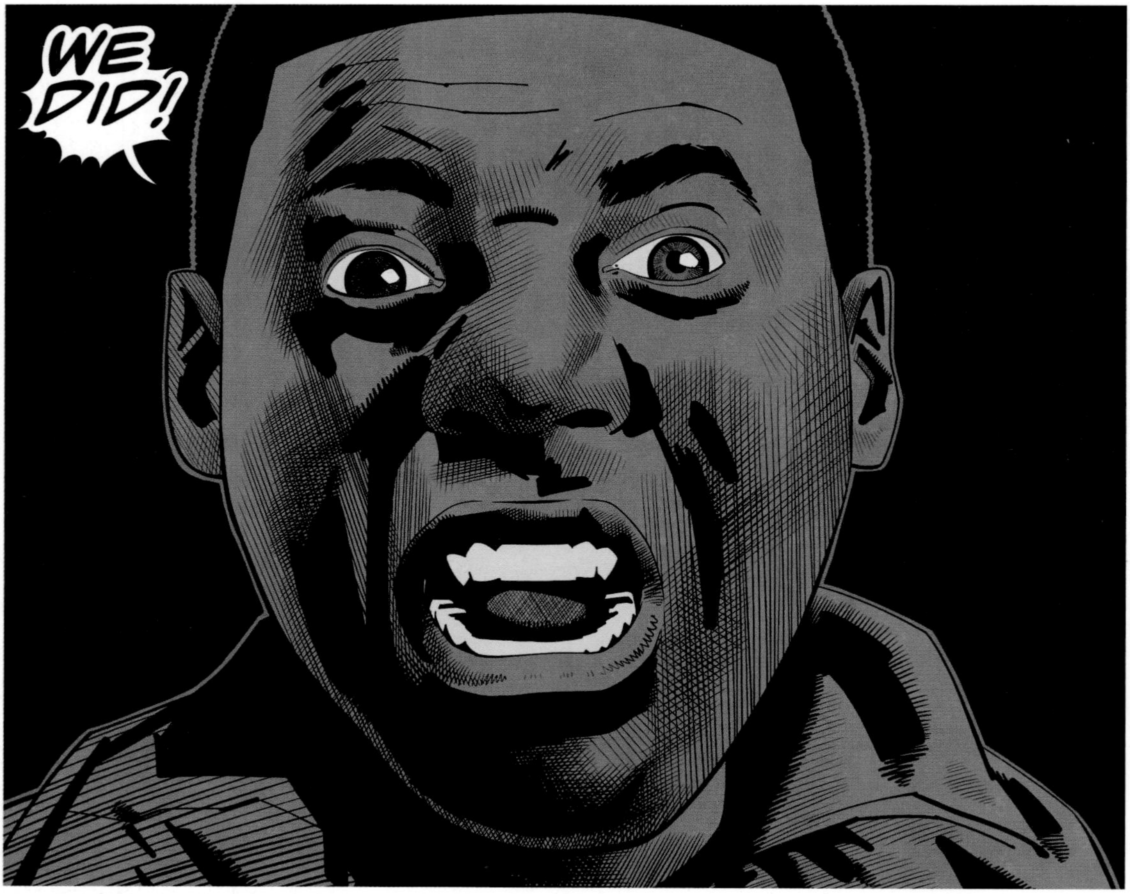
WE DID!

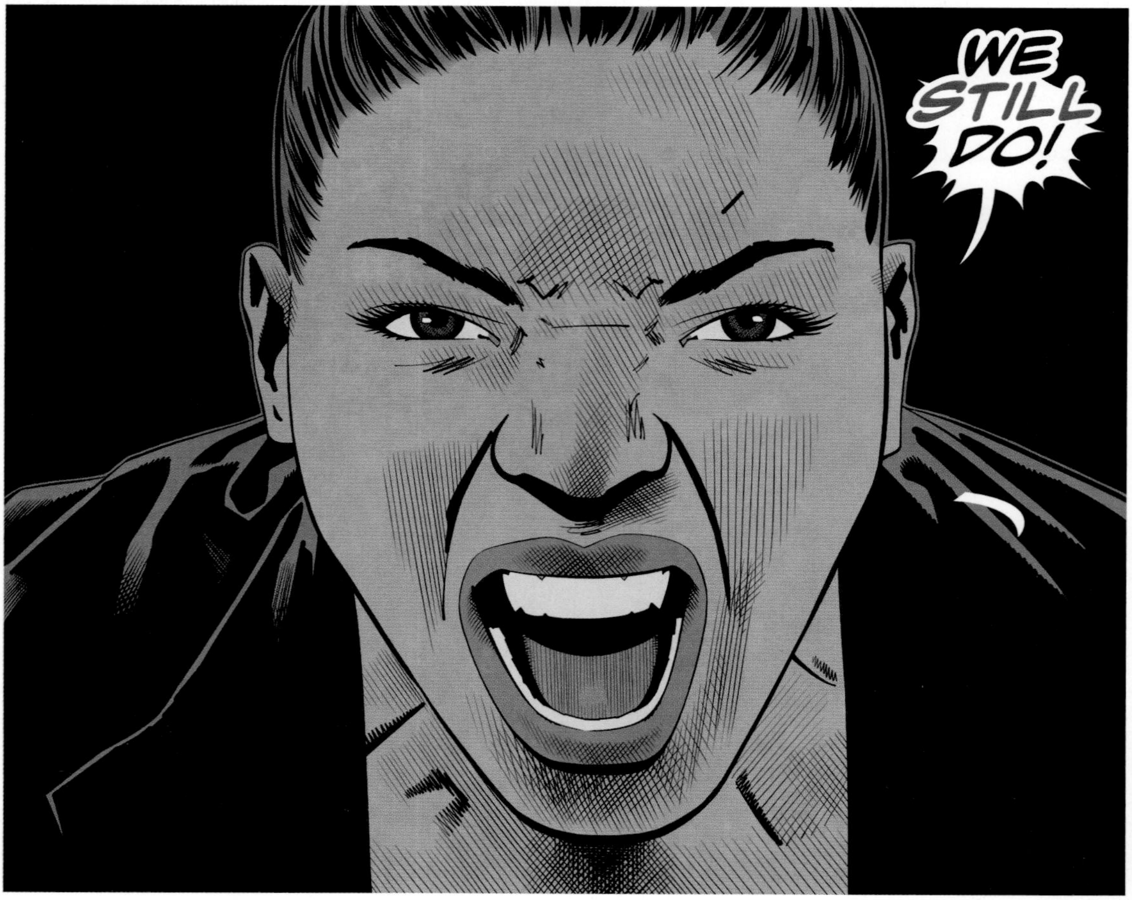
WE STILL DO!

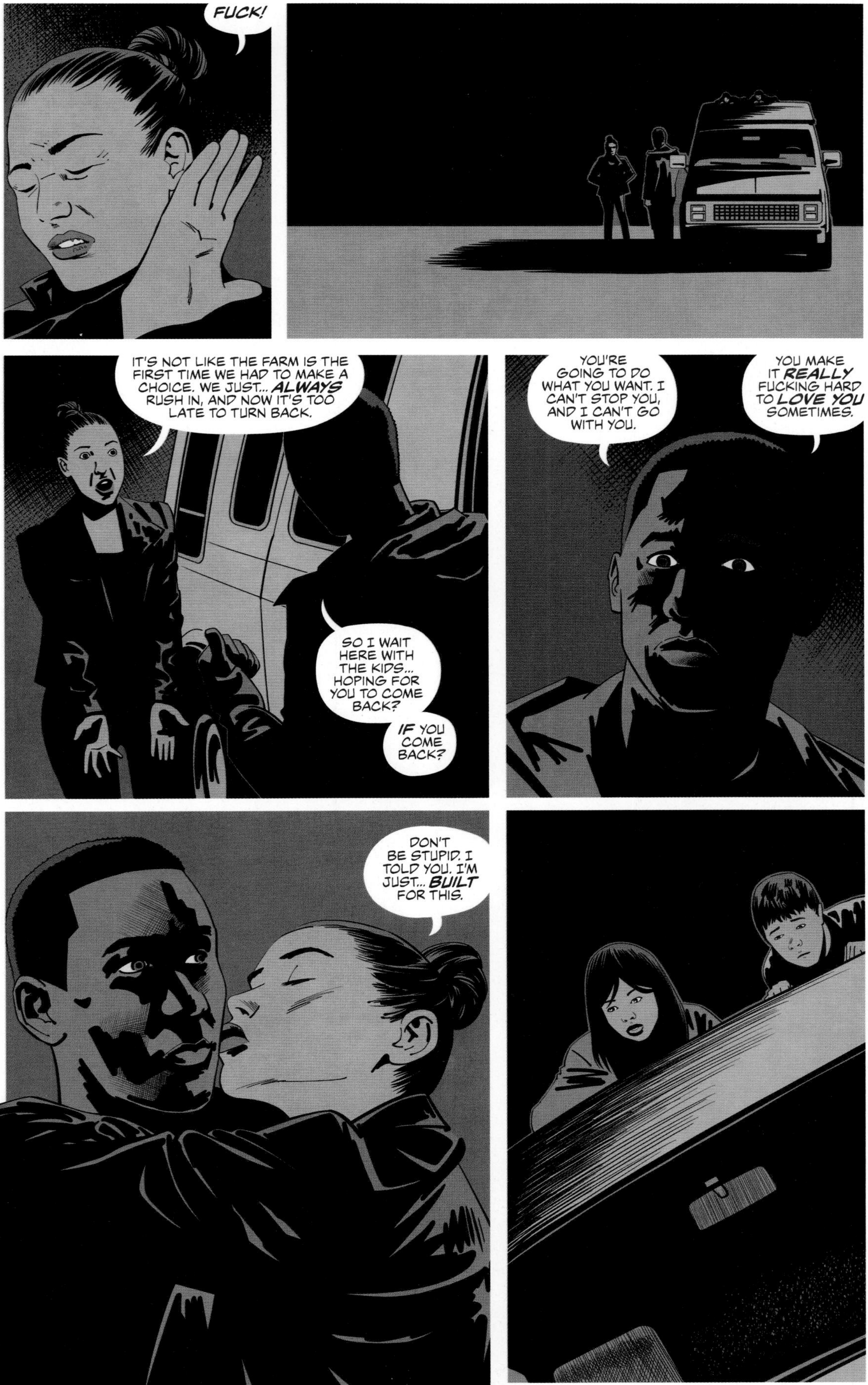
FUCK!
IT'S NOT LIKE THE FARM IS THE FIRST TIME WE HAD TO MAKE A CHOICE. WE JUST... ALWAYS RUSH IN, AND NOW IT'S TOO LATE TO TURN BACK.
SO I WAIT HERE WITH THE KIDS... HOPING FOR YOU TO COME BACK?
IF YOU COME BACK?
YOU'RE GOING TO DO WHAT YOU WANT. I CAN'T STOP YOU, AND I CAN'T GO WITH YOU.
YOU MAKE IT REALLY FUCKING HARD TO LOVE YOU SOMETIMES.
DON'T BE STUPID. I TOLD YOU. I'M JUST... BUILT FOR THIS.

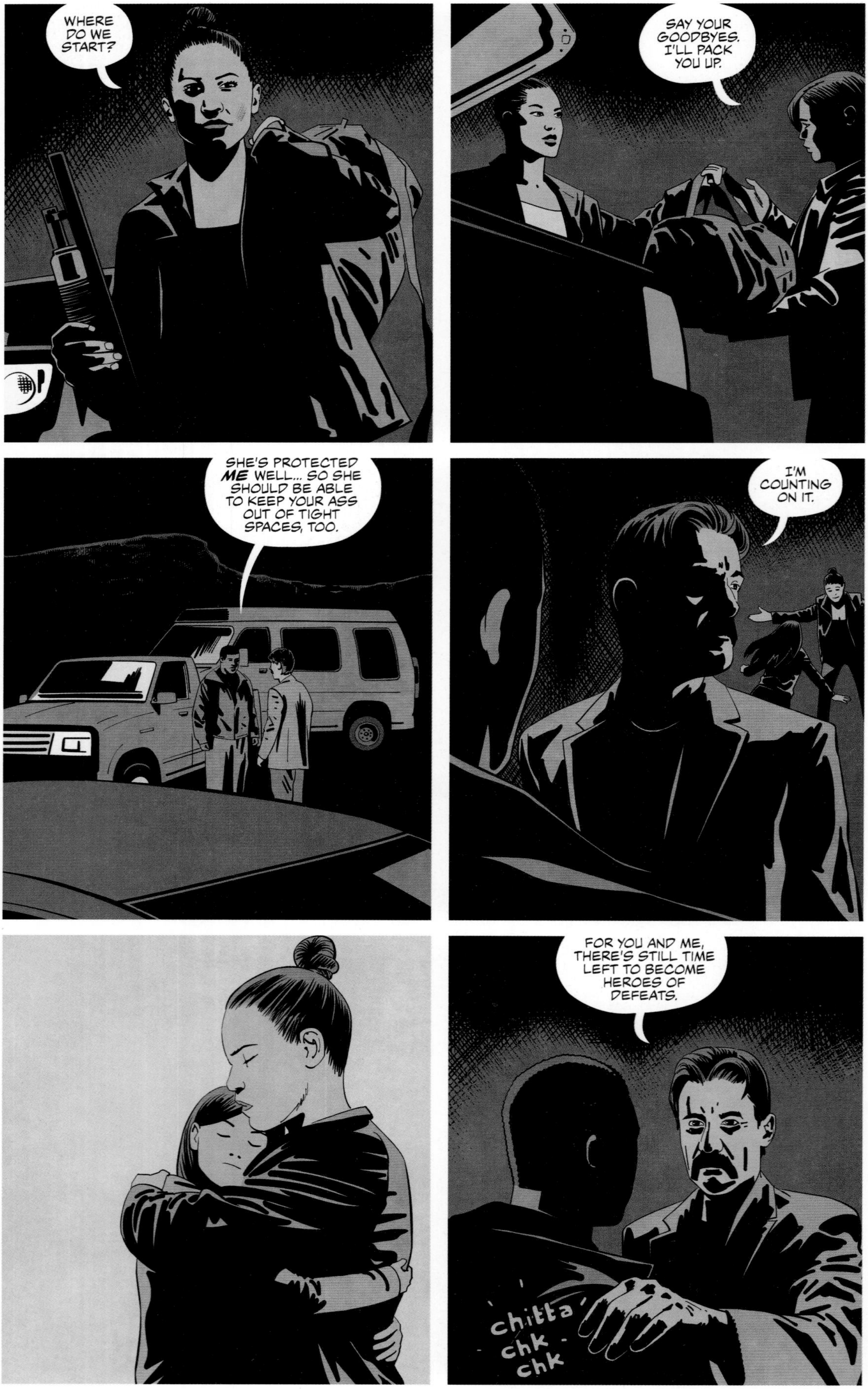
WHERE DO WE START?
SAY YOUR GOODBYES. I'LL PACK YOU UP.
SHE'S PROTECTED **ME** WELL... SO SHE SHOULD BE ABLE TO KEEP YOUR ASS OUT OF TIGHT SPACES, TOO.
I'M COUNTING ON IT.
FOR YOU AND ME, THERE'S STILL TIME LEFT TO BECOME HEROES OF DEFEATS.
chitta chk chk

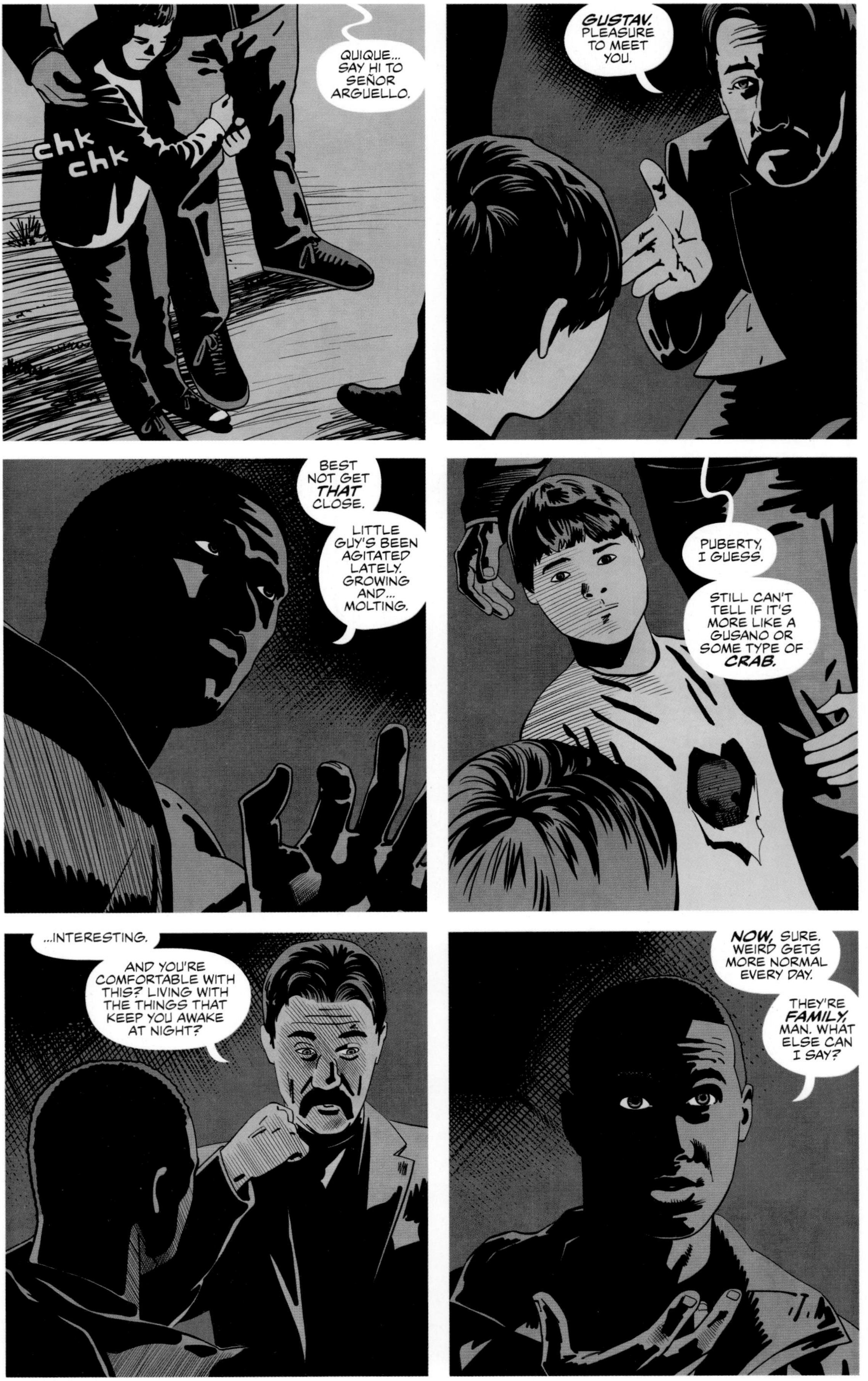
QUIQUE... SAY HI TO SEÑOR ARGUELLO.
chk chk
GUSTAV. PLEASURE TO MEET YOU.
BEST NOT GET THAT CLOSE.
LITTLE GUY'S BEEN AGITATED LATELY. GROWING AND... MOLTING.
PUBERTY, I GUESS.
STILL CAN'T TELL IF IT'S MORE LIKE A GUSANO OR SOME TYPE OF CRAB.
...INTERESTING.
AND YOU'RE COMFORTABLE WITH THIS? LIVING WITH THE THINGS THAT KEEP YOU AWAKE AT NIGHT?
NOW, SURE. WEIRD GETS MORE NORMAL EVERY DAY.
THEY'RE FAMILY, MAN. WHAT ELSE CAN I SAY?

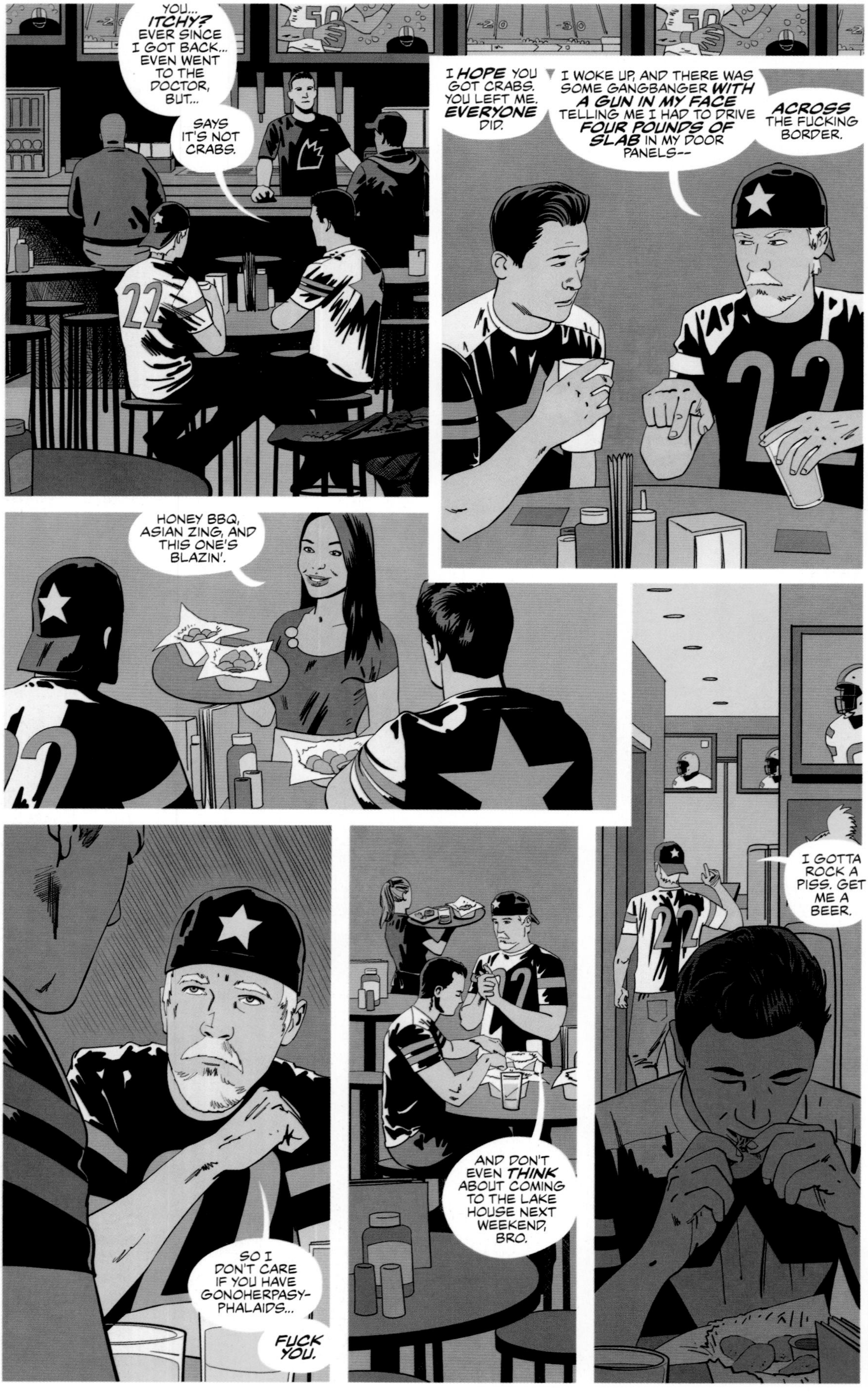
YOU... ITCHY? EVER SINCE I GOT BACK... EVEN WENT TO THE DOCTOR, BUT...
SAYS IT'S NOT CRABS.
I HOPE YOU GOT CRABS. YOU LEFT ME. EVERYONE DID.
I WOKE UP, AND THERE WAS SOME GANGBANGER WITH A GUN IN MY FACE TELLING ME I HAD TO DRIVE FOUR POUNDS OF SLAB IN MY DOOR PANELS--
ACROSS THE FUCKING BORDER.
HONEY BBQ, ASIAN ZING, AND THIS ONE'S BLAZIN'.
I GOTTA ROCK A PISS. GET ME A BEER.
SO I DON'T CARE IF YOU HAVE GONOHERPASY-PHALAIDS...
FUCK YOU.
AND DON'T EVEN THINK ABOUT COMING TO THE LAKE HOUSE NEXT WEEKEND, BRO.

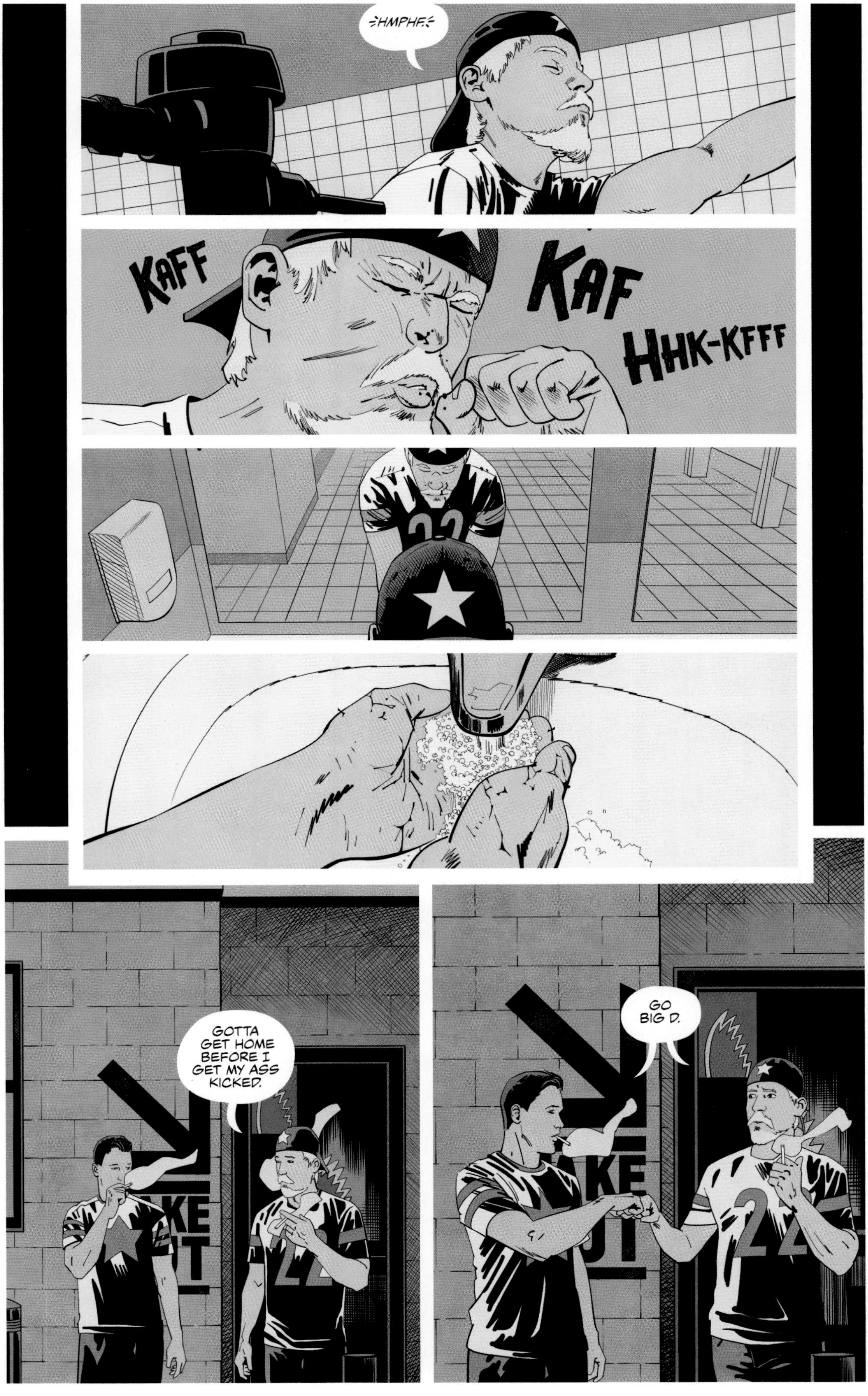
HMPHF
KAFF
KAF
HHK-KFFF
GOTTA GET HOME BEFORE I GET MY ASS KICKED.
GO BIG D.

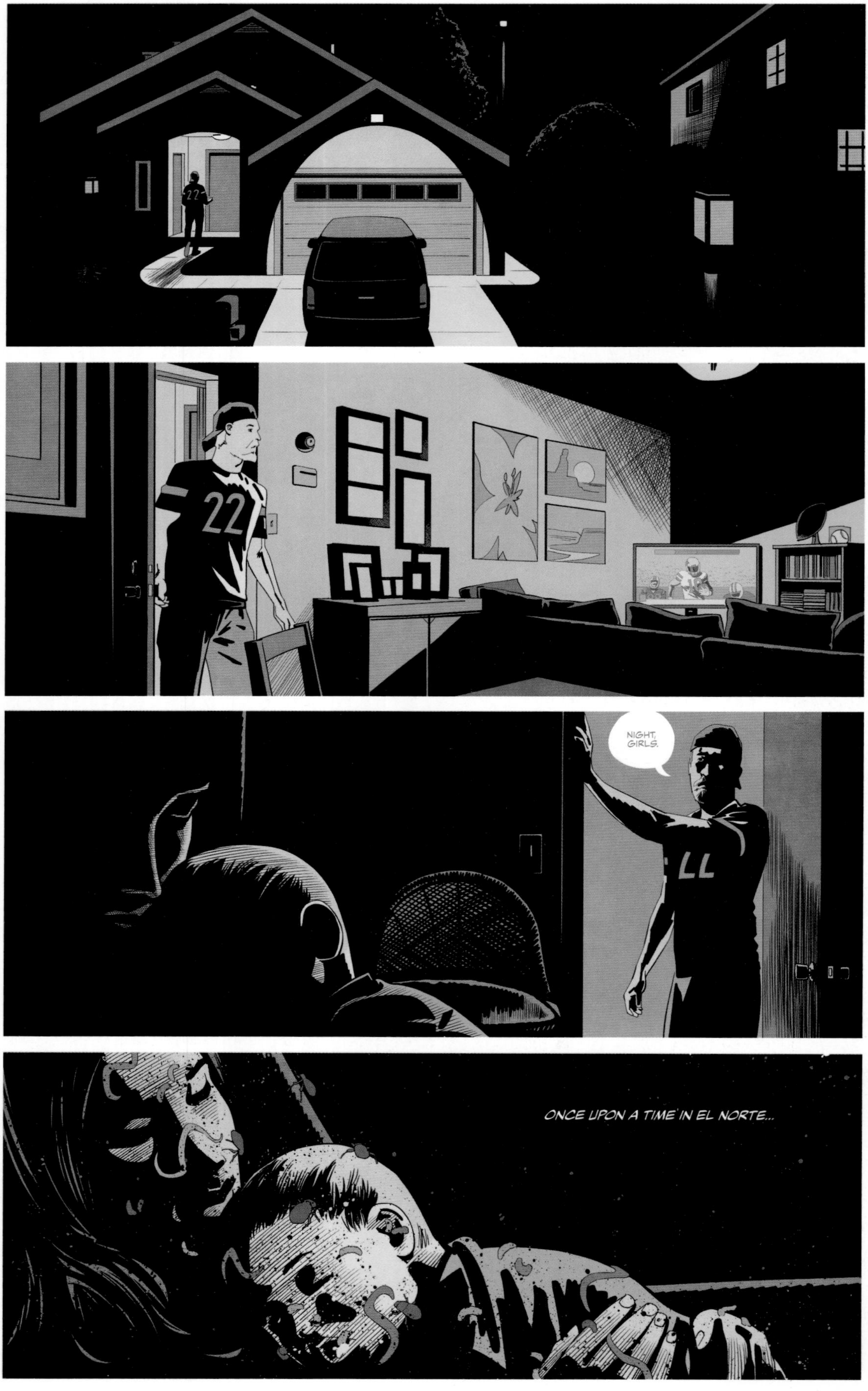
NIGHT, GIRLS.
ONCE UPON A TIME IN EL NORTE...

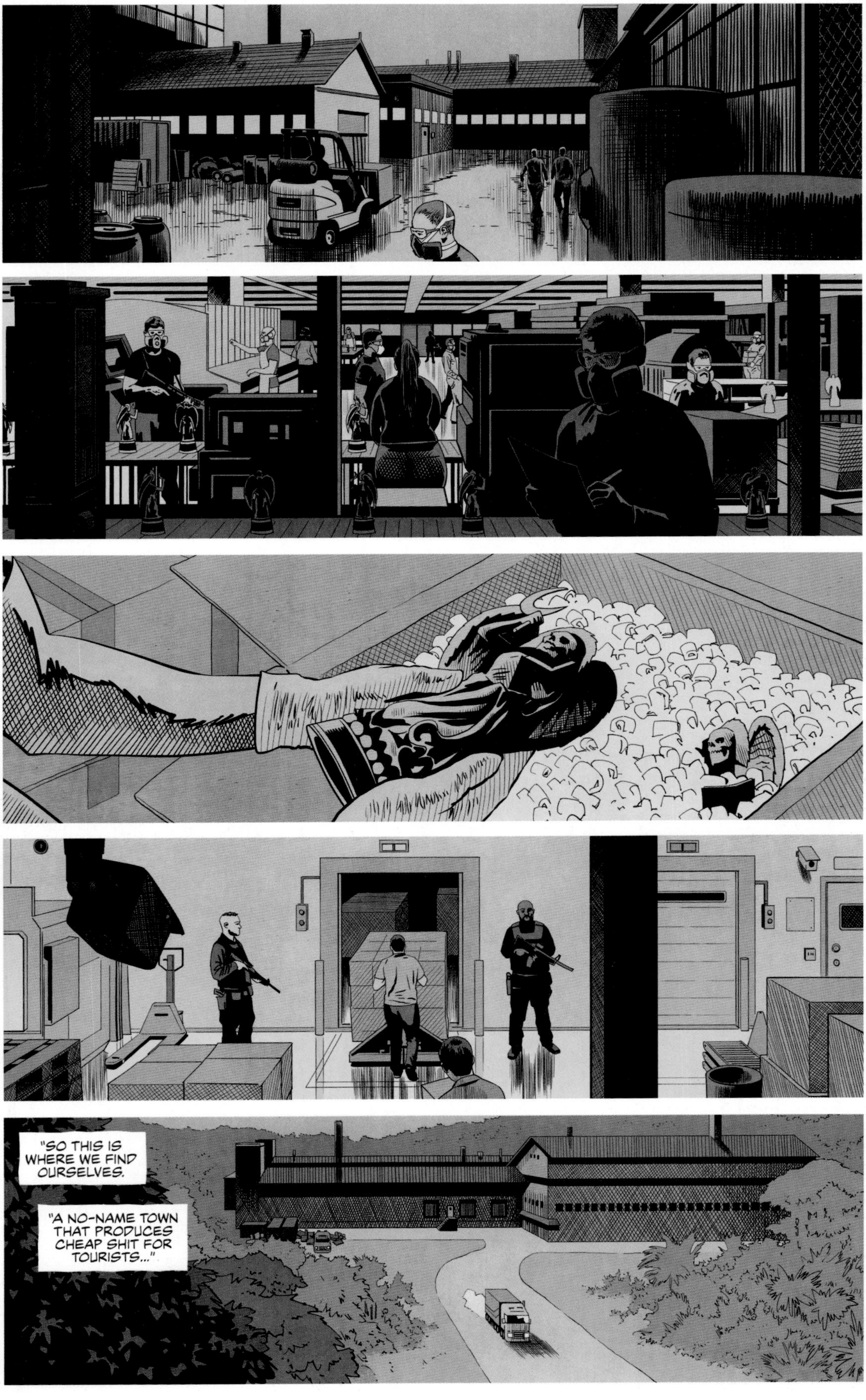
"SO THIS IS WHERE WE FIND OURSELVES.
"A NO-NAME TOWN THAT PRODUCES CHEAP SHIT FOR TOURISTS..."

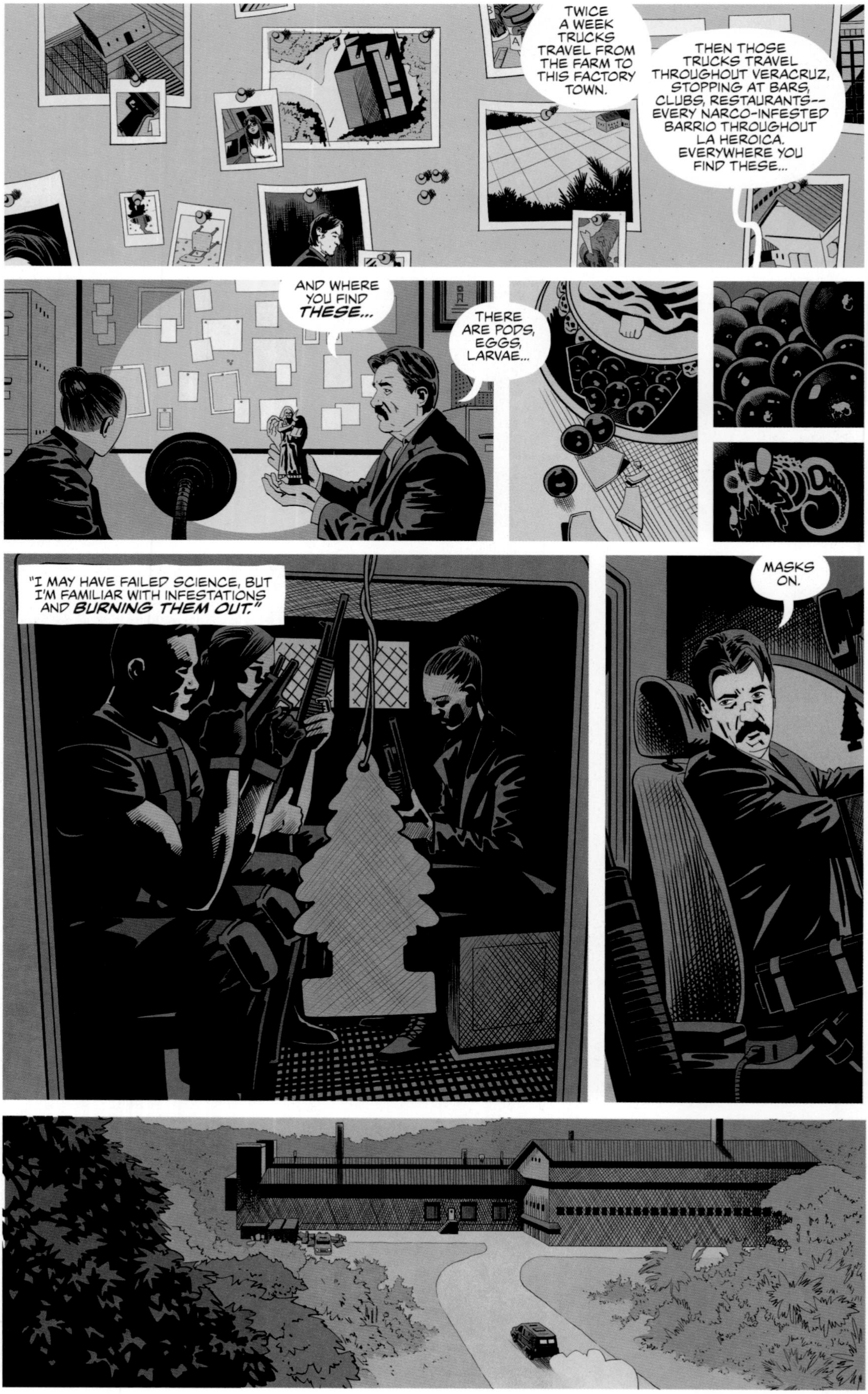
TWICE A WEEK TRUCKS TRAVEL FROM THE FARM TO THIS FACTORY TOWN.
THEN THOSE TRUCKS TRAVEL THROUGHOUT VERACRUZ, STOPPING AT BARS, CLUBS, RESTAURANTS-- EVERY NARCO-INFESTED BARRIO THROUGHOUT LA HEROICA. EVERYWHERE YOU FIND THESE...
AND WHERE YOU FIND ***THESE...***
THERE ARE PODS, EGGS, LARVAE...
"I MAY HAVE FAILED SCIENCE, BUT I'M FAMILIAR WITH INFESTATIONS AND ***BURNING THEM OUT.***"
MASKS ON.

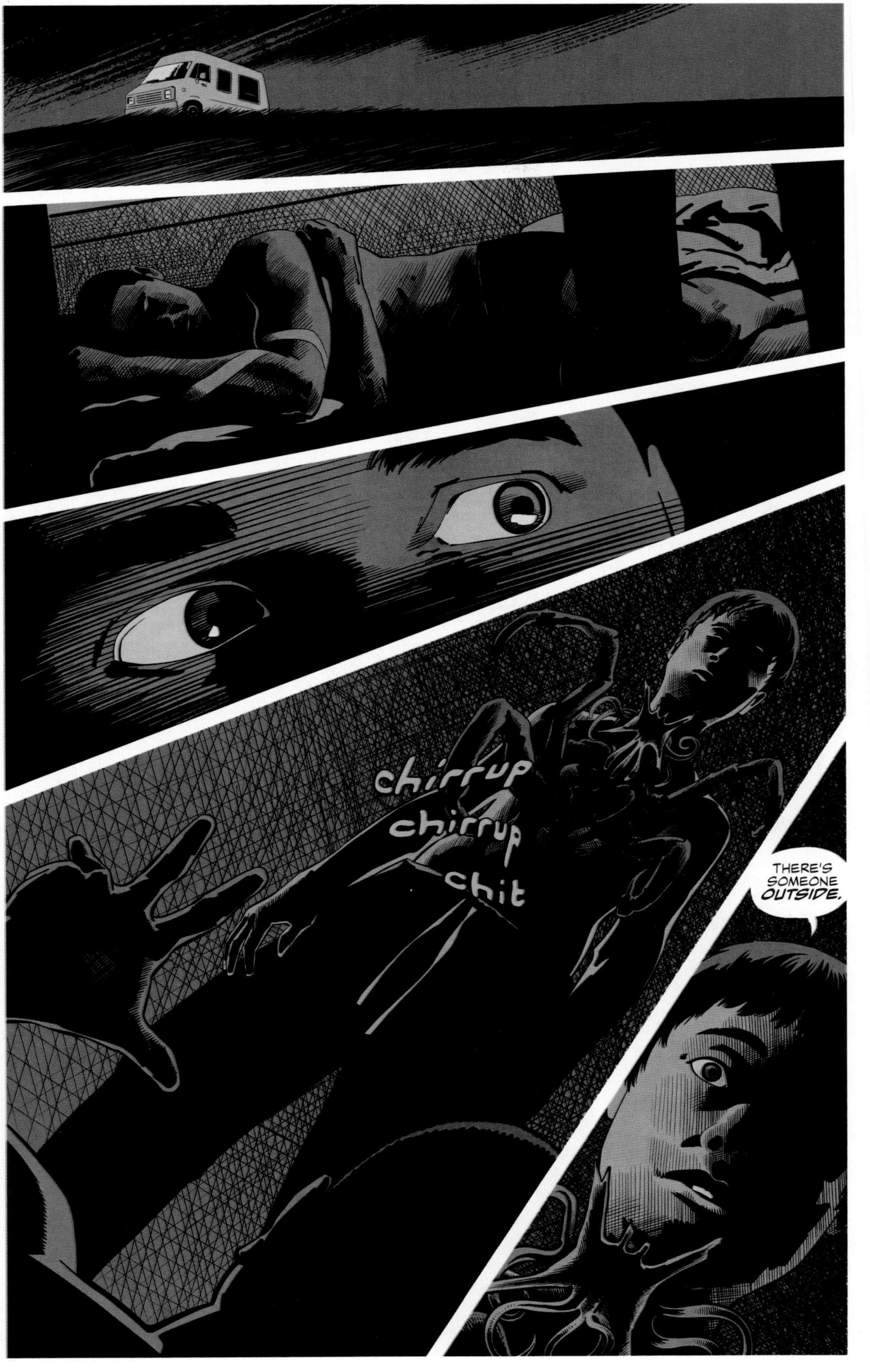
chirrup
chirrup
chit
THERE'S SOMEONE OUTSIDE.

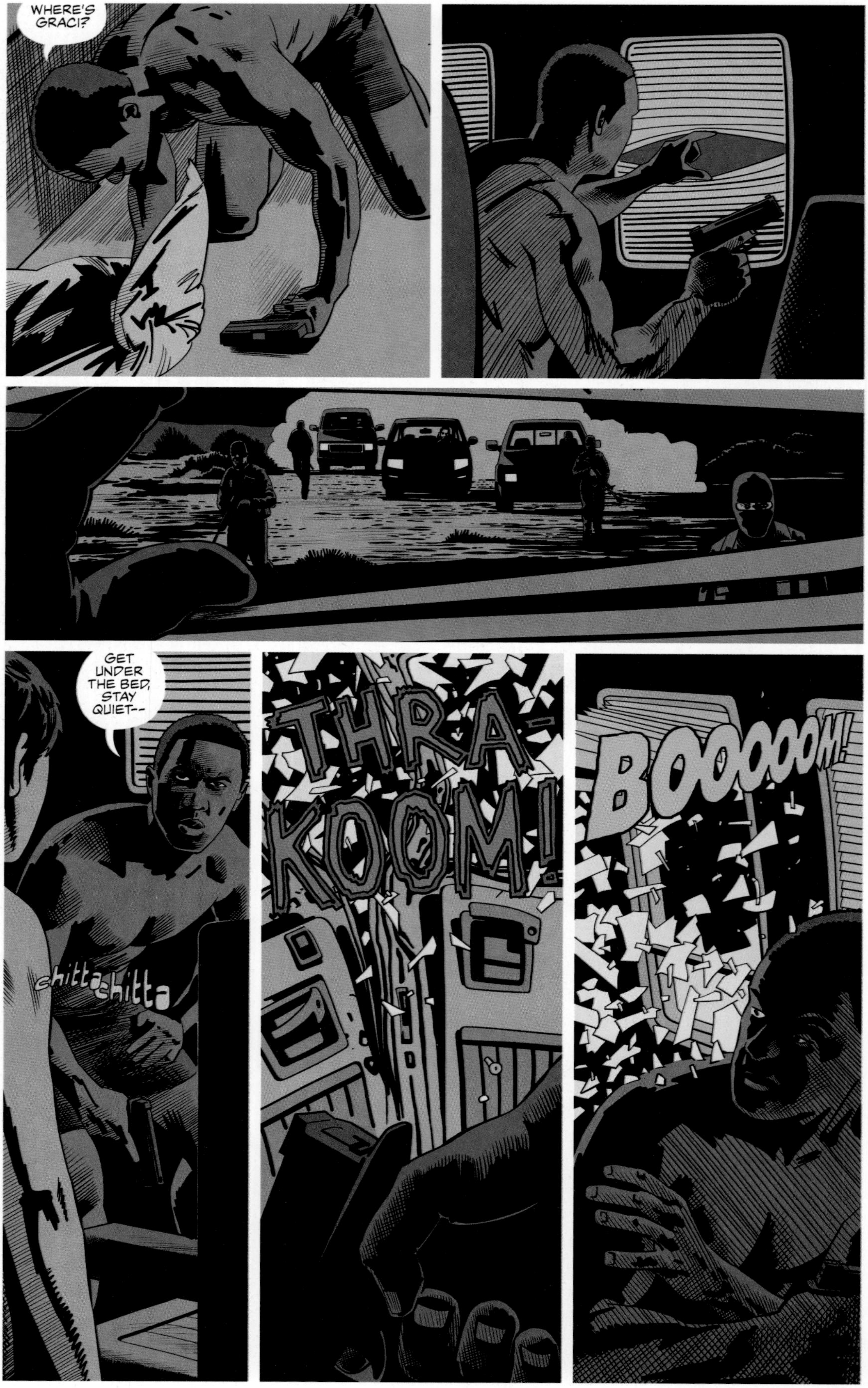
WHERE'S GRACI?
GET UNDER THE BED, STAY QUIET--
chitta chitta
THRA-KOOM!
BOOOOOM!

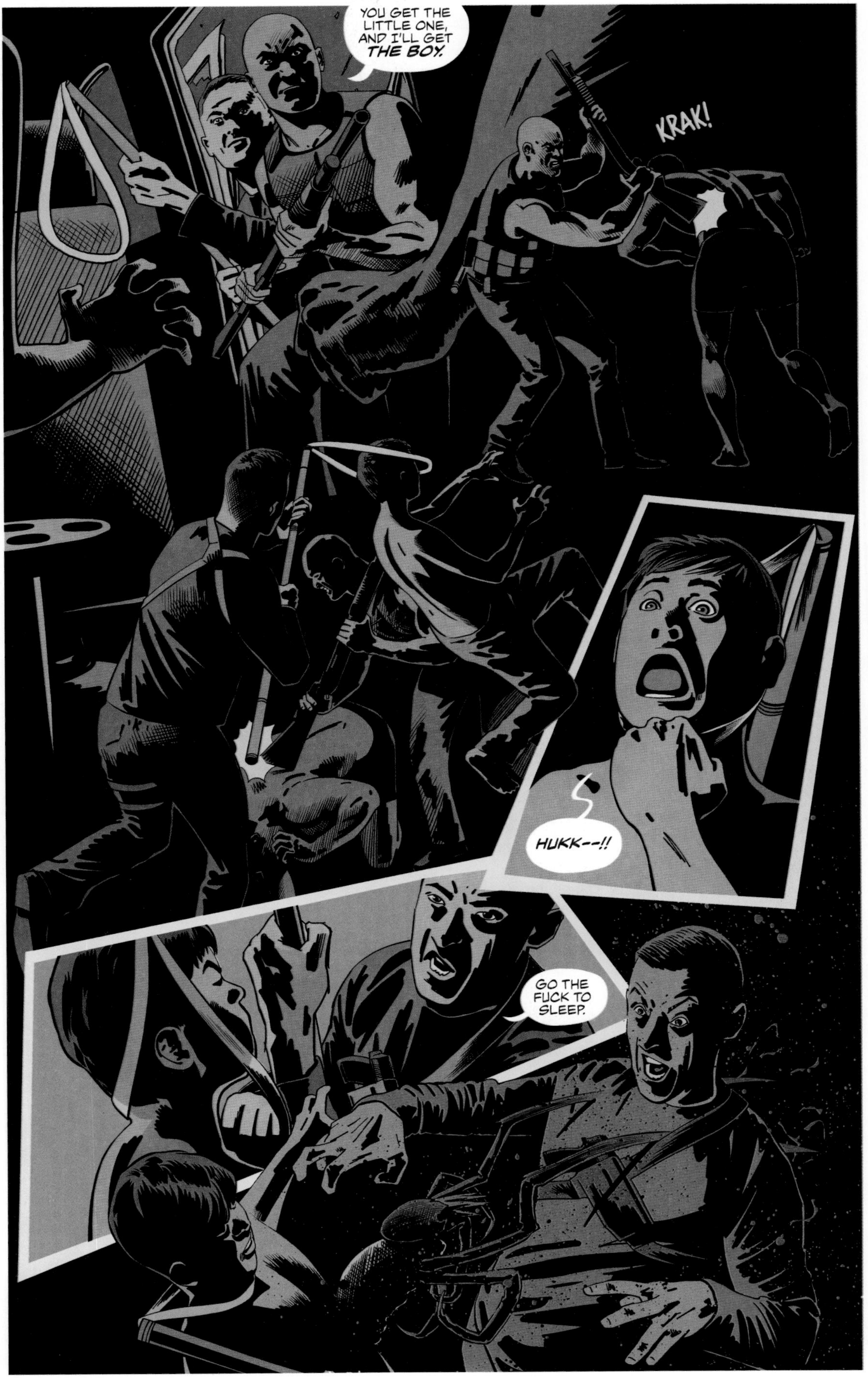
YOU GET THE LITTLE ONE, AND I'LL GET THE BOY.
KRAK!
HUKK--!!
GO THE FUCK TO SLEEP.

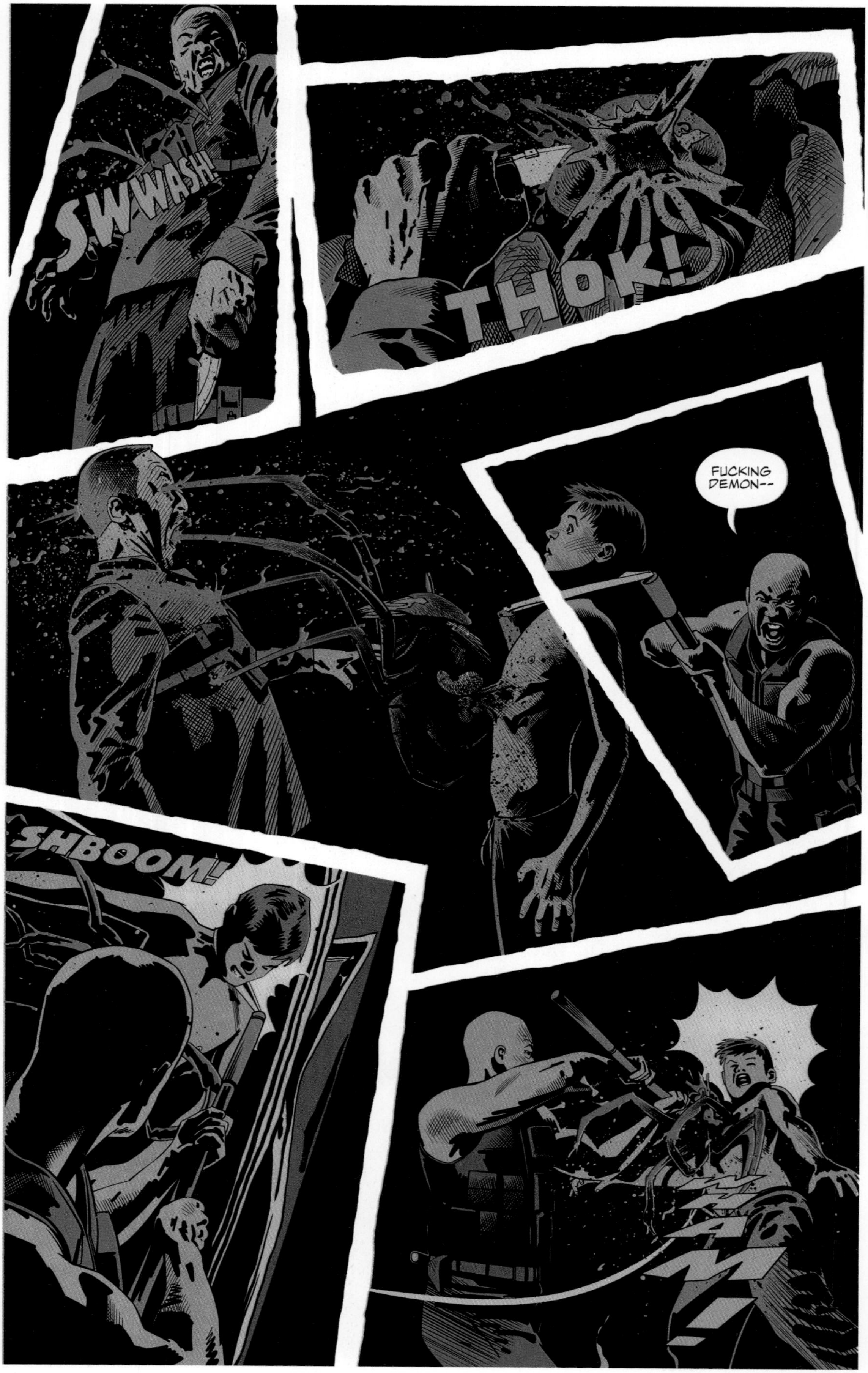
SWWASH!
THOK!
FUCKING DEMON--
SHBOOM!

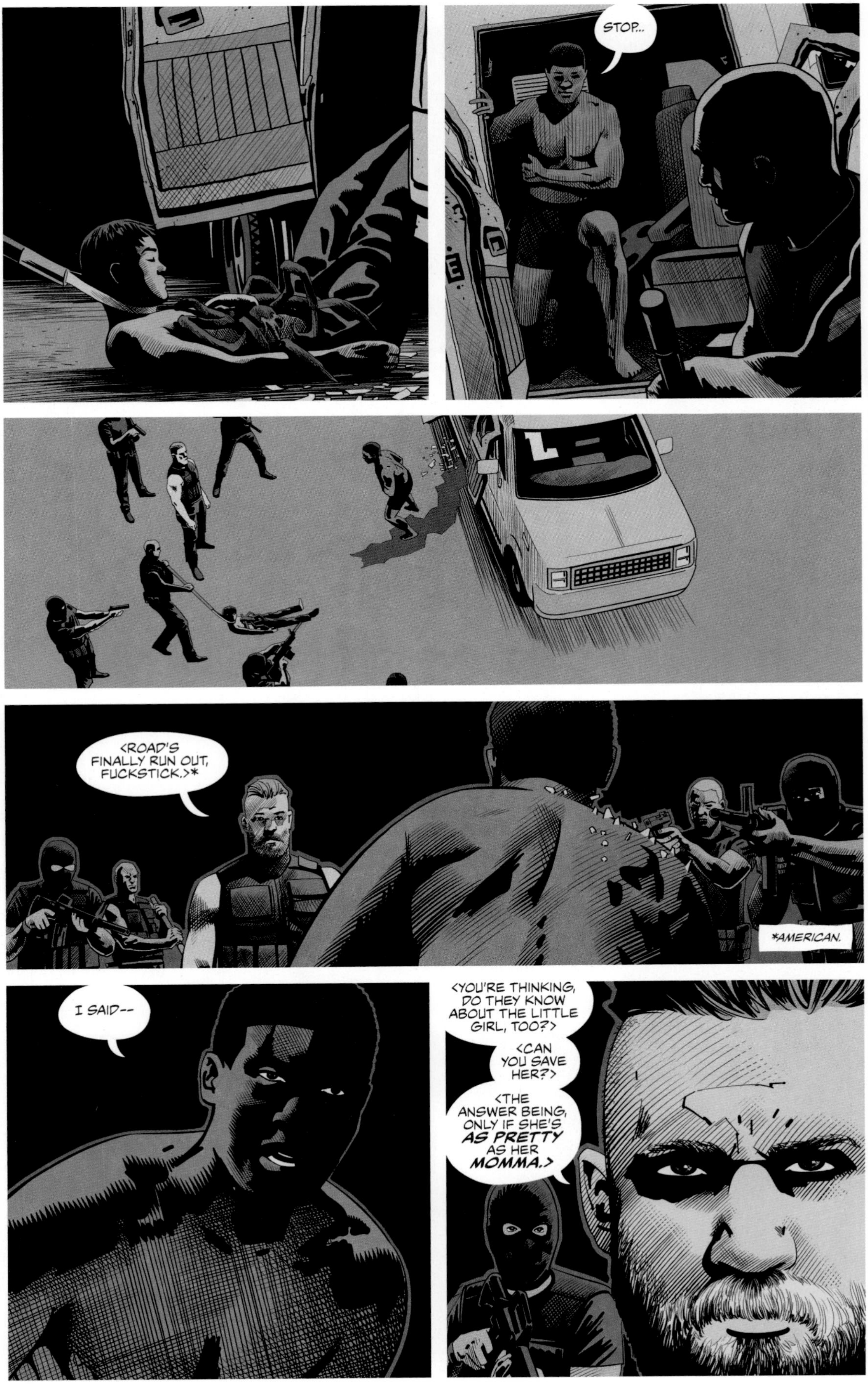
STOP...
<ROAD'S FINALLY RUN OUT, FUCKSTICK.>*
*AMERICAN.
I SAID--
<YOU'RE THINKING, DO THEY KNOW ABOUT THE LITTLE GIRL, TOO?>
<CAN YOU SAVE HER?>
<THE ANSWER BEING, ONLY IF SHE'S AS PRETTY AS HER MOMMA.>

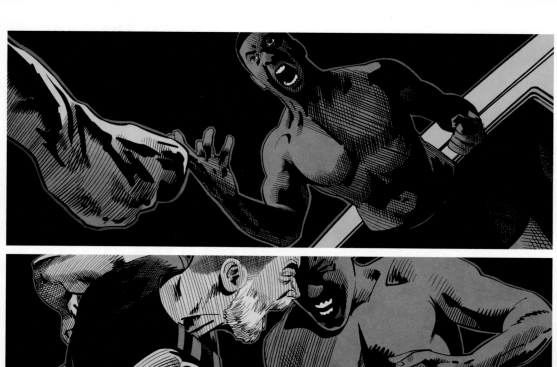

THMP!

UFF!

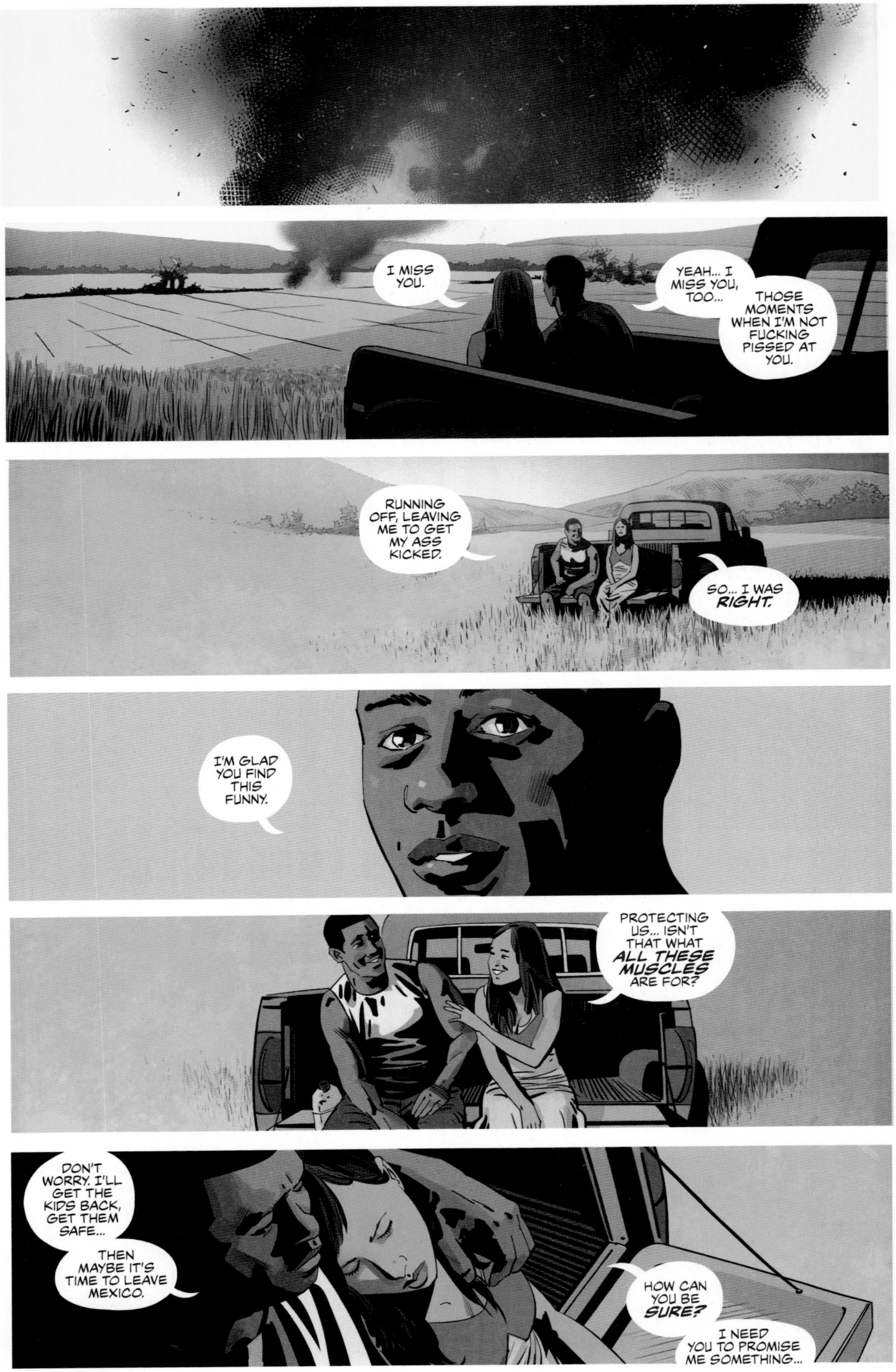
I MISS YOU.
YEAH... I MISS YOU, TOO...
THOSE MOMENTS WHEN I'M NOT FUCKING PISSED AT YOU.
RUNNING OFF, LEAVING ME TO GET MY ASS KICKED.
SO... I WAS RIGHT.
I'M GLAD YOU FIND THIS FUNNY.
PROTECTING US... ISN'T THAT WHAT ALL THESE MUSCLES ARE FOR?
DON'T WORRY. I'LL GET THE KIDS BACK, GET THEM SAFE...
THEN MAYBE IT'S TIME TO LEAVE MEXICO.
HOW CAN YOU BE SURE?
I NEED YOU TO PROMISE ME SOMETHING...

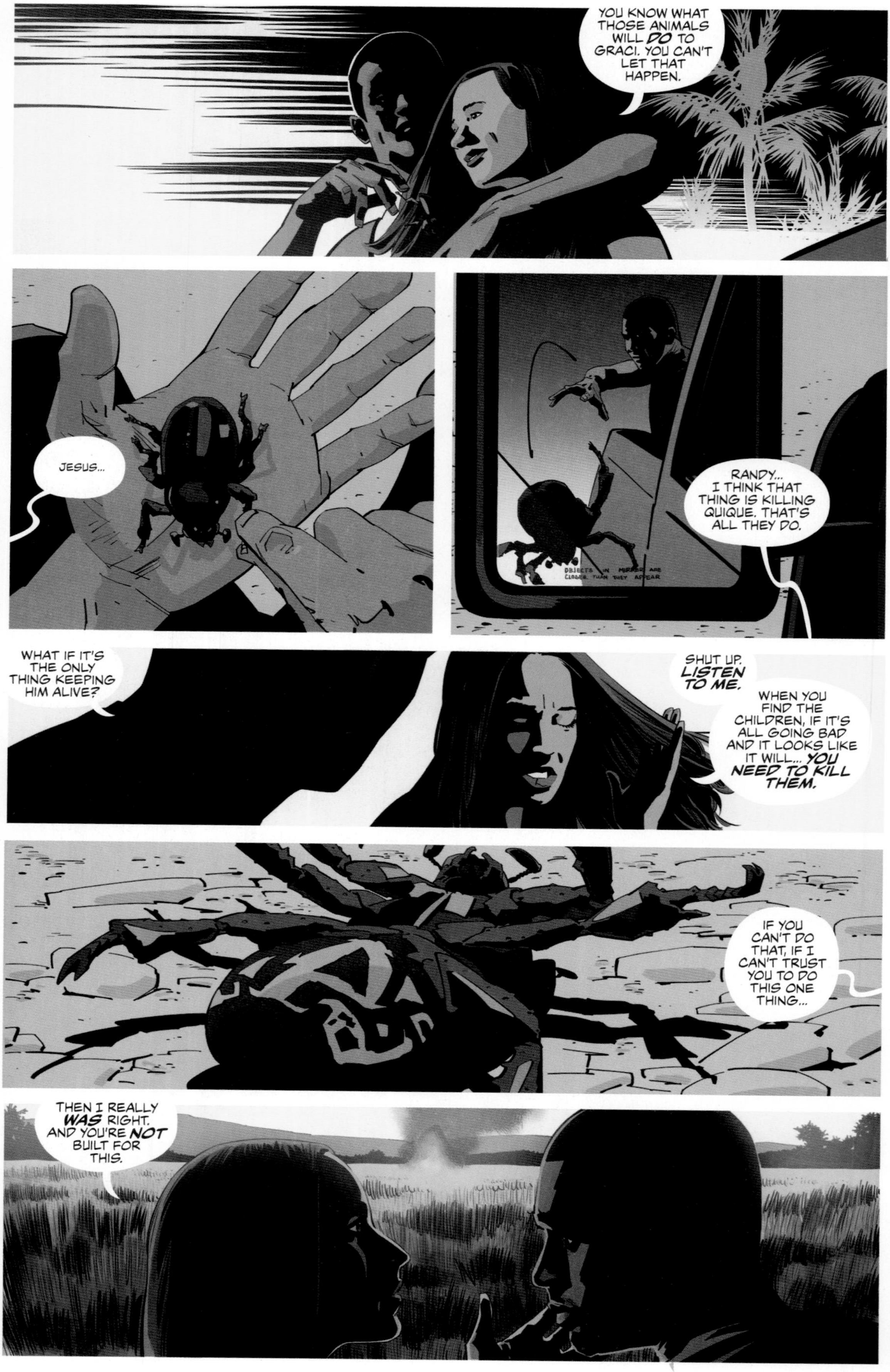
YOU KNOW WHAT THOSE ANIMALS WILL DO TO GRACI. YOU CAN'T LET THAT HAPPEN.
JESUS...
RANDY... I THINK THAT THING IS KILLING QUIQUE. THAT'S ALL THEY DO.
OBJECTS IN MIRROR ARE CLOSER THAN THEY APPEAR
WHAT IF IT'S THE ONLY THING KEEPING HIM ALIVE?
SHUT UP. LISTEN TO ME.
WHEN YOU FIND THE CHILDREN, IF IT'S ALL GOING BAD AND IT LOOKS LIKE IT WILL... YOU NEED TO KILL THEM.
IF YOU CAN'T DO THAT, IF I CAN'T TRUST YOU TO DO THIS ONE THING...
THEN I REALLY WAS RIGHT. AND YOU'RE NOT BUILT FOR THIS.

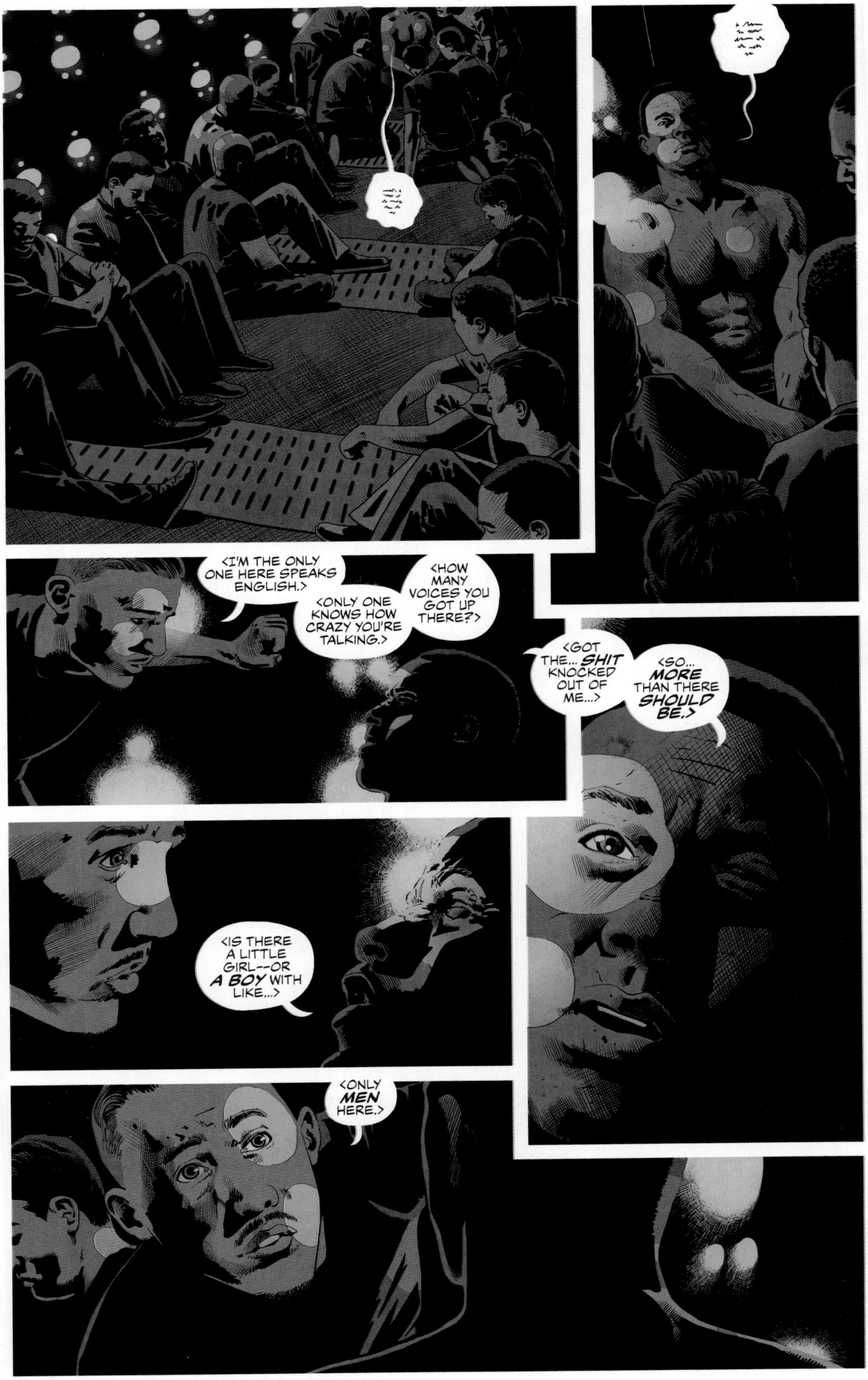

<I'M THE ONLY ONE HERE SPEAKS ENGLISH.>
<ONLY ONE KNOWS HOW CRAZY YOU'RE TALKING.>
<HOW MANY VOICES YOU GOT UP THERE?>
<GOT THE... **SHIT** KNOCKED OUT OF ME...>
<SO... **MORE** THAN THERE **SHOULD BE.**>
<IS THERE A LITTLE GIRL--OR ***A BOY*** WITH LIKE...>
<ONLY ***MEN*** HERE.>

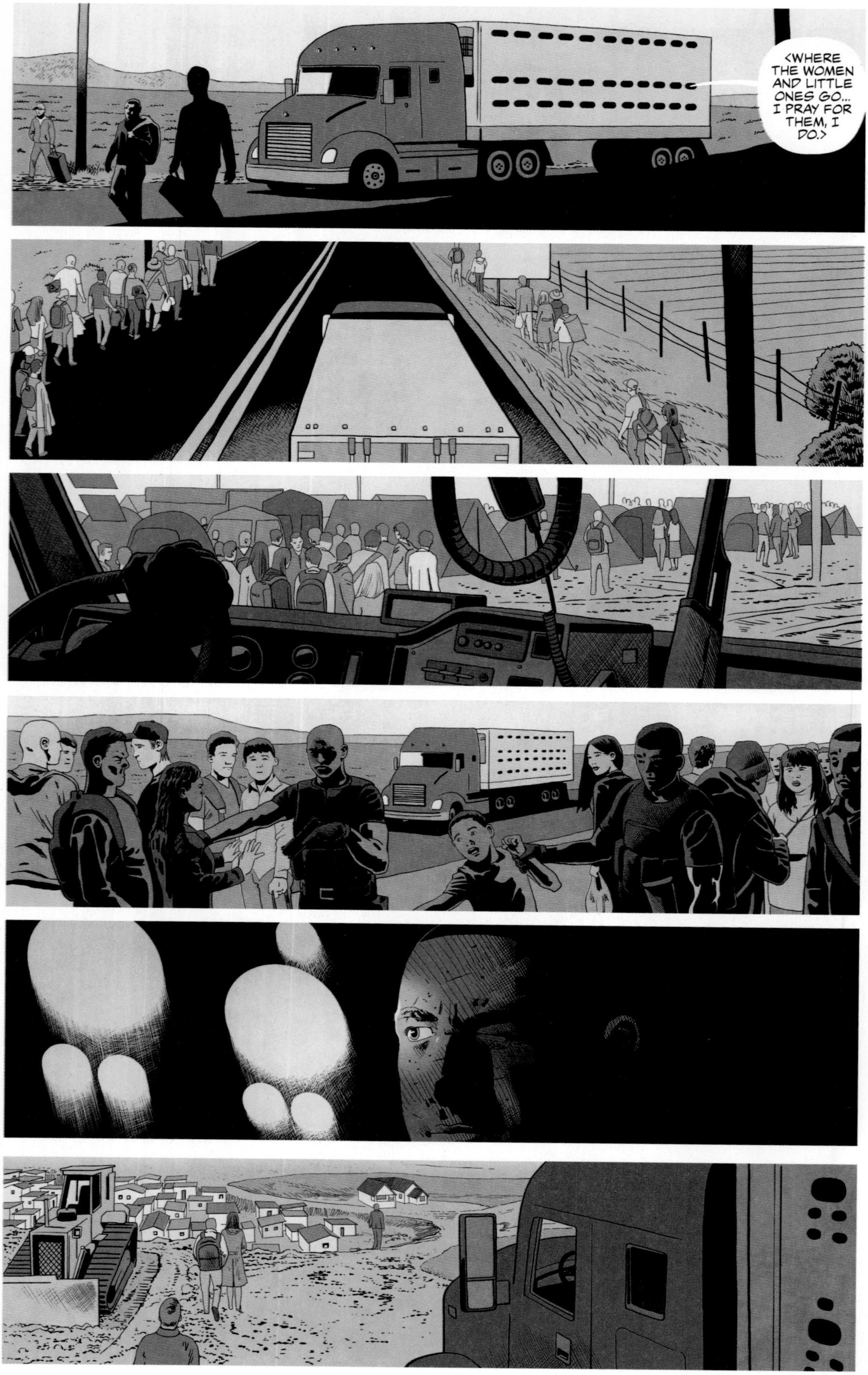
<WHERE THE WOMEN AND LITTLE ONES GO... I PRAY FOR THEM, I DO.>

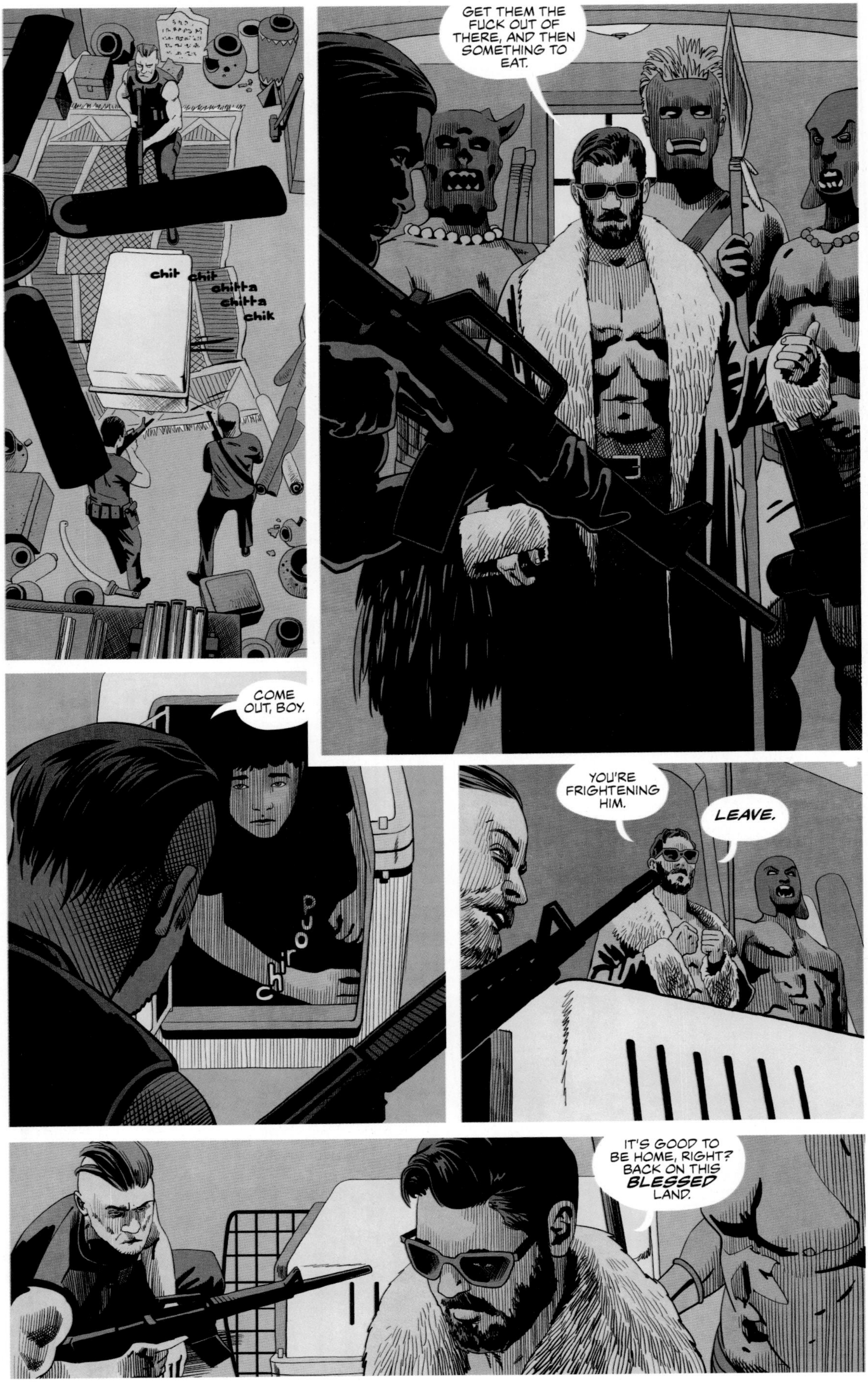
chit chit chitta chitta chik
GET THEM THE FUCK OUT OF THERE, AND THEN SOMETHING TO EAT.
COME OUT, BOY.
chiroup
YOU'RE FRIGHTENING HIM.
LEAVE.
IT'S GOOD TO BE HOME, RIGHT? BACK ON THIS BLESSED LAND.

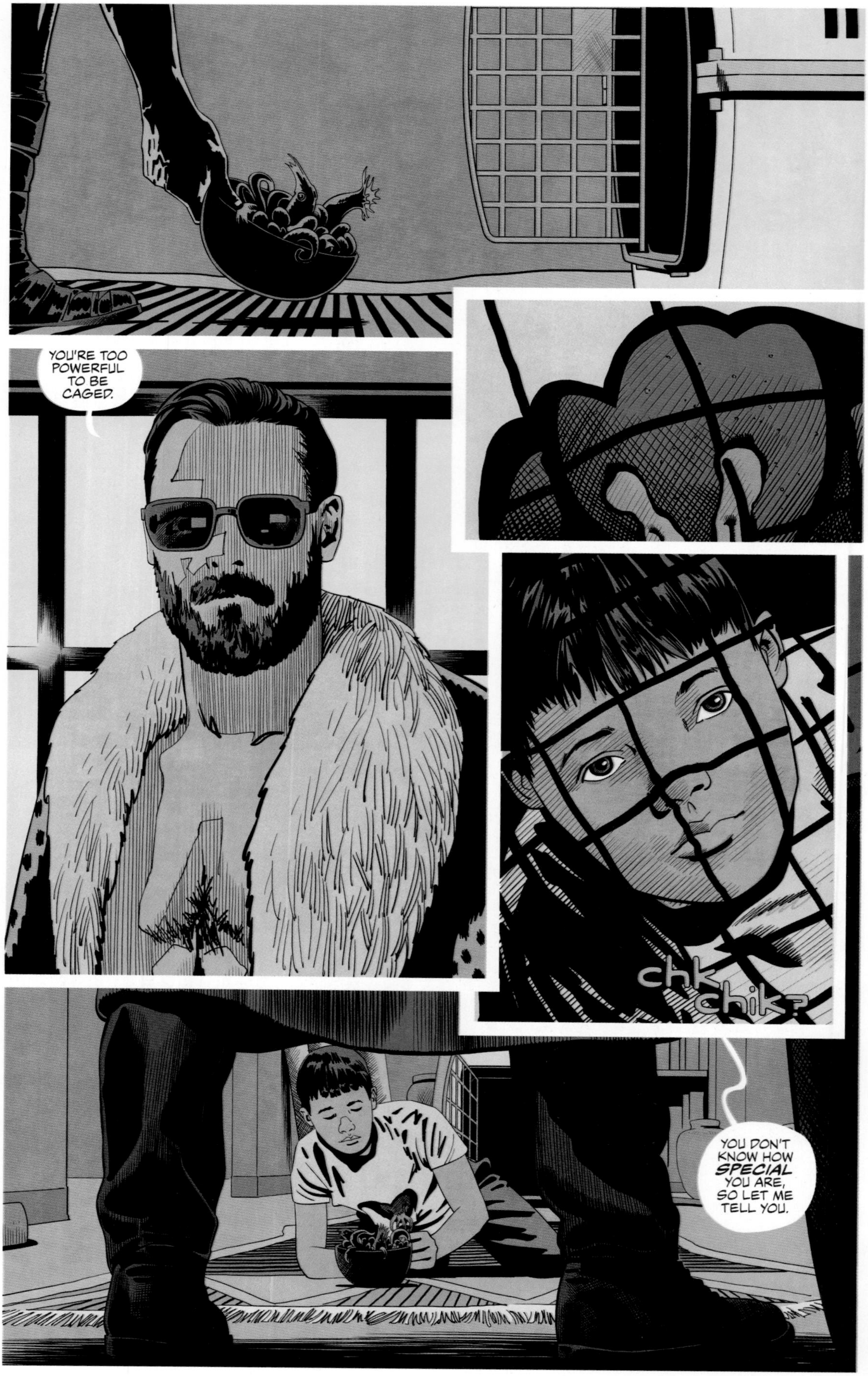
YOU'RE TOO POWERFUL TO BE CAGED.
chk chik?
YOU DON'T KNOW HOW SPECIAL YOU ARE, SO LET ME TELL YOU.

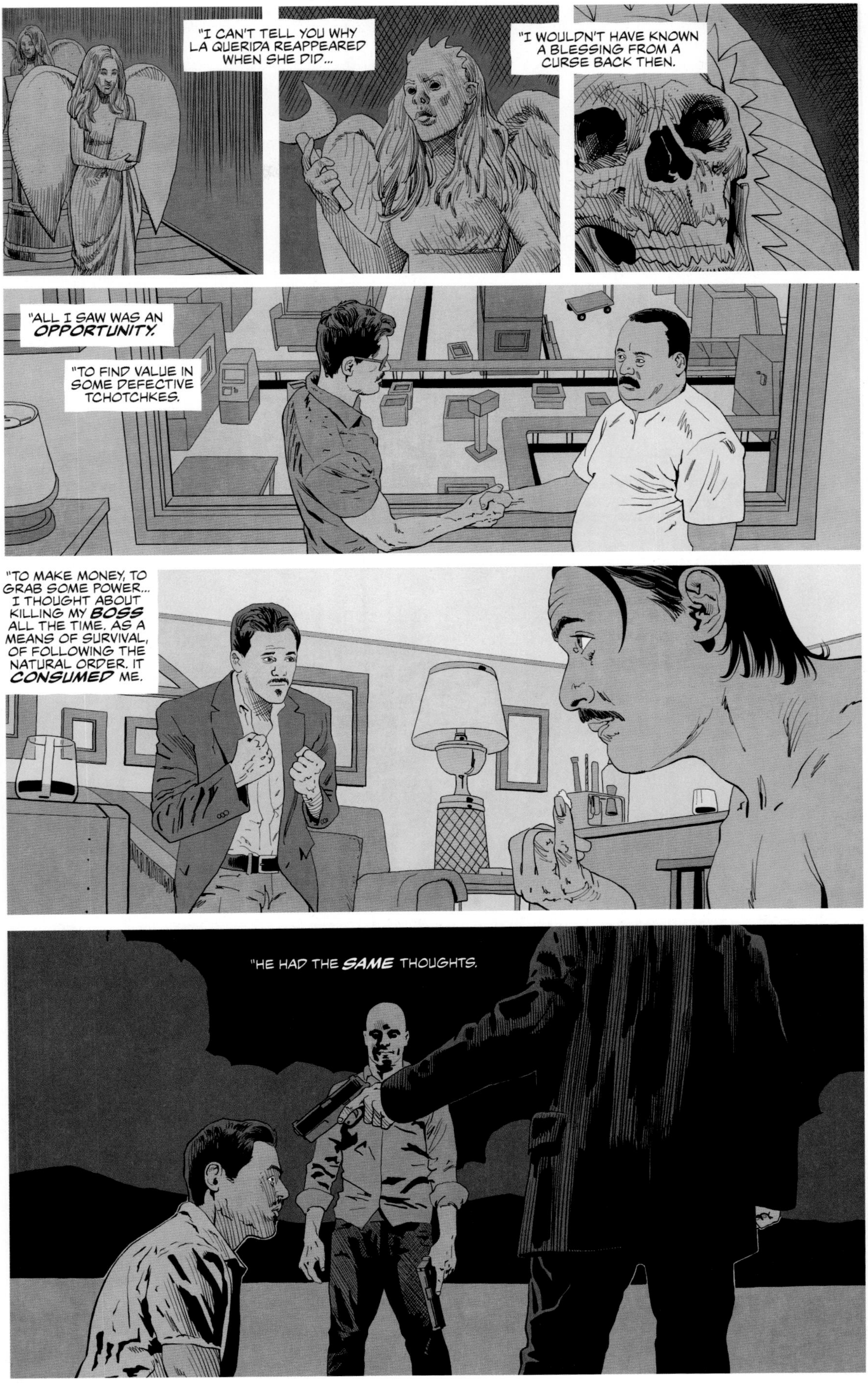
"I CAN'T TELL YOU WHY LA QUERIDA REAPPEARED WHEN SHE DID...
"I WOULDN'T HAVE KNOWN A BLESSING FROM A CURSE BACK THEN.
"ALL I SAW WAS AN OPPORTUNITY.
"TO FIND VALUE IN SOME DEFECTIVE TCHOTCHKES.
"TO MAKE MONEY, TO GRAB SOME POWER... I THOUGHT ABOUT KILLING MY BOSS ALL THE TIME. AS A MEANS OF SURVIVAL, OF FOLLOWING THE NATURAL ORDER. IT CONSUMED ME.
"HE HAD THE SAME THOUGHTS.

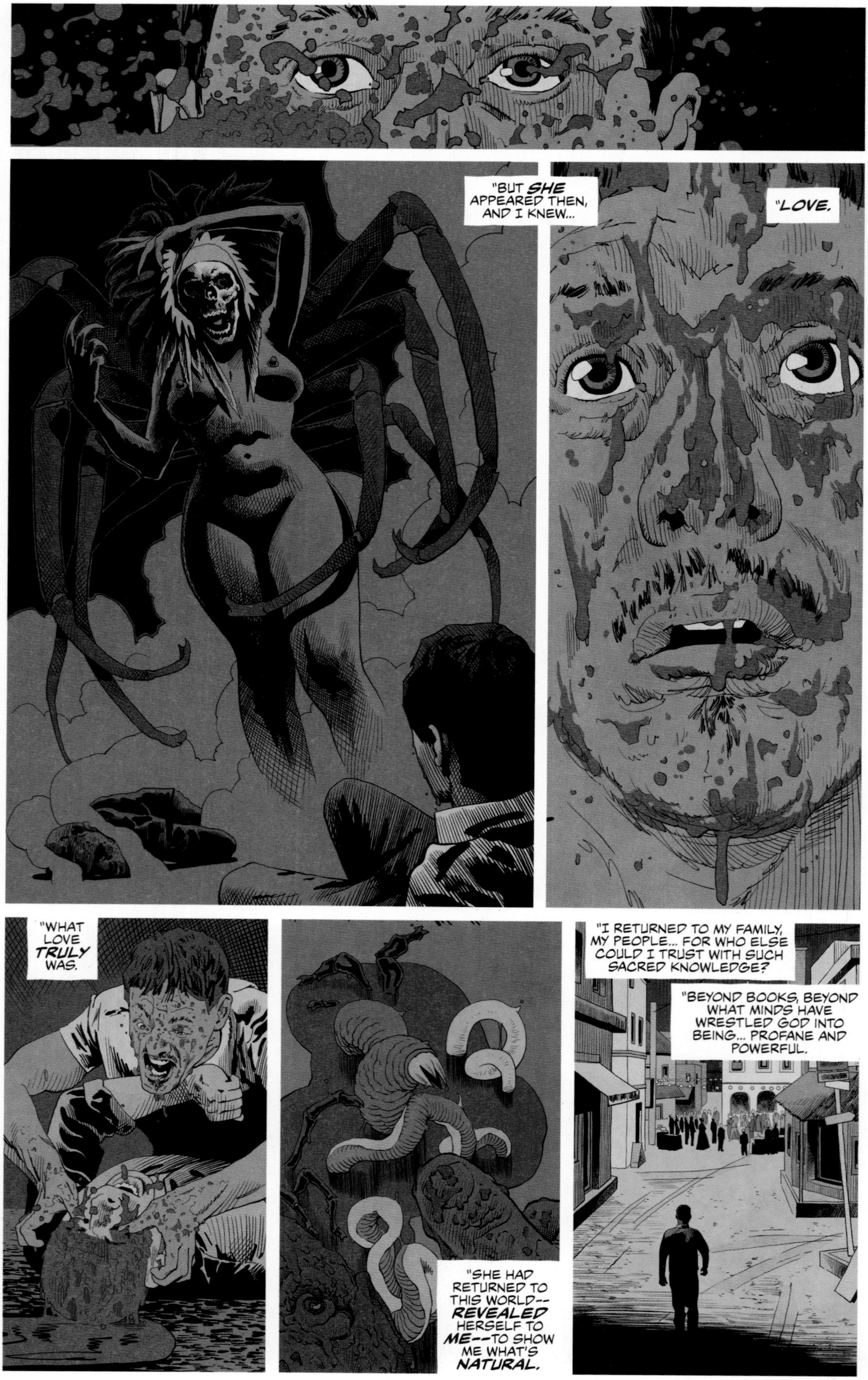
"BUT SHE APPEARED THEN, AND I KNEW...
"LOVE.
"WHAT LOVE TRULY WAS.
"SHE HAD RETURNED TO THIS WORLD--REVEALED HERSELF TO ME--TO SHOW ME WHAT'S NATURAL.
"I RETURNED TO MY FAMILY, MY PEOPLE... FOR WHO ELSE COULD I TRUST WITH SUCH SACRED KNOWLEDGE?
"BEYOND BOOKS, BEYOND WHAT MINDS HAVE WRESTLED GOD INTO BEING... PROFANE AND POWERFUL.

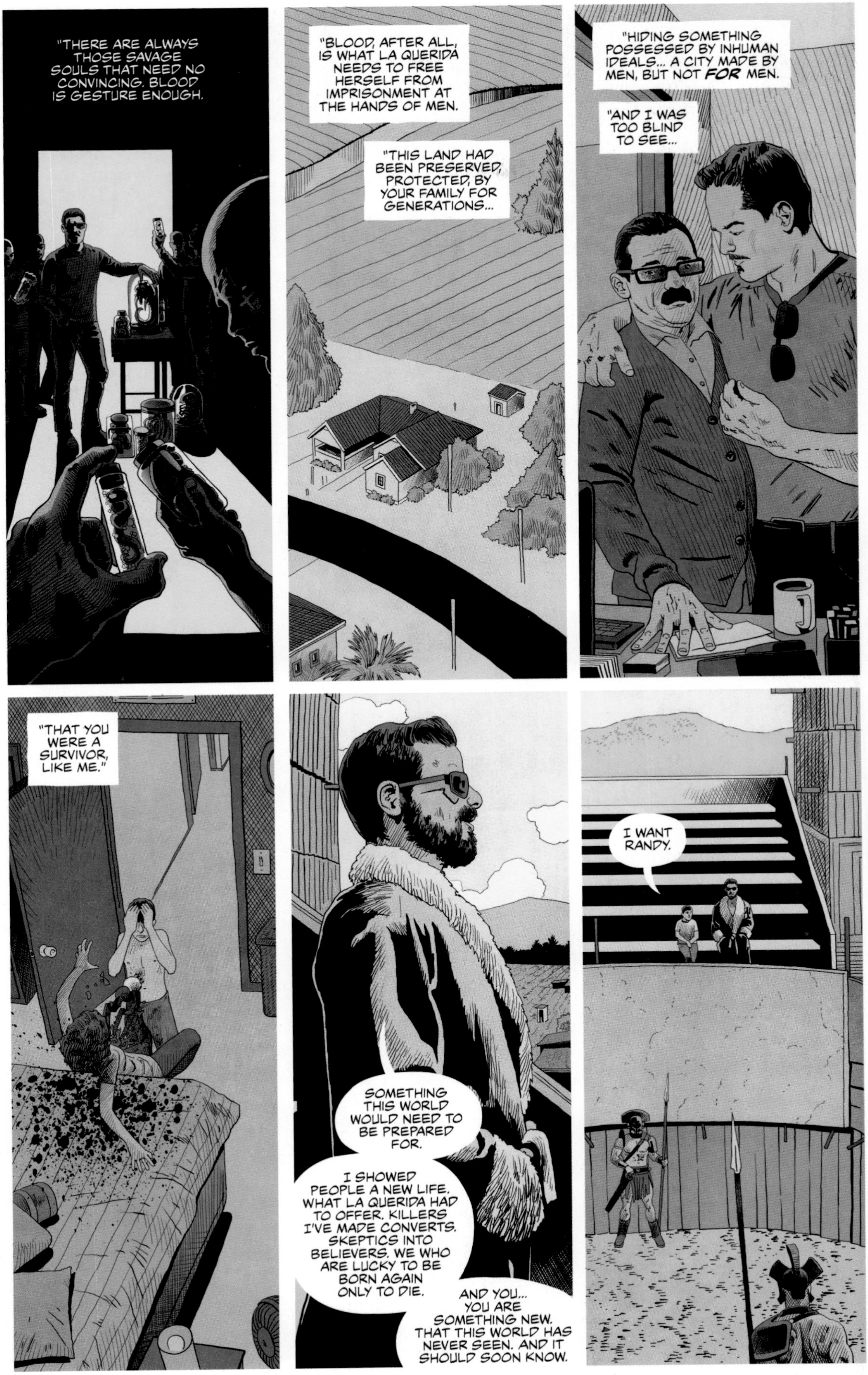
"THERE ARE ALWAYS THOSE SAVAGE SOULS THAT NEED NO CONVINCING. BLOOD IS GESTURE ENOUGH.
"BLOOD, AFTER ALL, IS WHAT LA QUERIDA NEEDS TO FREE HERSELF FROM IMPRISONMENT AT THE HANDS OF MEN.
"THIS LAND HAD BEEN PRESERVED, PROTECTED, BY YOUR FAMILY FOR GENERATIONS...
"HIDING SOMETHING POSSESSED BY INHUMAN IDEALS... A CITY MADE BY MEN, BUT NOT FOR MEN.
"AND I WAS TOO BLIND TO SEE...
"THAT YOU WERE A SURVIVOR, LIKE ME."
SOMETHING THIS WORLD WOULD NEED TO BE PREPARED FOR.
I SHOWED PEOPLE A NEW LIFE. WHAT LA QUERIDA HAD TO OFFER. KILLERS I'VE MADE CONVERTS. SKEPTICS INTO BELIEVERS. WE WHO ARE LUCKY TO BE BORN AGAIN ONLY TO DIE.
AND YOU... YOU ARE SOMETHING NEW. THAT THIS WORLD HAS NEVER SEEN. AND IT SHOULD SOON KNOW.
I WANT RANDY.

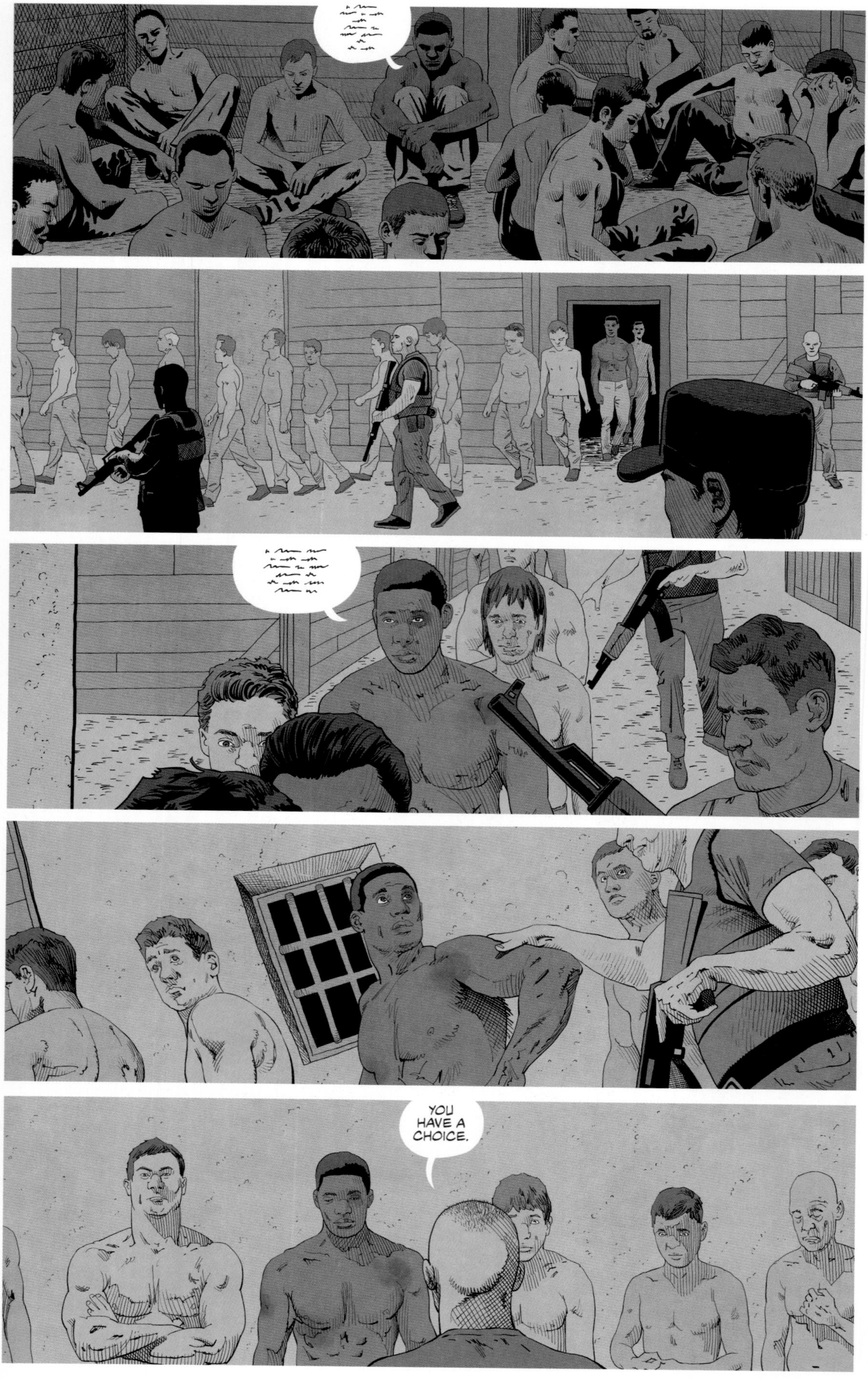
YOU HAVE A CHOICE.

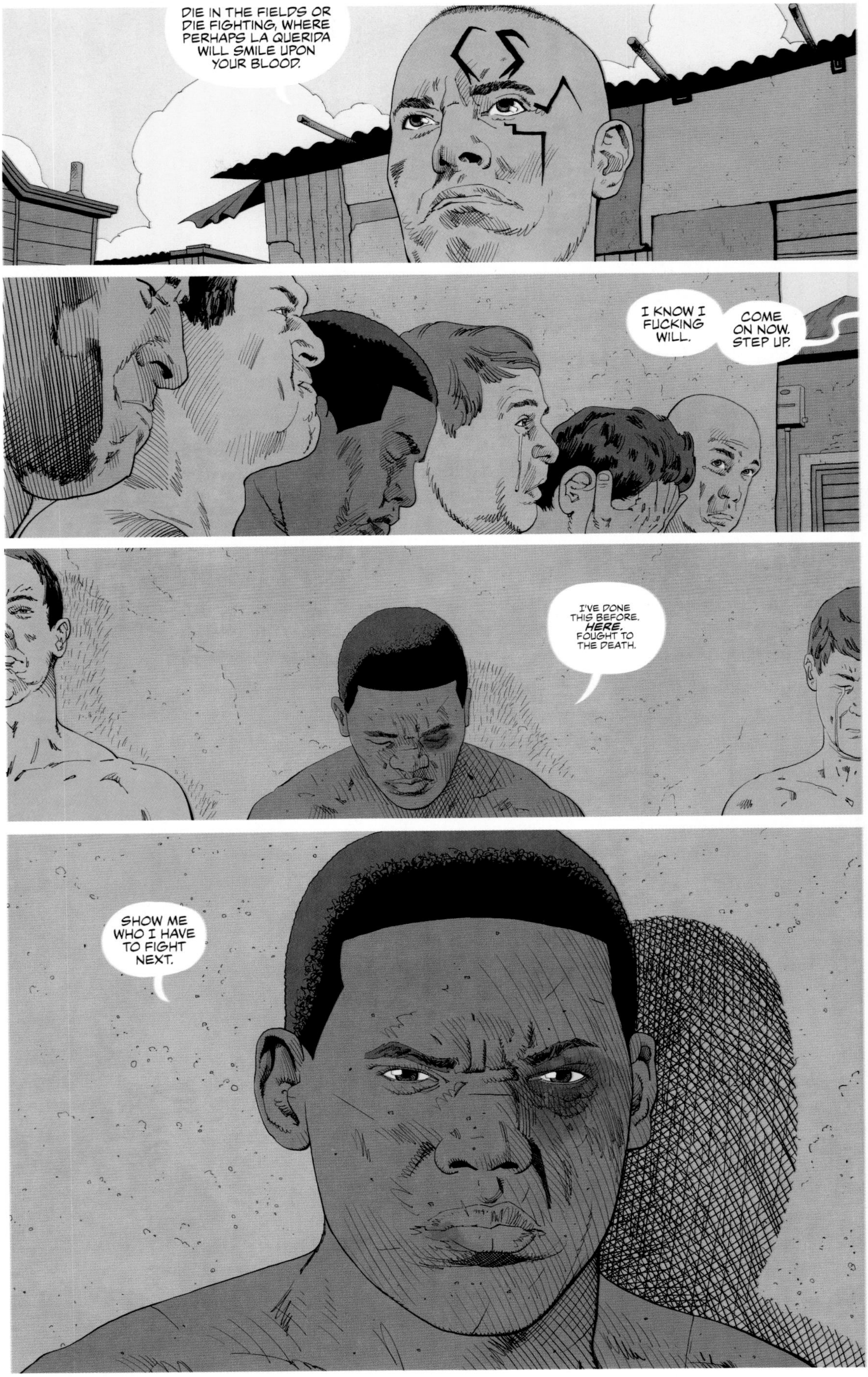
DIE IN THE FIELDS OR DIE FIGHTING, WHERE PERHAPS LA QUERIDA WILL SMILE UPON YOUR BLOOD.
COME ON NOW. STEP UP.
I KNOW I FUCKING WILL.
I'VE DONE THIS BEFORE. *HERE.* FOUGHT TO THE DEATH.
SHOW ME WHO I HAVE TO FIGHT NEXT.

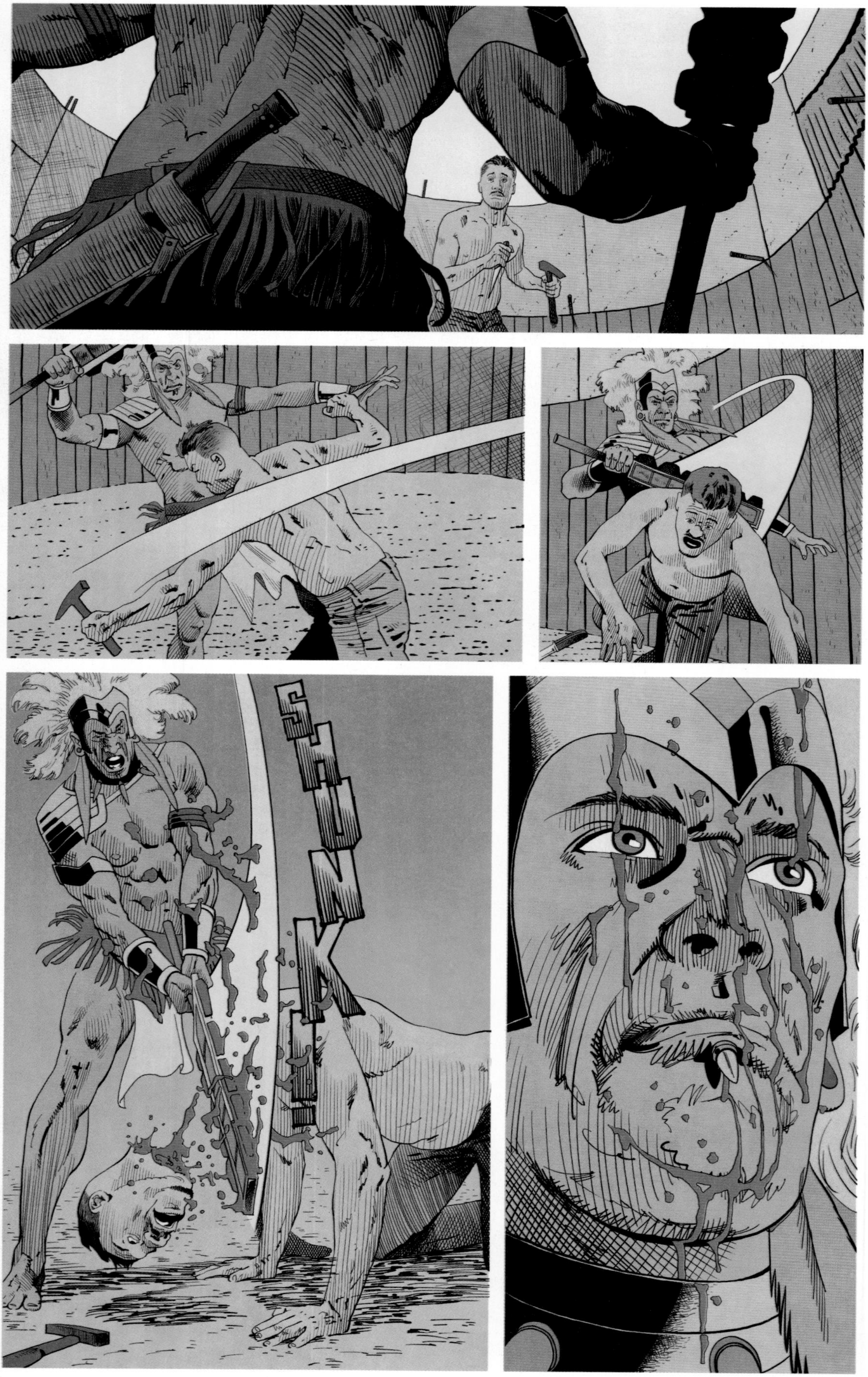
SHUNK

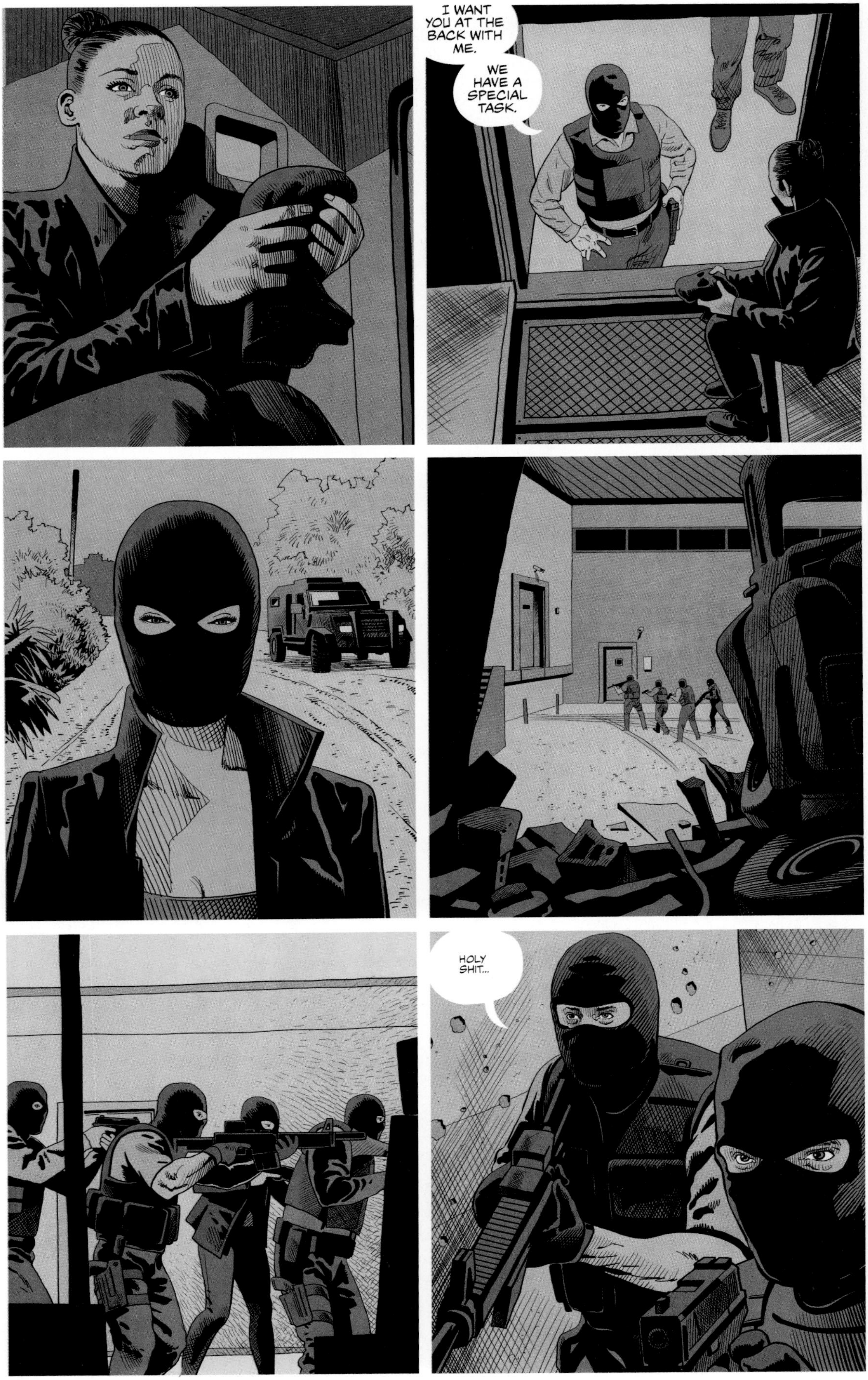
I WANT YOU AT THE BACK WITH ME.
WE HAVE A SPECIAL TASK.
HOLY SHIT...

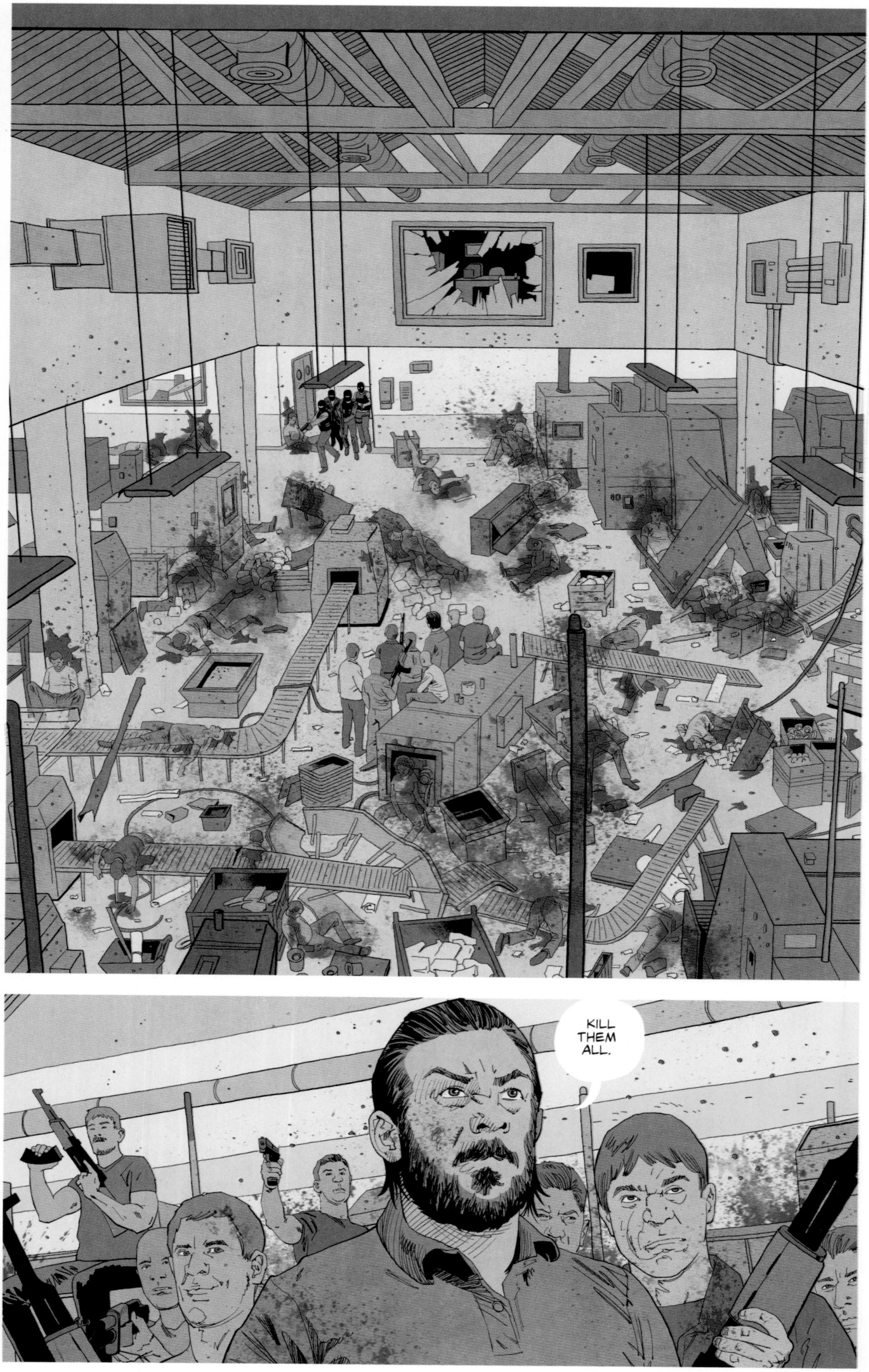
KILL THEM ALL.

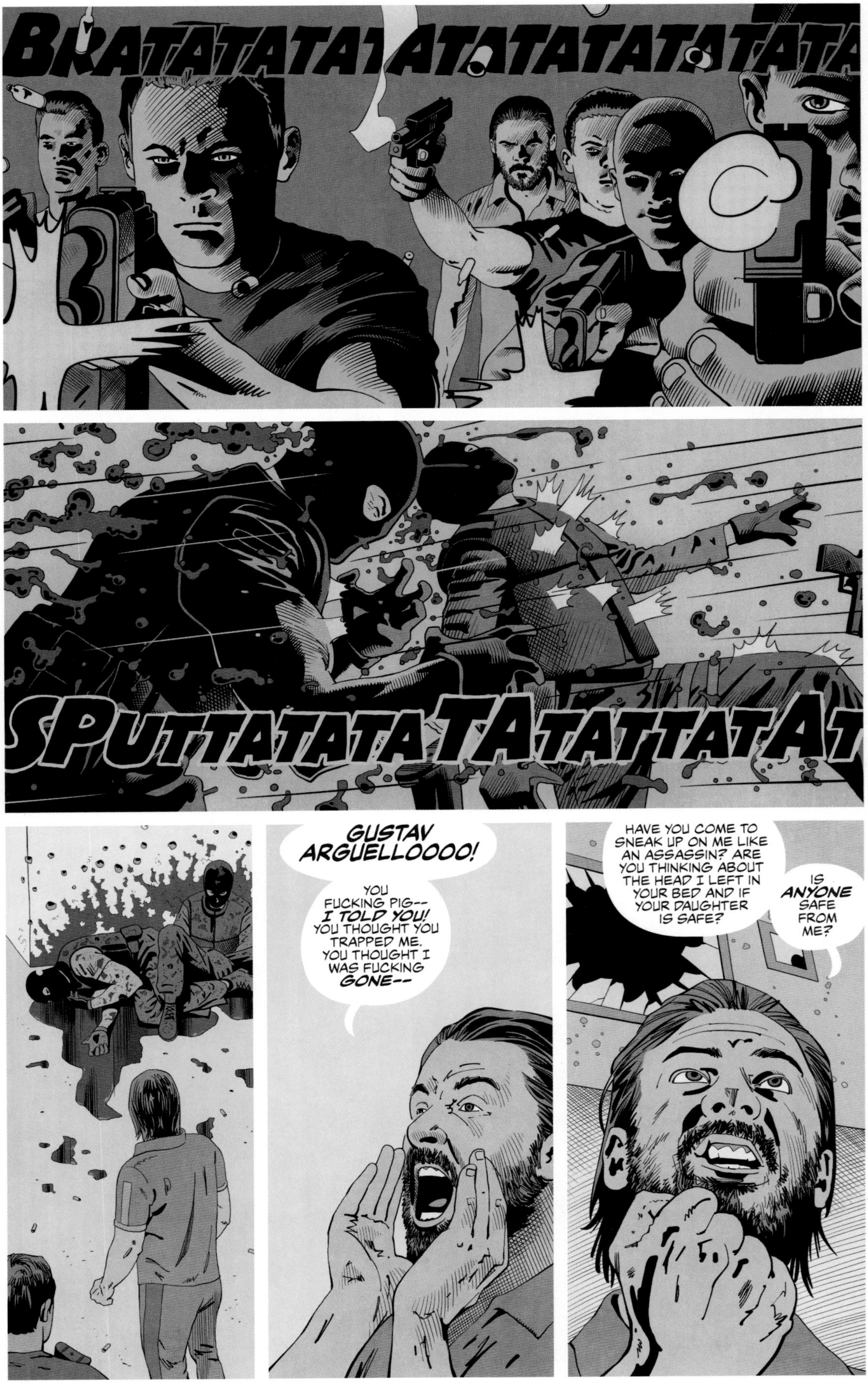
BRATATATATATATATATATATATA
SPUTTATATATATATTATATAT
GUSTAV ARGUELLOOOO!
YOU FUCKING PIG-- I TOLD YOU! YOU THOUGHT YOU TRAPPED ME. YOU THOUGHT I WAS FUCKING GONE--
HAVE YOU COME TO SNEAK UP ON ME LIKE AN ASSASSIN? ARE YOU THINKING ABOUT THE HEAD I LEFT IN YOUR BED AND IF YOUR DAUGHTER IS SAFE?
IS ANYONE SAFE FROM ME?

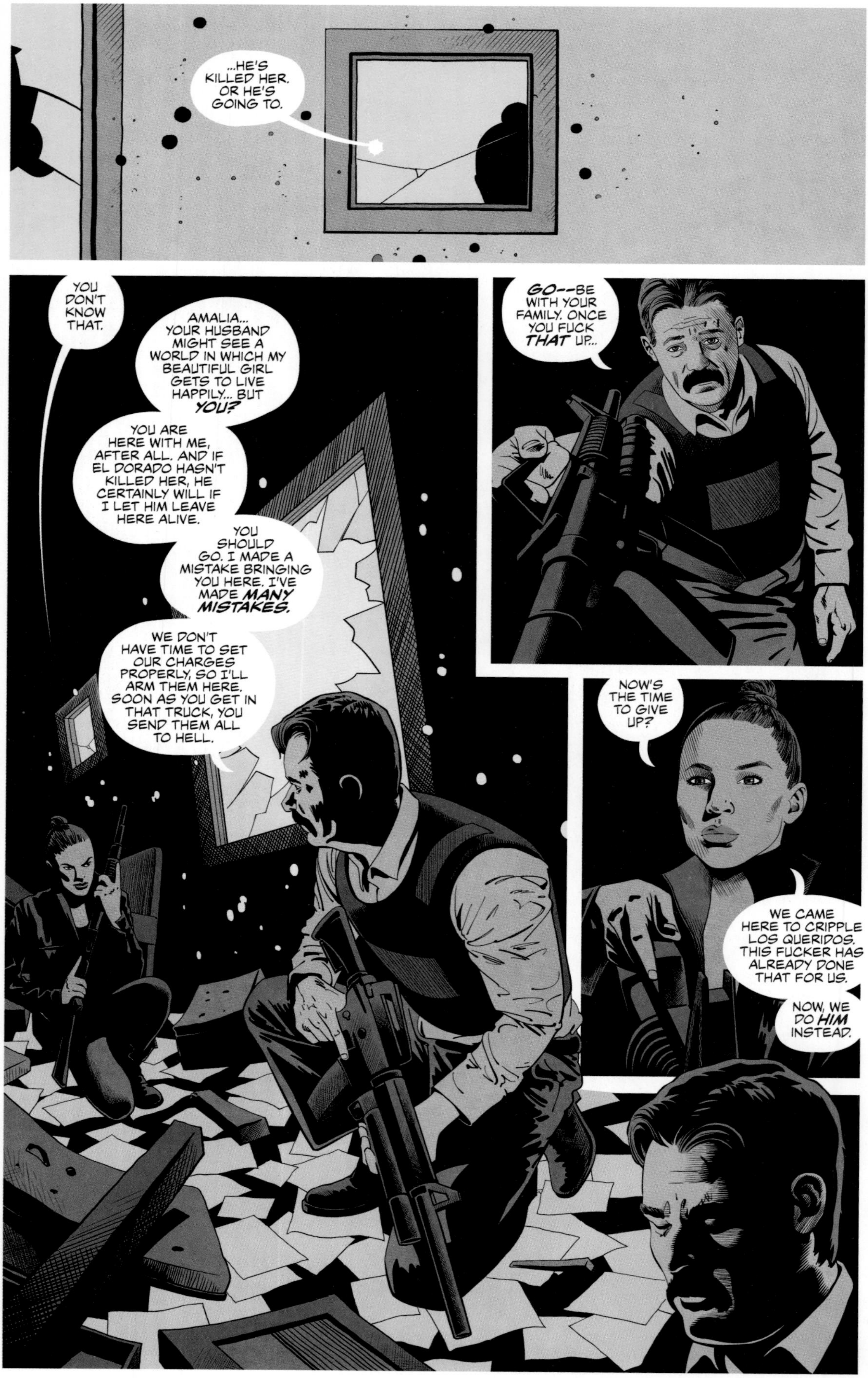
...HE'S KILLED HER. OR HE'S GOING TO.
YOU DON'T KNOW THAT.
AMALIA... YOUR HUSBAND MIGHT SEE A WORLD IN WHICH MY BEAUTIFUL GIRL GETS TO LIVE HAPPILY... BUT *YOU?*
YOU ARE HERE WITH ME, AFTER ALL. AND IF EL DORADO HASN'T KILLED HER, HE CERTAINLY WILL IF I LET HIM LEAVE HERE ALIVE.
YOU SHOULD GO. I MADE A MISTAKE BRINGING YOU HERE. I'VE MADE *MANY MISTAKES.*
WE DON'T HAVE TIME TO SET OUR CHARGES PROPERLY, SO I'LL ARM THEM HERE. SOON AS YOU GET IN THAT TRUCK, YOU SEND THEM ALL TO HELL.
GO--BE WITH YOUR FAMILY. ONCE YOU FUCK *THAT* UP...
NOW'S THE TIME TO GIVE UP?
WE CAME HERE TO CRIPPLE LOS QUERIDOS. THIS FUCKER HAS ALREADY DONE THAT FOR US.
NOW, WE DO *HIM* INSTEAD.

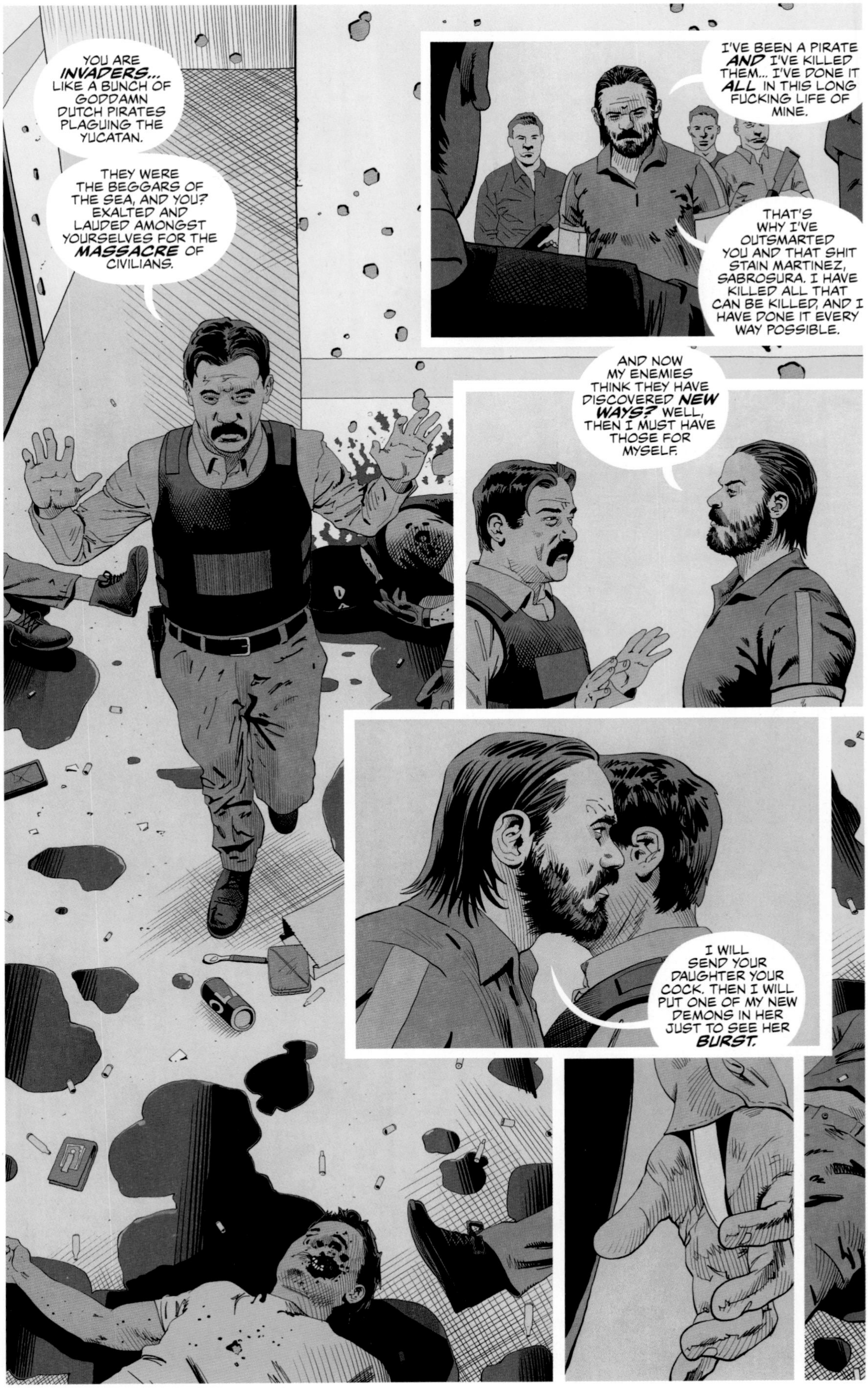
YOU ARE INVADERS... LIKE A BUNCH OF GODDAMN DUTCH PIRATES PLAGUING THE YUCATAN.
THEY WERE THE BEGGARS OF THE SEA, AND YOU? EXALTED AND LAUDED AMONGST YOURSELVES FOR THE MASSACRE OF CIVILIANS.
I'VE BEEN A PIRATE AND I'VE KILLED THEM... I'VE DONE IT ALL IN THIS LONG FUCKING LIFE OF MINE.
THAT'S WHY I'VE OUTSMARTED YOU AND THAT SHIT STAIN MARTINEZ, SABROSURA. I HAVE KILLED ALL THAT CAN BE KILLED, AND I HAVE DONE IT EVERY WAY POSSIBLE.
AND NOW MY ENEMIES THINK THEY HAVE DISCOVERED NEW WAYS? WELL, THEN I MUST HAVE THOSE FOR MYSELF.
I WILL SEND YOUR DAUGHTER YOUR COCK. THEN I WILL PUT ONE OF MY NEW DEMONS IN HER JUST TO SEE HER BURST.

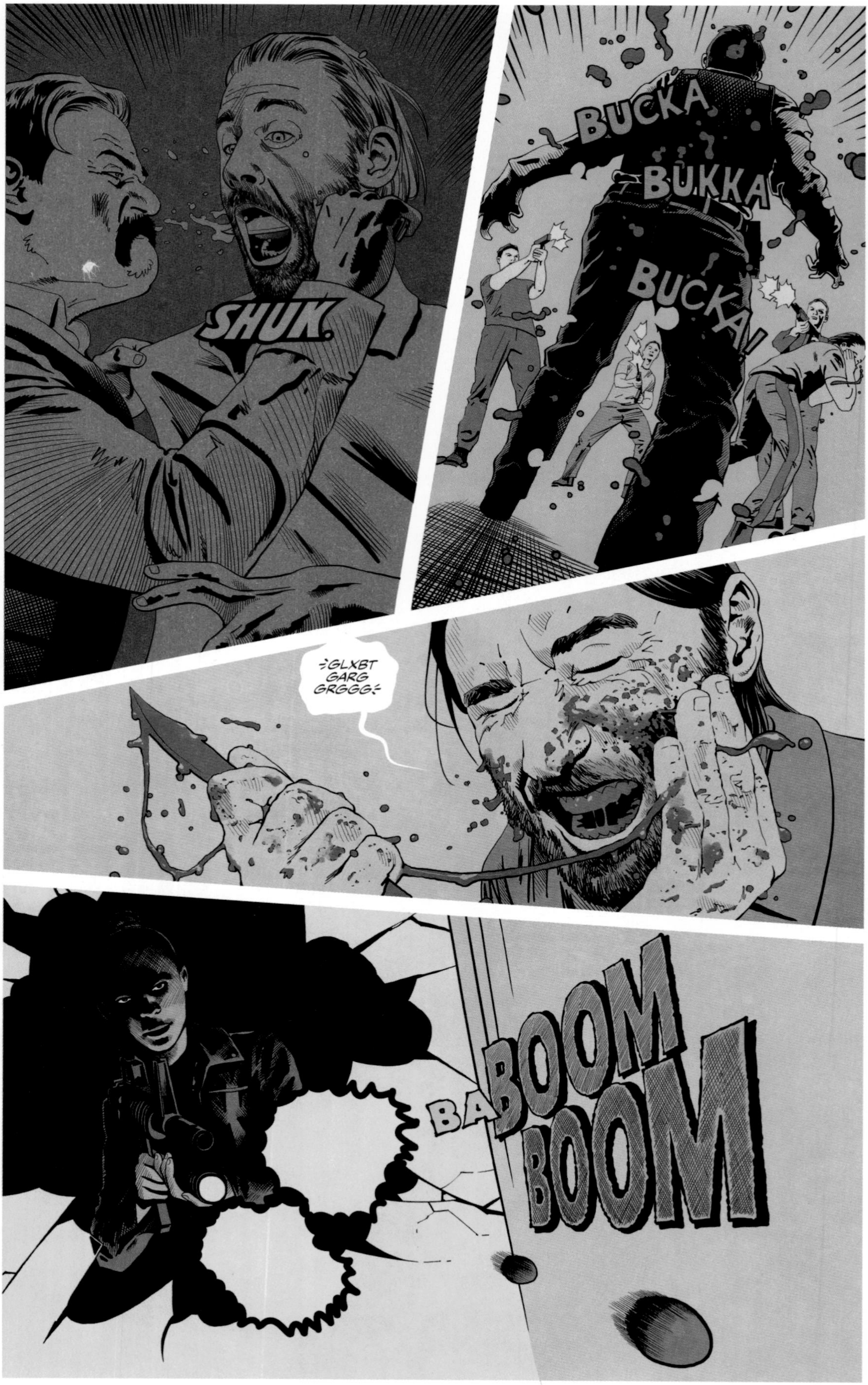
SHUK
BUCKA
BUKKA
BUCKA!
GLXBT GARG GRGGG
BA BOOM BOOM

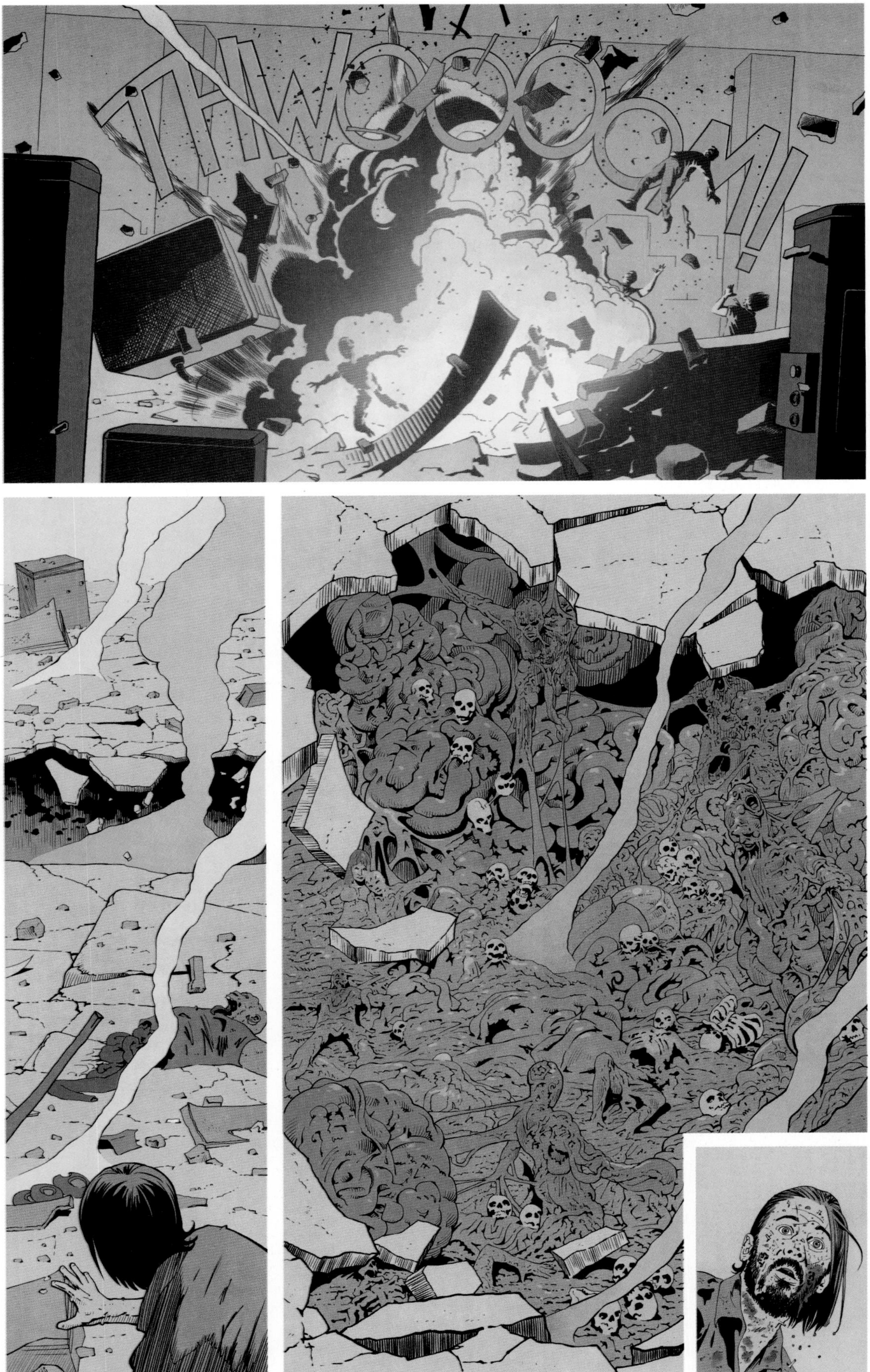
THWOOOOM!!

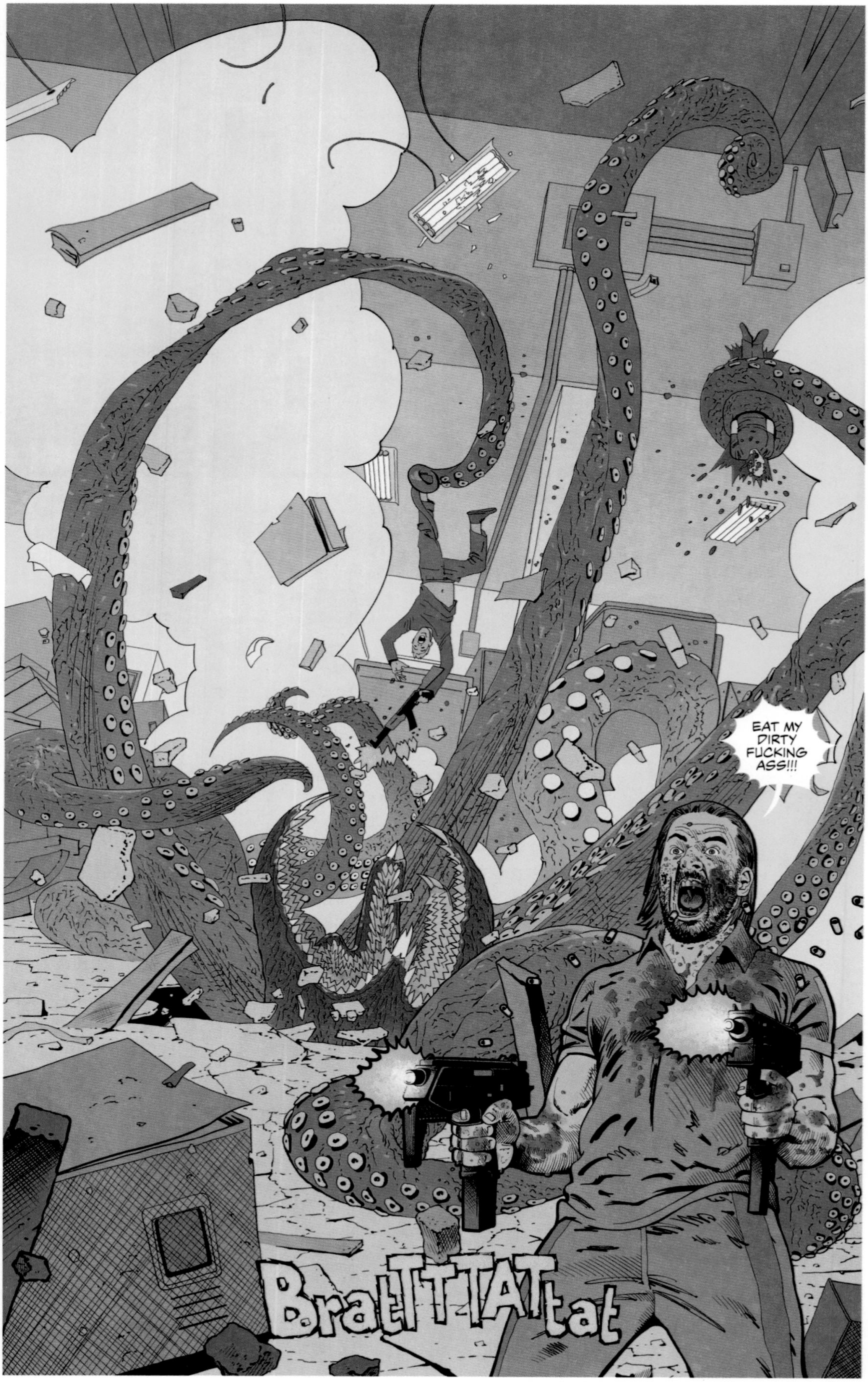
EAT MY DIRTY FUCKING ASS!!!
BratTTTATtat

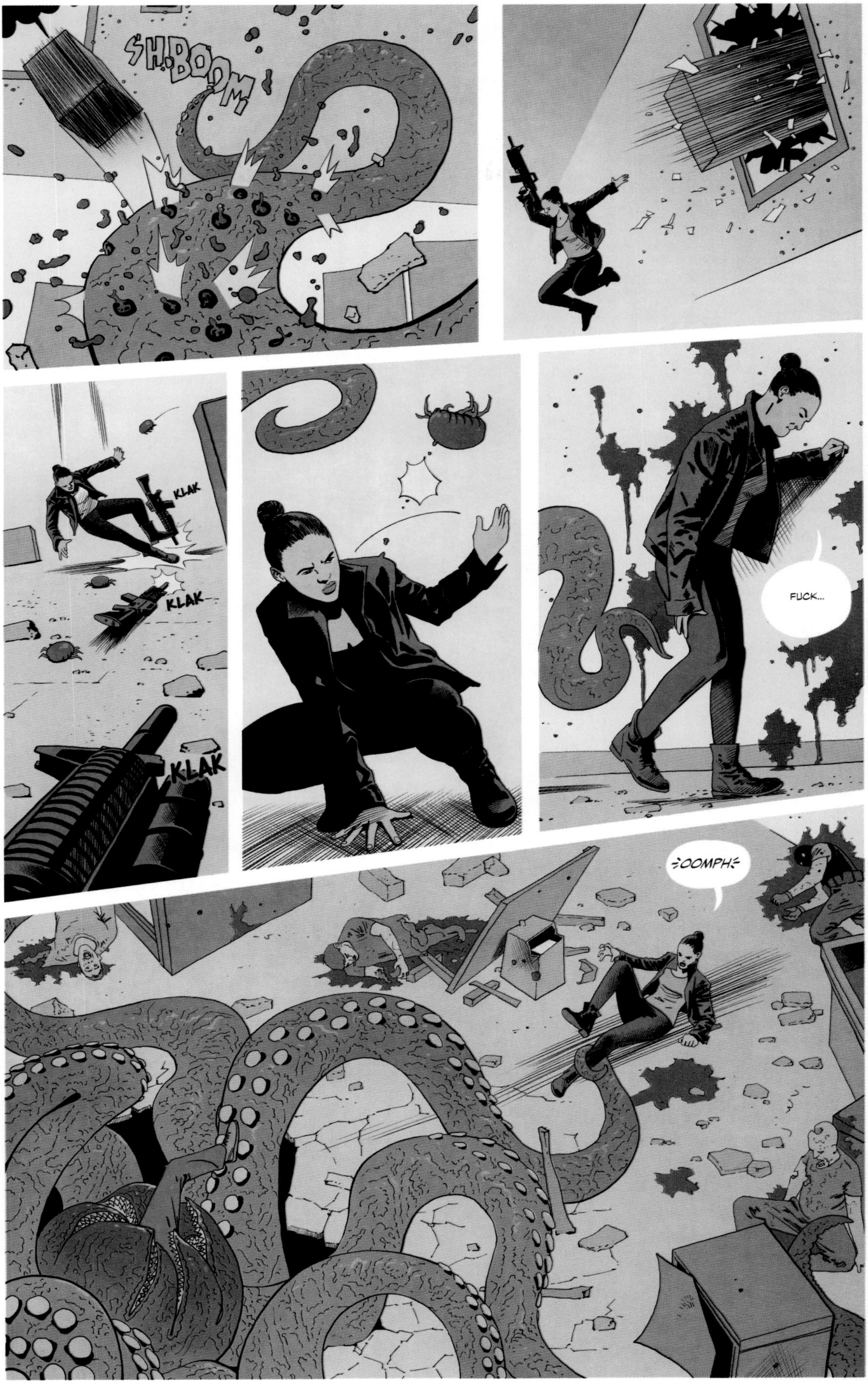
SHBOOM
KLAK
KLAK
KLAK
FUCK...
OOMPH

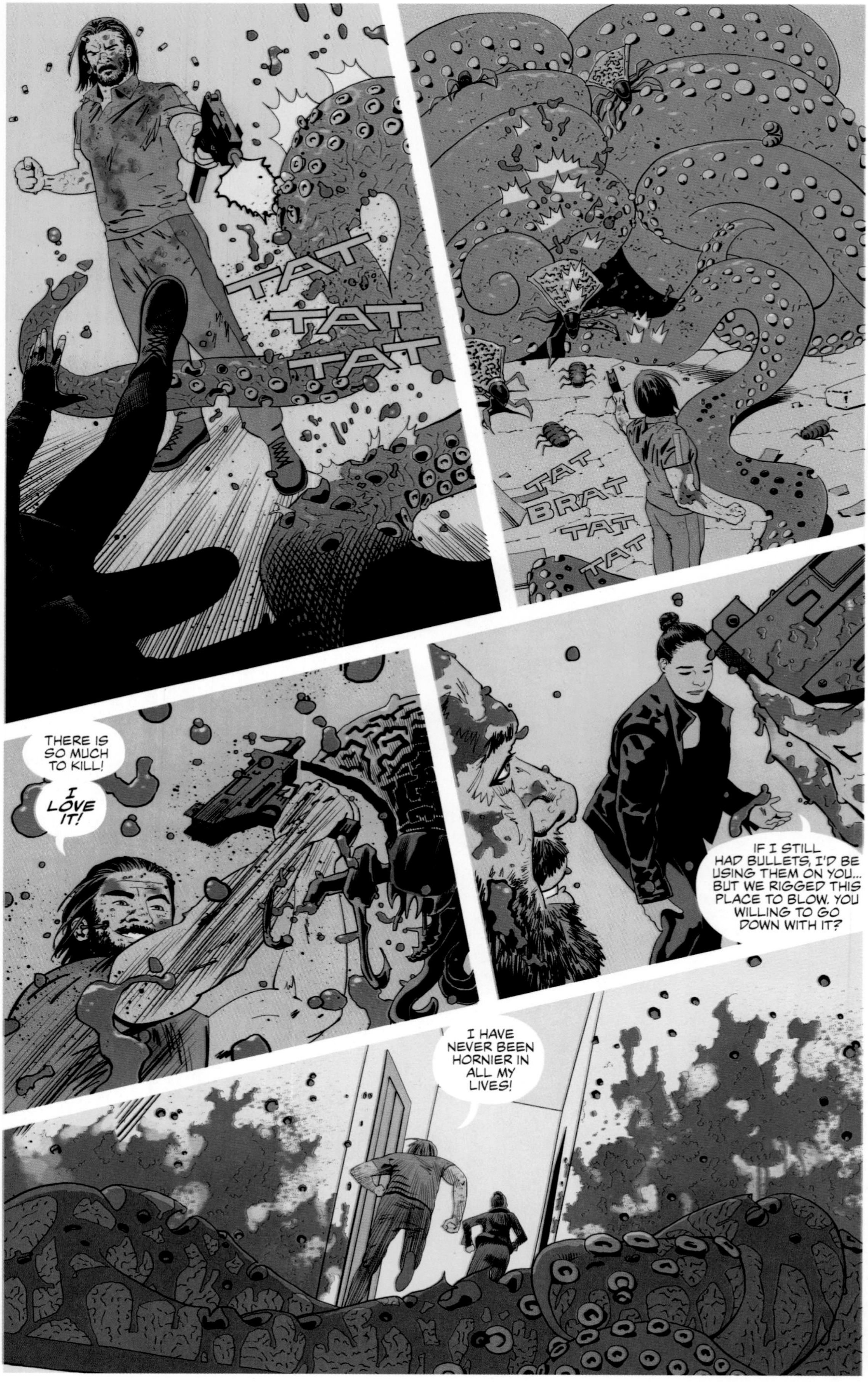
TAT
TAT
TAT
TAT
BRAT
TAT
TAT
THERE IS SO MUCH TO KILL!
I LOVE IT!
IF I STILL HAD BULLETS, I'D BE USING THEM ON YOU... BUT WE RIGGED THIS PLACE TO BLOW. YOU WILLING TO GO DOWN WITH IT?
I HAVE NEVER BEEN HORNIER IN ALL MY LIVES!

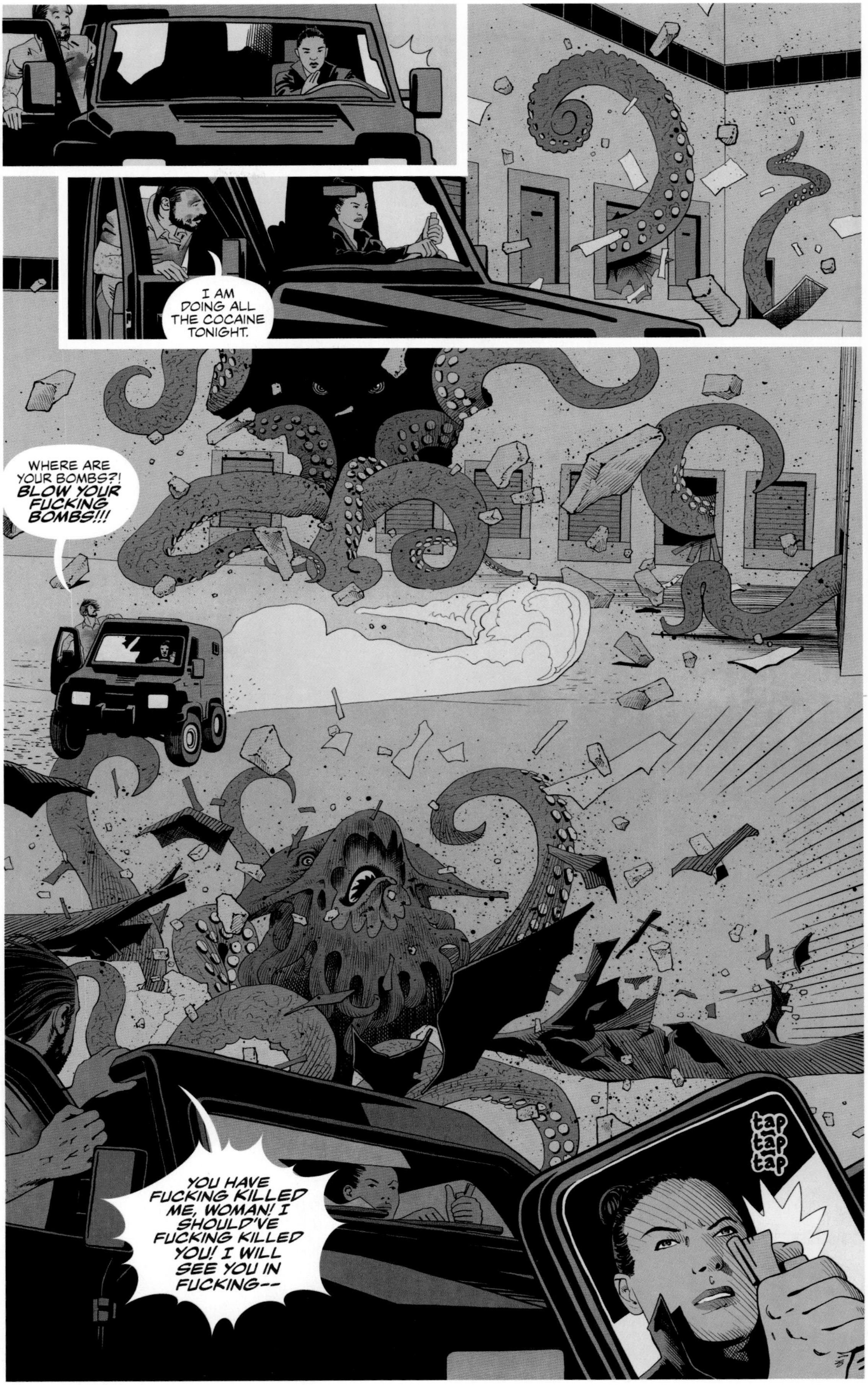
I AM DOING ALL THE COCAINE TONIGHT.
WHERE ARE YOUR BOMBS?! BLOW YOUR FUCKING BOMBS!!!
YOU HAVE FUCKING KILLED ME, WOMAN! I SHOULD'VE FUCKING KILLED YOU! I WILL SEE YOU IN FUCKING--
tap tap tap

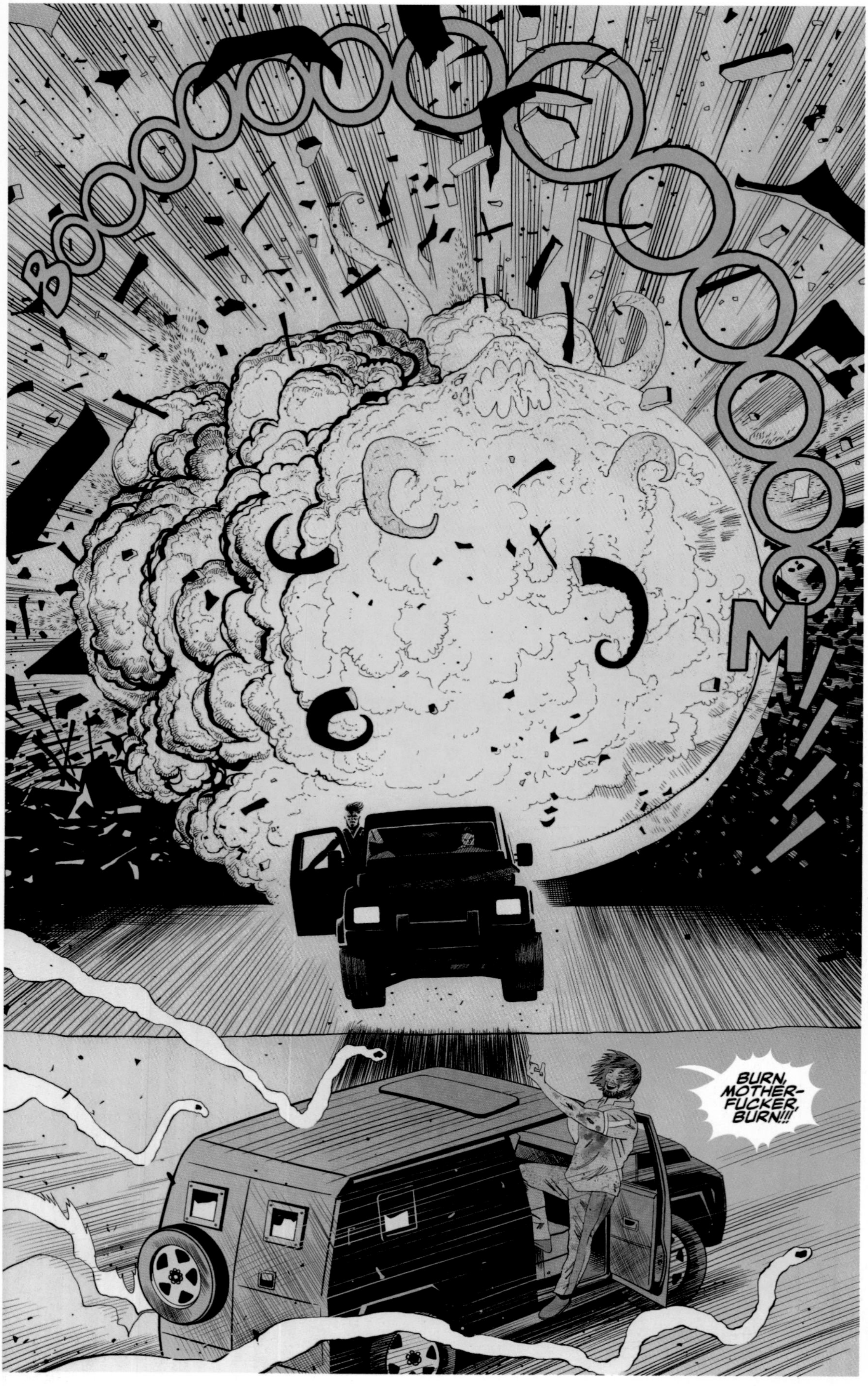
BOOOOOOOOOOOOOOOOOM!!!
BURN, MOTHER-FUCKER, BURN!!!

KRAK!

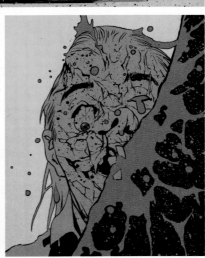

Skrrttt

≿HHURRRK≾

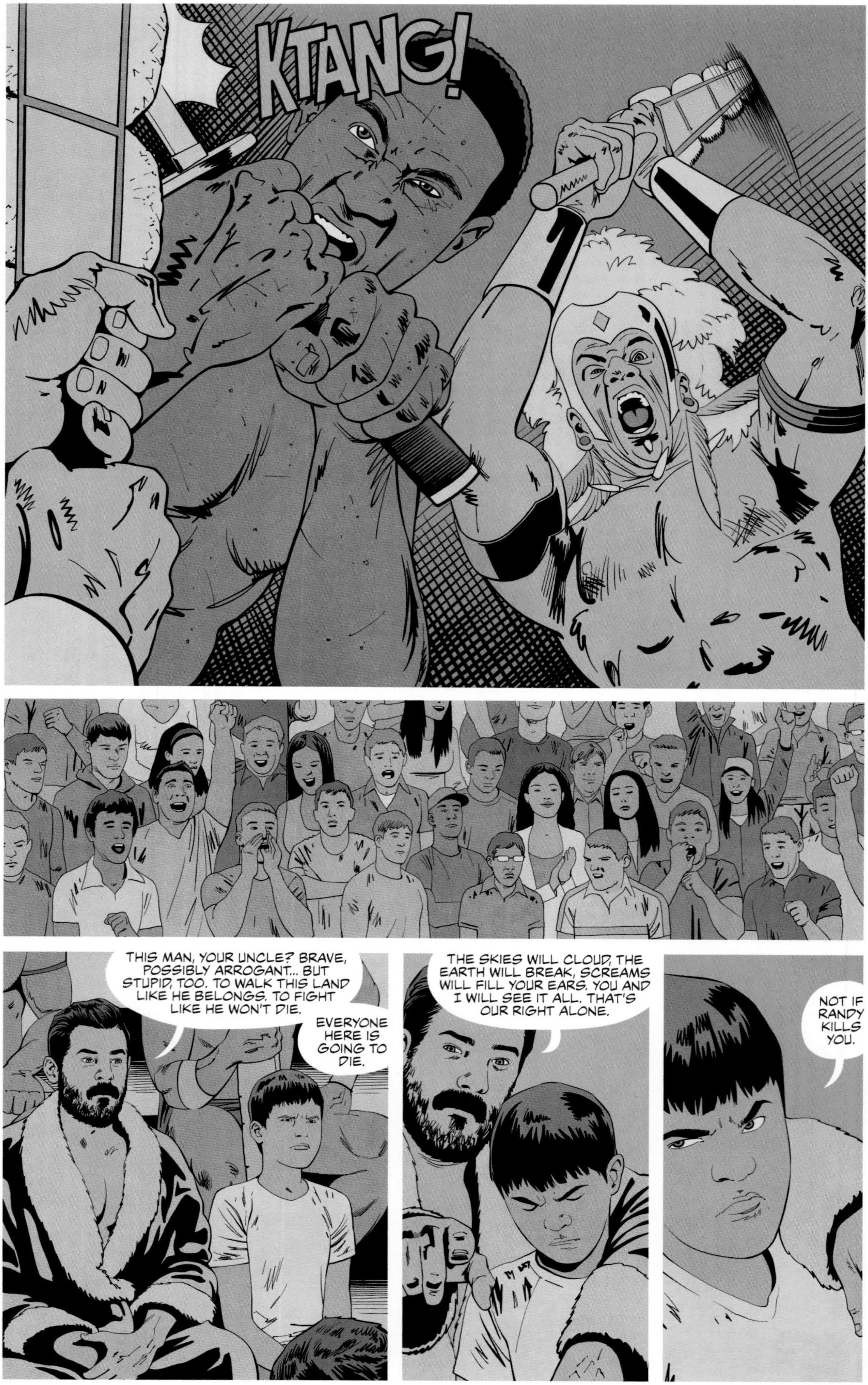
KTANG!
THIS MAN, YOUR UNCLE? BRAVE, POSSIBLY ARROGANT... BUT STUPID, TOO. TO WALK THIS LAND LIKE HE BELONGS. TO FIGHT LIKE HE WON'T DIE.
EVERYONE HERE IS GOING TO DIE.
THE SKIES WILL CLOUD, THE EARTH WILL BREAK, SCREAMS WILL FILL YOUR EARS. YOU AND I WILL SEE IT ALL. THAT'S OUR RIGHT ALONE.
NOT IF RANDY KILLS YOU.

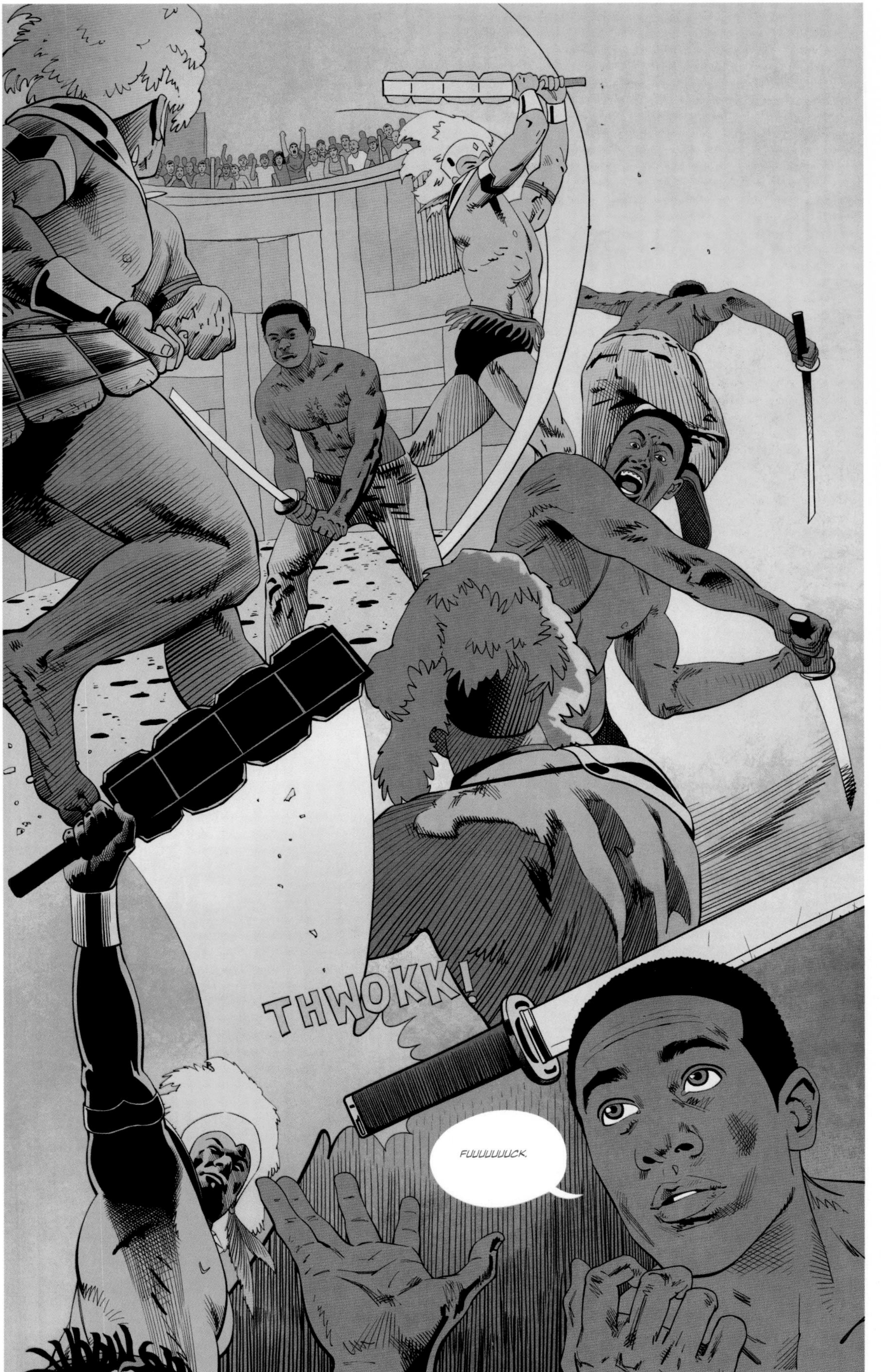
THWOKK!
FUUUUUUUCK.

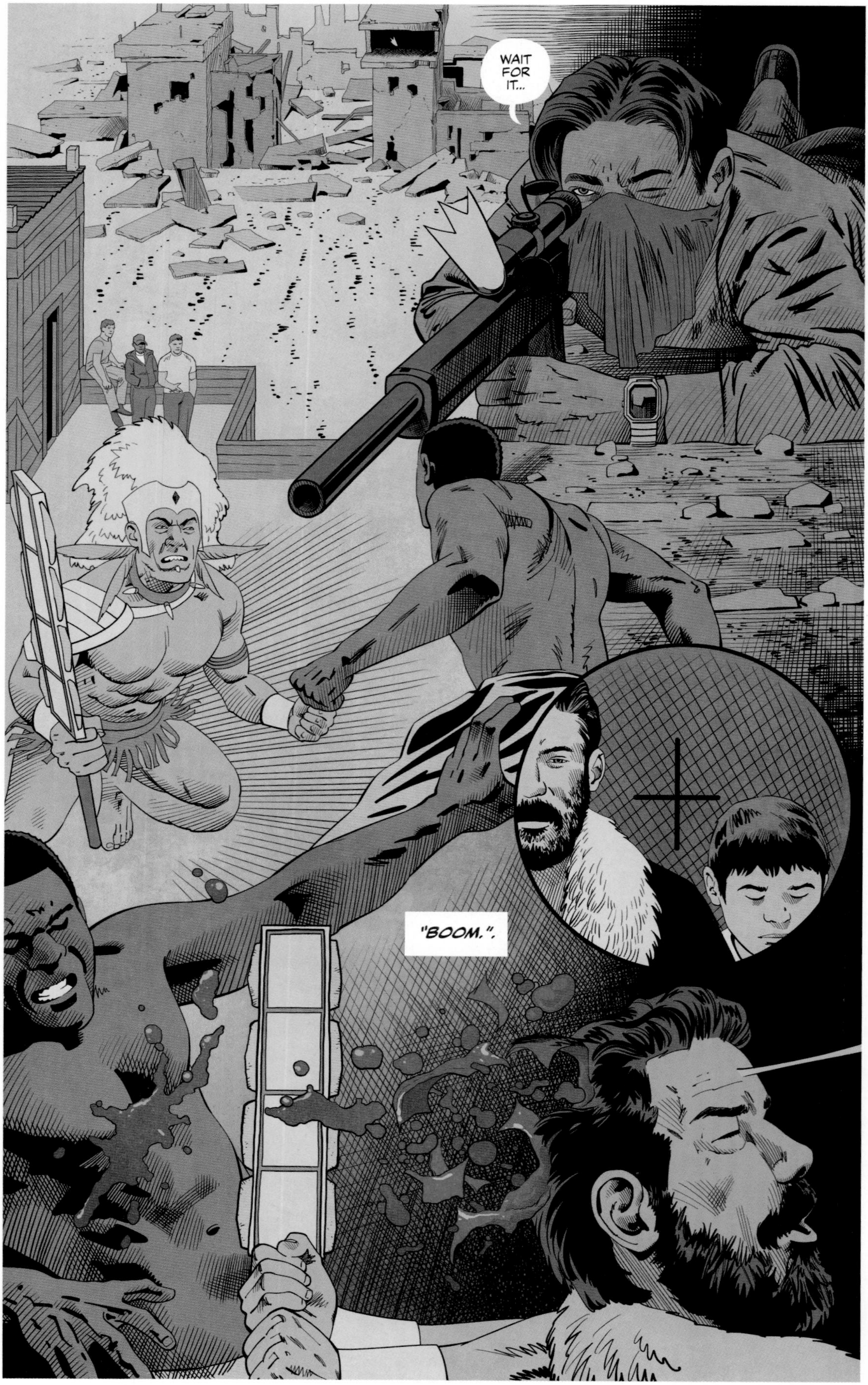
WAIT FOR IT...
"BOOM.".

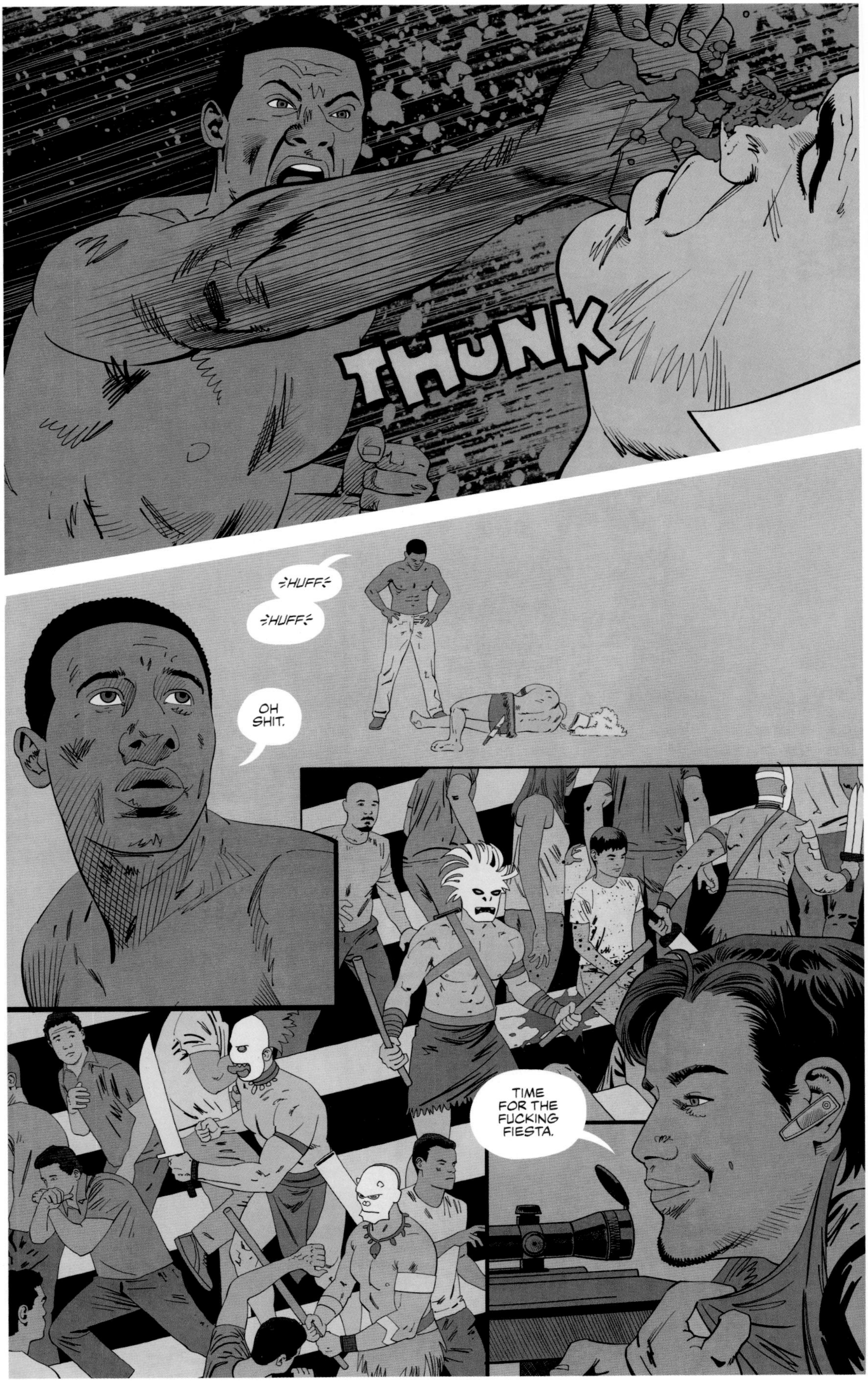
THUNK
HUFF
HUFF
OH SHIT.
TIME FOR THE FUCKING FIESTA.

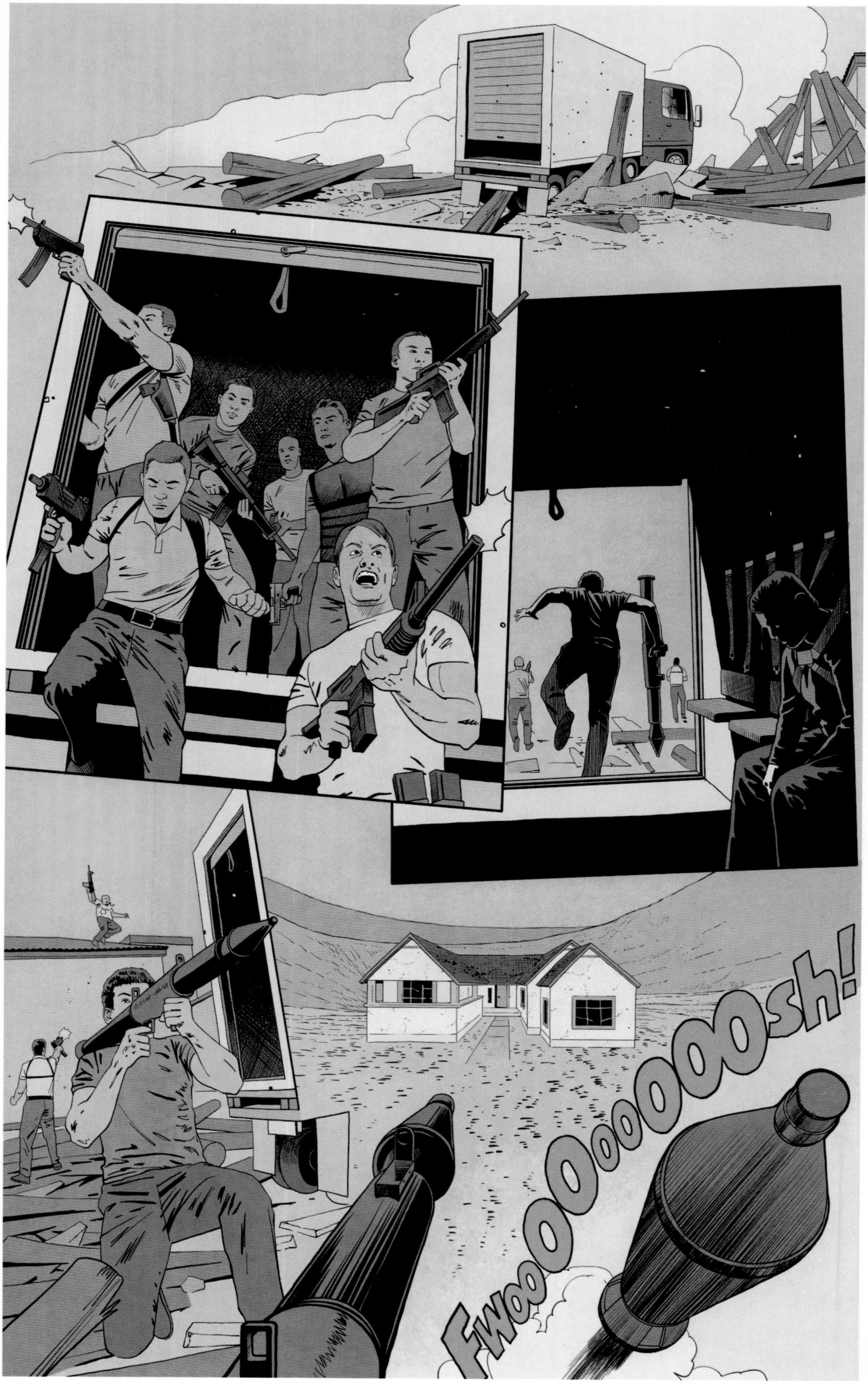
FwooOOooOOOOsh!

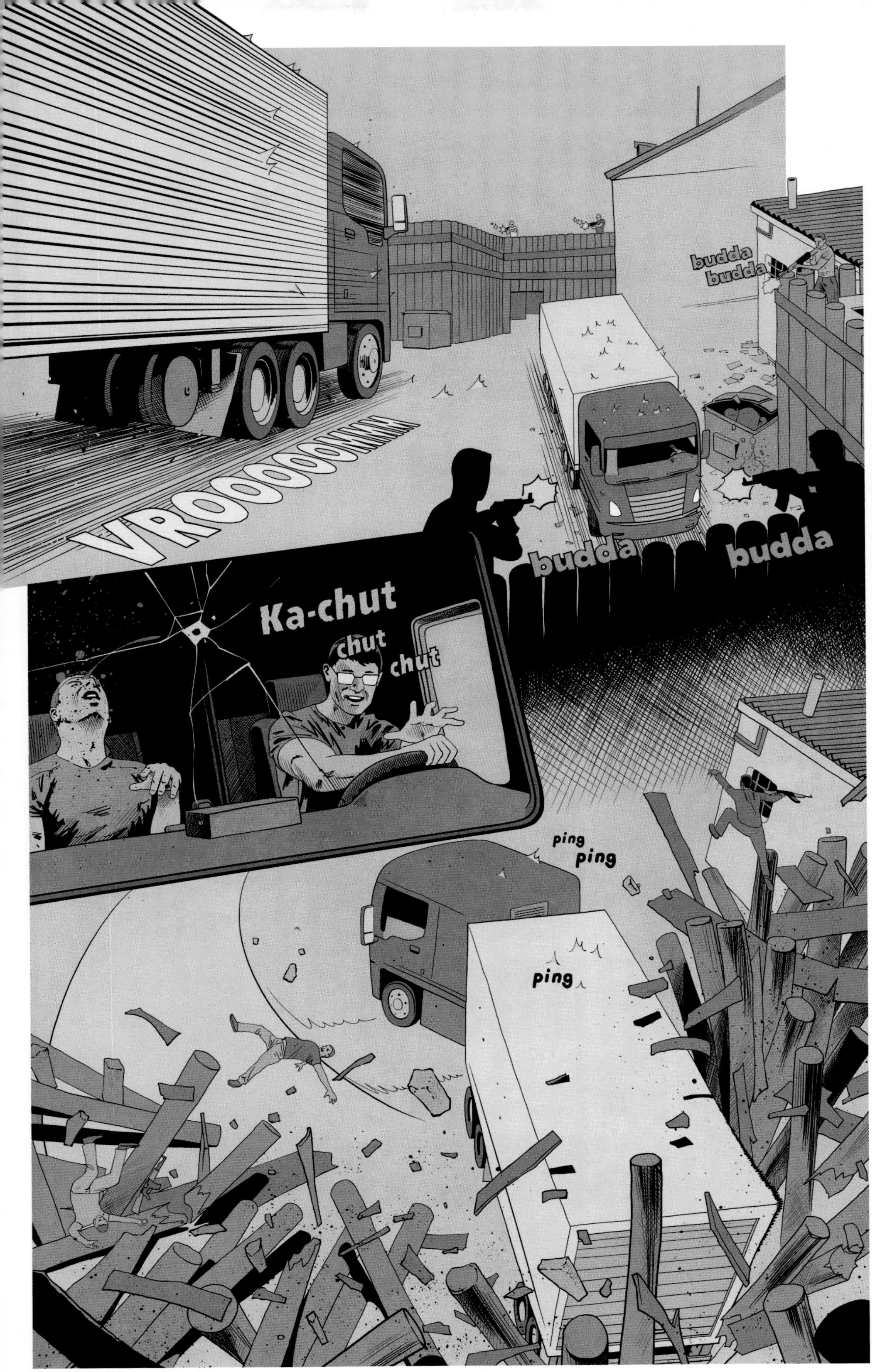

budda
budda
VROOOOOOHMMH
budda
budda
Ka-chut
chut
chut
ping
ping
ping

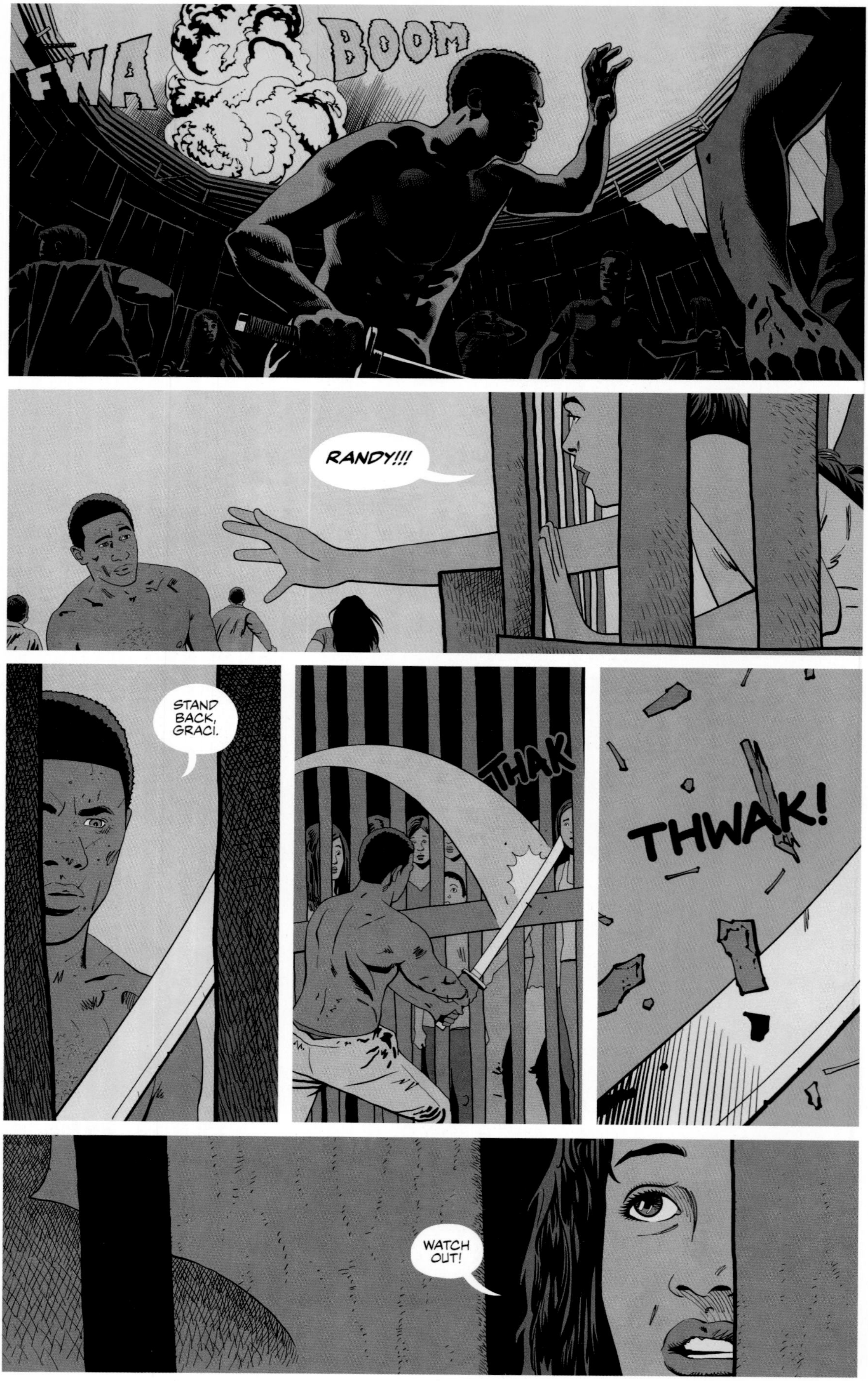
FWA
BOOM
RANDY!!!
STAND BACK, GRACI.
THAK
THWAK!
WATCH OUT!

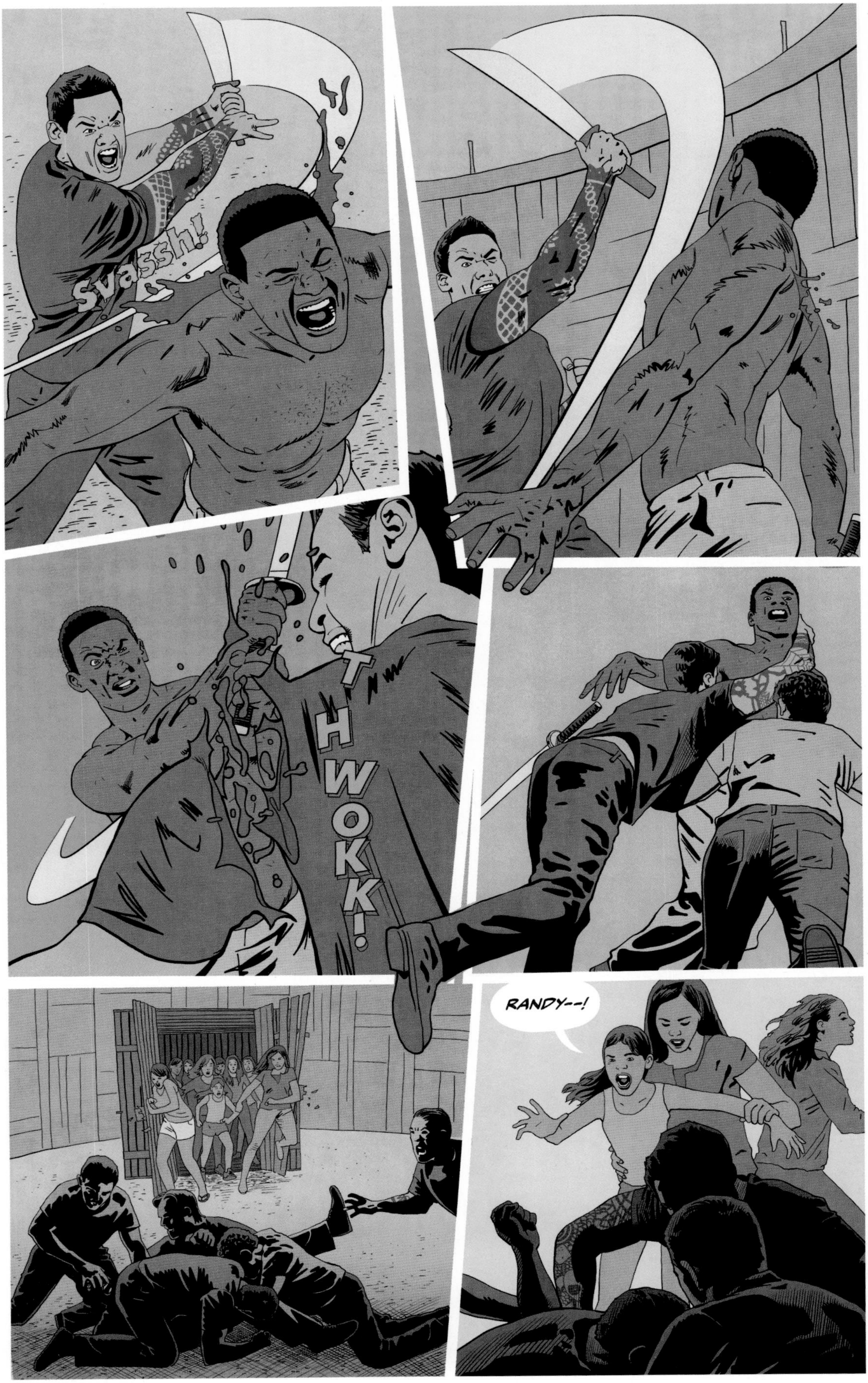
SVASSH!
THWOK!
RANDY--!

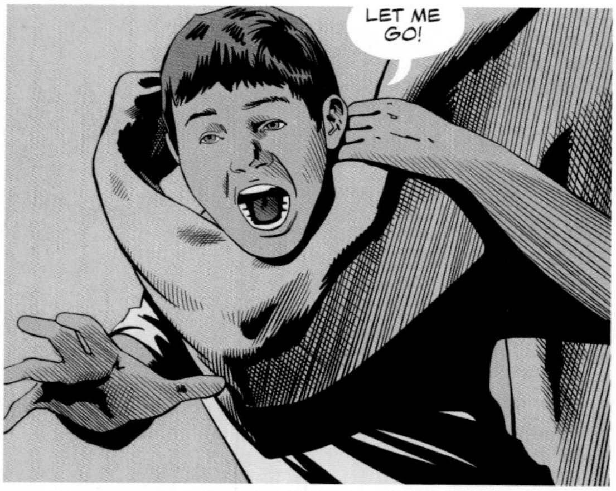
LET ME GO!

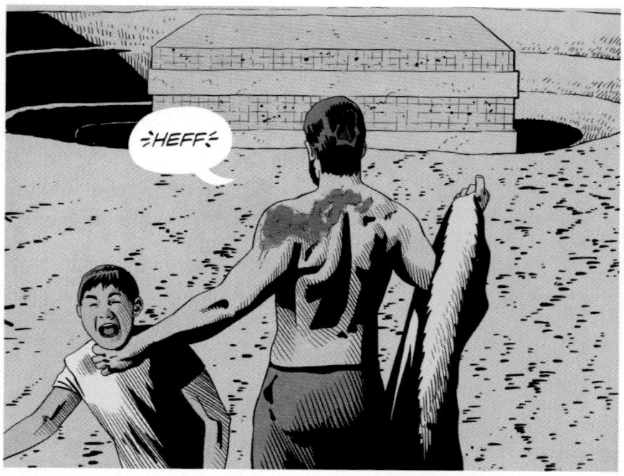
HEFF

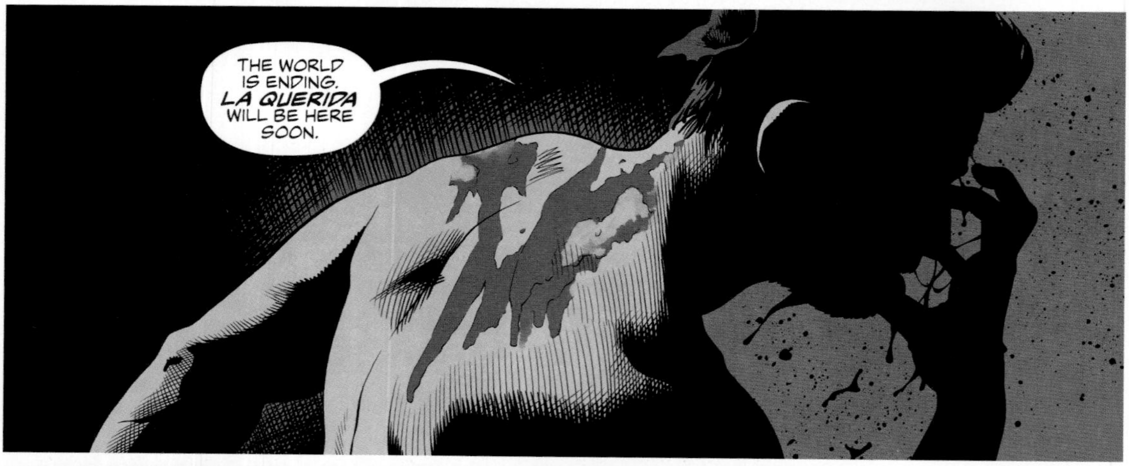
THE WORLD IS ENDING. LA QUERIDA WILL BE HERE SOON.

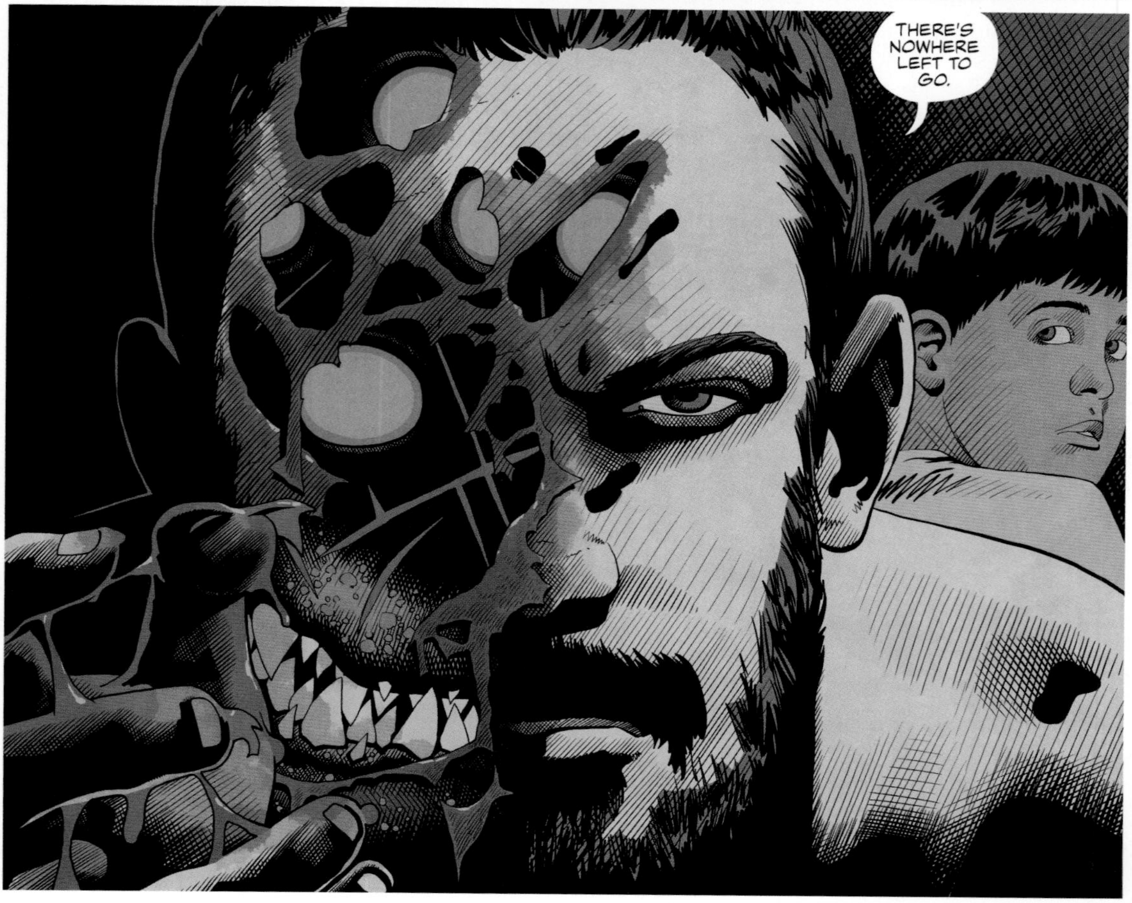
THERE'S NOWHERE LEFT TO GO.

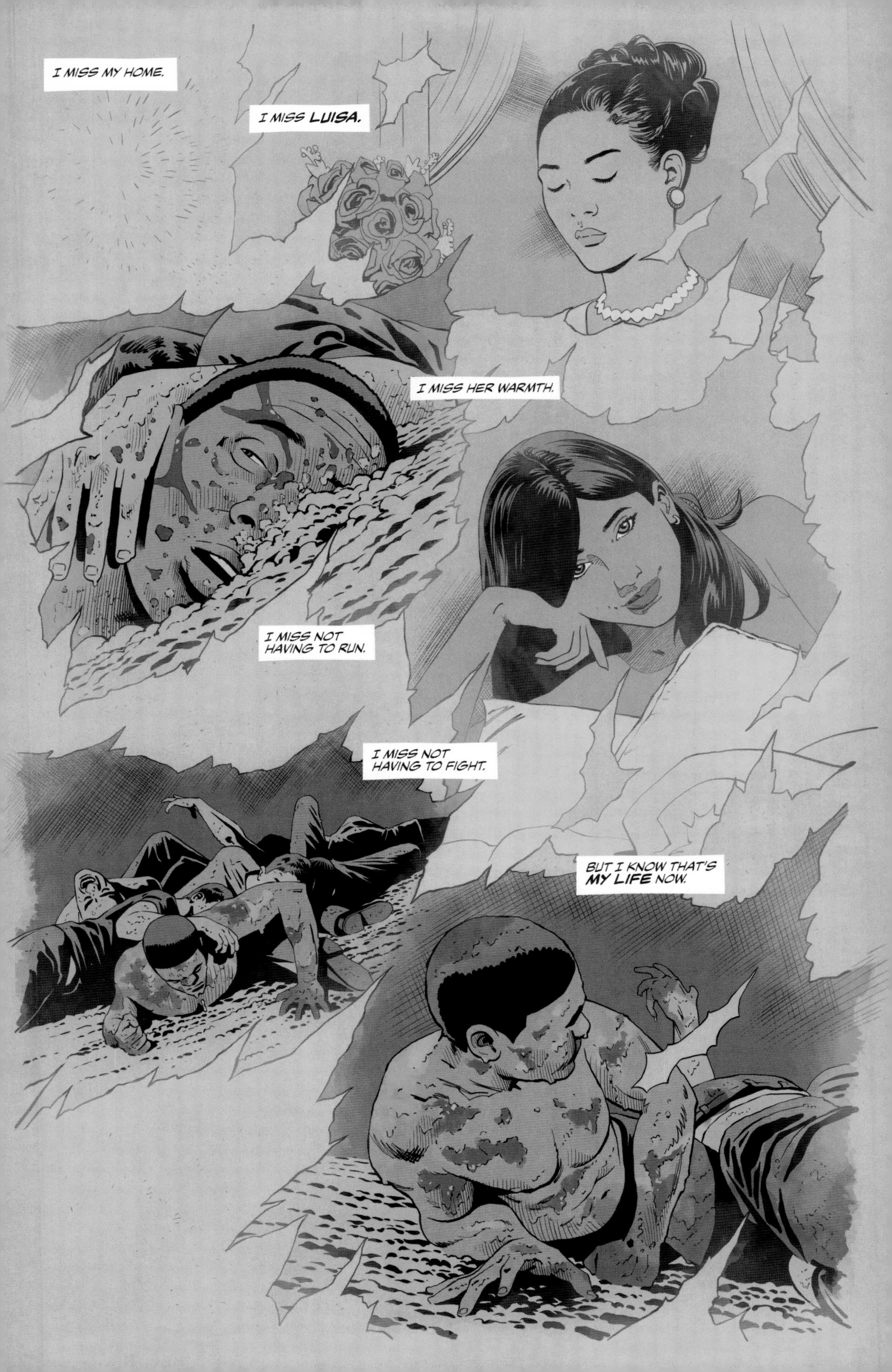
I MISS MY HOME.
I MISS LUISA.
I MISS HER WARMTH.
I MISS NOT HAVING TO RUN.
I MISS NOT HAVING TO FIGHT.
BUT I KNOW THAT'S MY LIFE NOW.

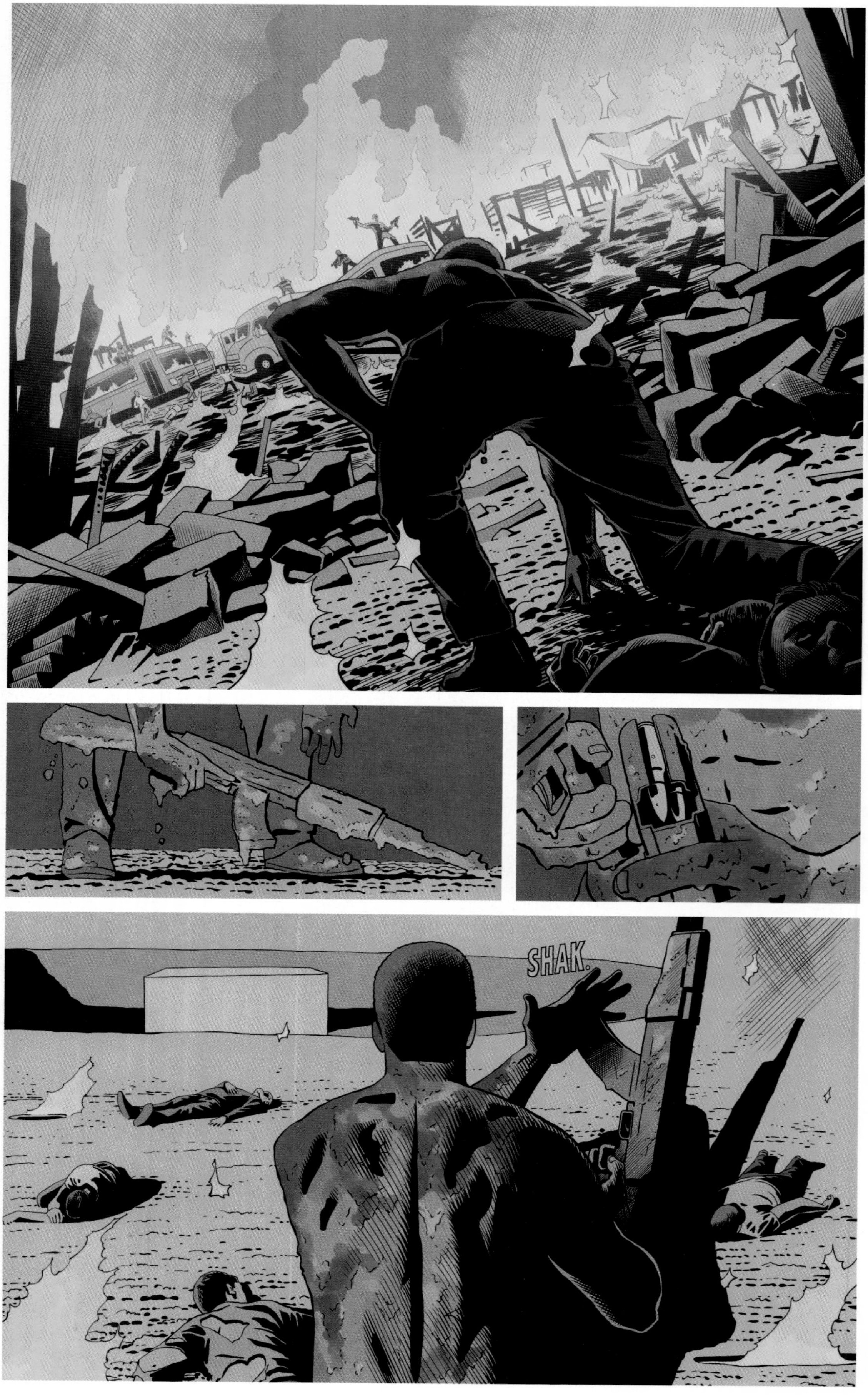
SHAK.

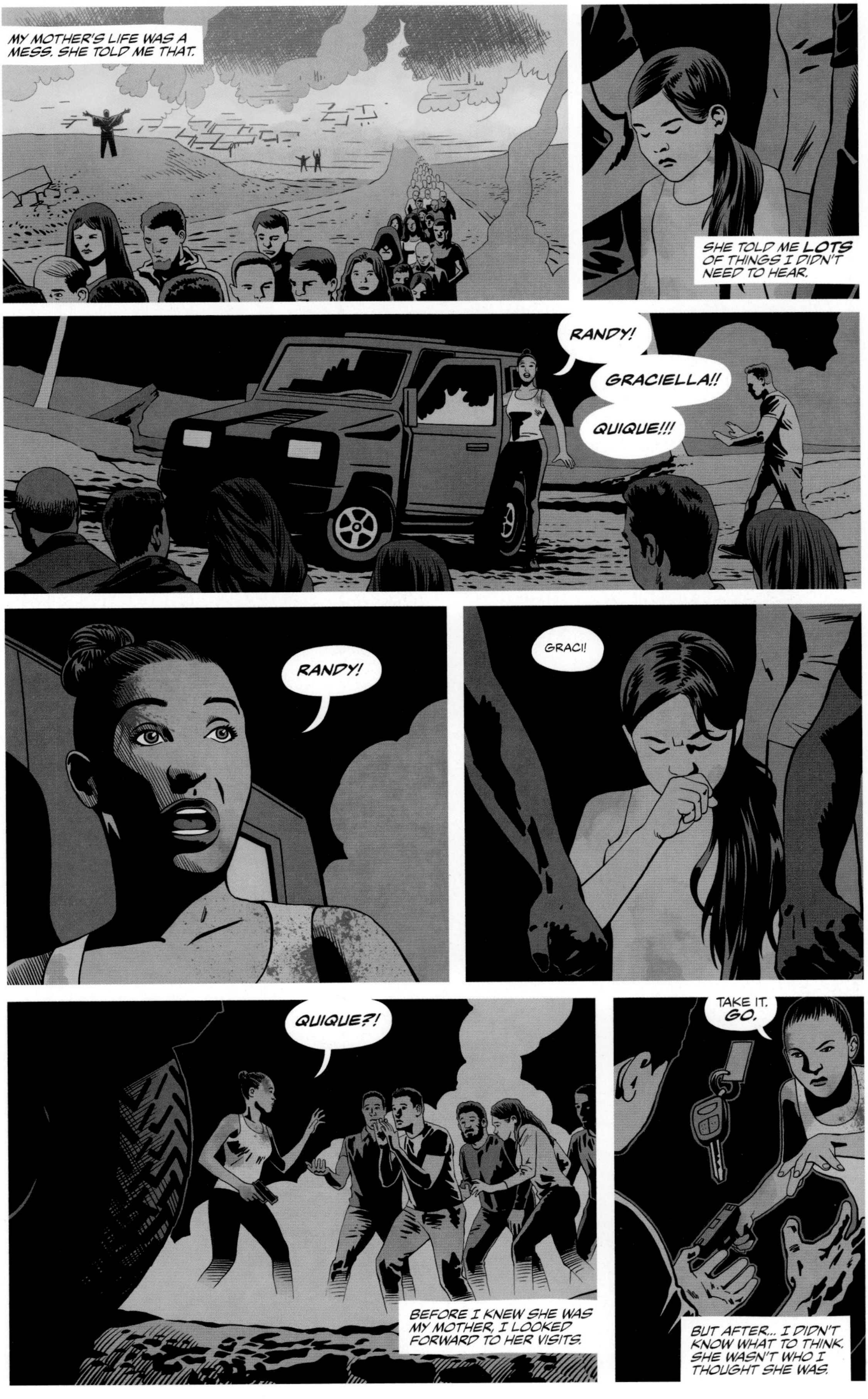
MY MOTHER'S LIFE WAS A MESS. SHE TOLD ME THAT.
SHE TOLD ME LOTS OF THINGS I DIDN'T NEED TO HEAR.
RANDY!
GRACIELLA!!
QUIQUE!!!
RANDY!
GRACI!
QUIQUE?!
BEFORE I KNEW SHE WAS MY MOTHER, I LOOKED FORWARD TO HER VISITS.
TAKE IT. GO.
BUT AFTER... I DIDN'T KNOW WHAT TO THINK. SHE WASN'T WHO I THOUGHT SHE WAS.

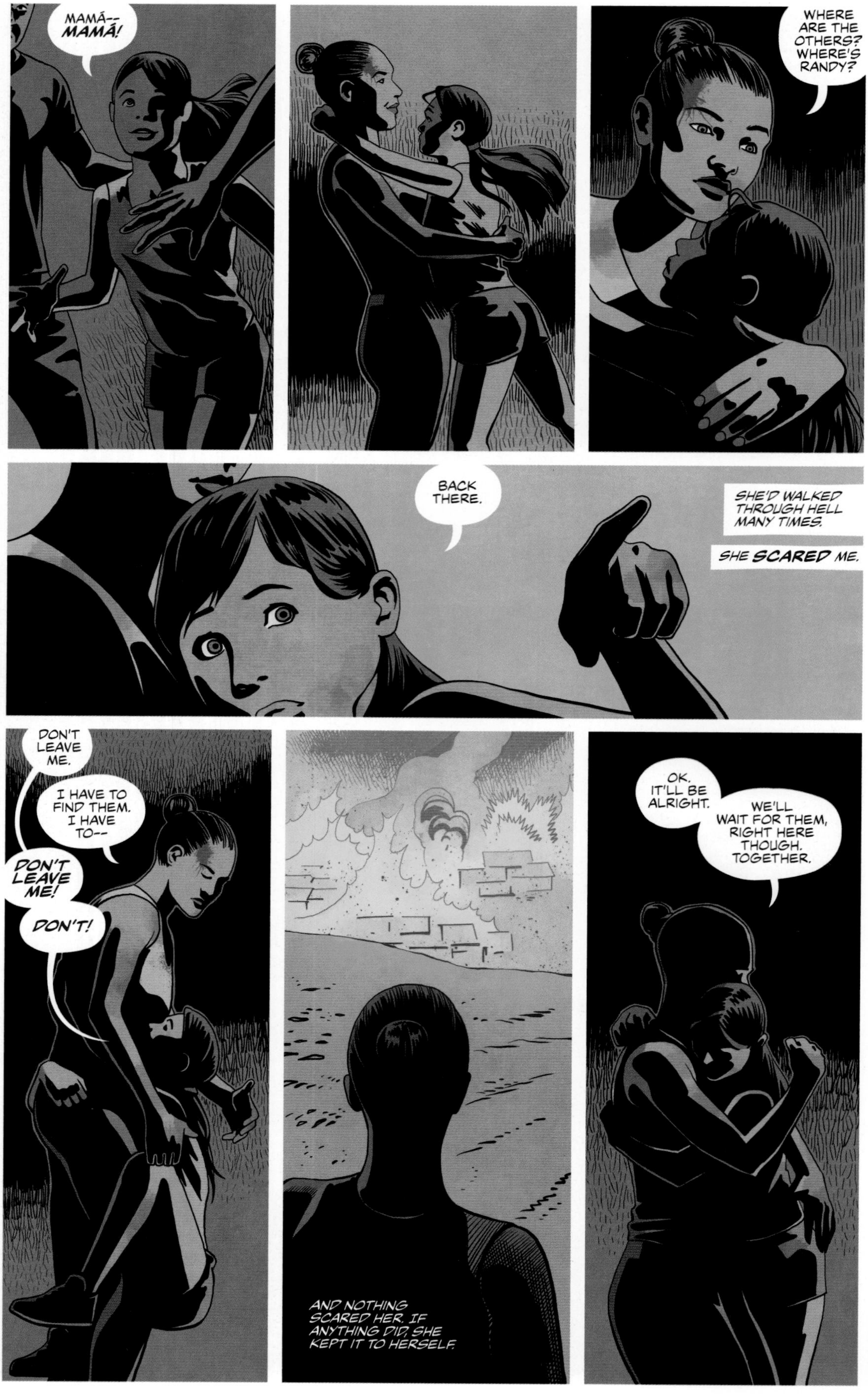

MAMÁ-- MAMÁ!
WHERE ARE THE OTHERS? WHERE'S RANDY?
BACK THERE.
SHE'D WALKED THROUGH HELL MANY TIMES.
SHE SCARED ME.
DON'T LEAVE ME.
I HAVE TO FIND THEM. I HAVE TO--
DON'T LEAVE ME!
DON'T!
AND NOTHING SCARED HER. IF ANYTHING DID, SHE KEPT IT TO HERSELF.
OK. IT'LL BE ALRIGHT.
WE'LL WAIT FOR THEM, RIGHT HERE THOUGH. TOGETHER.

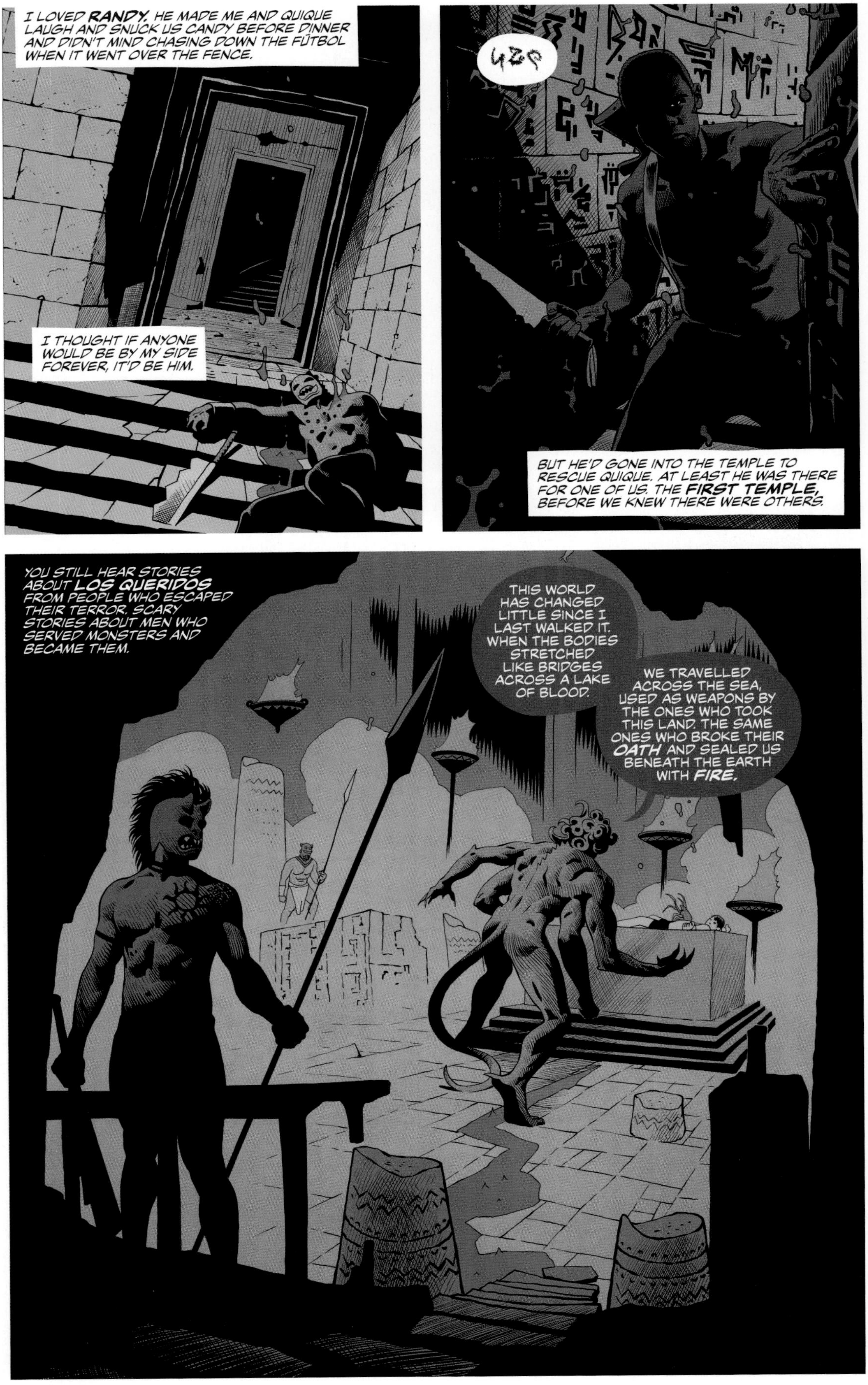

I LOVED **RANDY.** HE MADE ME AND QUIQUE LAUGH AND SNUCK US CANDY BEFORE DINNER AND DIDN'T MIND CHASING DOWN THE FÚTBOL WHEN IT WENT OVER THE FENCE.
I THOUGHT IF ANYONE WOULD BE BY MY SIDE FOREVER, IT'D BE HIM.
BUT HE'D GONE INTO THE TEMPLE TO RESCUE QUIQUE. AT LEAST HE WAS THERE FOR ONE OF US. THE **FIRST TEMPLE,** BEFORE WE KNEW THERE WERE OTHERS.
YOU STILL HEAR STORIES ABOUT **LOS QUERIDOS** FROM PEOPLE WHO ESCAPED THEIR TERROR. SCARY STORIES ABOUT MEN WHO SERVED MONSTERS AND BECAME THEM.
THIS WORLD HAS CHANGED LITTLE SINCE I LAST WALKED IT. WHEN THE BODIES STRETCHED LIKE BRIDGES ACROSS A LAKE OF BLOOD.
WE TRAVELLED ACROSS THE SEA, USED AS WEAPONS BY THE ONES WHO TOOK THIS LAND. THE SAME ONES WHO BROKE THEIR **OATH** AND SEALED US BENEATH THE EARTH WITH **FIRE.**

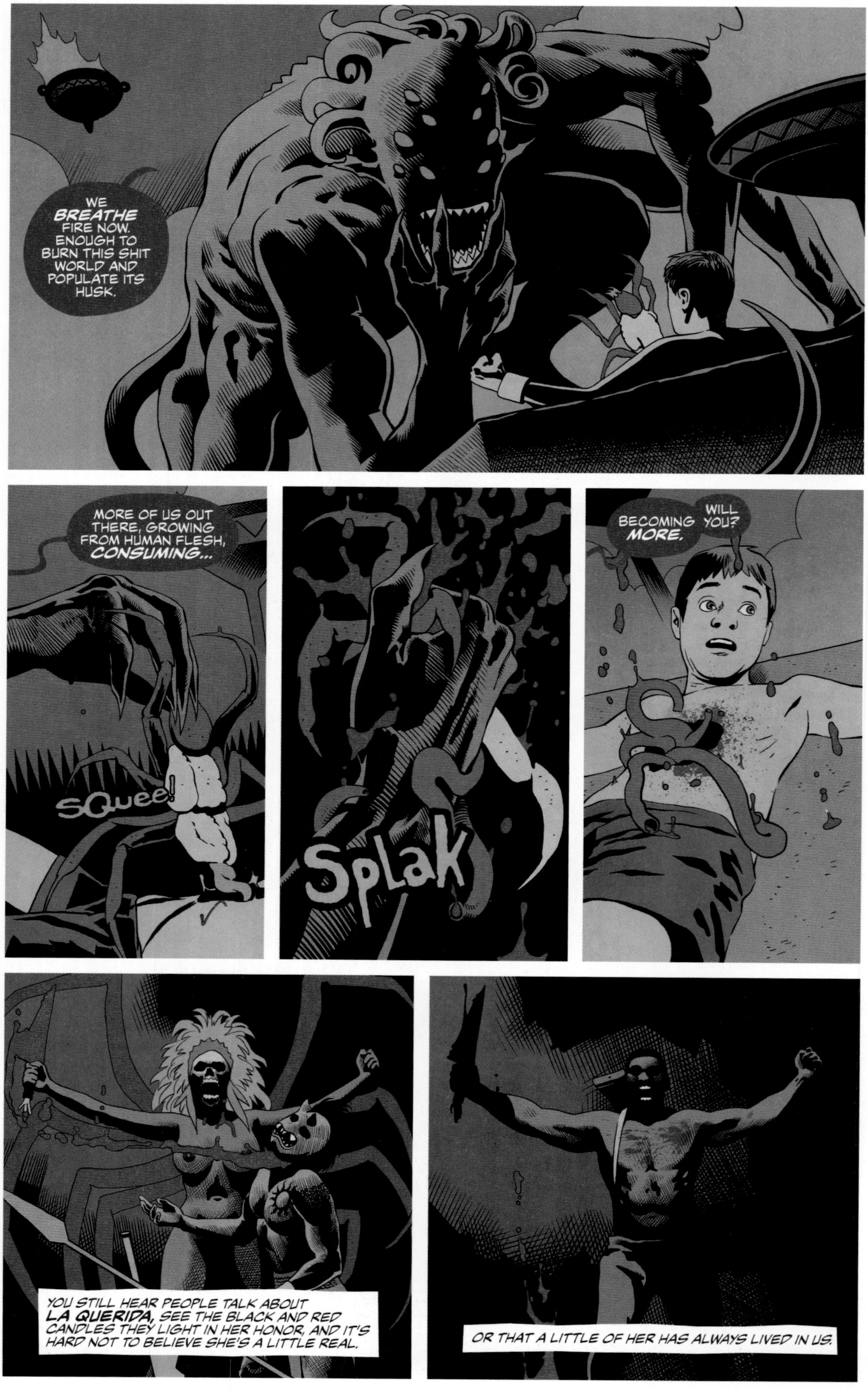
WE BREATHE FIRE NOW. ENOUGH TO BURN THIS SHIT WORLD AND POPULATE ITS HUSK.
MORE OF US OUT THERE, GROWING FROM HUMAN FLESH, CONSUMING...
sQuee!
Splak
BECOMING MORE.
WILL YOU?
YOU STILL HEAR PEOPLE TALK ABOUT LA QUERIDA, SEE THE BLACK AND RED CANDLES THEY LIGHT IN HER HONOR, AND IT'S HARD NOT TO BELIEVE SHE'S A LITTLE REAL.
OR THAT A LITTLE OF HER HAS ALWAYS LIVED IN US.

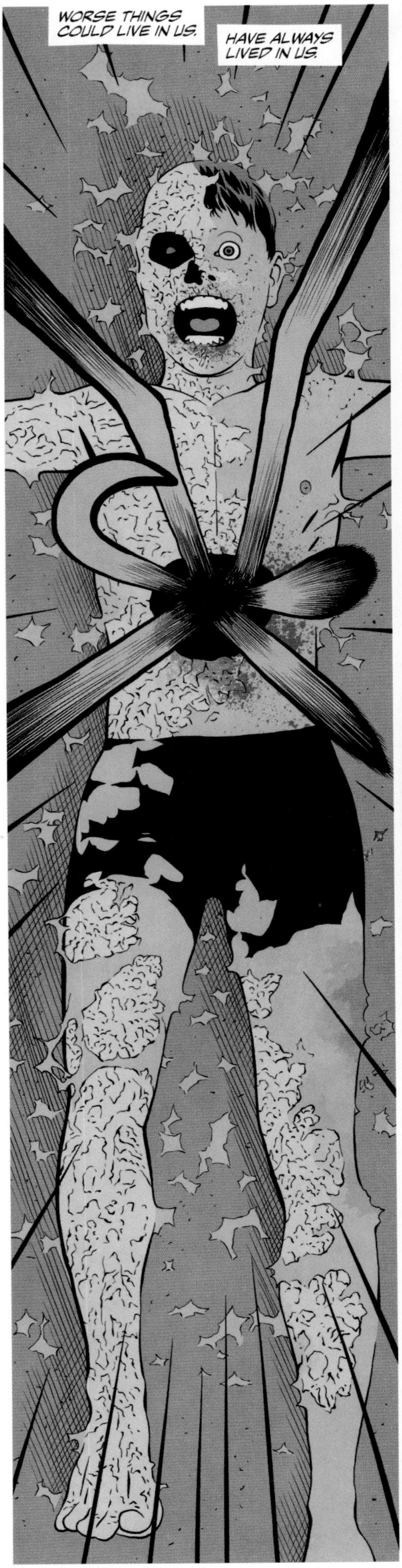
WORSE THINGS COULD LIVE IN US.
HAVE ALWAYS LIVED IN US.

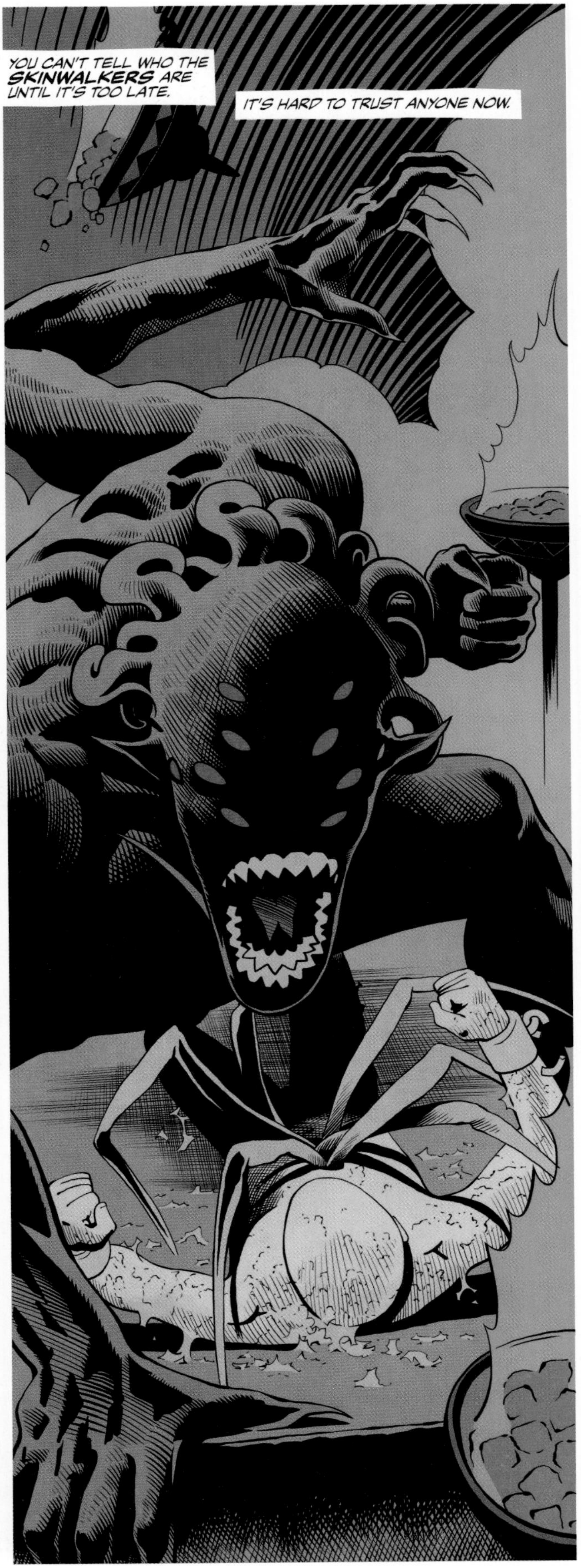
YOU CAN'T TELL WHO THE **SKINWALKERS** ARE UNTIL IT'S TOO LATE.
IT'S HARD TO TRUST ANYONE NOW.

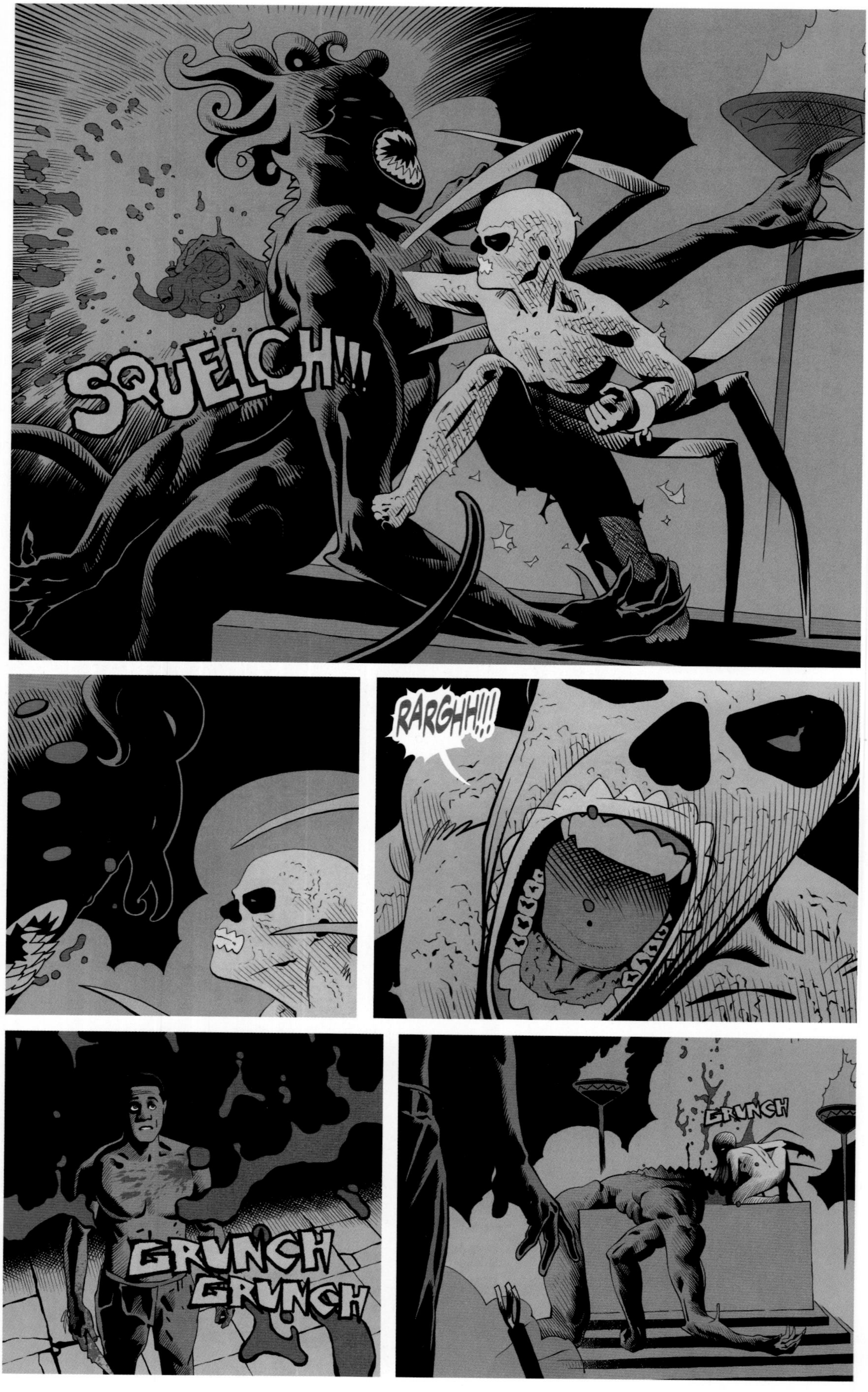
SQUELCH!!!
RARGHH!!!
GRUNCH
GRUNCH
GRUNCH

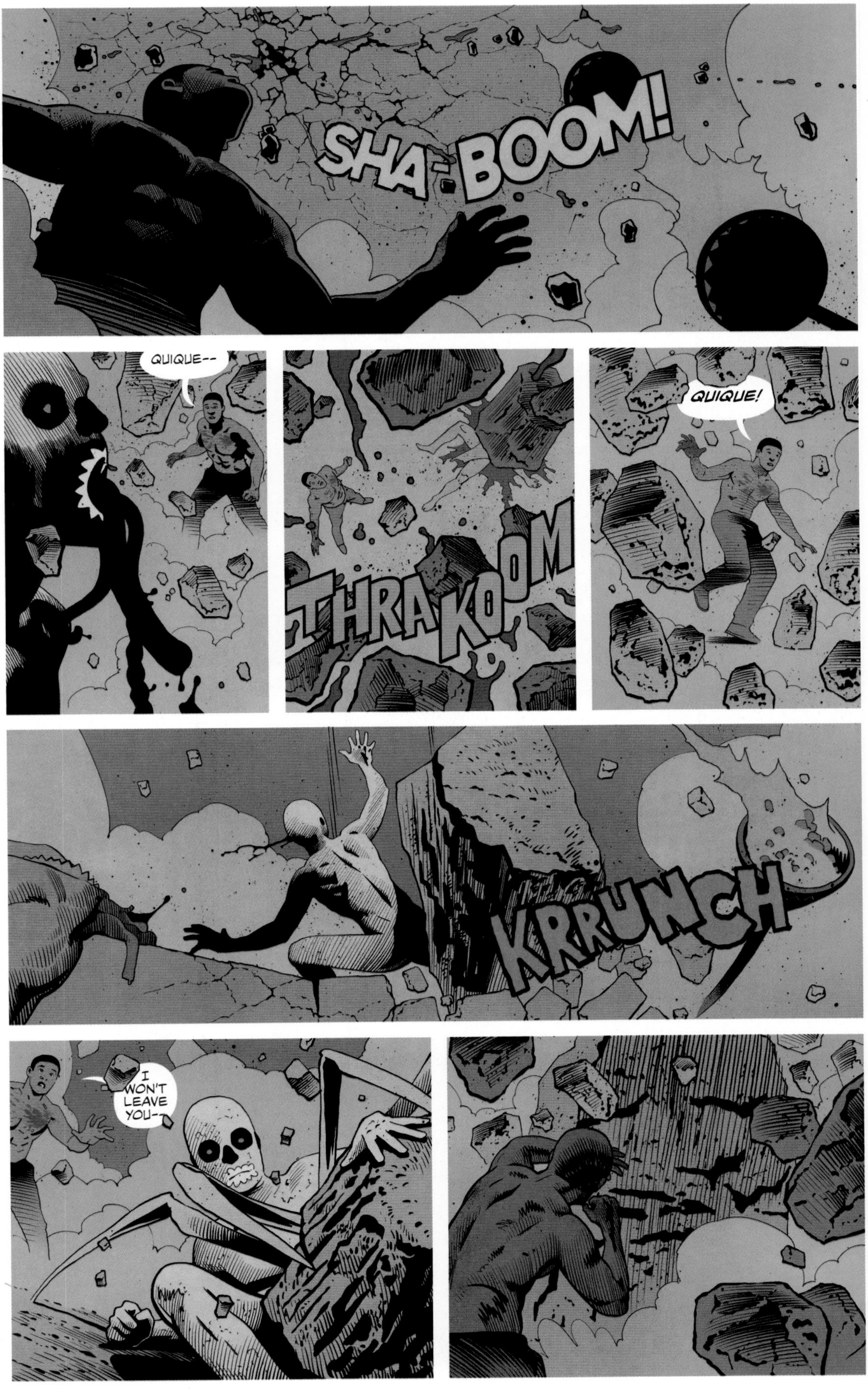
SHA-BOOM!
QUIQUE--
THRAKOOM
QUIQUE!
KRRUNCH
I WON'T LEAVE YOU--

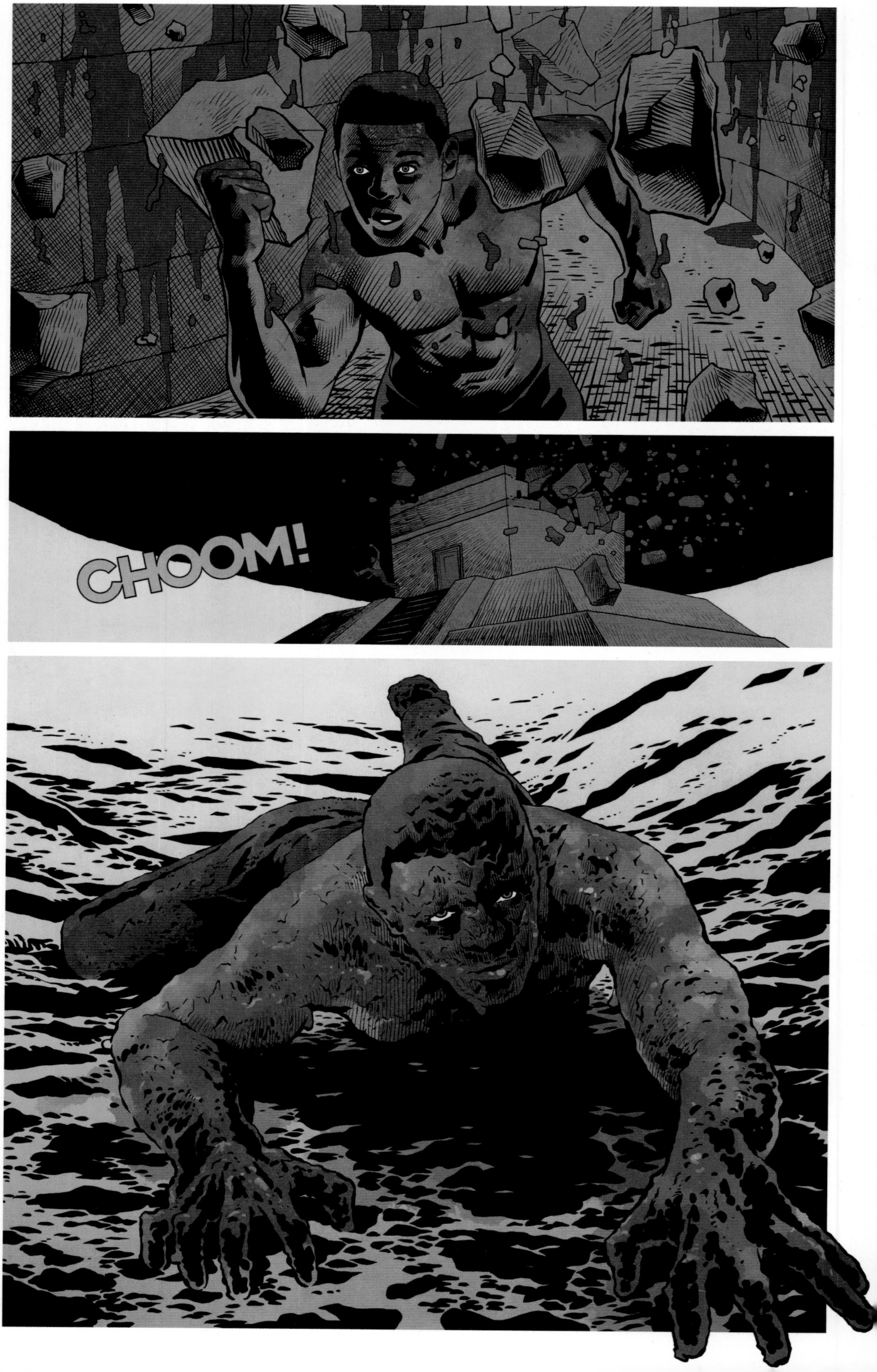
CHOOM!

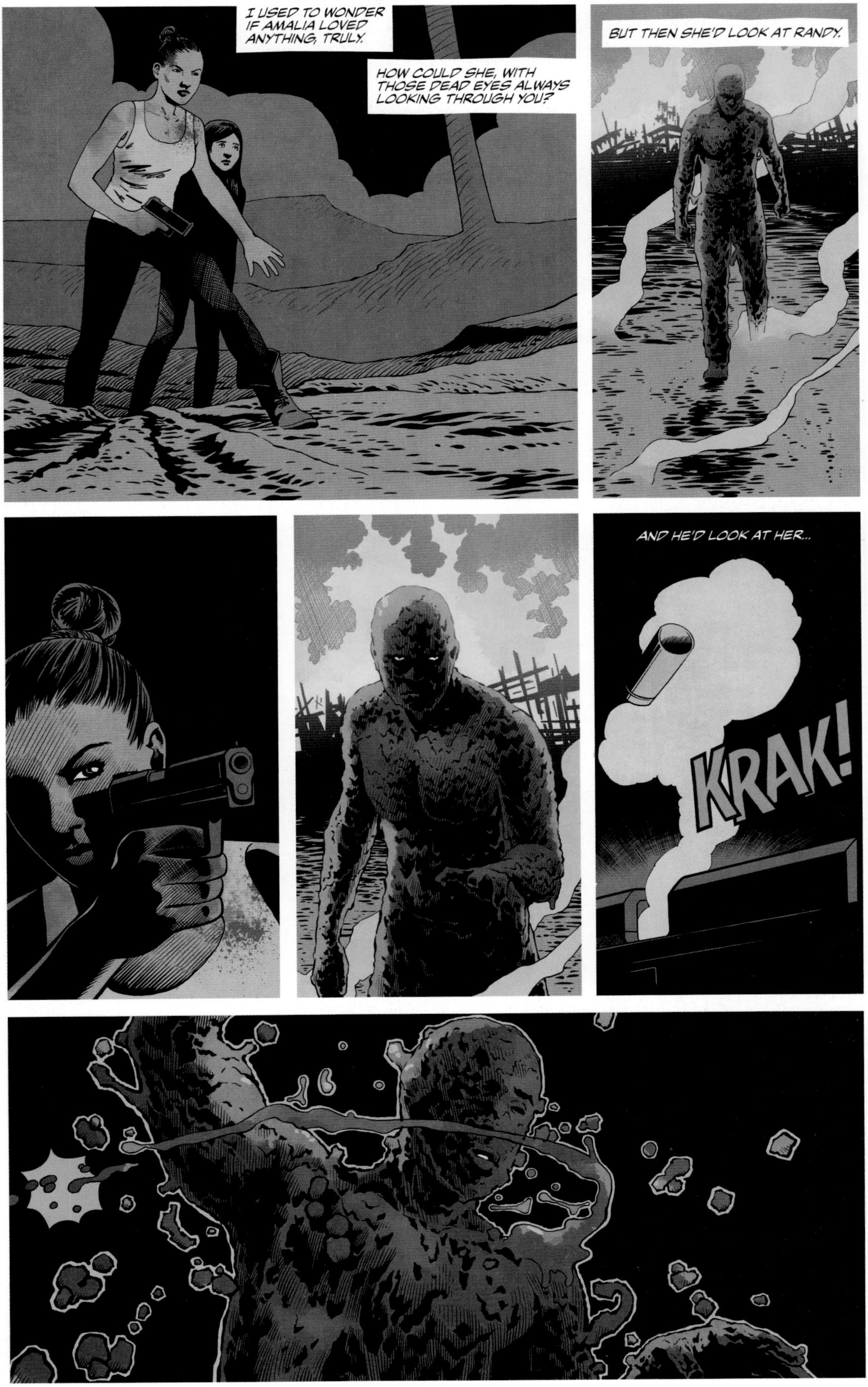
I USED TO WONDER IF AMALIA LOVED ANYTHING, TRULY.
HOW COULD SHE, WITH THOSE DEAD EYES ALWAYS LOOKING THROUGH YOU?
BUT THEN SHE'D LOOK AT RANDY.
AND HE'D LOOK AT HER...
KRAK!

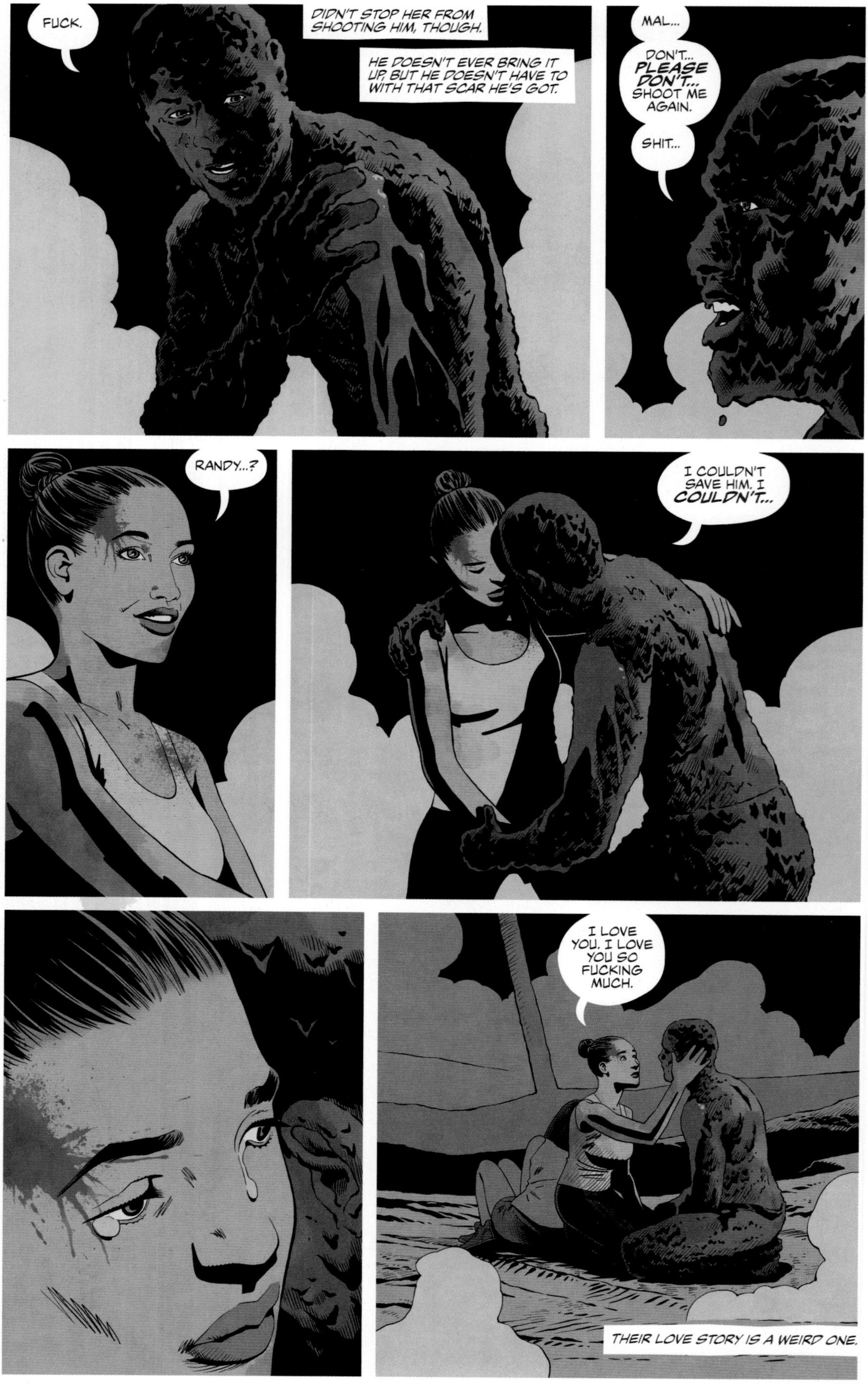
FUCK.
DIDN'T STOP HER FROM SHOOTING HIM, THOUGH.
HE DOESN'T EVER BRING IT UP, BUT HE DOESN'T HAVE TO WITH THAT SCAR HE'S GOT.
MAL...
DON'T... PLEASE DON'T... SHOOT ME AGAIN.
SHIT...
RANDY...?
I COULDN'T SAVE HIM. I COULDN'T...
I LOVE YOU. I LOVE YOU SO FUCKING MUCH.
THEIR LOVE STORY IS A WEIRD ONE.

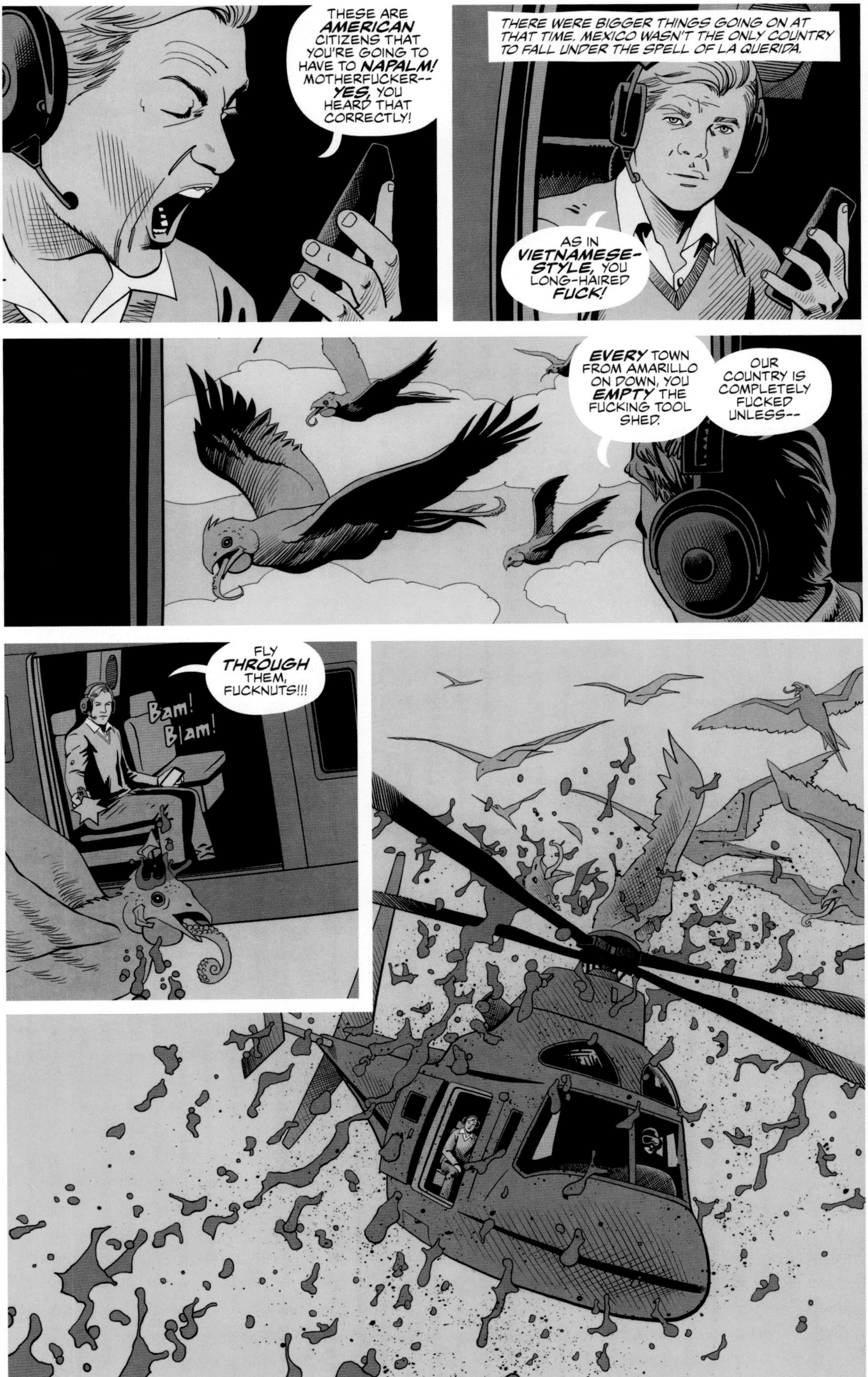
THESE ARE AMERICAN CITIZENS THAT YOU'RE GOING TO HAVE TO NAPALM! MOTHERFUCKER-- YES, YOU HEARD THAT CORRECTLY!
THERE WERE BIGGER THINGS GOING ON AT THAT TIME. MEXICO WASN'T THE ONLY COUNTRY TO FALL UNDER THE SPELL OF LA QUERIDA.
AS IN VIETNAMESE-STYLE, YOU LONG-HAIRED FUCK!
EVERY TOWN FROM AMARILLO ON DOWN, YOU EMPTY THE FUCKING TOOL SHED.
OUR COUNTRY IS COMPLETELY FUCKED UNLESS--
FLY THROUGH THEM, FUCKNUTS!!!
Bam!
Blam!

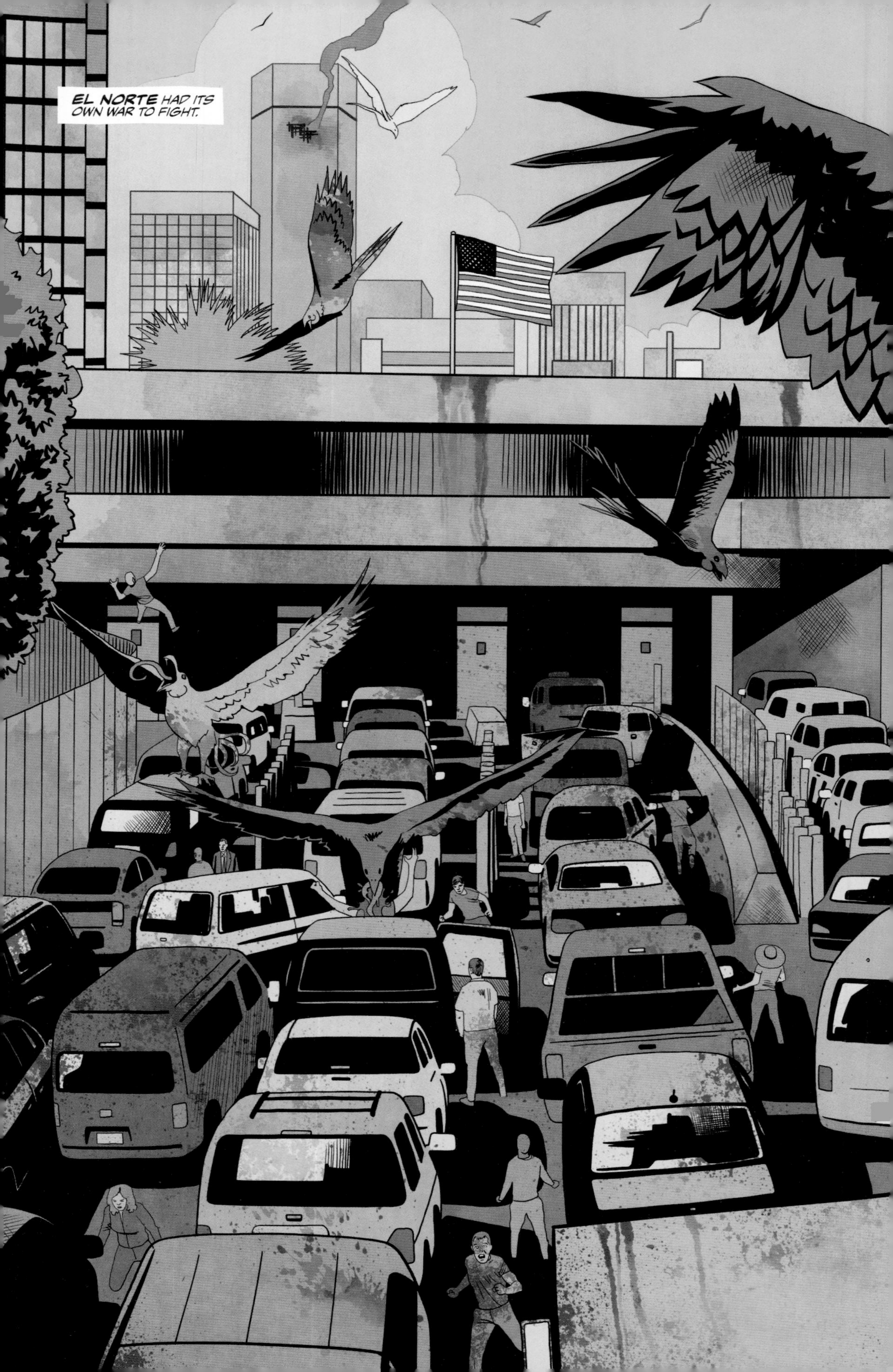
EL NORTE HAD ITS OWN WAR TO FIGHT.

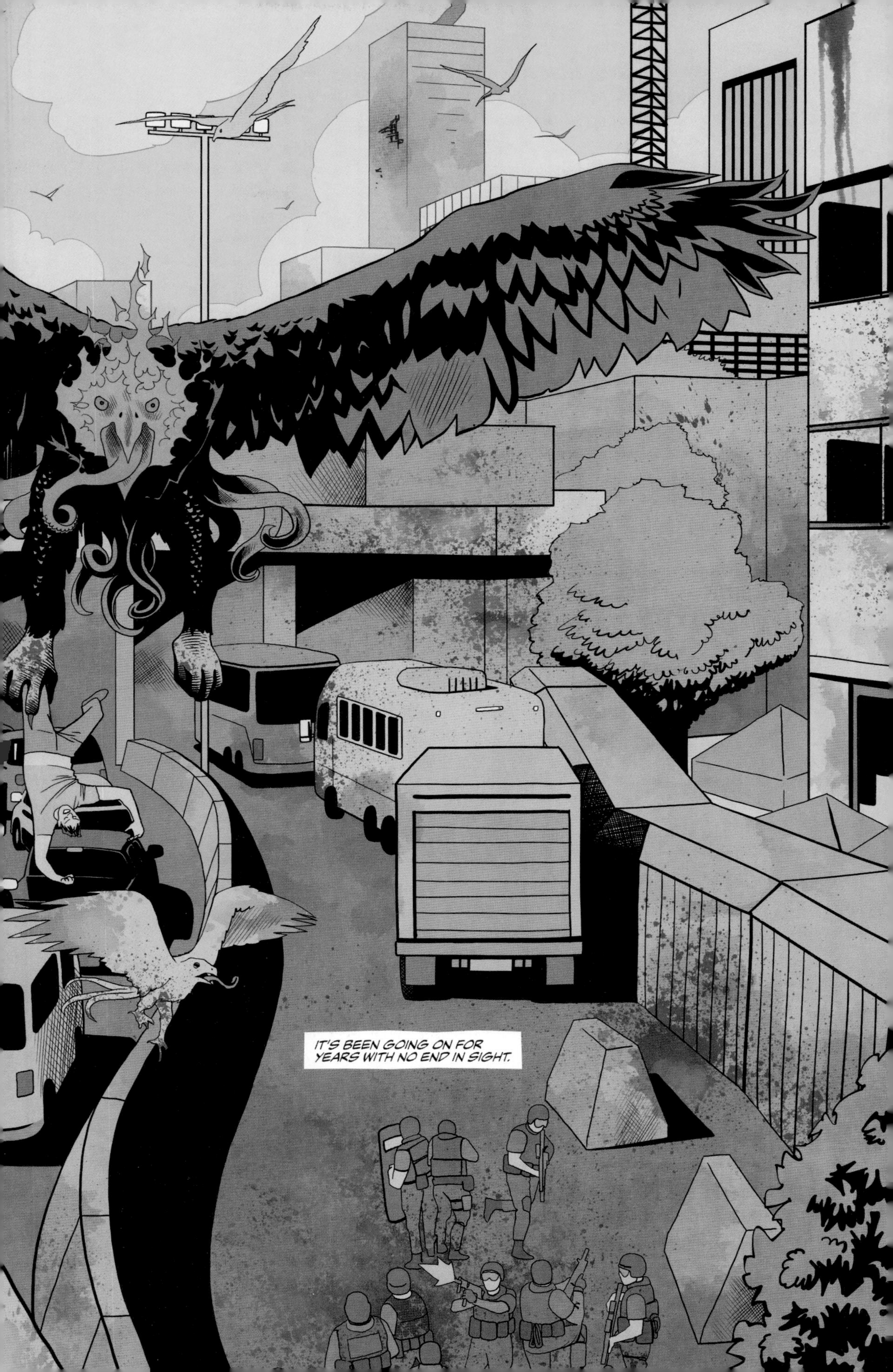
IT'S BEEN GOING ON FOR YEARS WITH NO END IN SIGHT.

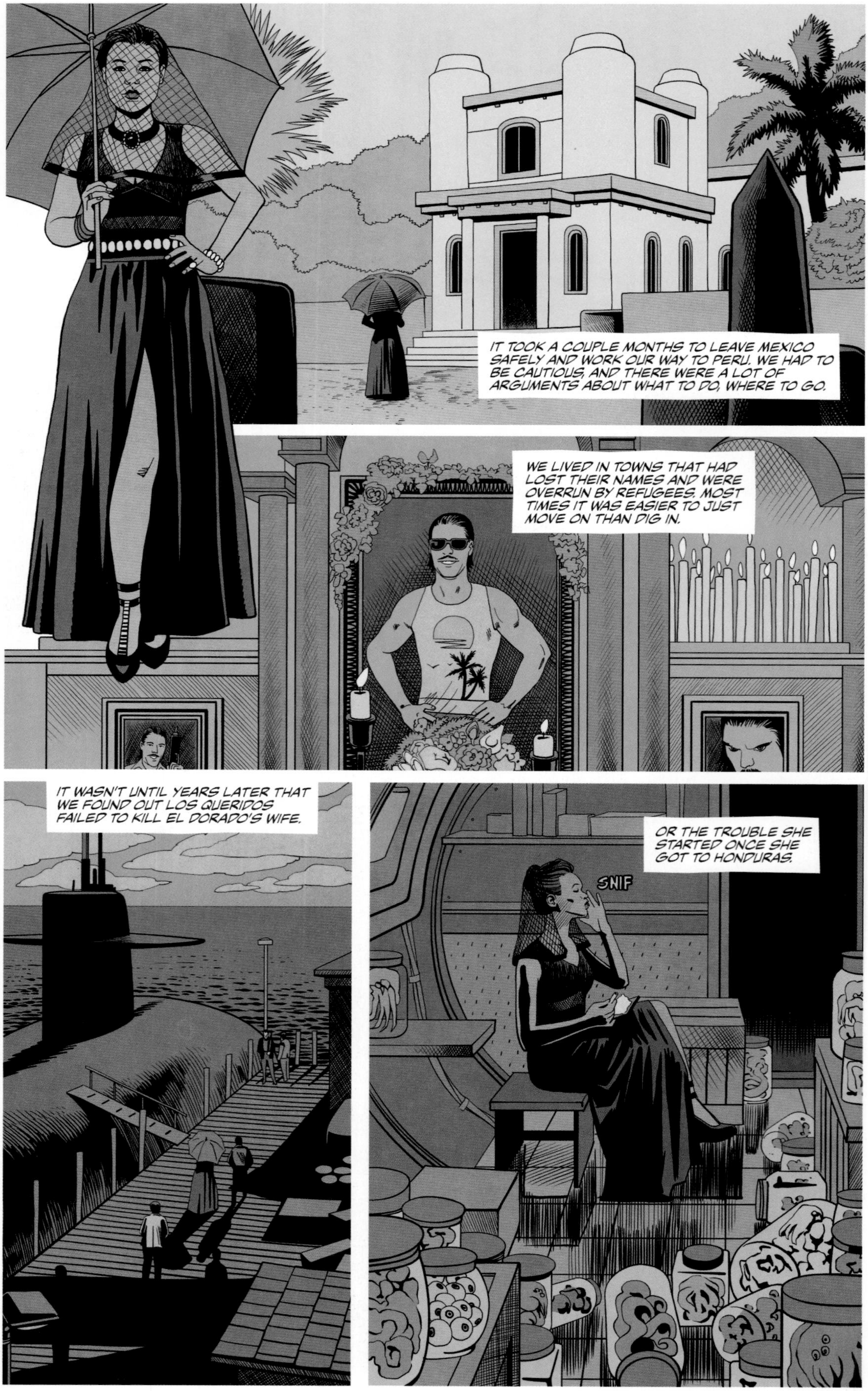
IT TOOK A COUPLE MONTHS TO LEAVE MEXICO SAFELY AND WORK OUR WAY TO PERU. WE HAD TO BE CAUTIOUS, AND THERE WERE A LOT OF ARGUMENTS ABOUT WHAT TO DO, WHERE TO GO.
WE LIVED IN TOWNS THAT HAD LOST THEIR NAMES AND WERE OVERRUN BY REFUGEES. MOST TIMES IT WAS EASIER TO JUST MOVE ON THAN DIG IN.
IT WASN'T UNTIL YEARS LATER THAT WE FOUND OUT LOS QUERIDOS FAILED TO KILL EL DORADO'S WIFE.
OR THE TROUBLE SHE STARTED ONCE SHE GOT TO HONDURAS.
SNIF

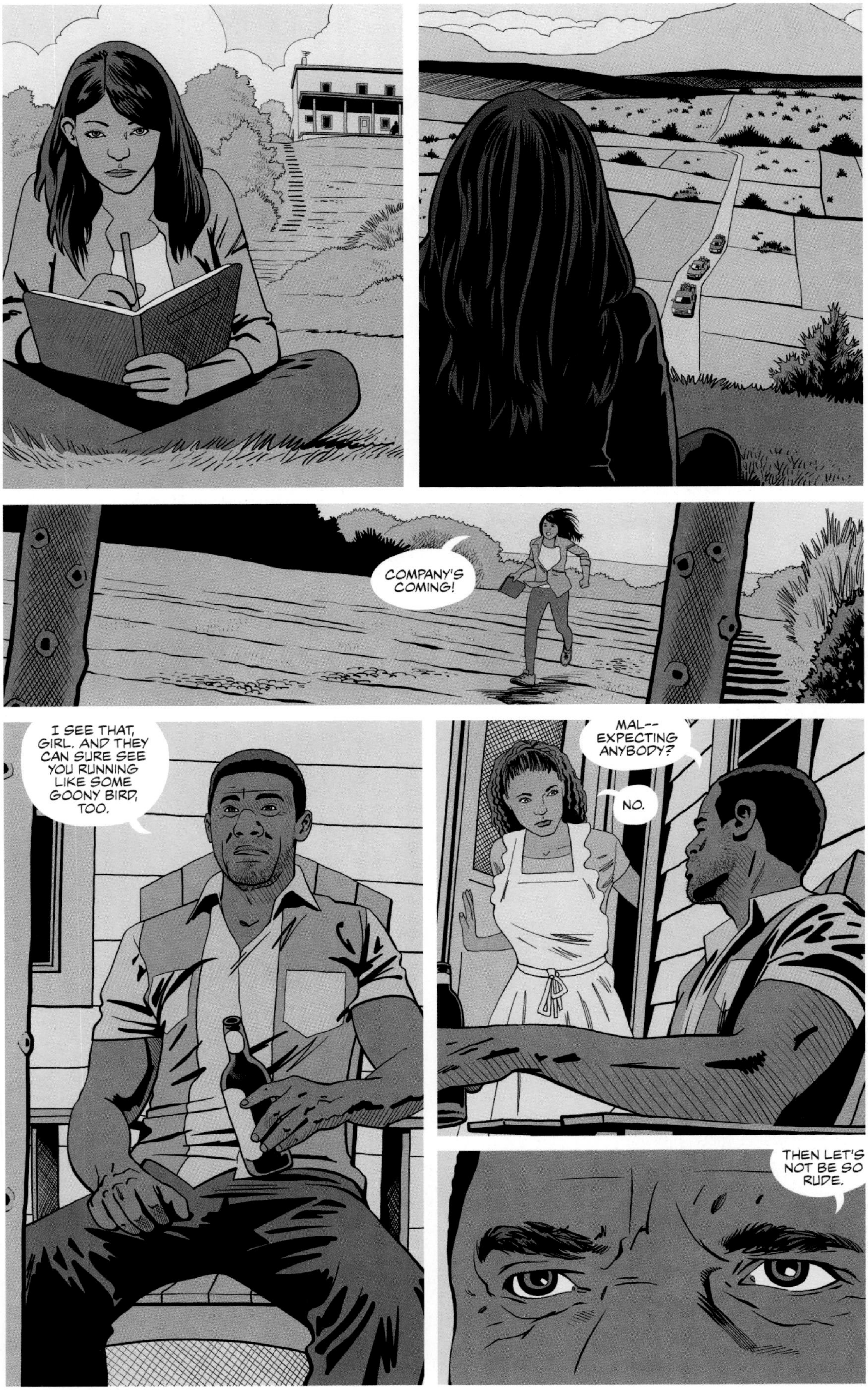
COMPANY'S COMING!
I SEE THAT, GIRL. AND THEY CAN SURE SEE YOU RUNNING LIKE SOME GOONY BIRD, TOO.
MAL-- EXPECTING ANYBODY?
NO.
THEN LET'S NOT BE SO RUDE.

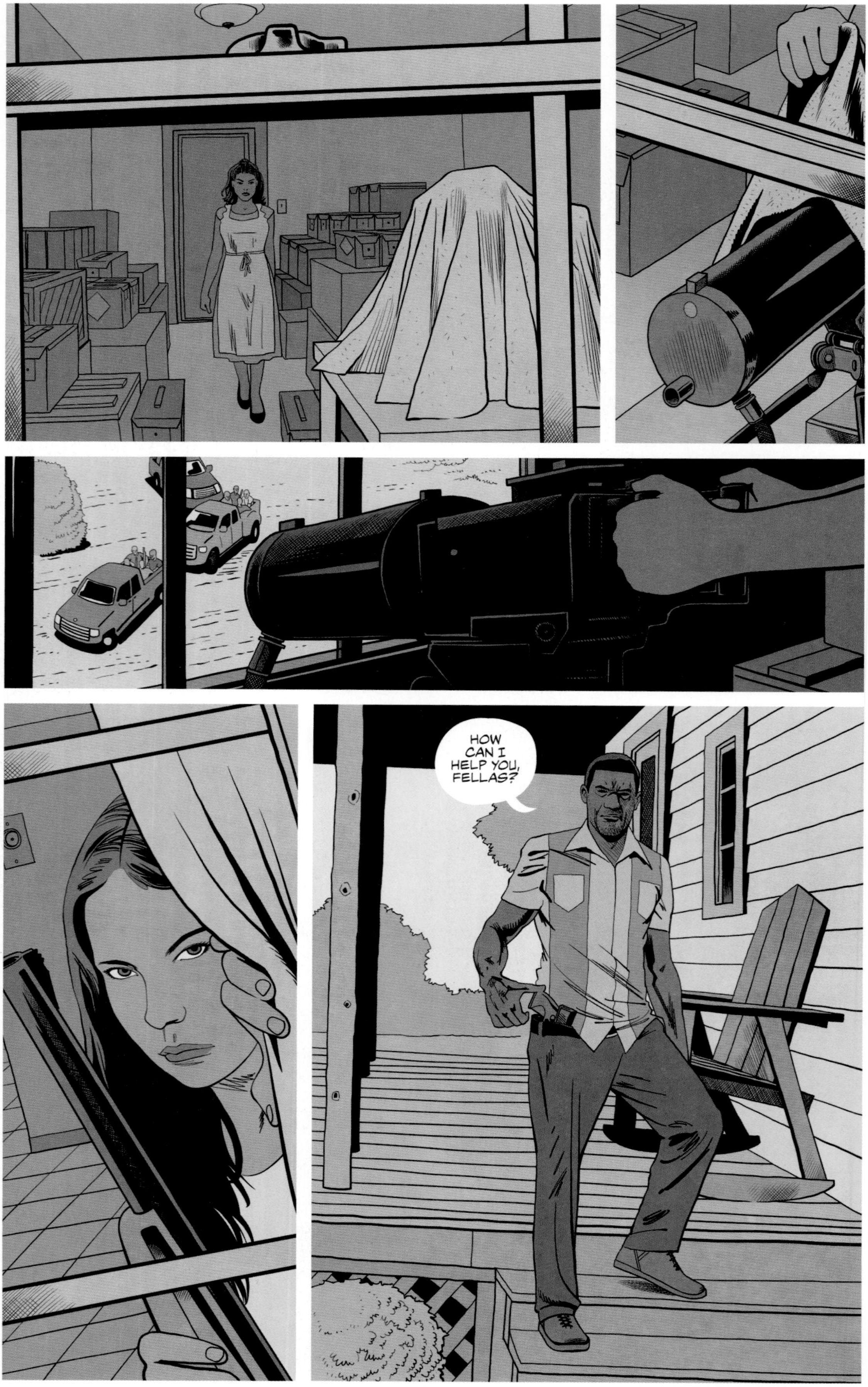
HOW CAN I HELP YOU, FELLAS?

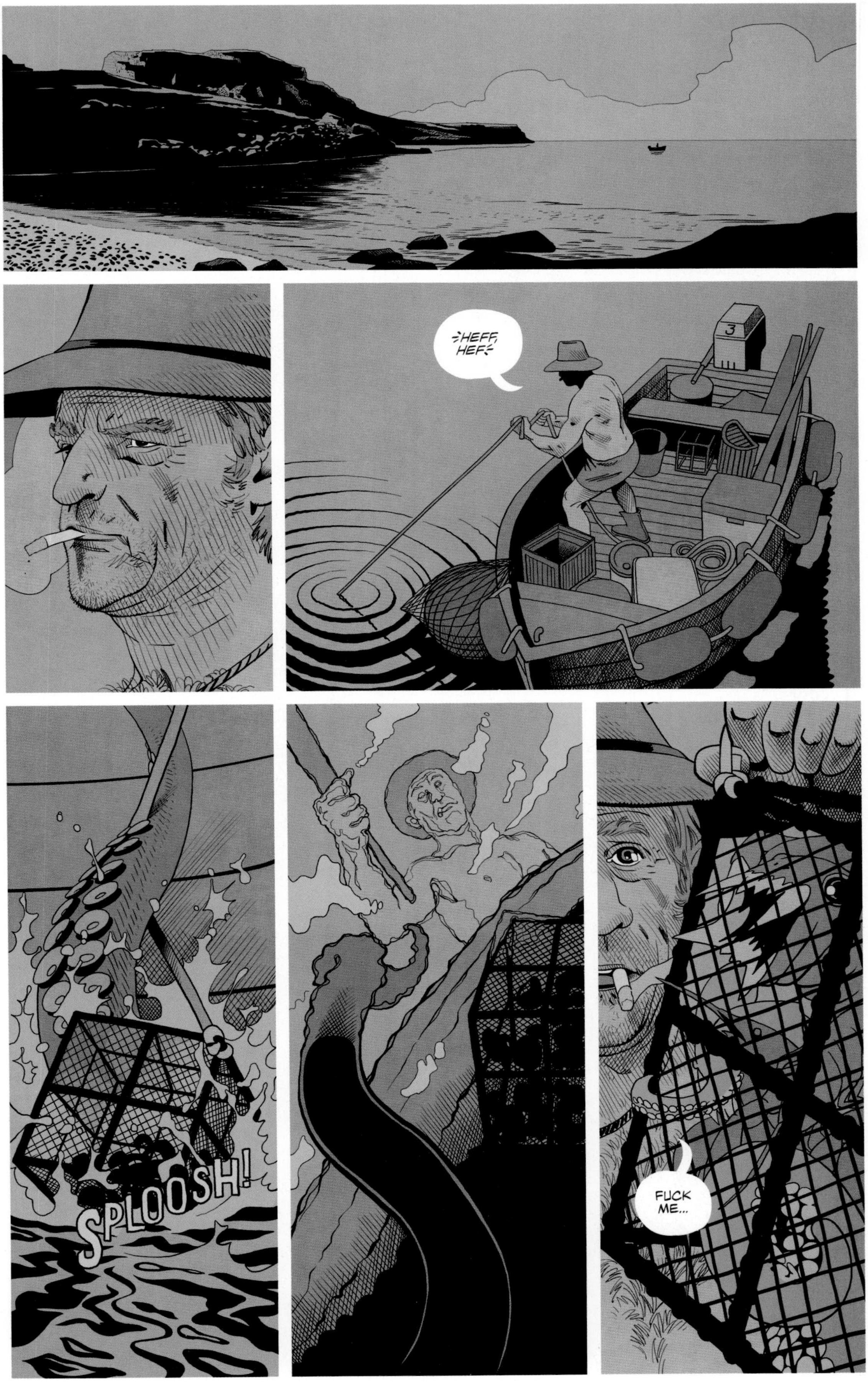
HEFF, HEF
SPLOOSH!
FUCK ME...

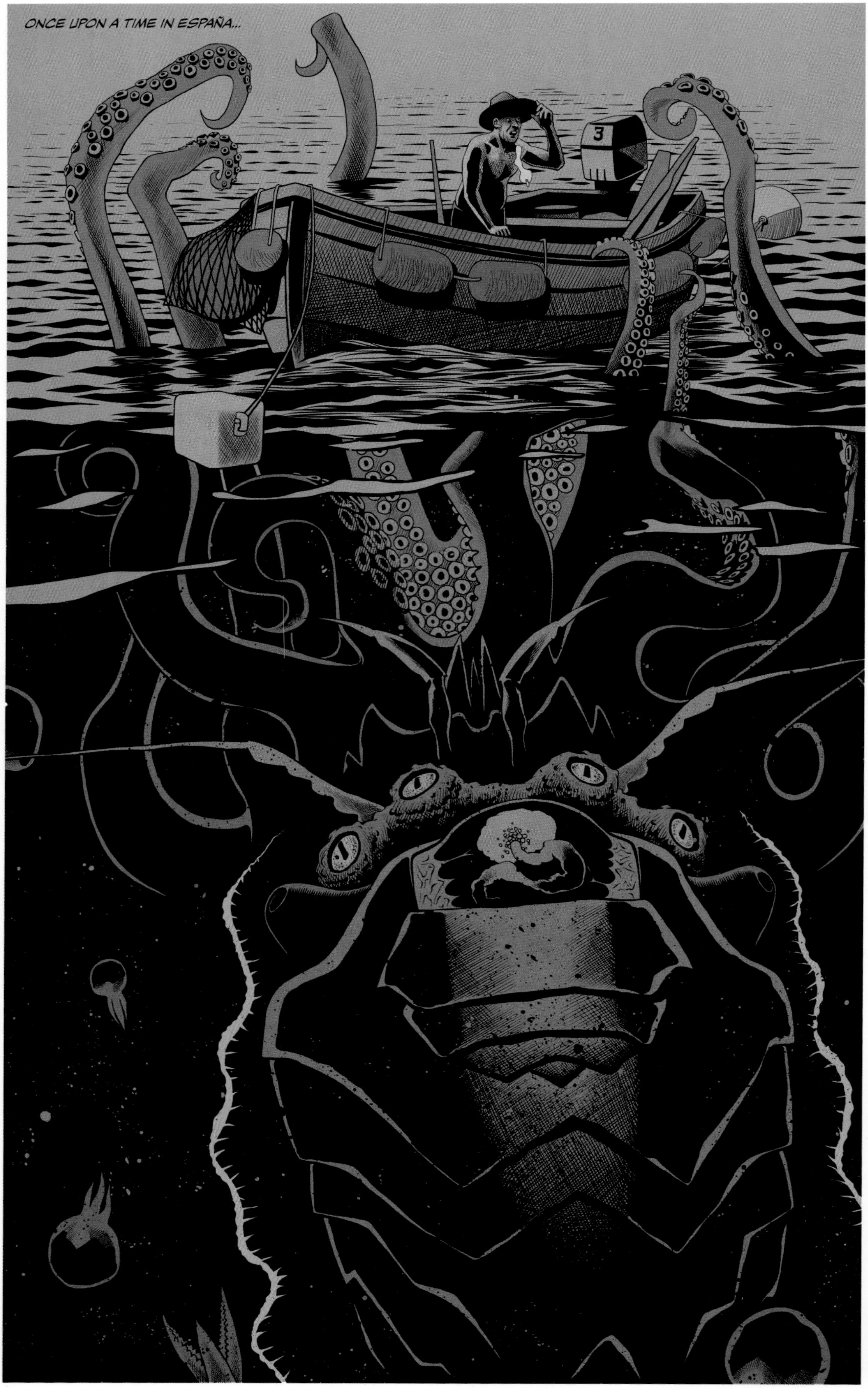
ONCE UPON A TIME IN ESPAÑA...

THE
END

For more tales from ROBERT KIRKMAN and SKYBOUND

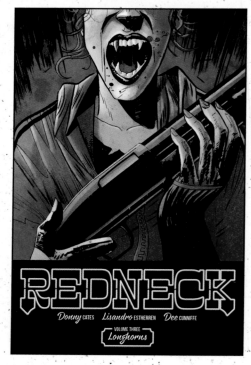

VOL. 1: ARTIST TP
ISBN: 978-1-5343-0242-6
$16.99

VOL. 2: WARRIOR TP
ISBN: 978-1-5343-0506-9
$16.99

VOL. 1: DEEP IN THE HEART TP
ISBN: 978-1-5343-0331-7
$16.99

VOL. 3: LONGHORNS TP
ISBN: 978-1-5343-1050-6
$16.99

VOL. 2: THE EYES UPON YOU
ISBN: 978-1-5343-0665-3
$16.99

VOL. 1: HOMECOMING TP
ISBN: 978-1-63215-231-2
$9.99

VOL. 2: CALL TO ADVENTURE TP
ISBN: 978-1-63215-446-0
$12.99

VOL. 3: ALLIES AND ENEMIES TP
ISBN: 978-1-63215-683-9
$12.99

VOL. 4: FAMILY HISTORY TP
ISBN: 978-1-63215-871-0
$12.99

VOL. 5: BELLY OF THE BEAST TP
ISBN: 978-1-5343-0218-1
$12.99

VOL. 6: FATHERHOOD TP
ISBN: 978-1-53430-498-7
$14.99

VOL. 7: BLOOD BROTHERS TP
ISBN: 978-1-5343-1053-7
$14.99

VOL. 1: FLORA & FAUNA TP
ISBN: 978-1-60706-982-9
$9.99

VOL. 2: AMPHIBIA & INSECTA TP
ISBN: 978-1-63215-052-3
$14.99

VOL. 3: CHIROPTERA & CARNIFORMAVES TP
ISBN: 978-1-63215-397-5
$14.99

VOL. 4: SASQUATCH TP
ISBN: 978-1-63215-890-1
$14.99

VOL. 5: MNEMOPHOBIA & CHRONOPHOBIA TP
ISBN: 978-1-5343-0230-3
$16.99

VOL. 6: FORTIS & INVISIBILIA TP
ISBN: 978-1-5343-0513-7
$16.99

VOL. 1: A DARKNESS SURROUNDS HIM TP
ISBN: 978-1-63215-053-0
$9.99

VOL. 2: A VAST AND UNENDING RUIN TP
ISBN: 978-1-63215-448-4
$14.99

VOL. 3: THIS LITTLE LIGHT TP
ISBN: 978-1-63215-693-8
$14.99

VOL. 4: UNDER DEVIL'S WING TP
ISBN: 978-1-5343-0050-7
$14.99

VOL. 5: THE NEW PATH TP
ISBN: 978-1-5343-0249-5
$16.99

VOL. 6: INVASION TP
ISBN: 978-1-5343-0751-3
$16.99

VOL. 1: "I QUIT."
ISBN: 978-1-60706-592-0
$14.99

VOL. 2: "HELP ME."
ISBN: 978-1-60706-676-7
$14.99

VOL. 3: "VENICE."
ISBN: 978-1-60706-844-0
$14.99

VOL. 4: "THE HIT LIST."
ISBN: 978-1-63215-037-0
$14.99

VOL. 5: "TAKE ME."
ISBN: 978-1-63215-401-9
$14.99

VOL. 6: "GOLD RUSH."
ISBN: 978-1-53430-037-8
$14.99